Fall of the Walker King

Walking Between Worlds
- Book III -

Fall Of The Walker King

Walking Between Worlds
- Book III -

J.K. Norry

Fall of the Walker King
Walking Between Worlds Book III

ISBN 978-0-9907280-7-8

Second Edition, Published Fall 2019

www.SuddenInsightPublishing.com
Indie publishing for the Indie Author

Acknowledgements

This book was done as quickly as we could possibly do it without compromising the quality. The well-oiled machine that Sudden Insight Publishing has become over the last couple of years is a special thing to be a part of. For the first time ever, I can be sure that I can publish at least one or two books every year. Therefore, my biggest thanks go to my partner-in-all-things, my "Awesome Girl". All of those slick covers, and print and ebook formatting, and likely the reason you have this book to begin with, are due to her talents and hard work. Thank you, Dawn… for so much.

I'd also like to thank Dawn's parents, Pat and Judy Marshall. Nobody has gotten more bookmarks out there than Judy, and no one has stood in line at the grocery store listening to her talk about my books more than Pat. I appreciate the support, and the bang-up job you did raising a wonderful daughter…thanks!

There are many angels in the indie publishing world, and the army that they form together is fighting for a better experience for writers and readers alike. It's a battle worth winning, and a force I am proud to be a part of. I would like to thank everyone who has helped make this trilogy possible, but that would be a book in itself. Rather, I will extend special thanks to a special few…

Thanks to Angela B. Chrysler, for your refreshing enthusiasm and relentless support. You show the way with your own work, and helped so much with ours. No one knows how you do it all, but we're all glad you do.

Is there a prime example of an indie author that's writing great books while striking a perfect balance between sleek professionalism and warm accessibility? There is, and his name is Adam Dreece. Thanks, Adam, for classing up the place with your tireless efforts.

Thanks to C.L. Schneider, who reached out in the very beginning of all of this to teach us and help us navigate this wonderful new world. I feel the warm embrace of a positive community around me, and am grateful that you did so much to bring me into these now-familiar folds.

To my angels, and my demons…thank you for your guidance and your love, and the blessed gift of silence.

To The One…and The Other…thank you. For everything. Literally.

FOR DAWN...

CHAPTER 1

William stood at the center of the Heavenly space, his head bowed and his gloved hands clasped before him. He had heard of the Walker Council, of course, but he had never had occasion to stand before them. He had also never imagined that meeting them one day would mean standing trial before them on that day.

He wore his custom spelled armor, yet he felt completely vulnerable. He could call upon his key or his weapon with a thought, yet he felt completely defenseless. Paul had told him a little about the council, that an ancient angel with dark skin seemed their best chance at an ally. Yet when William looked upon the first eight unfamiliar faces, he saw nothing but a bunch of stern and ugly old white guys.

The ninth face was old and ugly and white as well, but it was not unfamiliar. Andre had somehow transmuted from Watcher to angel without a break in consciousness. William wondered if making the rules and breaking them whenever you wanted was the best way to run a governing body. It certainly didn't seem to be the way angels should behave.

"We can read your thoughts, Walker." One of the round-faced, mostly bald men spoke venomously.

'*But are you listening?*' The Walker thought forcefully.

There was a sly smile on one face at that, and William saw friendly laughter behind the angel's eyes. He spoke next.

"We do not take action lightly or often, Walker," he said kindly. "The criticism we receive for our policy of non-interference is rivaled only by the criticism we receive on the rare occasion that we do interfere."

"My criticism never falls on anyone with the courage to stay their path or keep their word," William replied calmly. "There is no honor in breaking one's own code."

The angel seemed unperturbed, but he also seemed the only one.

"I can see why the Walker King chose you," he smiled.

"Calling himself a king does not make a man a king," another angel spat bitterly. "There has not been a Walker King for a great long time, and if Walker Paul was the great Stone Walker, he failed to fulfill his own grand prophecy."

"We found Walker Paul's soul, then?" The angel with the mirthful eyes turned in his seat to address the speaker.

"Of course not," the speaker crossed his arms and frowned. "He was destroyed by dragon fire, along with Ximena."

"You're sure about that?" The smiling angel was clearly amused with the exchange.

"Of course," he replied tartly. The other angel was clearly not amused. "We would have found them by now."

"Did we not seal up the realms in between?" His dark luminous eyes twinkled mischievously, and he looked pointedly at William.

"Is this conversation appropriate during this trial?" Andre spoke up, leaning forward and trying to catch someone's eye.

"You were told not to speak," the angel's merry eyes went cold. "You are too close to this matter, and too new to the Council."

Andre settled back in his chair and folded his arms sullenly.

"And yet you have a point, Angel Andre." The two angels were clearly battling for control. Now the dour one was smiling, thin-lipped and humorless. "Walker William is on trial."

"Can we all just stop using that word?" The jovial angel spread his hands. "We already know the outcome of these proceedings. The only three responsible for the destruction of souls seem to have been destroyed completely themselves. Walker William will not be rehumanized, or punished in any other way. In fact, we—"

"Enough!" The dour angel slammed his soft fist into the soft woven light that made every inanimate shape in the room. "If you suspect that they have not been destroyed, you should not speak so blithely about it."

"Very well." The angel with the easy smile folded his hands calmly before him. "I will admit that the evidence points to Ximena and the Walker King being destroyed."

His dour face was turning red now. "And I am happy to get on with our business with Walker William if you will please stop calling that miscreant a king."

Walker William cleared his throat.

"I destroyed a soul," he pointed out. "I killed a dragon."

"No you didn't," Andre sneered. "Walker Paul killed that dragon after it gutted you."

The dour angel shot Andre an irritated glance.

"Besides—" he began.

"Andre destroyed a soul," William said calmly, holding the accused's gaze. "He murdered Mason."

"As I was saying," the unhappy angel's icy tone cut in, "even if you had killed a dragon, it would have been because you were following orders. That guilt would fall on Walker Paul, as Andre's guilt transfers to the Dragon Queen."

The more pleasant speaker cut in again.

"Now on to more peaceful matters," he said. "Walker William, you no doubt remember Walker John?"

"Of course." William nodded tersely. He saw no need to share his assessment of the man. In getting to know other Walkers, he had learned that the appointed leader had struggled with what little authority he had had. On the other hand, nearly every Walker had treated the self-proclaimed Walker King with a respect that bordered on reverence. He looked from one self-righteous glowing face to the next, thinking how impossible it would be to explain what they did not wish to understand.

The jovial angel was looking less than jovial, and William tried to quiet his whirling mind.

"We are prepared to offer you the position vacated by Walker John," the dour angel said. "You seem to be someone the Walkers are willing to listen to and able to follow."

"They followed me when I followed the Walker King," William cut in. "Why would they follow me if I become your stooge?"

"Just because we can read your thoughts does not mean you need to express them all with such brash disdain," the happy angel didn't look happy at all as he spoke. "Surely you can step back far enough from your imbalanced emotional state to see that we are all just trying to make the best of a bad situation."

William took a deep breath and did not voice his next several thoughts.

"What if I refuse?" he asked.

"Then you will be rehumanized." The dour angel seemed pleased at the prospect. "Your memories of your life as a Walker will be erased and you will live out your mortal life as a normal man."

William felt his eyes go wide. "My memories will be taken?"

"It's a new policy," the dour angel said dismissively.

Andre looked left and right, then decided to venture a comment.

"Also," he said, "your Guide and your Watcher will be relieved of duty and released from their consciousness to properly pursue their after-earth life."

The Walker did not like to make decisions based on the feeling that he had no other choice. He thought of the men and women he had fought beside and loved; the Walkers he had trained, and the Guide whose touch made his heart sing. William knew he could not allow himself to be swayed by anger, but what about love?

"Walker William." The angel's smile was lighting his features again. "If I may…what would Walker Paul want you to do?"

The fluidity within him turned to stone. "What are my duties as a servant to this council?"

"As leader of the Walkers," the angel's smile was unperturbed, "you will assist in training new Walkers, you will find new Walkers to replace those we have lost and you will explain the new rules to all of the Walkers. Furthermore, you will assist in rehumanizing the Walkers we have deemed no longer fit for service and finding suitable replacements for them as well."

"You will also report to the Council daily," the unhappy angel added with a wry smile.

"Daily?" William frowned.

"We have seen what a Walker can do in a day," he shot back. "You will report daily."

The happy angel sighed, allowing his practiced look of infinite patience to fray.

"For now," he amended.

William addressed him. "What are the new rules?" He wished he had paid attention when the trial had begun; William had assumed that none of this would matter by the time they had tried him, and had not paid attention to their introductions. He didn't remember any of their names.

"Walkers are once again forbidden from interacting with each other," he began, then his smile broadened. "Stephan, Walker. My name is Stephan."

"My job would be a lot easier if I could let Walkers work together, Stephan." William tried to hide his irritation at feeling so violated.

"The walls between worlds have become dangerously thin due to recent events." The dour angel refused to be left out of the conversation. "One of those events was the gathering of a Walker army; another was excessive walking between worlds, including unauthorized entry to above and below; still another was the destruction of souls and the misplacement of millions of demons. Every dire consequence the Council is now dealing with would have been prevented by keeping Walkers from gathering. Only the Walker Leader may interact with other Walkers."

"And only on official Walker business," Stephan tried to lighten the blow by smiling. It didn't help.

"Walker movement is restricted as well," the other angel went on.

"Walkers shall not go above or below the seven layers of reality that make up the Earth dimension."

William narrowed his eyes. "I don't even know what that means."

"Ask your Guide," Stephan responded. "And let all of the Walkers know: we will be keeping an eye on them, particularly the surviving members of the army."

"Violations will not be tolerated," added the dour angel, "and punishment will not be lenient."

"No need to threaten those who have not yet committed any transgression." Stephan waved his hand in William's general direction, and something took shape in his hand. "Take that scroll to the new Queen of Hell. We have not been able to establish a clear line of communication with her as of yet, but she is bound by law to update your key to match your new position."

William frowned. "By what law?"

The dour angel leaned forward and narrowed his eyes hatefully at the Walker. "By highest law. By Council law."

"And what if she kills me?"

Stephan shook his head. "It is highly doubtful. We would be obligated by law to bring her to justice."

William almost laughed. "And who would take her place?"

Now the dour angel looked downright pleased with himself. "The Council would act as Hell's governing body until Creator appoints a replacement."

CHAPTER 2

Cal curbed the wheels of his shiny black Acura and killed the engine. He turned to Sarah.

"I'm sure there's just some kind of mix-up," he smiled his charismatic grin.

"Mason has been missing since last night," Sarah frowned. "He hasn't returned my calls or yours. I can't get ahold of Mikie, either. I don't know why, but I just have a feeling that something is terribly wrong. Call it woman's intuition, I just can't shake it."

"Why can't it just be intuition?" Cal let his smile fall as his hand fell on the door handle. "When I figure something out, I don't say I used 'men's logic'. Nor do I think that only women are prone to intuitive impulses."

Sarah's eyes were wide and unblinking. "Um….sorry?"

He wouldn't let it go.

"Besides," he pressed. "You weren't using intuition, you were using logic. You can't get ahold of two guys who are usually at your beck and call, so you're worried."

"You don't have to do this," Sarah had her fingers on the handle that would let her out of the car.

"Sorry," Cal relaxed. "Let's go inside and see if anybody knows anything." He had driven all the way up here, after all.

"Do you need to do some coke or something?" Sarah asked politely. "Don't mind me if you don't have enough to share."

Cal looked up and down the empty street they were parked on.

"Okay," he shrugged. "I have plenty, if you want some."

Sarah sighed. "That would be great. I have a bottle of tequila in my purse. You want a drink?"

"Let me see the bottle," he said. It was a tall rectangular bottle, and he turned the cap to make sure it was on tight. Then he flipped it over to see how much flat surface was on the bottom. There was enough for the two sizable bumps he shook from the baggie onto the bottle.

Cal liked to close his eyes when he snorted coke. There was always a pleasant internal fireworks show when the powder hit his mucous membrane, even if it was just a little bit. He hated to miss the show, but he did not dare to close his eyes. Not since last night.

When Cal closed his eyes, he saw memories of Mikie. Scenes played out in his head, ordinary moments he had spent watching Mikie play his guitar or talking with the band or snorting Cal's coke. It annoyed him to see the dead man animated behind his closed eyelids, annoyed him so much that it ruined the fireworks.

That wasn't all he saw, though. Sometimes when he closed his eyes, Cal saw Mikie as he had seen him last night. Pale and lifeless and lying in a pool of his own blood, Mikie's eyes stared into nothingness in that picture. When that image appeared to him, it did not annoy Cal. To say it pleased him would be like saying Cal kind of liked his cocaine.

When the image that awaited behind his eyes was the image of Mikie's lifeless corpse, Cal felt a smile tug at the corners of his mouth and a primal need tug at the crotch of his pants. The feeling that came with that picture made the fireworks show of cocaine look like a handful of lame sparklers.

So he kept his eyes open while he positioned his snorter tube over the bump, while he pushed one nostril closed with his fingertip, and while he snorted the white powder up his nose. He handed the upturned bottle and the tube to Sarah. She had no problem closing her eyes to do the bump, or to take a long drink of the clear intoxicating liquid. After, she leaned back into the passenger seat and held the bottle out to Cal. It was right side up and uncapped.

It was barely noon, and Cal was not much for drinking even at appropriate hours. Of course, he had snorted a fat line this morning before he even brushed his teeth; but that was different.

"Maybe later," he smiled. "Thanks."

Sarah capped the bottle and it disappeared again into her purse. They were both out of the car and on the sidewalk when they noticed the sign.

It was written in black marker on brown cardboard, in letters that ranged from six inches high to twelve. The sign looked like it had been scrawled by a child or an enraged adult.

It said "Closed until further notice".

Cal looked at all the glass panes on the storefront, trying to see through the cardboard that covered every square inch of transparent surface. He stepped back and looked up.

"The sign is gone," he said.

Sarah stepped back to stand beside him and look up. It was easy to see where the sign had been: four jagged craters of concrete showed where anchor bolts had held it in place.

Taking two swift steps forward, Sarah was knocking on the glass door before Cal realized she had moved. He couldn't take his eyes off the damaged concrete. His mind wondering what could have torn the sign off like that, he imagined a tractor or heavy crane coming in the night or wee morning hours. It seemed doubtful. Of course, it seemed a lot more likely than a ten or eleven foot monster with supernatural strength ripping the sign from its moorings.

It was only four bolts; why not just unbolt them?

Sarah was rapping loudly on the glass again. Cal tore his eyes from the pitted overhang to step up beside her.

"Looks like nobody's home," he observed.

She looked at him, frowned, then stepped forward and knocked again. A flap of cardboard was pulled aside as she did, and a round red and black eyeball looked out through the hole. It was huge.

"What the hell was that?" Cal whispered.

"What?" Sarah's eyes searched the place where he looked. It was covered cardboard again.

There was the quiet sound of metal grating on metal, then the clicking and clacking of tumblers turning. Whatever was in there was unlocking the door.

Cal edged backward as the door inched open inward, putting Sarah between him and whatever owned that gigantic reptilian eye.

A black fedora appeared, followed by a familiar face. Cal breathed a sigh of relief.

Roche looked up and down the empty street.

"Get in here, you two," he growled.

As soon as they were inside, the club owner locked the door behind them. Cal felt a knot of tension start to form in his belly when the keys turned, felt it tighten further when Roche removed the key from the lock and slipped it in his pocket.

Sarah didn't seem to notice. She was turning a slow wide circle on what used to be the dance floor by night and coffee lounge by day. Now it was gutted and burnt, every surface flattened and blackened by flames. The stage was gone, the floor where it once stood littered with bent and burnt metal. The stale acrid stench of smoke and wet charcoal was thick and cloying as it climbed inside Cal's numbed nostrils.

"Oh my God, Roche," Sarah found her voice somewhere in the wreckage. "What happened?"

"Electrical fire," Roche said quickly. Too quickly for Cal's trained ear. People had lied to him far too often.

"Where did it start?" Cal asked, looking up at the remnants of the upper landing. It was nothing but twisted metal charred beyond usability or recognition.

"In an electrical circuit," the big man growled.

Cal didn't see any reason to point out that the response neither answered his question nor made real sense. He just shrugged and nodded. Whatever.

"You haven't by any chance seen or heard from Mason, have you?" Sarah crossed her arms and bit her lip.

"Your guitar wizard?" The club owner shook his big head. "I haven't seen him since the show ended last night. Great show, by the way."

"Thanks." Sarah looked about as enthusiastic accepting the compliment as Roche had been in giving it. "Did you happen to see where Mason went after the show?"

Roche shrugged.

"Last I saw he was headed upstairs, maybe to talk to Kris. Or Paul, he was up there too. I didn't see him after that, but I was busy closing up." He shrugged his beefy shoulders once more. "Sorry, kid."

"It would be silly to ask if you had heard from Mikie, wouldn't it?" Sarah was nervously biting her lip again. Cal found it kind of annoying.

"The no-show king?" Roche shook his head. "I haven't seen that guy for days."

They were all quiet then, and Cal and Sarah turned to gaze at the burnt wreckage again. It looked like a bomb had gone off where the coffee bar used to be, the bent stainless steel sink and appliances in pieces and stained black by smoke and fire. The shrapnel described a pretty clear concentric pattern around the scorched floor, which had long gashes cut into it in deep long sets of five. For all the crime dramas his cocaine-fueled mind may have payed way too close attention to, Cal could not for the life of him figure out what had happened here. He was pretty damn sure it wasn't an electrical fire.

"On a completely unrelated note." The sound of Roche's growling voice had a false ring to it. Cal turned to him.

The big man's beady black eyes were boring into him, and Cal thought of the big reptilian eye he had imagined earlier for some reason.

"The cops were here last night," Roche growled. "They said there was a report of gunshots, they found blood in the street."

"Oh my God," Sarah gasped. "What happened?"

"They didn't come till we were closed," he sighed. "They said the caller didn't want to identify themselves. They called nine-one-one from a payphone and said they heard shots fired a couple hours earlier in front of the Devil's Brew." Roche made a sour face when he said the name.

"Unbelievable," Sarah's eyes were wide and shocked.

"I know," Cal quipped. "Where the hell did they find a pay phone in the city?"

The club owner and the pretty singer looked at him darkly.

"You don't know anything about any shooting, do you, Cokey?" Roche's eyes seemed to be invading his mind more than awaiting an answer.

Cal knew how to lie.

"Of course not." He lifted his shirt to show his slim abdomen. "I don't need a gun. I'm good to my customers and they're good to me." He looked around the gutted room. "Do you know anything about the shooting?"

Roche strode to the door, fishing his keys from his pocket as he walked. Unlocking the door, he swung it inward and held it open.

"Get the hell out of here," he growled.

"I'm sure Cal didn't mean anything by that." Sarah was moving toward the door despite her protestations. Cal was already standing outside.

She paused in the doorway. "Will you please call if you hear anything? About Mason or Mikie?"

"Sure, kid." The big man sounded doubtful.

"I'm really sorry about your club." She was still standing in the doorway.

"Thanks, kid."

He was clearly waiting for her to get out of the way so he could close the door. Finally, she stepped one foot into the street. Roche began to close the door on her other foot as it paused in the frame.

"Hey, Roche?" She looked over his broad shoulder to eye the corpse of his business one last time. "Where's Jessica?"

The big man grimaced.

"That girl never belonged here," he sighed heavily. "She went home."

"Home?" Sarah pressed. "Where's home?"

Roche pushed the door shut, giving Sarah a moment to move her petite sandaled foot before it was smashed. She pulled her foot back and set it on the sidewalk to the clacking sound of the lock.

She was biting her lip in that annoying way and looking up at him uncertainly.

"Where to next?" he asked.

Sarah took her phone out of her purse, tried one number and then another with no results.

"I'm so worried, Cal," she said needlessly.

"I can see that."

"Will you stay with me at Mason's apartment tonight?" She blinked, her eyes going wide. "You can have the bed, I'll sleep on the couch. I just don't want to be alone."

Cal jangled his keys and pretended to consider it. There was no way on Earth he was wrapping himself in sheets that surely stunk of pot and stale cigarette smoke, maybe even Mason and Sarah's sex.

"I need to get home," Cal said, unable to think of an excuse as to why. "You're welcome to crash at my place. I have a spare bedroom."

She thought about it for a moment, long enough to start listing reasons why she shouldn't.

"It's an hour and a half drive one way," he said. "I can bring you back up tomorrow if you want, although traffic will be shitty on Seventeen in the morning and again in the afternoon."

"Okay." Sarah nodded, much to his dismay. "If you're sure you don't mind."

He waved his hand dismissively, and smiled charismatically. "Of course. I never have company."

Because I don't like company, he thought under the smile.

The Acura chirped as they approached it from opposite sides.

"Hey Cal, check this out." Sarah was kneeling carefully in her green sundress, looking at the side of his car.

Cal came around to her side of the car and knelt beside her. Together, they looked at the little round hole in the wheel well.

"Is that a bullet hole?" Sarah took a step away from the car.

"Well, hell," Cal muttered. "I guess I parked in the wrong spot."

"Are you going to report it?"

"Sarah," Cal regarded her coldly. "Do you know how I make my money? Besides managing a band that loses members at an average of one per day?"

"Well, you don't have to be a dick about it," she huffed.

Cal moved to the driver's side and opened the door.

"You coming?" He didn't wait for a response, just got in and closed the door and started the engine.

The other door opened, the dome light came on, and her summery scent filled the car. She began to buckle her seat belt, stopped mid-motion with the belt between her breasts.

"Cal," she said quietly, "did you have any involvement with the shooting Roche talked about?"

"Apparently," Cal snapped. "My car was caught in the crossfire, and now I have to fix it or cover it up. Does that count as involvement?"

Sarah pulled the tequila from her purse as he moved the car into the street. She gulped at it thirstily, then held it out to him.

What the hell. Cal took the bottle and tilted it as he drove. Maybe it would make him stop wondering what her face would look like if he smashed it against the dashboard.

The tequila burned his mouth when he drank it, burned his throat when he swallowed it, and burned his belly as he took another mouthful. He handed the bottle back to Sarah, noting that it had not burned away his morbid curiosity.

"An hour and a half?" Sarah hit the bottle again before stowing it. "Do you usually go that long without...y'know..."

She sniffled meaningfully.

"No," he laughed. "I do usually wait until I get on the freeway. Being a cokehead is not nearly as easy as being a pothead on the road."

Sarah laughed with him.

"Mason seems to think his car won't work unless he's smoking weed." She paused for thought. "I have a little, if you want some."

Cal made a face. "No thanks. You can if you want, just blow it out the window. No cigarettes, please."

"I don't smoke," Sarah responded with a shrug. "I take a drag every now and then, but I don't smoke."

She dug around her purse and came up with a little black cloth bag. Sarah untied the strings and widened the mouth of the bag with her careful worrying fingers. Soon she was packing a little bowl in a little glass pipe riddled with resin.

"Want some?" She was holding it out, along with a lighter. Cal could smell the fresh green scent. He didn't answer for a moment, savoring the aroma before it became a burnt smoky stench.

"No thanks," he said finally.

Sarah hit the little pipe, coughing at the end and spewing smoke all over the cab of the car.

Sighing, Cal rolled down her window from his control panel.

She puffed away at the weed pipe until they were on 280 and moving at the sixty-five miles an hour he had programmed into his cruise control.

"Let me know what I can do," Sarah said, putting the pipe and the little plastic baggie into the black stow. The cloth bag disappeared into her purse, and the air cleared at last.

Cal glanced at her. "What do you mean?"

"I take my job as passenger very seriously," she smiled. "I am here to deejay or pass the bottle or whatever the honored driver might need."

"Okay." Cal shrugged. "There's a CD case under your seat. If you flip it open, you will not find a CD inside. Rather, you will find a razor blade, a plastic straw cut to size, and a little bag of coke. Please cut us a couple of fat lines."

She reached under her seat with a giggle. When she set the case on her lap, half on her dress and half on her bare leg, she nudged him with her elbow.

"Great White, huh?"

Cal nodded. "My brother had to watch me a lot when I was a kid. To him, watching me meant buying an extra concert ticket or sneaking me into a show. I usually hated it, the muddled ugly sounds that a lot of people call a rock show. Great White was just different. They sounded clean and crisp, and I liked them. I don't have many CD's, but I have most of theirs. All the early stuff, with Jack Russell and his incredible voice."

"I'm familiar," Sarah was chopping up two decent lines. "White boy blues, that's what I always called them. They were pretty huge for a while, back in the day."

"Do you mind if my line is not fat?" Sarah seemed intimidated by the neatly cut rails.

He shook his head again. "Slide it over to my side, or just do how much you want."

"Nope, driver first." Sarah busied herself making her line into a thin skiff and his into a wide ridge. Cal glanced down at her lap, then back at the road. That was better.

She held the scarred plastic surface in front of her. "Is that too much?"

"No." Cal didn't bother to look over.

Then she was holding it in front of him and putting the plastic straw close to his nose with her other hand.

"I got it." Cal grasped the wheel at twelve o' clock, took the straw with his free hand. Balancing it out, he snorted half the line up one nostril and the rest up the other. That was nice; it was usually difficult to do while driving.

"Well thanks, Sarah," he said affably. "Aren't you nice to have around."

She giggled as she tooted the little line she had cut for herself. Before he knew it she was proffering the open bottle of tequila again.

Cal wondered while he drank if the bottle would break if he bashed it against her skull, or if the thick glass would hold up to a good pummeling.

He handed the bottle back. "Thanks."

"Want to listen to some music? Some Great White, maybe?" It looked like she was digging in her purse for the pot pipe again.

"Nah," he said. She was looking for the pot pipe. Cal cracked her window as she packed the bowl. "Damn girl, you know how to party."

A dark cloud passed over her face. "I'm so worried. I just want to feel numb."

"About Mason?"

She took a hit before she answered, held it in while she spoke.

"Totally. He's not just missing, Cal." She blew the smoke onto the dash, and it filled the cab of the car for a few seconds before escaping out the open window. "He was with another girl last night."

Cal raised his eyebrows and glanced at her. "Define 'with'."

Sarah blew another cloud of smoke at the dashboard. "He got a blowjob in the alley behind the bar from some slut."

He resisted the urge to laugh. Barely.

"You saw him?" he asked.

She nodded, putting the lighter's flame to the stinky weed.

"Did he see you?"

Sarah shook her head and exhaled, filling the car with white-blue smoke again.

"Are you guys supposed to be exclusive?" Cal opened her window a little wider.

"We're in a committed relationship, Cal," she said sarcastically.

"Does he know that?" Cal pressed. "Is he clear on all the rules he is supposed to be following? Sarah, is it possible that Mason is just spending time with someone else?"

"Mason needs me," Sarah retorted. She didn't sound so sure.

"A week ago he didn't need you," Cal shrugged. "A week ago he didn't even know you existed."

"So you think he's with that girl?"

"Nope." He shrugged again. "I think he's not taking our calls. I think I'll wait until he turns up to find out what's up. I think imagining what he might be doing is a waste of time."

Sarah sparked the flame and hit the pipe, filled the cab with smoke again.

"I think he's with that girl," she said.

"I understand why you're worried about Mason, sort of," Cal said. "But why Mikie?" Maybe talking about the guy he had successfully killed would take his mind off killing the girl beside him.

Sarah exchanged the pipe for the bottle again.

"Mikie is a recovered addict," she said soberly, taking a long draught.

He took the tequila from her and had a swallow. "Recovered from what? Every time I saw him he was drinking and smoking weed."

"Oh, he can handle beer and pot alright." Sarah had another sip from the bottle before capping it. "Just not the hard stuff. He was strung out on heroin for about a year. I've been worried about him ever since the other night when you gave him that coke."

"How long was he clean?" Cal was not enjoying the death mask behind his eyes nearly so much now.

Sarah frowned. "About a month."

He frowned back. "Why didn't anyone say something?"

CHAPTER 3

He shouldn't still be here.

Kris sat in the easy chair in William's living room, wondering what was going to happen to him. William's new Walker, Chase, was sitting nearby on the sofa with Daemon. They were talking excitedly, the unusual demon explaining things only Guides knew to the unlikely Walker. Chase seemed far more interested in the unseen worlds than most Walkers, and Kris had tuned the elementary conversation out quite a while ago.

Paul was gone, Brenna was gone and then reborn as Ximena and now she was gone too. William had survived, but there was no way of knowing if he would see another day as a Walker. Even Matt was gone, either killed in battle or lost in Hell. There were so many uncertainties, Kris clung to the one certainty he felt to his dead bones.

He shouldn't still be here.

Vanessa was busying herself about the house, using her newfound ability to touch on mundane housework. She seemed as calm and collected as usual, except for the worried furtive glances she shot at Daemon and Chase from time to time. They were too engrossed in conversation to notice.

She wouldn't even look at Kris. The Guide didn't blame her. He shouldn't still be here.

The angels had received some special dispensation to freeze time and extract the Walker army and the horde of demons from Hell. Jessica had shown up after the freeze, free to move about as she pleased. In the time it had taken to extract the Walker army, half had been torched by her fire.

The demon horde had been left behind when the mission went wrong; and now Jessica was the Queen of Hell, and Hell was overrun with demons. It was all Kris knew for sure, because he had seen it with his own frozen eyes. Well, he did know one other thing for sure.

He shouldn't still be here.

When a Walker died or was rehumanized, their Guide and Watcher passed naturally into the next life, usually as an angel in the lower levels of Heaven. The Walkers who were able to bear the burden of immortality for long centuries surely had Watchers and Guides that came into being in the higher realms. It gave Kris no comfort to think that many of the Walkers they had lost had been ancient, and would go on to becoming angels themselves.

Daemon shouldn't be here either. He claimed that when he had stepped into the dragon fire, he had appeared at Chase's side. Kris had no reason to suspect he wasn't telling the truth, but it still felt wrong.

The front door opening seemed a surprise to everyone but Chase, who was still more startled when someone suddenly materialized from thin air than he was when they used a door.

They all turned at the sound, and William walked into the room to find eight immortal eyes on him.

Vanessa crossed the room to take his motorcycle helmet and leather jacket from his hands and drop them unceremoniously to the floor. The helmet rolled to a thunk against a wall as she threw her arms about his shoulders.

"What happened?" Vanessa asked.

She stepped back as the others came forward, and they formed a semi-circle around William.

"Well, I'm not dead." William stated the obvious and stepped into the room. The semi-circle moved with him.

"Kris," the Walker looked at him, "you are to remain a Guide if you so choose. I have many keys to find Walkers for, and you may select the Walker you would like to Guide from those that will be made."

The Guide felt like a balloon with a fast leak. He deflated under the news, letting his sagging shoulders be his reply.

William gave him a smile. He looked around like he was checking to see if anyone outside the group could hear, then leaned in conspiratorially toward Kris.

"Or," William murmured, "you can help Vanessa Guide me until some of my current tasks have been completed."

The Guide sighed with relief. He could read between the lines; William didn't think Paul was gone, and he wanted Kris to help find him.

"Are you the new king?" Kris was surprised to hear hope in his voice.

"No." William leaned back and away from them.

"According to most of the angels, there never was a Walker King; at least not recently," he told them. "I am to lead the Walkers as Walker John did, individually and separately."

"Walkers can't gather again?" Vanessa folded her hands together in the sleeves of her robe with a teenaged grimace.

"It was helping Walkers, spending time together." She was clearly not pleased in her compassion. "I saw so many men and women relieve years of mental burdens just talking to each other. Fighting together made many Walkers forever friends."

"I know," the Walker responded plaintively. "The Council says it was thinning the walls between dimensions. That, along with excessive walking between worlds."

"What?" Kris sputtered. "Walkers can't walk between worlds anymore?"

William focused his attention on the new Walker and his unlikely Guide.

"Chase," he said, folding his arms before him. "Show me your key."

Daemon nodded encouragingly when Chase glanced to him. The new Walker held out his hand so the old Walker could see the open watch face.

"Can you feel the countdown?" William's arms were still crossed, his tone brusque.

He couldn't expect the Walker to be tuned in to the key enough to feel the countdown happening within him. Kris knew it had taken William years to even notice the organic second heartbeat that every Walker had inside. The Guide barely had time to wonder why William had asked when he saw the new Walker nod.

"Yeah, sure," Chase said. "We have about seven minutes."

Daemon edged forward. "He didn't want armor. Or a weapon."

CHAPTER 4

"I have found them, my queen." A hunched form approached the grand dragon throne, swathed in a dark and tattered robe. Her hood was pulled over her head, and her voice was a crackling ancient wheeze. The eyes that peered from the cowled shadows were dark and milky. Violet fire danced in that darkness, irises alive with an eerie glow punctuated by wide dark slits for pupils.

Curled up in a scaled ball on the throne, the dragon lifted her head from the coil of her body.

"Show me," she hissed.

A dragon must spend a good many years in its reptilian body, practicing to make words sound spoken rather than hissed. The throat is different, the mouth and nose all literally a completely different animal. Although her age showed in her scant seventeen foot length and her graveled papery voice, Jessica had remained in dragon form since transforming in Roche's coffee shop. All day she sat on her throne and issued orders and proclamations in that lizardly voice.

It may have been traumatizing beyond hope of recovery for a human to behold the new Dragon Queen in Hell, her raspy reptilian voice hissing the words that were bringing the dark realm to an even darker place. The devils and dragons bore up under it, and soon her callous reign became routine. Among the first of her proclamations was the promise of a life of ease to whomever found the souls of the Walker King and his bitch quisling.

"My Queen." The huddled form produced a crystal ball from the folds of her robe. A perfect clear orb, it was but the size of one of her gnarled fists.

Her bent fingers uncurled slowly, as much as they could, and the quartz sphere grew as they did. In the space of a breath, the crystal ball was the size of the woman's head. The weight of it bowed her withered arms.

Growing larger was not the only power that the quartz sphere possessed. As Jessica's reptilian head snaked closer, she could make out shadows and shapes moving amidst the crystal clarity. Coming closer still, she could hear sounds that grew louder the more intently she listened. They were the same sounds she would hear if she left this room and ventured out to the layered surfaces of the dark underworld. Countless fires crackled and popped, an interminable percussion section that never played the same beat twice. Wretched screams and piteous moans that could have belonged to demons or devils or dragons filled the air, as off-time with the beat as they were off-key with each other. Altogether it made for a hellish song that chilled the new queen to her dark dragon bones every time she heard it.

Her reptilian nose nearly touching the smooth crystal surface, Jessica's crimson slitted eyes narrowed as a shape shifted in the shadows and another moan rose above the others. Naked and trembling, the shape slowly rose from lifeless puddle of flesh to the shakily standing form of a human man. Another low moan, one of confusion, escaped his lips as he stood.

"Paul." The Dragon Queen's voice was an angry hiss, and the robed hag drew back.

"Closer!" Jessica raged at the woman. She couldn't understand why they couldn't use a giant flatscreen instead of this technological relic. In her short time on Earth, Jessica had seen humans take leaps and bounds in industrial ingenuity with a speed that rivaled any civilization that had risen before. She had gone for the Renaissance, and to continually secure the contract that had been drawn up to keep her mother both in power and in check.

First she had missed one; now she missed the other.

Arriving too late had broken her heart twice already. The new queen was not going to let it happen a third time. She gazed at the image and tuned in to the sound.

How can they not even have internet? she thought to herself for the thousandth time, then perished the thought.

"Mmmo," Paul's voice was low and unintelligible, but it was still Paul's. The shifting shades of dark red on the dragon's scales was from the candles that guttered nearby. The queen was as still as her own captive breath as she watched.

"Maul." It was almost a word this time, and Jessica's eyes widened as he turned and seemed to look right at her. He looked like Paul in every way, standing there naked and peering into the shadows. Yet his stance was not Paul's; the lost and wild look in his eyes belonged to an animal, and the way he stood looked like he either expected or craved violence. He continued to stretch and flex his muscles, as if his own naked sinewed body was unfamiliar to him.

His eyes stayed on the shadows, wild and watchful, and after a few moments Jessica saw why. They came alive around him, a half-dozen demons that were all taller and wider than the trembling wild thing. Talons and teeth were not the only weapons they had, and Jessica wondered where demons had secured swords as two of them advanced with gleaming curved blades.

The thing that looked like Paul dove at the bare feet of the monster closest him, not quite dodging fast enough under the swing of the demon's sword. A gash appeared on his bare shoulder, splashing blood on the demon as they went down together. Human stood over demon then, the hard-won sword in his hand.

Watching intently, Jessica noted with satisfaction that the man was still bleeding. It did not matter when he beheaded the prone demon and disarmed another; what mattered was that he did it ever-so-slowly, like a normal human should. There was no sign of supernatural speed or strength, and the beast that looked like Paul was still bleeding and already beginning to wane. Holding just one sword aloft was too much the task, and the tip dipped to the charred rock floor as his fate loomed ever closer.

Another figure stepped from the shadows, and Jessica's eyes danced with furious flames.

"Ximena!" she hissed, the name escaping her lips before she could recall it. Jessica continued watching the scene, oblivious to the stir caused in the throne room by the sound of that name.

Lost in the scene, the Dragon Queen watched Ximena and Paul battling the demons together. The taut grimace that had appeared when Ximena did turned to a wicked slow half-smile as they fought. The duo looked like two ordinary humans who knew as well as their onlooker that every swing of the sword only staved off the inevitable.

Jessica's smile grew as another group of demons emerged from the smoky shadows before the first had been properly dispatched. It turned to a grin as the two humans looked at each other, him baffled and terrified and her swathed in a sad resignation.

Ximena's voice sounded above the dreadful song that played eternally in the desolate landscape.

"Paul," she said, looking in the wild thing's eyes.

His blue eyes widened in wonder, and another unintelligible moan came from his lips.

"Paul," she said again, eyeing the demons as they gathered. "I love you."

They were upon them then, Jessica wondering how that voice could sound so much like the great Ximena and ordinary little Brenna all at the same time as flesh was rent from bone and life was plucked from them both. She watched Ximena bleed, again pleased at the red color as it flowed.

Neither of them healed as they were torn limb from limb, and the light fled both of their eyes long before the demons stopped flaying their flesh with long talons and sharp swords and chomping canines. For as long as it took for the slavering monsters to consume every bit of what had once been her two friends, Jessica watched and smiled.

When it was over, her laughter filled the room. It was dark and reptilian and humorless, the sound of the bitterness that consumed her. She eyed the room and its unfamiliar occupants suspiciously, swinging her long toothy snout in a slow semi-circle. All of them had voiced some doubt or glanced some uncertainty her way since she had taken the throne, but for the twin sentinel guards at the door and the three others that attended her constant court.

Those were the three she regarded with the most suspicion.

First was the devil girl with the bright orange slitted eyes who always smiled sweetly when the queen looked her way. She was just a devil, but Jessica couldn't pry into the lowest devil's thoughts like her mother had been able to. All she could see was the smile, and every time she saw it she trusted the pretty devil a bit less. Everyone had presented themselves to her, but Jessica could not remember most of their names any more than she could read their thoughts. That was not the case with her second problem.

Royal dragons are educated, and Jessica had received her own royal education in Hell. Laurentis had been an old dragon when Jessica first fought her way free of her leathery shell, and she had heard stories of his glory and his viciousness to accompany every history lesson on Hell's waves of war. He had always fought for the queen, a lethal shadow beside her that lived for the loyal pleasure of bringing her enemies to the ground and tearing them asunder. She didn't know what role he had played in her mother's rule; she had not lived under it for long. Jessica hoped that his honesty in revealing his true name and his habit of never speaking against her bode well; why tell her his name if he meant to betray?

The new queen was young, but she hadn't hatched yesterday. Jessica knew that the ancient dragon's mind was surely as complicated as the layered tunnels of Hell, and as unfathomable. Still, she couldn't help but think of an adage that she had heard many times growing up in the luminous wonder that Hell had once been.

Be wary of the devil whose lips would drip with lies; be warier still the devil who speaks truth and holds your eyes.

The words resounded in her head every time he gave her a solemn respectful nod across the royal room. Jessica had considered ordering his death or exile, but she didn't know if the remains of her mother's army would or could carry out the order. If the ancient dragon resisted, it could decimate what few forces and what little power she actually had. Humans and Earth had been the sources of her continued learning for the last few centuries, and she had picked up a thing or two living in the short-sighted realm. The first was that the mortal heart could neither contain nor understand the meaning of its own love; the second was another old saying, this one learned under blue sky.

Since Jessica had no friends to keep close, she did what she had to do and kept her enemies closer.

That thought brought her eyes and her attention to rest on her third source of suspicion. There was no mistaking that one's intentions, the first human she had ever seen in the lower realms. He lay there sweating profusely, his skin flushed to match the devils that surrounded him. Had they food or water for him, he would have refused it. Matt lay on the floor, in chains, awaiting death like a child waiting for the ice cream truck.

CHAPTER 5

"I'll take a pair of those leather pants," Chase eyed William's leggings. "Or some chaps. One way I'll be beating the girls off and the other way I'll be beating off the boys."

The new Walker seemed to be considering both options with relish for his own sweet forever moment.

William wondered why Chase's watery blue eyes still looked drunk, and why he still smelled of vodka. He was sure there was none in the house.

"Is that why you want me to carry a stick?" Chase's liquid gaze moved to the weapon Daemon had somehow gotten ahold of. "To beat off the pretty boys and girls? I don't need it; I'm a gambler, not a fighter. Let the lovers come."

William had lived a very long time, and patience had been a hard thing won over frustrating decades. He felt it wearing thin. A glance at Kris showed him that the Guide was lost in thought, his back turned to them.

"My outfit is my armor, that 'stick' is your weapon," William spoke brusquely, unable to take a liking to the flippant new Walker and unwilling to try. "With proper training, you can hold that 'stick' in your hand and cause it to transform into a sword or axe or a variety of other things."

His watery blue eyes widened at William's words, and Chase snatched the walking stick from Daemon's hands. The new Walker didn't close his eyes or ask for instruction or express the expected disbelief. He watched with the rest of them as the stick became a sword in his hands, and seemed to be the only one not surprised when it did.

Chase smiled at the gleaming blade. He was eyeing William's leather leggings again.

"So that's armor, huh?" he asked.

William nodded, extending his arm in the direction of his jacket and imagining his palm a magnet and the armor as a metal filing. The jacket leapt into his grasp, and William hadn't had to close his eyes either. He shrugged into it while the new Walker's smile broadened.

"William." Vanessa's voice was not reprimanding but cautious, and he did not turn at the sound. Instead William held out his arm and nodded to the new Walker and then to his shining longsword. She watched, along with Kris and Daemon, as Chase brought the sword down on the old Walker's armored arm.

It was always a marvel to expect a sharp blade to be stilled by what looked like ordinary leather; the surprise he could never get used to was how little of the blade's impact reached his arm. The armor truly was magickal, removing the force from the most powerful blow and staying even the keenest steel. As far as William was concerned, he felt but a light tap on his arm as the sword bounced harmlessly off his armor.

"Okay, I'll take the armor," Chase smiled wider than ever. "Full pants and jacket like you, please."

Daemon stepped forward, holding the dark folded overcoat out to him. Chase plucked the black cowboy hat off the top and tossed it aside, somehow making it disappear before it hit the floor. The new Walker kicked off his shoes and began to wiggle his feet into the dark cowboy boots. His nose was crinkled in contempt until he found the dagger waiting in the bottom of one of them.

Chase disappeared his sword with the unblinking ease of a veteran Walker and held the dagger aloft.

"That became standard issue during the Walker King's reign," William said proudly. "Dagger, axe, flashlight, short sword, bow, snare staff...all new Walkers get them, old ones are having them issued."

The new Walker cycled through the arsenal as the old spoke the words, until he ended up with a stringed recurve in his hand. Chase arced an eyebrow at William.

"Snare staff?" He echoed.

It appeared in William's hand as Chase said it, a simple wooden staff with a generous loop of leather dangling from the far end. In the next moment the new Walker held his own taming tool in his hand, only to disappear it in the following moment with as much ease as he had the first.

Chase took the dark oiled leather overcoat from the demon and shrugged into it, his face twisted in contempt again. He didn't look like a Walker, he looked like a homeless guy that happened upon some luck in the dumpster behind a western wear outlet. William was no more pleased with the way the new Walker looked than Chase himself seemed to be.

"Where did you get the biker gear?" he asked William.

"I made it," William responded. "I used my intent and the strongest needles I could find to turn my overcoat into more modern armor."

"Does it ever get damaged?" Chase seemed curious, not concerned.

"It's not much use against dragons," William admitted.

"You've battled dragons?" Once again, the new Walker seemed a great deal more intrigued than disbelieving or worried.

William nodded, the memory neither distant enough nor pleasant enough for him to talk about it.

"Did you get new armor?" Chase was onto something, and William saw what it was when he responded.

"No," William said. "I just imagined it whole again."

This time Chase did close his eyes, and when he opened them he wore leather pants and jacket and harness boots with twice the jangling chrome on them as William's. The jacket was similar to William's, but slimmer about the waist. The broad patch of leather on William's back was bare; Chase had imagined an emblem on his, a dark tricolor design that looked like the new Walker emerging from a fiery mist wielding a sword. Three swirling forms danced about him, the only blue in the picture that wasn't his eyes. Two dark words were emblazoned on the banner, one above the image and the other below. "Walker Chase" the words read, framing the dark beautiful art between them.

The new Walker showed William and the others his back, smiling over his shoulder at each of them in turn.

"Do you like my emblem?" he asked William.

William couldn't help but nod; he liked it well enough.

Moving to stand before a tall mirror, Chase looked himself over with what looked like drunken satisfaction to William.

"Mi gusto!" Chase exclaimed.

"Si," William smiled. "Mucho gusto."

Chase was beaming at him. "Hablas español?"

"Un poco," William smiled. "Tengo mucho que aprender."

"How old are you?" The new Walker's question was harder, even if it was in his native tongue.

"Pretty old," William admitted.

"How old?" Chase pressed him curiously.

William frowned, thinking back. "I was twenty-eight when I became a Walker."

"Twenty-six," Vanessa's voice corrected him gently. "Your Saturn never returned."

"And when was that?" The more answers Chase got, the more he wanted.

"Early eighteenth century?" William was asking his Guide a question more than he was answering the Walker.

"Seventeen-oh-six, by your people's reckoning." That phrase had been a barrier between them, all those years ago; now it was a private joke between them. The only people either of them had had for over a century were each other.

"Wow." Chase was lost in his own thoughts. "You must know just about everything, huh?"

"I have a lot to learn," William said again, in the language they all understood this time.

"Is that how you keep life interesting?" Chase asked.

William regarded the new Walker with the calm quiet demeanor he had come by over the centuries. There was a sharp mind behind those watery blue eyes. Chase was wrong, but not by much.

"I learn to stay sane," William stated simply.

The two Walkers continued to eye each other with curiosity. William decided it wouldn't hurt to elaborate; and someday, it might just help.

"I started to lose my mind around the hundred fifty year mark," William sighed. "I looked for a way to solve the problem before I couldn't see a problem anymore."

"Learning was not his first attempt at a solution." Vanessa was remembering too, solemn and sad in her thoughts of yesterday's yesterday.

The old Walker nodded his agreement. "The first was justice. When the cowboy way and the United States were both new, I embraced each equally. I tried to do right with my dwindling faculties. I lost human friends, my Watcher and my face before I learned my lesson."

Chase smiled. "What lesson?"

"Human affairs are for humans," William sighed. "I had carefully crafted a legitimate identity to do my meddling, and in learning to become someone else I found myself."

"Then you lost your face?" Chase was still curious. "Or did you mean you lost face? Tell me that story."

"I meant both," William replied. "That story is best left for another day. You have a job to do, new Walker."

That distasteful look came over Chase's face again.

"Prepare yourself," William counseled him, though Chase had everything he needed waiting on his thought. "I need to speak with my Guides."

Chase glanced about the room, his curiosity pursuing a new path. "You don't happen to have any vodka, do you? I sent Daemon out for some earlier, but I think it was a bad batch or something."

William shook his head, fighting the urge to smile.

"Didn't Daemon tell you about your healing ability?" he asked.

"He did," Chase nodded as he answered. "He didn't tell me that I couldn't drink anymore."

"You can drink." William gave a rare shrug. "It just won't have any affect."

Of all the things that often disturbed a new Walker, that one rarely disturbed them the most. This new Walker was more than just disturbed at the news; Chase looked horrified. His eyes looked sharp and clear for the first time, wide in fear.

"You haven't been drunk in over three hundred years?" At long last, something had mystified Chase. "No wonder you went crazy."

"Almost," Vanessa spoke for William, kindly. "He almost went crazy."

"It didn't stop Paul." Kris spoke up, roused from his sullen thoughts by something. They all turned to look at him, William last. Still sitting with his back to them, he had half-turned on the sofa.

The Guide shrugged.

"From drinking," he clarified.

William felt the defensive muscles that had crowded together in his shoulders relax as he grasped the Guide's meaning.

"Paul?" Chase echoed the name that reverberated in all of their thoughts. "Didn't I meet him? Where is he?"

They were all lost in their own memories or supposings for a long still moment. It was William who finally answered.

"The Walker King was burnt to nothing by dragon flame, as we all watched helpless." His tone was stern and solemn again, and begged no more questions as much as his suddenly turned back demanded it. William needed to talk to his Guides, and time was of the essence.

Kris, Vanessa and William seemed grateful to hear Chase express his next concern aloud as they leaned together.

"Hey!" the new Walker exclaimed, caught in a fresh wave of panic. "What about my tattoos?!"

William heard the demon begin to explain that Chase was doomed to an unmarked future as he addressed the Guides in a low voice.

"The Council doesn't see everything," he told them in hushed hurried words. "It may be because I have no Watcher, it could apply to all Walkers; I don't know."

"I don't have a Watcher," Kris noted quietly. "Or a Walker."

William nodded. "You two could work together to—"

"To guide William." Vanessa spoke loudly, startling both of them. They turned to see the others looking on and listening. Chase had one boot and sock off, his jacket and shirt flung to the floor, and his pants puddled about his ankles. Damon stood beside him, arms crossed.

The new Walker did not seem interested in what they had been talking about at all. Instead, he looked furious. He glared at William as if he alone were responsible for the dark frown that clouded his countenance.

"My tattoos are gone." Chase was obviously not pleased.

"Put your clothes on," William responded. "Let's go."

CHAPTER 6

It was a long dark climb through an unfamiliar pain as he came awake, a desperate groping for his own name and the source of the dull ache. He remembered all at once.

He was Cal, and the pain was tequila.

At least he was in his own bed and had plenty of cocaine, if his splotchy memory served. The pusher thought about laying there and moaning for a few seconds, trying to remember the last thing he remembered. He decided to roll over and get up and do some cocaine. No matter what ailed him, that always seemed to help.

When he nearly rolled over on top of Sarah, more memories came rushing back. Awake and naked, she lay on her side with one arm bent to hold her head. Her eyes were clear and wide and green, and they went even wider when she blinked.

"Good morning, lover," she cooed, smiling.

She began to reach out to touch him or ruffle his bedhead or something, and Cal rolled the other way to launch himself off the mattress. He was naked too, so he tugged on a fresh pair of boxers after pulling them from the drawer.

"I have work to do," Cal faced her for a moment in his underwear before he turned to open the sock drawer.

Sarah laughed. "You're a drug dealer. What do you have to do at nine A.M.?"

"Well, for starters," Cal grabbed the slacks he had been wearing last night and fished in the correct pocket the first time. He held aloft a baggie of powder. "Some cocaine."

"And then?" Sarah was still naked, laying there looking enticing.

"Then I need to re-up." Cal was too busy cutting a line to look.

"Is your guy really up this early?" she asked.

Cal nodded, already holding a tube over a line. The nightstands and dresser all had glass tops, and the dresser always had a cheap pen with all of its mechanisms removed on it or in a drawer.

"My guy's always awake," he said between snorting powder up one nostril and then the other. Out of kindness or generosity or reflex, he gestured to what remained on the glass surface. Sarah refused with a smile and a shake of her head, so Cal tooted that one as well. He tried to hide his surprise, both at her being alive and being naked.

Sarah stretched languidly, pelting his mind with more recollections of the night before. Her slender body and soft skin called to him with delectable memories and delightful imaginings. And fresh surprise that her heart still beat.

"Do you at least have time for breakfast?" she asked.

Pulling on fresh slacks and securing the fastenings, Cal considered the thought. He still felt like he had been hit by a tequila truck rather then drink a small portion of one's contents. He knew what was in the fridge; it was his.

"Eggs and toast is all I really have." He slid his feet into one of the five identical pairs of leather shoes lined up in his closet under the dark array of buttoned shirts.

Sarah pulled on the crinkled shirt Cal had worn yesterday as he chose a fresh one from the closet.

"What about coffee?" Sarah approached him from behind as Cal made a show of ignoring her attention and buttoning up the charcoal softness.

"Yeah, just warm up the Keurig and pick a brew." Cal answered as brusquely as he could.

"Do you want some?" Sarah's bright mood kept shining despite the deliberate distance he was keeping as he moved toward the bathroom.

"Yeah, just a little sugar."

A minute later she was setting the brew on the counter next to the toothpaste. Sarah kissed Cal on the back of the head as he bent to spit in the sink.

"There you go," she giggled into his mussed hair. "Just a little sugar."

When he came into the kitchen Sarah was staring into the open refrigerator. She had rolled up the sleeves of his midnight shirt so he could see her slight hairless forearms, and every bit of her legs and most of her ass showed under it. None of the buttons were fastened, and she swept one side back to put her lightly balled fist on one of her slim hips. One side of her was bare as she turned her attention to him, one leg bent from her body to remind him that she was pretty everywhere.

"This is the cleanest barest bachelor fridge I've ever seen," she said, enjoying watching him watching her.

There was a loaf of sprouted whole wheat bread, a tub of organic butter from free range cows, and a carton of brown free range organic eggs on the otherwise clean shelves. Cal didn't have to look; he knew there was some satisfactory portion of each item to feed them both, none of the items expired.

"Have you seen a lot of bachelor fridges?" Cal always liked to hold a mirror up when he felt he was being criticized.

"Yeah." Sarah shrugged, unperturbed. "I've been in a lot of bands."

It was easy for her to find the egg pan and the toaster oven, and Cal had the pleasure of watching someone else put together his customary morning fare.

"Is that all you eat, then?" She found the silver and set a place on the small dining table for each of them.

"I like to eat out." Cal sipped his coffee.

"Yes you do!" Sarah was upon him then, covering the hair he had just wetted with kisses. She was rubbing his shoulders, and it felt good. "You're awfully good at it too."

He let her purr against his back for a few more seconds, then Cal reminded her. "The eggs, Sarah."

Kissing him atop the head one last time, she finally moved away from him and toward the stove.

"Aren't you Mason's girl?" Cal asked her back.

She cooked in silence for a few more minutes, then set two plates on the table and pulled out a chair.

"I'm Sarah's girl," she smiled across the table at him. "If Mason can have fun, then I can too. Isn't that what you said last night?"

Cal still wasn't completely clear on every detail of the previous evening's events, but he had obviously not been raped or anything. Why hadn't he just killed her, like he had thought about so many times? Not once had he wondered what color her nipples were or what she tasted like in thick drops, but he knew those things now. Cal had imagined bashing her head in or stabbing her, and the thought of cleaning that up seemed simpler.

Cal salted his eggs with ground Himalayan sea salt and peppered them with organic peppercorn and ate them slowly. His head was still pounding, and the deliciousness of the scant meal was lost on his pummeled palette. Watching Sarah across the table was like watching the sun come up over the horizon. Her face and eyes were clear and bright, and she smiled at him between every bite she took.

"Don't you feel any semblance of what I am enduring?" Cal had to stop eating for a few minutes; his stomach had more to say than he did.

Sarah popped her last bite of toast into her mouth and smiled at him while she chewed it. After sipping at her coffee, she shook her head.

"I don't get hangovers," she blinked, and her pretty green eyes went wide. "You should smoke some weed. It's a pretty common remedy for a hangover, you know. It might help you get your appetite back too."

They both looked at the scattered remains of food on his plate.

"Unless you don't like the way I cook." The sunshine on her face was obscured by sudden clouds.

"No." Cal pushed the eggs around in the bit of yellow goo that hadn't hardened in the heat, dipped his toast in the perfect mess and contemplated the dripping slice.

"It's perfect." He set the browned bread on the plate. "I'm just not hungry."

His stomach gurgled loud enough for her to hear.

"Aww." Sarah cocked her head prettily to one side and blinked.

Cal watched her eyes widen, and shrugged.

"How much pot do you have?" he asked.

Sarah beamed. "Enough to smoke all day and sit around watching nature documentaries or detective shows."

His apartment did not advertise Cal's drug use, unless glass tables in every room tipped the observer off. It did speak of his neat and tidy nature, his taste in furnishings and an ability to afford those tastes, and his love of nature and crime drama. The only thing he watched were the channels that showed endless animal or taped off scenes, and the only DVDs he ordered were the ones they advertised as he watched. All of them were proudly displayed behind clear glass under his enormous wall-mounted flat screen.

"I went out on the balcony and smoked some while you were sleeping." Sarah was clearing the dishes and then parting the long curtains that obscured the sliding glass. Sunlight speared through the clear pane to stab a fresh wave of agony through Cal's brain.

"Aaaah!" His voice was a thin high-pitched wail of agony. "I'm melting!"

Sarah giggled as the screech died out, sliding the door on its track. It produced another screech, a reminder to Cal that he had ignored the outer area for some time.

"I cleaned out the spider webs too," Sarah said as she screeched the door home again. Looking at her was hard; the sunlight behind her mostly nude form lit her like an angel, burned his eyes and stabbed his skull.

"Close the curtains, please." Cal squinted at the clean floor.

"You don't want to smoke out on the deck?" She was still bathed in painful luminosity.

"I want you to close the fucking curtain," he gritted.

At last, only scant unnatural light bathed the room. Cal got up and gestured to the open doorway that led to the living room, following Sarah to the couch.

"Ooh, the leather is cold." Sarah wiggled her ass around on the sofa before settling in. "And soft."

She sat sideways when she did settle, her knees toward him as Cal joined her.

"I can't believe it." She held the glass pipe out to him. It was packed with a fresh green flower. "I'm about to smoke out Cal…hey, what's your last name?"

He coughed on the first puff, but only a little. It wasn't his first time or anything. On the second he held it in for a few seconds, and Cal felt his face reddening as he handed the pipe and lighter back. He also felt a pleasant wave wash over his whole body, and he sighed out the smoke with a smile.

"Drake." He turned the smile her way. "Thanks."

"One more." She was holding an item in each hand. "Then you should take your shirt off so I can sit behind you and rub your shoulders. What do you want to watch?"

Cal hit the pipe once more, then remembered the other appetite that could be affected by nature's remedy.

"I want to watch you take your shirt off and then come over here and take my clothes off too." Cal smiled hungrily as she advanced on him.

Splendidly naked, Sarah knelt before him and started unbuttoning his shirt. Cal brought his hands to either side of her face, brushing back the hair that hung down both sides of her head until he had gently coaxed every strand behind her ears. Tracing feather touches down her neck and across her shoulders, Cal leaned forward and kissed her forehead. The next soft kiss landed on the tip of her nose, and the next on her waiting lips. She stared at his open eyes while their mouths met, blinking and then letting them go green and wide again.

Her fingers still worried at his buttons, while his traced the curves of her shoulders and back with gentle care. When she had freed the last one, she pushed his shirt back over his shoulders. As soon as they were exposed she kissed them, one shoulder and then the other, while his feathered touch came back to her soft pale cheeks.

Cupping her face in his hands, Cal kissed her again.

"So gentle," she murmured, smiling softly as he was touching her.

More shards of memory flashed in his mind, some of the ways he had taken her last night.

"Is that okay?" Cal brushed back a strand of hair that had escaped from behind her ear.

She kissed him again.

"Oh, yeah," she glowed. "Multifaceted is as important as highly skilled."

He tasted her lips, her neck and her bare chest while she reached over him to gently massage his shoulders.

As his touches and kisses moved to encircle her nipples without touching them just yet, Sarah collapsed slowly backwards onto the soft leather. Her breasts moved away from him as she laid back, the nipples erect while the rest glowed from the wet sheen of his carefully placed kisses. When her back came to rest on the cushion, she stretched a leg to either side of him and lifted her belly and hips to meet the next wave of affection.

Cal responded in kind, the speed and pressure of his touch increasing as his kisses did. He kissed her stomach as it fell away from him, grasping her legs to put one over each of his shoulders. Tasting her calves and inner thighs, Cal breathed in her scent and swallowed her flavor as he kissed a hungry radius around her moistening mound. Each of his hands grasped a slim buttock, kneading her flesh in firm revolving grasps. His face just over the blossoming junction of her widened thighs, Cal inhaled her again and breathed close to her. Sarah shuddered at the wind, and again when his tongue moved to lightly taste her.

Unable or unwilling to wait, Sarah pressed her whole body towards him while spreading her legs further. One of her feet found the floor and the other dangled over the back of the couch while soft layers of flesh moved to his mouth. Cal opened his mouth to encompass her, meeting her eyes as he sucked and licked.

Again, she did not want to wait. Sarah tangled her fingers in his drying hair and dragged him hungrily upward so he would move inside her as they kissed again.

CHAPTER 7

Kris stood facing Vanessa in the wake of the Walker trio's departure. It had been pleasantly reminiscent to watch William put one gloved hand on Chase's shoulder and the other on Daemon's and then see them fade from view. The Guide had grown accustomed to feeling the weight of Paul's hand falling on him to wrench him from one world to another. He had all but forgotten that he had his own key that hung round his neck when he wanted it to.

The other Guide was holding her own golden key, looking at him expectantly. Her question was not of the mission at hand or what steps they must take, however.

"Are you alright, Guide Kris?" Her dark eyes spoke concern.

"I shouldn't still be here," he muttered.

"Pardon?" Vanessa cocked her head to the side.

"Nothing." He shrugged. "Nothing I need to wallow in, anyways."

The forever youthful Guide beckoned him to the nearby sofa to sit. She settled her weightlessness with an open square of cushion between them.

"My friendship does not invite wallowing," she smiled. "I only sense that you carry a burden whose weight may diminish if given voice. An ear not lent in judgement can both ease such a burden and forge bonds of friendship."

Kris sighed. "I tried to control Jessica."

"What do you mean?" Vanessa asked.

"I tried to use the things you taught me to stop the woman I loved from exercising her own free will." Kris let the storm that pelted his heart cloud his countenance.

"You speak of the red dragon that burned the Walker King, yes?" she asked. "The one you call Jessica?"

Kris nodded.

"Even a dragon that small is hundreds of years old," Vanessa reminded him. "Your scant training and practice would have been no match for a mind like that. You mustn't feel bad that you were unable to stop her."

"I don't," he responded with bitter haste. "I feel bad because I tried to."

"Paul might yet live if you had succeeded," she pointed out.

Kris shrugged. "Somehow I don't think so. Paul didn't either. He expected to die in Hell."

"Did Jessica have a good heart?" she asked.

"It felt good when it wrapped me up in its love." Heavy clouds continued to darken his face.

"Perhaps if you had stopped her she would have come to thank you for it one day. Perhaps your attempt has not been filed in a completely evil category in her complex mind." Vanessa spoke calmly to him, smiling gently the entire time. "Perhaps the burden you carry is misplaced, for where you see a reason for shame I see a source of pride. You tried to do the right thing, even if it meant stopping someone you loved from acting to do the wrong thing. Your love for her and Paul nearly saved them both, one from the pain of death and the other from the burden of having inflicted it."

"So," Kris peeked through the clouds, "we're right back to looking at the fact that I failed."

"Have you given up?" Vanessa glanced around, reminding him that someone could very well be listening.

Kris shook his head, resolute.

'Then you have not failed.' Vanessa smiled as her sweet voice sounded in his head. *'Where to, King of the Guides?'*

He reached out his hand, and she grasped it over the empty cushion. They both smiled, her in grateful memory of his teachings and him at the weight that had indeed been eased.

"Was that your nonjudgmental assessment?" He smiled as her fingers curled around his. "Because it sounded a little judgy."

Vanessa made a face and a sound that she had surely seen on a teenaged girl in a high school television drama. It was shockingly out of character for the young wise Guide.

"What-ever!" Her eyes and her voice danced with mirth. "I'm only seventeen! Of course I'm judgmental!"

Kris was laughing as they shifted, and forgot to close his eyes. It wasn't so bad, a flash of colors and they were holding hands in the clouds.

'You are a good friend, Guide Kris.' Her voice was her own again as it sounded in his head. *'To me, to Paul, and even to the tempestuous dragon that holds your heart.'*

Squeezing her hand in thanks, he let his fall to his side. "They can't listen in here, I don't think."

They both looked around, their eyes falling on the strange doorless structure nearby at the same time.

"There are two devils in there." Kris spoke first.

Vanessa nodded. "So I have heard."

"I plan to speak with them."

She reached out her hand again. "Then I intend to join you."

A moment later they stood in the secured space within the secured space. There were bunks and bottles strewn about, slept on and drained. The two occupants turned to the Guides as they appeared and began to advance on them. They stopped almost immediately, regarding the two robed visitors together. Kris let go of her hand.

The room stunk of sweat and sage, brimstone and beer. Kris tuned out the smells, throwing Vanessa a glance at the same time the captives shared one.

"Where is the Walker King?" One of the devils spoke, balling meaty fists at his side and raising an eyebrow to make the question an aggressive one. His voice was a low throaty growl, his eyes lit with red.

Kris paused, exchanged another look with Vanessa.

"Please say it isn't true." The other devil's voice was higher and thinner, and the Guide was surprised to hear fear in it. He was even more surprised to see one devil reach out and grasp the other's hand, giving or seeking comfort.

"It's true, isn't it?" The larger devil grumbled and shook his head. "Paul is dead."

"Walker Paul was killed by the dragon queen's daughter." Vanessa spoke while Kris wondered at their concern.

"And the true queen?" High and thin went to piercing and shrill as the smaller devil clenched the other's hand. He looked around, cautious even when gripped by anxiety, then spoke the name aloud. "Ximena?"

"She was with him," Vanessa responded. "She was burned to nothing by the same flame."

One devil left the other's side, but only for as long as it took to fish an unlabeled bottle of beer from under one of the tumbled bunks. In less than a minute they were holding hands again and passing the bottle.

"Where did you get all this beer?" Kris finally spoke.

The devils looked at each other, surprised by his surprise.

"Paul," the bigger one grumped. "He bought us the ingredients and we brewed the beer. Where did you think 'The Devil's Brew' was made?"

Both of the devils nodded in time, solemn and respectful as they thought back. The smaller one had the bottle, and tipped it to let a few drops splatter on the luminous floor. Shooting him an annoyed glance, the other took the bottle and let go his hand.

"For the Walker King," came the meek voice of the slight devil, as he cringed away and reached out tentatively at the same time.

The big devil grumbled something under his breath and upended the bottle. Brown liquid pooled on the flowing floor before being absorbed to nothingness at their feet.

"For the Walker King," he echoed, tossing the empty container aside and taking the other devil's hand again.

"Wasn't he your captor?" Kris was doing his best not to look or sound befuddled.

"He was our friend!" The small demon's shrill voice split the air. "Don't look so surprised, Guide. The only devils that could fight up here were on our way up and pretty high already. We all volunteered, because we were all ready to leave Hell behind. One more death and many of us were slated not just to move up but to move on."

The other devil grimaced. "We devils on the way up know that death speeds us along, especially when we die for a good cause. We have come to the place where we value life too much to take our own, but where we also understand that life has a purpose higher than any individual."

Kris couldn't believe he was about to ask a devil what the meaning of life was, but he did it anyway.

"And what is the higher purpose of life?"

"Love," the devils answered in unison, moving closer together.

Vanessa nodded her agreement. Kris frowned.

"You were Paul's Guide, yes?" The smaller devil seemed the chattier of the two.

Kris nodded.

"Did he not take you to see the light?" he asked.

Kris nodded again.

"Paul took you to see the Great Spirit?" Vanessa's eyes were round with wonder.

Kris shrugged. "Yeah, I guess so."

The devil nudged the big one with an elbow. "He met God, and he's still agnostic."

He grumbled with laughter while the talkative devil went on. "You saw the light. You talked to it, it answered. What did it sound like? Why did it speak? What was the general impression you got from it?"

The answer to all of his questions were the same.

"Love," Kris acknowledged after a moment, frowning once more.

Kris decided it was time for him to start asking the questions. "How do you two know so much? About me? About Paul? About Ximena?"

The two devils drew back at the sound of the name, their black on scarlet eyes going wide.

"What?!" Kris demanded. "Ximena, Ximena, Ximena! You think I haven't tried summoning her?! She's one of my best friends!"

Silence reigned in the wake of his rant, and Kris was breathing heavy while his heart beat fast though neither process was a necessary part of his existence. The odors of the room assaulted his senses once again, sleep and brimstone and beer and probably violent devil sex from the way they clung to each other. Kris shut off his breathing and stilled his dead heart.

"Sorry." Kris spoke calmly. "Can we start over? I am Kris, and this is Guide Vanessa. What are you two called?"

The smaller devil stepped forward and extended a taloned hand. "I am Rikar, this is Yarson."

Vanessa shook the proffered hand while Kris considered the condition of the room and the absence of a sink. Then he shook it too. What the hell; he was already dead. Rikar went on in his high-pitched voice while they exchanged handshakes with beefy Yarson.

"Devils can see," Rikar explained, "in a way that humans can't. No, scratch that. Devils learn to see in a way that most humans don't learn. Only the humans on the borders of Heaven or Hell can usually see without trying, and the rest don't live for long enough to develop it. While your television and publications and internet connect your world's denizens, Hell is in a technological dark age that has few benefits. Some say the sight is one of those benefits, that if we were digitally connected to each other as so many humans are we would lose the sight."

"Bullshit," Yarson grumbled.

"I saw it with my people." Vanessa spoke softly, and all eyes turned to her. "Humans do not have to be on the brink of devil or angel to see the Great Spirit and have it guide them in all things. True seers do walk between worlds in their own way, but they can bring others to that doorway as well. Maintaining a connection with Mother Earth and Father Sky was a way of life for my people when I lived. My people still live, but very few of them see even in ritual what we learned to see every day."

Rikar was nodding. "Indigenous humans can often see as well."

"See what?" Kris did not feel like he was learning anything.

"Everything," Vanessa smiled, "and love."

Rikar nodded again. "Anything you want to see, anything of interest to you. Unless it's protected like this place. Yeah, and love. Lots of love."

"So you saw them die?" Kris wondered why they would ask about it if they could just peek in.

Yarson shook his head while Rikar spoke.

"No," he said. "There was a white-out when we both tried to look, like someone is trying to hide something."

"The Council paused time," Kris pointed out. "Could that have anything to do with it?"

Rikar's shrill laughter split the air. "The Council could not stop time; that would stop space. They paused everyone in Hell, not time itself. Time must always flow, Guide."

Thinking of time made Kris think of his friend.

"What did you talk to Paul about?" he asked them.

"Everything," Rikar responded. "Life, the Universe. Everything. Heaven and Hell and demons and devils."

"And God?" Kris ventured.

Rikar nodded. "And God. Nearly everyone in the Universe is a pretty big fan, Guide. Besides you, of course."

"Did Paul have the sight?" the Guide asked.

Again the big devil nodded while the smaller spoke.

"Not at first," Rikar answered. "He did in the end though, either because he meditated so much or because his soul was rising so fast. Once he took you above he was wide open. We did so hope it would be enough."

Kris sighed. Paul had seemed awfully happy for a guy who saw the end was near, especially when he held Ximena in his arms.

"Do you know what her and I are up to?" Kris asked.

Yarson let go the smaller devil's hand to go fishing about under a bunk. The Guide was momentarily alarmed, and shared a look of concern with Vanessa. It evaporated when the devil stood holding another unlabeled and unopened bottle.

"You had better be here to enlist our help finding the Walker King and Ximena and restoring their places of power." Yarson suddenly had some things to say. "Otherwise we are going to drink this last beer and use it to send each other to the next life. We may not remember it, but we want our souls to know that we did right by all the realms."

"Paul said he would come back for us if he could," Rikar said. "He wouldn't let us help fight in Hell, because he knows how dragons treat turncoats. He said that when the war was over he would help find a place for us, or help us make a better home here."

Yarson had drunk nearly the entire frothy contents of the bottle he had opened, and he passed the last few ounces to his horned companion. He bent to pull a stack of leather and metal from under another bunk, then began choosing pieces and strapping them to himself and Rikar. By the time the smaller devil had consumed the last drops, both devils stood armed and armored before the Guides.

"Where to first, Guide King?" Yarson grumbled.

"Can you see Paul now?" he asked the sighted pair.

The devils moved their heads in negation.

Kris tried to keep the frustration from his voice and his face. "Then what makes you think he's not gone for good?"

"You, Guide," Yarson growled.

Rikar nodded. "You yet live, and have the powers of a Guide. The keys generated by Walker Paul's platinum key still exist, and one of them hangs yet about your neck. That means the platinum key continues to exist, and that it is still attached to the Stone Walker."

"What about the other keys? Matt's didn't save him." Kris didn't want to spend any more time counting how many friends he had lost than necessary, but there it was.

"Matthew yet lives as well," Rikar assured him. "Perhaps we all owe our continued existence to that great devil. His sight was always on another level altogether. Matthew left his key behind on Earth, so the new dragon queen could not get ahold of him and it and mis-use them both. He saw the future coming as surely as the Walker King, and even more clearly. Matthew placed himself in her captivity as deliberately as he left his key with the Original Walker Devil."

"Roche has Matt's key," Kris repeated, "and Matt is Jessica's prisoner in Hell."

The devils nodded together.

"And dragons are especially cruel to those they view as having betrayed them?" he asked.

"Matthew left Hell with a promise to never return until his soul's downward distant future brought him back," Rikar answered with a shrug. "He came back with an army of Walkers. It's easy to see how some would see betrayal in that."

Yarson grunted and shifted his weight, his settling armor clanking loudly.

"Matthew is a patriot of the Universe," he said in his low graveled voice, "as are Ximena and Paul."

"As are we." Rikar tossed the empty bottle aside and grasped Yarson's hand again. "Where to, Guide?"

"I have to rescue Matt." Kris frowned. "I need to try to talk to Jessica."

The devils both drew their swords from the scabbards on their hips. Kris shook his head and spread his hands.

"I think I have a better chance alone," he told them. "I would like you to go with Vanessa to start looking for Paul and Ximena."

Although they exchanged a doubtful look, the devils put their blades away.

"Where?" Rikar asked, his face still crimson concern.

"Where can you not see?" the Guide asked.

It was Vanessa that answered. "Personal spaces and between realms. The walls within which the Walker army battled demons are beyond the vision of all but a special few. They are also inaccessible to most Walkers. My golden key will not open those doorways."

"No worries." Rikar held up a platinum key that Kris could swear he hadn't been holding a moment earlier. "The Walker King made us his Agents."

Kris shook his head, bemused. "You could have gone anywhere, anytime. Why did you stay here?"

Yarson grimaced happily. "The Walker King asked us to wait here."

"He left us a bunch of beer and forever and each other," Rikar bobbed his horned head in happy agreement. "Where would we go?"

Kris looked the three of them over before thinking of Jessica. He felt good about leaving the devils with the Guide, and lighter for having a clear purpose. He smiled. "Good luck."

Rikar's laughter followed him to Hell with his words. "Good luck to us? No, Guide, good luck to you. You are the one that needs it."

CHAPTER 8

The demon that Chase's timepiece counted down to had brought them back to streets familiar to both of the Walkers. Daemon marveled at the lights and sounds of the biggest little city in the world as William instructed the new Walker in living just above the humans around them. They passed pedestrians without any of them taking notice, and one rushing young man stepped right through Chase as he concentrated.

"Good," William nodded. It appeared as though the new Walker was going to excel at all of the training most balked at. William watched him scanning the scene, looking as much the Walker as he was probably ever going to in his emblemed biker gear.

"See that young woman?" he asked Chase. "The one in the black dress?"

"You mean the hooker?" The new Walker watched the attractive woman that they were here for. She wore a great deal of make-up, accenting her blue eyes and carefully coiffed blonde tresses. The early afternoon sun shone through her hair and the high arch of her suede stilettos as she turned in place, asking men whose clothes looked like they could afford it if they wanted a date as they passed.

Chase must have seen the frown that William tried to keep from his lips.

"Sorry," he smirked. "Would you prefer 'prostitute'?"

"How you see the world is your choice, to be informed by your Guide." William spoke the familiar sentence before he realized who he was referencing. Daemon stood near his Walker, still engrossed in the energy of the new city. He was accustomed to not being seen or heard and being completely alone in his world. William had no illusions that the demon was not paying attention to their exchange. He did have to remind himself that that was a good thing.

William cast his gaze again toward the streetwalker. "I see a young woman."

"Me too," agreed Chase. "A young woman who is a hooker. She is also a sister and a mother and a daughter."

"How do you know that?" William wasn't sure if he was calling his bluff or if he really believed him.

Chase pointed. "She has three demons that have the most influence over her. One is obsessed with her daughter discovering what she does and following in her footsteps or hating her. The older one is constantly worrying her over her parents or brother finding out, and the one we are here for is the one that feeds on her misplaced sadness."

This time William let the frown touch his face. "Misplaced?"

Instead of answering, Chase dug in his pocket and pulled out a wad of bills. He counted them and shoved them back in his leather jeans, then began walking up the street away from his Guide and Maker.

William caught up easily, falling into step beside him. "What are you doing?"

Holding up the ticking timepiece as he walked, Chase said, "It's time."

He turned when he neared the intersection, closing his eyes as a group of pedestrians surrounded him in passing. William watched three wispy forms whirlwind into the small crowd as they passed, and saw Daemon concentrating on the moving group much like Vanessa did when she was re-minding folks. Chase was one of them suddenly, walking in their world and trailing behind the handful of people that made no notice of his appearance. He tipped the hat he wasn't wearing at William as he fell into step beside him again.

"What are you doing?" William knew the new Walker couldn't answer without drawing attention to himself. He pressed on anyway in the time he had. "You need to separate her from the big demon and cut off its head. There is no need for you to interact with her."

And that was all the time he had.

Chase walked up to the young lady, his chains clanking and his leather creaking, and stopped before her.

"Hi," he smiled. "I don't usually do this, but you look like an especially sweet girl and I had to ask."

Chase had her attention. William decided to go with it, and step in at the last second if he needed to.

When she smiled, it was especially sweet. Her voice was sweet too. "How can I help you, honey?"

The new Walker scanned the street, though he hadn't before addressing her. He leaned toward her.

"The anti-depressants I take make me unable to get…y'know, hard," Chase spoke in low confidential tones. "It's okay; I don't want it either, nor do I want to want it. I do long for a woman's sweet touch sometimes, but I have no one. I have almost three hundred dollars. I was hoping we might go somewhere private and you could just…hold me."

It looked like Chase had met his long-time girlfriend there on the street as William watched. She took his hand and put it around her waist, cuddling up to him and kissing the new Walker's cheek. Her lips left the perfect imprint of the kiss, and she giggled and wiped it away with her thumb. With one arm around Chase and the other stretched across her shapely body to hook her thumb in his front pocket, she clung to him lovingly and led him up the street at the same time.

"I have a room," she smiled.

"I only have about a half hour," Chase said. "Is it close?"

She nodded and pointed to the hotel across the street. It was part of the casino that dominated that side of the block, but the lobby and hotel entrance were the closest part of the structure. William paced them invisibly as they crossed the paved lanes, watching her demon walking along beside her. She was young and looked much like her host, as was so often the case with a person's primary demon. Her hair was dark where her host's was blonde, and her eyes were scarlet and black where the young lady's were blue and white. Dressed more modestly than her creator, the demon wore a plain full-length black leather dress that showed no cleavage and little leg. Her black heels were low, and made no sound as she walked in time with the couple.

Waving at the concierge as they crossed the colorful lobby, the young woman thought she was alone in the elevator with her customer. Snuggling up close to him after pressing the button for floor twenty-three, she looked up at Chase while her demon and William looked on. The demon began to chant, her voice sad and distant as her gaze. Daemon stood in a far corner, silent.

"Cameras and Charlie won't keep you safe," the demon murmured quietly. "If this guy or any guy kills you then that's it. How hard will the cops look? How sad will your family be?"

She seemed to be drugged or dazed, and even as William looked right at her the demon did not acknowledge him. Curious, he looked harder and saw the smaller monsters that rode the woman's shoulders. One male and one female, they sat and stared dully at nothing. Each of them was ensconced in a cloud of spiraling energy, and when William looked back at the largest demon he saw a similar form swirling about her head. The demon went on mumbling half-heartedly while Chase smiled at the young woman and spoke quietly to her. Daemon watched William watching, a slight smile on his lips.

"You have a great energy," he said, squeezing her shoulder softly. "What's your name?"

"Angela," she purred, moving even closer to him. "What's yours?"

"John." he smiled.

A bell dinged lightly when they reached her floor, and Angela led Chase by the hand up the carpeted hallway.

William hesitated as she keyed the entry, but Chase beckoned him to follow while she stepped into the room with her back to them both. The whole assemblage somehow made it through the doorway before it closed, Chase and Angela with all the demons that came with them preceding William.

The first thing the new Walker did was walk to the nightstand and pile all the bills in his pocket there. Then he turned to her and opened his arms, and she stepped into them. She traced lazy lines down his back while he caught his fingers lightly in her hair, and she leaned her head to lay it on his chest.

"You want me to take my clothes off, baby?" she cooed.

William shifted uncomfortably and glanced at Daemon.

The demon watched his Walker with careful concentration.

"Only if you want to," Chase answered, to William's relief. "Why don't you take off your shoes. I'd like to pile up a couple pillows and lie back while you rest your head on my chest and rub my belly or play with my hair or whatever you do when you are being affectionate."

It was strange watching them interact. Chase seemed the practiced professional with his mind on business; Angela made every indication that she wanted to be here, that this was for her. When Chase laid back, she climbed halfway on top of him for a few moments and kissed his forehead and his cheeks with slow sweetness. Settling her head on his chest, she looked up at him and smiled.

"I like your energy, too." Her voice was a whispered enchantment, as were the light patterns she drew over his heart. "You seem like a pretty great guy."

Chase sighed and returned her smile, then leaned back further into the stacked pillows. He closed his eyes and stroked her hair. Angela's head dropped lower on his chest, and she sighed.

"You put me at ease," Chase spoke in a measured slow voice. "I feel so relaxed with you, so comfortable and so very relaxed. I feel like I could just close my eyes and drift off and when I woke up everything would be better. I feel like I could just relax and sleep."

The old Watcher watched the young lady's face as the new Walker spoke. The first sentence visibly put her at ease, the next had her yawning and curling up closer to Chase. As he spoke the third sentence she closed her eyes sleepily, and by the end of the fourth Angela was breathing deeply and adrift in another world.

Chase scooted himself out from under her and stood next to the bed looking right at the young woman's largest demon. She stared numbly at nothing, her quiet rant nothing but a silent movement of her lips.

"Make sure she doesn't wake up, please," Chase said quietly, and the swirl of energy that encompassed the demon's head uncoiled to swirl about Angela's instead.

Slowly, the demon came out of her stupor and looked around. William knew that the day a demon became the objective of a Walker's countdown was generally the first time it interacted with a demon hunter since it's creation. Yet somehow they always knew a Walker when they saw one, and that their numbered days had come to an end. It didn't stop them from trying to take over their host or attack the Walker, and William waited to see which this one would try to do first.

The demon's eyes widened; and as he had expected, the demon moved toward the sleeping young woman.

William gave Chase a chance to move, and he did. The new Walker put himself between the demon and her host, taking the horned monster in his arms and holding her close as he had her creator. The sudden embrace took the demon by surprise as much as it did William, and for a moment she stood still next to him. She struggled then, but only for a moment. Soothing wordless sounds dripped from Chase's lips, and she melted into his arms.

"That's it," the new Walker murmured, smoothing her hair. "Just relax. We are not here to hurt you."

The demon looked up at Chase, her scarlet eyes round with great misery and a touch of wonder.

Chase smiled a kind and open smile down at the pretty demon. Looking in her eyes, he asked, "Why are you so sad?"

Although her eyes filled with tears, she shook her head. "I'm not sad. She is."

She pointed at the dozing young lady.

Chase shook his head, but he didn't argue.

"Why is she so sad?" he asked.

"Because she doesn't listen to me!" Her voice became a hiss on the last few words. After she had spoken them, the demon moved even closer to Chase.

"She can't hear you like I can," he smiled. "She doesn't know how sweet your voice is or how wise your words are. All she hears is judgement, and that makes her sad. That isn't what you want, is it?"

Her eyes went round again, this time in a kind of innocent shock. "No, I don't want that. I want her to be happy. I love her."

The demon's voice actually sounded sweeter now. She spoke of love as well, and William always took that as some indicator of wisdom. Watching the scene, the old Walker no longer held his sword ready in his mind or his body prepared to move. He was relaxed and observant, not wondering what might go wrong but simply curious how this was going to turn out.

Still holding her close and stroking her hair, Chase spoke again to the demon. "What do you want her to know? I can tell her when she wakes up."

The demon nodded, anxious and excited. "Tell her she needs to stop being a prostitute."

"Okay," Chase cooed to her. "Why is that?"

She looked up at him strangely, and William felt the same look on his own face.

"Well, it's wrong," she said.

"Okay," Chase said again. "And why is that?"

The demon blinked rapidly several times, and William thought of a computer screen flashing nonsense while its hard drive fried. If it was possible for him to pay any closer attention to the exchange than he already was, he did. He watched the demon open her eyes wide at last and answer.

"Well, it's illegal for one." She sounded uncertain.

Chase nodded his agreement. "It is in Reno. Not in most of Nevada though, right?"

Now she was nodding, agreeing with him.

"Did you know that's how it is in most of the world? I didn't know this for the longest time," Chase spoke in the tone of a confessional, still holding her close, "but most civilized countries throughout history and today have always considered prostitution a healthy part of a happy society's structure. It happens whether it's legal or not, and enlightened governments regulate and tax it like any other legitimate business exchange. Prostitution is good for the economy, and in a fair market only those who wish to practice or partake are involved in it. The countries that make prostitution illegal are only creating a more dangerous market for all parties involved by making it a black market. Testing and regulations are eliminated by that market while human trafficking is an inevitable by-product of it."

Chase looked down at her the whole time he spoke, his voice calm and measured stating his case. The demon seemed to be drooping in his arms under the weight of the words, and the new Walker appeared to be holding her up.

"I'm sure Angela knows all that," Chase went on calm and quiet. "I can't fail to mention it even if she doesn't. The way I see it, the only good that comes of her job being illegal is giving the justice system more money by packing our courts and fining participants or packing private prisons with non-violent populations."

He supported her sagging weight. "What should I say if she brings up valid points? Doesn't she usually work at a brothel, in a county where it's legal? Has she ever been arrested?"

At the carefully placed questions, the demon seemed to come back to herself. Perhaps she did not quite hear the first two, or maybe she didn't want to answer them.

"No," she spoke as quietly as Chase, and in the same cadence. "She has never been arrested. I've heard a beautiful voice singing of the thing you speak, mostly when I am drawing the most energy from her. I don't listen, I can't listen; she has to hear *me*."

"She does," Chase soothed her. "She hears you in her own way. What else do you say to her?"

"Even if it's not illegal, it's still wrong," she hissed.

"Does she not enjoy it?" he asked plaintively.

"Not always," she spat, her voice still a hiss. She relaxed a little then, and added, "Usually she does, though."

"Is she mean or underhanded with her customers?"

"No." The demon shook her head, resolute. "She makes people happy. She is good at what she does. It's just *wrong*."

Chase stroked her hair. "Who is it wrong for? How is it wrong? Please help me understand, so I can explain it to her when she wakes up. Angela seems like a smart girl."

Straightening in his arms, she hissed, "That's not her real name!"

"I hope not." The new Walker smiled. "My name isn't John, either. I still feel like we connected. That means she is either good at what she does or just a genuinely kind person. Either way, I can't bring her arguments that aren't logical in some way. What else do you tell her?"

"It's dangerous," she said, in a voice full of concern. "So many hookers get murdered and left in the desert."

"How many?" His voice was open and curious, not interrogating.

"She could get beat up." The demon tried a different track.

"Has she ever?" Chase was curiously concerned.

"No," The demon seemed to be deflating in his arms again.

"Has she been robbed?" he asked.

She shook her horned head, not trusting her voice.

Chase took her by the shoulders and stepped back, still looking in her eyes. Forced to stand on her own, the demon was visibly smaller than before. Nonetheless she tottered under her own diminished weight, steadied only by his hands on her shoulders. Her black and scarlet eyes swirled with the intoxication of her first real interaction.

"I had to ask myself a question when I started gambling for a living," Chase confided. "I had to make sure that I understood the inherent risks, and that they were worth the benefits I got from gambling. I realized then that most real dream jobs have a similar set of pitfalls, and that the only people who realize big dreams are those that go ahead despite those pitfalls. The Universe made me a good gambler, and designed me to be happy when I'm doing it. When I finally embraced those facts, I somehow embraced the dark side of what I love at the same time."

The demon was swaying to the rhythm of his words.

"Does she not make good money?" Chase wondered aloud. "Does she squander it?"

She shook her head, glancing at the sleeping woman. Her swirling dark eyes seemed full of compassion, devoid of judgement. "She sends her little girl to a private school. She owns her condo outright. She saves and spends whatever she makes raising her daughter."

Eyes narrowing, she seemed to be trying to garner support from the young woman's other demons by glaring at them. They sat on her shoulders, stupefied, swirling spirits dancing about their heads like the one dancing about Angela's.

"Her daughter," she spat, her voice turning sad again. "What if she finds out? And her parents? Or her brother?"

Chase shook her just a little, to regain her attention. When her eyes were on his again, he spoke softly once more.

"Are those your concerns, truly?" he asked.

"No," The demon looked at him, trying to recapture his embrace by moving closer. "You sound so much like that voice that sings whenever I talk to her."

Chase took her in his arms again and stroked her hair. Her head fell to his chest, and Chase rested his chin lightly between her horns. He made eye contact with William across the room and smiled at him.

The old Walker just watched, as stupefied as the little demons.

"That voice is a light," Chase said quietly. "It's a type of angel. It's here to remind her of all the good things that exist in this issue for her."

Suddenly stiffening, the demon broke the embrace and stepped back. "An angel? Then what am I?"

For the first time, she rushed to a mirror and saw her own crimson skin and scarlet eyes. She screamed.

"Am I evil?" she gasped.

Her eyes were wide and unbelieving and she whirled in place, looking behind her at her tail and then the new Walker.

"No," Chase opened his arms to her again. "You have kept her safe and practical by voicing your concerns. Your voice gave her a realistic set of issues that she had to either overcome or succumb to. You helped her to overcome them by persisting in your duties."

The demon's eyes found the floor as she resisted the magnetic pull of the Walker's proffered embrace. William could actually see energy, a warm amorphous cloud, reaching out from Chase's chest to engulf her lovingly.

"Do you know what I was about to do to her?" Her voice was low and full of shame, her gaze still on the carpet.

"Yes," Chase said. "Do you still want to do it?"

Her eyes found his again quickly. "No."

"Do you want to say anything to her?" he asked.

She nodded and approached the sleeping woman. William was at the ready, but he suspected Chase was too. He stood relaxed and watched.

"I'm sorry," she began, casting a glance at both Walkers and then touching the young lady's hand. "I was here to help you. I got so caught up in being right I didn't see how what I was doing was wrong. I love you, sweetie. I wish nothing but the best for you and your little girl. If she and your family cannot see what a good person you are, or accept what you do, that is their decision and their path. I think it's time for me to go."

The devil stepped back, and Chase moved between her and her host. He took hold of the thick cord of energy drifting in the air between them, trailed it to where it attached to the sleeping woman, and pulled it gently from her body. It was like he had pulled an electrical cord from a wall socket, then activated it's retracting mechanism. The smoky tendril collapsed to disappear into the demon's chest. Tears streamed down her cheeks as she spread her arms and stood back.

"I am ready, Walker," she said calmly.

A light appeared over the sleeping woman's head, dim at first. It brightened and grew at the same time, floating to the floor as it took form. When the light hit the carpet, feet formed and the illumination coalesced into humanoid form. She was the mirror image of the demon, with a soft glow about her to replace the horns and tail.

"He's not here to kill you," she said to the demon. The light reached out her hand and took the demon's in it while black and scarlet eyes stared unbelieving at her.

William stood and watched, as close to disbelief as he could get after all that he had seen.

Chase moved to put his hand on the inert woman's shoulder. He nodded to the three swirling forms.

Purposefully, the constantly shifting shapes drifted from swirling about sleepy heads to hover in the air. They swirled and shifted in place, one a couple feet off the floor, the next a couple of feet above that and the last eye level to the onlooking Walker. A square portal appeared at each vortex, and the shapes moved around them. Framing them like windows, the things that Chase called the spirits held the portals in place while holding them open as well.

The light glanced at the windows, each offering a sublime glimpse into a different world. William could see that the lower opening was alight with flames and roiling with smoke. In the center, the second window showed him what looked like rolling hills on a sunny day. The landscape was unlike any William had seen, and no sun hung in the sky to provide the daylight that illuminated the natural scene. At eye level, William stared into a heavenly hallway made of light and cloud. It looked as much like Heaven as Heaven had looked in the times he had been there, but it was different too.

"Do you feel drawn to one of them? The light spoke to the demon as if she were the only person in the room.

She nodded, her horns bobbing with the motion.

"I feel drawn to all of them." The demon shifted her wide eyes between the portals and the light. A transformation had taken place in her. She was not angry or sad or afraid, tension did not knot her muscles or twist her visage. Lips smiling, eyes shining, the demon looked happy.

"Why do you feel drawn to them?" the angel asked. Her voice really was musical, light and lifting in soft sweet song. "What does the lower one make you feel?"

The demon's smile softened. "I would be with my kind there, many of them. I see none like you, though. If your place is not there, I don't want to be there."

Her smile was angelic as her haloed form.

"I will go where you go," she answered, "unless or until you would have it otherwise."

"Should we go there?" The demon was hesitant, considerate.

The light smiled. "How does the second make you feel?"

"It draws me as well," the demon answered. "There are many like me there, and many like you as well. Is that where you would like to go?"

Still smiling, the luminous lady with the musical voice answered her question with another of her own.

"What of the highest doorway, my dear?" the angel asked. "What do you feel pull you towards that one?"

"It's empty," The demon replied. "It's beautiful and bright and wonderful and…empty. There are some like you there, but not many. There are none like me."

Pivoting in place to address her heavenly counterpart straight on, the awed demon whispered, "Why is it so empty?"

Her words were spoken kindly, and the angel never once glanced at William as she began to speak. Somehow every word struck him like a hammer's blow to his heart just the same as the Walker listened to the first light he had ever bothered listening to.

"Walkers are important," the angel answered, "but they have never learned the specifics of their true function. From the First Walker to the modern Walker, all of them have been warriors either in life or at heart. They learned to do what many of the demons of yesterday needed, and they met rage or frustration with their own violent solution. There was a time when Walkers did not know to separate a demon from its host, and humans fell ill every time a Walker killed one. Many of those that found peace at last from a lifelong issue would die shortly thereafter, as they tried to feed a connection that led to another world."

She let out a sigh and continued. "One day people will be amazed to find that Walkers used to behead all demons, even nonviolent ones, and leave their lights behind with no balance and no direction. Perhaps they will remember that you were the first demon to find its way home to Heaven through a Walker. They will certainly remember the Walker. When the enslaved lights in Heaven and demons in Hell are free, when we have found our places between the worlds where we belong, when the pain of walking between worlds becomes the pleasure of countless hearts carrying

Walkers to right the wrongs of yesterday's ignorance, one name will sound on the lips of every being that tells the tale."

Turning from her carbon copy, the light looked lovingly at Chase. "Walker Chase, let me be the first to thank you."

Chase had climbed back under the sleeping young woman's bodily embrace. He was looking down at her while stroking her hair gently, and William wondered for a moment if maybe he hadn't heard.

Looking up finally, the new Walker spoke low so as not to wake the spiritually sedated lady in his arms.

"Thank you," he said quietly. "That was beautiful."

A lively chatter erupted from the two demons sitting on the young woman's shoulders.

"Can I come with you?" one demon asked, his voice as small as his body.

The other demon nodded empathetically. "We are as connected to you as we are to her, maybe more. We can help, we can *help!*" Her voice went high at the end as her eyes rolled back in her head. The thought of worthwhile service seemed to spark the divine within her, and she gazed with pleading eyes that mirrored the other's.

The light beamed. "You may do whatever you wish."

When they had entered, the hotel room had seemed spacious and well-appointed. It began to feel a bit cramped for William as the demons stepped from her shoulders. Each miniature monster gave their host a long wistful last glance before wrapping little hands around their connecting cords and giving them a firm tug. When the flowing tendrils snapped into them, they grew to full adult size as they stepped to the floor.

Almost immediately, two more lights appeared to join them. One by one they walked towards the trio of portals. Two portals collapsed as they approached, and three spirits suddenly swam about a tall doorway.

Heaven beckoned from beyond. William could hear its song calling to him, a tune he ought to know by heart at this point. He knew the doorway wasn't for him, however, and he stepped forward for only one reason.

"Excuse me," he said, polite but firm.

The doorway's luminescence was obscured by the first of them passing through it. Two more moved through the portal while the light that had spoken turned to him.

"I have so many questions," William said.

Her smile came again. "Ask the lights. What one knows, we all know."

All of them had disappeared through the heavenly gateway but the light and her counterpart. The demon waited, glancing between her angel and the door.

"Why have none of you spoken to us before?" he pressed.

"You never asked," she shrugged.

That shrug and those words were painful twin sledgehammer blows to the old Walker's heart.

"I'm so sorry." It was all he could think to say.

"Don't be." The angel's smile lifted him. "Many of the demons you sent on should have gone with violence. Not all of them, though. Now not all of them will."

William nodded the firmness of his resolution.

The angel turned, took the demon's hand, and walked through the doorway. Immediately after they passed, the lighted rectangle collapsed. Swirling through the air, Chase's helpful spirits turned into a tornado of rapidly whirling light and then disappeared.

Chase was already speaking quietly to the sleeping young woman.

"Angela," he murmured, stroking her hair. "Soon you are going to wake up feeling refreshed and renewed. You will know that you are safe and that all is well as you come awake. Wake up now, Angela."

When he said her name, her eyelids fluttered but remained closed. They fluttered again when he spoke of her waking, and opened wide when he fell silent.

Sitting up straight, she looked at Chase.

"I'm so sorry," she said. "I think I fell asleep."

Chase yawned and stretched. "No worries, I think I did too."

"I'm so sorry," she said again. "I can't take your money."

"Nonsense." Chase stood beside the bed and stretched once more. "That was wonderful. How do I find you when I switch my prescription?"

Her business card was simple and professional-looking, a pink rectangle with red hearts all around her embossed black first name and number. It appeared in her hand like Walker magick, and she handed it to Chase.

They were in the hallway, the young woman on the other side of the closed door, when William asked the new Walker the first of many questions on his mind.

"How did you know to do that?"

Chase shrugged. "I didn't do much. I just let it happen. Do you think she'll mind that I took all the vodka from the mini bar?"

CHAPTER 9

Jessica's reptilian eyes watched the stooped form make her way slowly across the room. The wait was interminable, and the dragon thought of how many times she could burn the old hag to ashes in the time it took her to reach the queen. Jessica thought more than once that the crone seemed to be approaching her with deliberate slowness. Pushing the thought from her mind, she moved forward to watch the clear orb appear from the worn folds of robe. Eyes narrowed and jaw clenched, Jessica stared as it grew in the hag's slim veiny hands.

"Did you find it?" Jessica hissed. "Did you find the stone? Where is it?"

Something in the shadows of the dark cowl moved back and forth in negation. Words issued then from the darkness.

"The stone is nowhere to be found, my queen," she answered, low and slow. "It must have been destroyed."

"Then what am I looking at?" As Jessica asked the question, her eyes focused on the image within the orb. She resisted the urge to gasp, or say that damned name again. Instead she concentrated on watching the nude young woman that seemed unaware that she was under observation. The woman searched the shadows with her eyes, chose a direction and began walking. Then she stopped and turned at the sound of her name.

Jessica could hear it too, a distant voice calling out over and over. She leaned in closer to the crystal ball.

"Ximena!" This time they both heard it clearly, and Ximena pivoted in place to begin running in the direction of the voice.

It called out again as she ran, then came clear and loud as she rounded a wide turn in the endless tunnel.

"Ximena." Paul opened his arms to her as soon as he saw her, and she moved naturally into his embrace.

He grasped her shoulders. "Do you remember?"

Ximena's eyes were dark and round and confused.

"Remember what?"

Paul sighed. "You spoke of how death speeds us along our upward and downward paths, how a soul progresses more quickly when each mortal coil is shed."

Ximena nodded. "Often the soul is propelled in another direction or lost, depending on the death and how it is handled. Why would I speak of such things?"

"What's the last thing you remember?" he asked.

She looked up at him, her eyes full of dark light.

"We were frozen," she replied. "And Jessica killed us."

Paul shook his head. "We came back. We came back here or somewhere similar, in the walls between layers of Hell. We found each other, or you found me."

"Then demons killed us both." Ximena nodded, remembering.

"We came back and they killed us again," Paul reminded her. "Maybe several times, I don't remember."

Ximena smiled. "Then I told you to get away, to find me when I came back."

Paul's frown mirrored her smile. "The demons killed you, and I ran like a coward."

Ximena's smile broadened as she took his hand.

"Don't you see, my love?" she asked. "You saved us both."

Paul shook his head. "That's what you said before, and that's why I did it. I still don't understand."

"We keep forgetting," she explained. "Every time we die, our souls leap forward along their paths but our memories are lost. Like humans, we keep dying and forgetting in an endless cycle."

He nodded. "How do we break the cycle?"

"Like this." Ximena squeezed his hand. "One of us survives to find the other and remind them who they are. And then…"

She trailed off.

"Then we switch." Paul grimaced.

Both of them started at the same time, listening to the sudden sound of footfalls close by.

Paul let go her hand. "Go, sweetie. Run."

There was no time for a long fleeting last look in each other's eyes, no opportunity for his lips to touch hers in this lifetime. They both heard sounds approaching, and she turned her back to him and ran.

She made it twenty feet before a demon stepped from the shadows to seize her. Paul ran towards them as Ximena struggled in the monster's grasp, only to be tackled by an even larger demon. A sea of crimson flesh washed over them both in a violent wave, and they watched each other die up close while the dragon queen watched from far away.

Jessica turned to her manacled captive

Swathed in rags and a sheen of sweat, his skin was flushed with the heat to make him look a little less human and a little more like the devils that surrounded him. Despite the queen's efforts to ensure his discomfort, despite the heat that should have been too much for any human to handle, the prisoner appeared to be in an emotionally sublime state.

"Where is your key, Matt?" the dragon queen hissed.

He spread his hands, the chains clanking with the motion.

"Like I keep saying, Jessica, if I had my key I would be long gone." He smiled, letting his hands and the chain fall. The sound was dry and raspy, like his voice.

"What do you know?" she demanded.

"I know that your powers are to your mother's what hers were to Ximena's." Matt raised one hand again to hold his thumb and first finger an inch apart. "Small by comparison."

Matt grinned, his hair plastered to his head as sweat ran in rivers down his face. "I know you cannot walk between worlds without a key, and that you can't forge them as your mother did. I know you want Ximena's powers, and that if your search for the stone doesn't kill you then finding it surely will."

Drawing back as if to strike, the dragon queen drew in a lungful of fiery breath.

Matt straightened, spreading his arms.

"By all means," he smiled. "Kill me."

The dragon looked around the room, baleful eyes burning with rage.

"I can't wait to see what happens when you lose your few remaining wits and kill me," Matt chuckled. "Will I go back to Earth and find my key? Will I regain my devil's form and all my powers? Either way, I will come back for you, and I'll wager that everyone in this room is as curious as I about that day."

"Shut up!" she hissed. "I will throw you in the dungeon, traitor! You will rot in there for an eternity!"

"Not in this body," he laughed. "I would expire in there even sooner."

Her rage became a calm one. "I ran those dungeons when I was here. I may be lacking in some of my mother's abilities, but I am uniquely skilled in inflicting pain and prolonging life. Do not test me. I know that your human form does not age for some reason, and I know the limits of the fragility that binds you. I am not blind, Matt, or stupid. You are a fool not to fear me."

"And you are twice the fool," Matt chuckled darkly. "First for thinking that I might fear pain, second for not seeing that the only eternity you should be concerned for is your own. Your dark path leads to your own flame being snuffed out forever. Look ahead and you will see."

"The future is not set," she hissed.

"Isn't that what your mother used to say?" Matt smiled.

Jessica's smoothly scaled paw caught him in a backhand that stretched taut his chain, raised a series of welts, and sent him to the floor unconscious.

CHAPTER 10

Kris eyed the familiar landscape warily.

It seemed darker, more dense with smoke. Miniature fires danced in and out of existence all around him, sputtering to life only to disappear in a dark plume of noxious vapor. When the Guide had last been in Hell, he could see far enough to have tossed a scorched stone as hard as he could and watch it fall. Now he could see perhaps a dozen paces before anything that may lie beyond was obscured in the miasma. Hell had gone from desolate barrenness to post-apocalyptic wasteland since the Guide had been here last. He hadn't liked it here before; being here alone, with the place in such a state, did little to put him at ease.

None of that mattered. The Guide knew what he had to do. His key had brought him as close to the dragon queen as it could; the rest was up to him. His sense of direction was flawless so long as he held a destination in mind, and the Guide traversed the scorched footing following its internal beacon.

It wasn't long before he heard the sound he had fervently hoped not to hear. The leathery flapping of wings got louder as he listened, and in almost no time at all a thirty foot long blue dragon burst from the roiling smoke overhead to land a few yards from the Guide.

Kris spread his hands defensively.

"I'm just here to talk to the Dragon Queen," he said.

The dragon transformed before his eyes, and a stunning dark-haired she-devil faced him suddenly.

"You are the Guide Kris, are you not?" Her voice was beautiful and feminine, but her tone was flat and her intent hard to read. Kris hoped that her transformation was a good sign, that she might be here as an escort.

He nodded. "Yes, I—"

"The Dragon Queen has a message for you," she cut him off.

In the next moment she was a dragon again, puffing up her chest and unhinging her jaw.

Kris closed his eyes as flame leapt from her maw, going to the first place he thought of.

He blinked his eyes open in a dark and empty room, his hands searching his robe for burn marks or fire. It was a full minute before he realized where he was. Looking around, confused, Kris thought first that he shouldn't be here and then that this room shouldn't be here.

There had been an open invitation when he was alive, one he had never accepted. He was especially glad to have stayed away now that he was here. The room was creepy in its familiarity, and he stayed only long enough to decide whether to walk into another room or into another world.

Stepping into the hallway, the Guide wondered if perhaps no one was home. That made it even more strange, an empty house that was both full of his memories and absent from them. Then a sound came to him, a soft sobbing coming from downstairs, and Kris followed it until he came upon its source. His mother sat on a large L-shaped sofa in the living room, adrift in a sea of memory. There were photo albums and loose pictures arranged all about her, and Sharon spent more moments gazing at images than finding a place for them. An egg salad sandwich sat on the coffee table within her reach, one small bite taken from it. From the looks of it, the sandwich had been there a good long time.

Sharon had looked awful at his funeral; she had taken a turn for the worse. Her eyes stared unfocused and possibly unseeing at one picture after another while tears leaked from them to stream unchecked down her cheeks. Where she had been chubby and flabby, she was now emaciated and flabby. The tracks of her tears dipped into the open-mouthed undernourished concavities that her cheeks had become.

There was no room on the couch nearby, no place to sit even if Kris had wanted to. Feeling the dark waves of her reality staining his heart, Kris fell enough to see the demons he would have normally tuned out. There were a half-dozen little monsters lounging about on the angled back of the sofa.

Seeing them meant hearing them, and hearing them meant hearing his own name in their dark chants.

"…your son Kris deserved better…"

"…you lied to your son and your husband every day…"

"…Kris would have been better off with no mother…"

"…your whole life was a lie…"

"…it's all your fault…"

"…Kris and Doug are both gone because of you…"

The Guide clenched his fists at his side.

"Enough," he said, willing the demons to see him.

Continuing their collective cacophony, the demons ignored him. They were not accustomed to being addressed.

"I am Kris," he said loudly.

Two of the demons glanced up at him. The Guide took a step forward.

"Look at me," he said to them. "Look at the image you use to haunt her with and then look at me standing before you."

They all stopped and looked him over. The two that had first glanced his way continued watching him while the others went back to chanting their mantras and sucking Sharon dry.

"I am a Guide," Kris said to the two demons. "I am not dead. I walk between worlds."

They peered at him closely.

"What is going on?" Kris demanded. "Where's my…"

The Guide trailed off.

"Where's Doug?" he finished.

The two little horned monsters looked at each other and back at him. Kris realized they both kind of looked like him. One had his relaxed mannerisms, and the other had an eerily familiar countenance. Similar features, with longer hair. One of them shrugged, and the Guide fought the urge to smile.

"After the funeral, on the flight back to Portland, Doug wouldn't talk to her at all," the shrugging monster said. "When they got home he packed a couple bags and left."

Kris frowned. "Did he say where he was going?"

"No." The horned head moved in negation. "He just stopped at the doorway, looked at your mom and said, 'I'm sorry, I can't do this anymore.' Then he left. Your mom thinks he went to Lisa's, but she won't even look out the window and check."

"What do you mean?" The Guide was still frowning.

"Your parents sold their house in San Francisco and bought two here, next door to each other. Shortly thereafter your Dad brought Lisa up here to live in the house next door, just like she did in the city."

Kris nodded. He had heard most of it; he hadn't known the house was right next door. He looked at his mother, wondering if he should feel bad that he didn't feel bad for her.

"He's not really my dad." Kris said quietly.

"Who told you that?" The demon that looked so much like him spoke, sitting up straight suddenly.

Kris shrugged. He didn't want to seem pompous telling them that they probably wouldn't believe him if he told them any more than he wanted to explain if he did tell them. He had uttered that name enough times today.

"I'm okay," Kris said. "That's all that matters. I can't tell her that, and she can't really hear you, but I leave you two in charge of helping her. She's no saint, but she doesn't deserve this."

He took one last look around the room at her sagging figure, and shook his head. "No one deserves this."

He had thought he would appear in another house, perhaps the one next door. Instead the Guide found himself in the back seat of a convertible sitting next to a demon.

This time the monster noticed him immediately. It was the demon Paul had faced the night of Kris' funeral, scarred and one-armed but definitely not dead.

Kris scooted away as much as the cramped rear seat would allow. He watched the demon watching him for an awkward forever moment, then he frowned.

"I thought you were dead," the Guide said.

The leather vest that the demon wore had three buttons on it, but none were fastened. His lone remaining hand moved aside half of the garment, and Kris could see that the demon's entire torso was a grotesque network of scars. He held up the crimson stump, rounded to an awkwardly bulging mound of jagged bone covered in darkened flesh, as if to make sure Kris had noticed it.

"Almost," the demon said, smiling.

His canines flashed gold, and his jaw canted unnaturally.

The demon leaned forward, put his one good hand on the shoulder of the man in the front driver's seat. He looked like he was gently massaging the man with a reassuring hand. Continuing the comforting contact, the demon turned his attention once again to the Guide.

"I was wrong about him, you know," the demon said.

Kris nodded his quiet agreement.

"You were wrong about him too," the demon added.

Kris nodded again.

"The only reason he stayed with your mom was you." The one-armed monster's voice was kind, almost human. "He was so proud of you, even when you shut him out. Every day he hoped you would call or come visit. He never talked to anyone for more than thirty seconds before he mentioned his smart and successful son in San Francisco."

Kris smiled. "I wasn't really all that successful."

The demon returned his smile. "You were to him. From what I've heard, you've made quite a few waves in the Afterlife. King of the Guides? Dating the Dragon Princess?"

The Guide shrugged. "That's all gone now."

'Is the Walker King truly dead?' The same voice that had been sounding in his ear suddenly sounded in his head. Kris started, his dead gray eyes going wide.

'I'm not sure.' Kris kept his face composed while his thoughts whirled.

The demon's face broke out in a wide grin, his long gold canines glinting in the sunlight.

'If I can help, let me know.' The voice came again, startling the Guide for a different reason. *'I owe the Walker King my life. I was given the chance to undo the damage I did over the years as best I could. That means the world to me. That means my life to me.'*

For the first time, Kris noticed that Doug had a passenger. He could only see the back of her head, but long silky black hair told him that it wasn't Lisa.

"Have you been helping him?" The Guide thought it wise to speak harmless thoughts aloud; anyone could be watching.

The demon nodded, glancing at Doug.

"New job, new car, new outlook," his gold teeth glinted the demon's pride.

"New girl?"

The demon shrugged, the third demon today to make Kris think of his own mannerisms.

"There are a few others," the demon answered.

"Have you seen my mom?" Kris asked. "What about Lisa?"

Gold teeth blinked light as the demon smiled again.

"Your mother has always been so absorbed in her own thoughts about herself, I'm surprised if she has paid any attention to his absence." The demon watched Kris to see if he was wrong.

It was the Guide's turn to shrug. He wouldn't admit that the thought had flitted through his mind that Sharon got just what she deserved, but he wasn't going to pretend that it hadn't either.

"I know Lisa better than you," the demon admonished him kindly. "She was never after a commitment, and she has never wanted all of the responsibilities of a full-fledged relationship. Lisa always wanted to be the other woman; she still does."

Kris really couldn't find a victim in all of this. He wondered why he kept trying to.

"He's not even really my dad," Kris muttered quietly.

The demon didn't seem completely surprised.

"Have you met your biological father?" he asked Kris.

Kris shook his head.

"Is that database not accessible to the King of the Guides?"

Kris laughed out loud, despite himself. He didn't know if he liked the demon because he reminded Kris of Doug or of himself. Musing quietly to himself, he thought it might be both.

"I could find out pretty easy," the Guide acknowledged. "It doesn't really matter."

The demon seemed to be actively massaging his host's neck over the seat. His eyes were on the back of Doug's head as he spoke a quiet question.

"How do you think he would feel if he knew?" the demon asked.

Kris shrugged. "He'd probably be pretty pissed off at my mom."

Still looking straight ahead, the demon asked, "Would he?"

In that moment, Doug turned to grin at the woman in the passenger seat. Although his eyes were hidden behind dark sunglasses, Kris knew they were crinkled to sparkling almond shapes with the smile. A thousand memories assaulted his mind, Doug's smile the consistent star of his childhood. When something went well for Kris, he would always grin and say, "See? You can do anything!" or something along those lines. If something went wrong, Doug would smile that same smile and say something like, "Wait till they see what you do next; it'll be so brilliant no one will even remember this."

The Guide thought of Doug's guileless charm, the seemingly carefree attitude he had. For the first time, Kris considered that Doug was more than a happy simpleton; that maybe he was deliberately making the best of every moment.

Kris thought of what Doug might say if he were to discover that they were not truly linked by blood. He had answered from a place of his own cynicism before; now he tried to look at it through the filter of Doug's rosy paradigm.

"He wouldn't be mad at my mom," Kris smiled softly. "He would probably say that he was lucky and proud to have raised me as his own."

A sound broke loose from him, a laugh or a sob, and a tear rolled down the Guide's dead cheek. His next words were choked with emotion, a bittersweet happy sadness.

"Not long ago," Kris sputtered, "I would have said 'The stupid fool would probably thank my mom, find some silly reason why it had to happen that way, and move on.'"

"And now?" the demon prompted.

Kris wiped his tears with the sleeve of his robe.

"Now I think that it's time that I realize that I was the lucky one." Kris sighed after he spoke, looking at the happy driver living in his decidedly happy moment. A knot that had taken a lifetime to tie unraveled in him in that sweet forever moment, and he sighed again.

Kris turned to the demon.

"Tell Doug…" he began, then started again.

"Tell my dad that he was the greatest man I ever knew." The Guide spoke slowly, so he wouldn't cry. "Tell him that if I had lived long enough to grow up a little more, I would have realized it. Tell him that I'm sorry."

"He won't hear me."

Kris looked at the driver, the passenger, the soft leather seats they all sat in. His eyes found the demon last.

"I think he will," the Guide smiled.

There seemed to be a glow about the demon, a golden haze of light that outlined his entire body. His glinting canines seemed dull by comparison.

"Did I help?" he asked, his voice full of hope.

Kris nodded. "You helped."

The demon glowed even brighter.

"What's your name?" the Guide asked.

His eyes went wide, the only answer the demon had to a question he had never considered.

"No one ever gave me one." The demon's voice fell to a whisper. "Would you name me, Guide Kris?"

Kris smiled. "A name does come to mind."

"What name?" The demon seemed to have forgotten how to blink, his eyelids lost in anticipation. "Why?"

"Simon," Kris answered. "It means he who talks to God, or he who listens to God, or messenger of God."

The Guide would have bet everything he had that the demon's eyes couldn't widen any further.

He would have lost.

"I don't speak to God," the demon said breathlessly. "Or at least, God doesn't speak to me."

"My dad doesn't believe in God," Kris said.

The demon nodded. It wasn't news to him; he had been there when Kris had accused Doug of being wishy-washy for calling himself agnostic.

Kris had been a new atheist, with the hubris of any thirteen-year-old with an idea they thought was their own.

"Neither do you," the demon pointed out with a shrug.

"God is love," Kris said to his own surprise. "You speak of love, you act with love, you glow with love. That is why the name Simon came to mind."

Lowering his hand from his host for the first time in a good long stretch of minutes, the demon lowered his head as well. When he looked up, Kris saw that his black and scarlet eyes were full of tears.

"Thank you," he breathed. "In my own thoughts, I will call myself Simon. If anyone ever asks my name, I will tell them I am called Simon."

Simon dropped his head again, before the tears could fall.

"Thank you," he said once more, the words muffled into his chest.

Kris wasn't sure if he thought of it first, or if he felt cold metal against his bare chest under the robe first. He clawed gently at his throat, separating the two chains. Usually his key existed only in the Guide's mind, where he kept it for safekeeping. Sometimes he wore it around his neck, when he intended to or when it had reason to call attention to itself. Now there were two, and it did not surprise him at all; he knew what the second one was for.

"Simon." The Guide fished the platinum key and chain from his robe and held it out to the awed demon. "Would you be my Agent?"

As Simon's eyes widened once more, Kris finished his request silently. *'Will you help me find Paul? And Ximena?'*

The demon beamed brighter than ever as he took the key.

CHAPTER 11

William clasped his key in his hand, looking around at the scorched terrain it had taken him to. He had no way of knowing that Kris had stood not a dozen steps from where his harness boots were now planted not so long ago. He had no way of knowing what to expect as the leathered flapping of dragon wings drew closer. He stood his ground, gloved hands empty but blades at the ready in his mind.

The dragon did not keep him waiting long.

It emerged from the choking smog, flapping its wings backward to lower itself to the ground. Big and black, it made William think of the killing machine that had seemed so eager to do Ximena's bidding. He knew this beast was different, smaller and slower while still far too large and fast to put him at ease. His sword was so close to appearing out of reflex, William forced himself to breathe.

"I am Walker William, appointed leader of the Walkers," he said clearly, his voice raised but not threatening. "I seek an audience with the Dragon Queen."

For a moment it looked like the beast was going to answer him. William leaned forward, almost imperceptibly.

The dragon's eyes narrowed and it breathed in deeply, almost reluctantly. It hesitated for so long that William thought maybe it wasn't about to breathe fire at him. Then the flames leapt forward, and the old Walker shook his head sadly in the moment he had before the inferno reached him. Then he disappeared.

CHAPTER 12

Cal watched the giant screen through a dull hazy fog, his tan eyes shot with a network of blood. He felt Sarah's head on his lap, thought absently about how he would get the blood off the leather if he killed her here, then put his wandering attention back on the gigantic ant on the wall. His hand brushed absently through her hair.

"Thanks for getting stoned with me." Sarah's sleepy voice drifted up from his lap.

Cal smiled. He thought she had dozed off; she actually was waiting for an ad break to talk. Leaving the remote control where it lay on the arm of the couch, he pressed the mute button to silence the selling sounds.

"I thought you didn't like weed at all." Sarah's voice was still quiet, but louder for the silence.

"I take a CDB capsule every night before bed," Cal said, stroking her hair consciously now. "It helps me get better sleep, it supposedly assists in tissue regeneration. The part in the capsules doesn't get you high, I think they separate the THC or something. Cannabis can be processed and used in a number of ways, like cocaine and heroin and many other chemicals nature provides. Did you know that the coca leaf is actually very nutritious and gives you a light energetic buzz when you eat it? Or that cocaine in some form or another has been used by the medical profession virtually since there was one?"

Sarah rotated so her head looked up at him while still resting in his lap. She raised an eyebrow doubtfully.

"Not today," she objected. "Not in the U.S."

Cal chuckled. "You've never heard of lidocaine? Or procaine? Or novocaine?"

Sarah blinked, her eyes going round. "Is that why you love cocaine so much?"

"Nah." He waved off her question, moved agitatedly in his seat. All this talk about his constant companion had him itching for the tasteless numbness. When she didn't move at his subtle series of wiggles, Cal took his hand from her hair and rested it on her throat.

All he had to do was squeeze, really. Sarah would surely fight back, but she would certainly fail in her vulnerable position. Cal thought of watching her gasp for breath as her eyes went impossibly wide one last time. He imagined her tense and flailing in panic one moment, overcome with peace at his violent hands in the next.

He tapped her shoulder, and Sarah sat up.

"It's the same with a lot of drugs," Cal spoke as he stood. "The only thing the United States is behind on is psychedelic studies and their medicinal application. Other cultures understand that psychedelics are the secret ingredient to making effective treatment programs for every addiction imaginable, but ours is focused more on getting people strung out in large quantities with no real hope of ever leading a normal balanced life again. People do heroin every day in hospitals all over the country, but they call it morphine. Oxycontin is one of the popular pill forms, even easier to take at home or work or while driving, but it's still essentially heroin. Coca-Cola tastes different than any cola in the country is allowed to, because they have a special dispensation to use coca leaves with the active component removed to flavor their classic beverage. That brand name is a wide moat for competitors to cross, but a special ingredient that only you can legally obtain is piranhas in the water."

Crossing the carpet as he spoke, Cal slipped into the bedroom for a few moments. When he came back into the living room wearing his boxer shorts and a smile, one of his hands clutched his customary kit. Cal continued talking as he approached Sarah and the sofa.

"Alcohol is the only legal mind-altering substance in our country for some reason, despite being more lethal and physically damaging than most drugs." Cal sat down. "You want to know why I love cocaine?"

Sarah nodded, her pale green eyes wide as they eyed the items that Cal set on the glass coffee table.

"You want some?" he asked, emptying white powder on the clean transparent surface. Setting the bag down, he picked up the razor to start lining it up.

"Can I put it on a fresh bowl and smoke it?"

"If you want," he nodded, picking up the tube.

He snorted what he had laid out, watching Sarah clear the remnants of what they had smoked in her little pipe. Breaking up the little bits of cannabis, she packed them loosely in the bowl. She held it out when she was finished, and he tipped the bag generously. The leafy little mountain became a snow-capped peak.

She proffered him the pipe.

"Go ahead," he smiled.

Cal knew the taste in the back of his throat and the energetic prickles that tickled his skin would be overwhelmed by the combination. He savored his clear-headed relaxed state while he watched Sarah smoking.

"My big brother had a lot of influence on my upbringing," Cal recalled aloud. "When I found out he was smoking weed in high school, I freaked out and begged him to stop. Tyler sat me down and had a talk with me that changed my whole way of thinking. I'll never forget it. He asked me if I believed in Santa Claus. I laughed at him, and said that was for stupid little kids. Then he said something else that stuck with me."

He reached out and took the pipe from her. Most of the mixture was charred black, but a third was green and white. Touching the flame to the special blend, Cal inhaled deeply. He blew out the smoke and filled his lungs once more before passing it back to her.

Sarah stared at the pipe dully as she held it, her eyelids drooping to make her wide green eyes look the size of a normal person's at last. Setting the pipe on the table, then the lighter, she turned her attention back to Cal.

"What did he say?"

Her voice came at him through cotton, or clouds. The molasses in his head dripped through circuits designed for electrical impulses. Cal stared at Sarah, resisting the urge to puddle into a pool of laughter.

He smiled at her, his mouth twitching from the effort.

"Tyler told me that most stuff is like Santa Claus," Cal said, remembering. "He said that it's easier to tell your kids pretty lies than the truth. Most of the things even full-grown adults believe end up being pretty lies, that they believe because someone told them something when they were little kids that they never bothered to examine in adulthood."

Cal paused, looking back over what he had said to make sure it made sense. His thoughts were slippery and sticky at the same time, and somehow looking backwards wiped the entire slate clean. When he looked at Sarah, he tried to look wise instead of like someone watching the caboose to his train of thought disappearing over the horizon. A part of his mind tried to run after it, to catch it. The rest of him looked on in amused resignation.

They looked in each other's eyes, still together.

"What was I talking about?" Cal said at last.

Sarah grinned and blinked three times. Her eyes went up and to the left, then up and to the right, disappearing for the most part under heavy lids. Her smile fell to a frown as the realization that she had forgotten as well hit her. She giggled, then snapped her fingers.

"Santa Claus!" she exclaimed, like a child hearing reindeer hooves on the rooftop.

"Yeah," Cal smiled lazily. "Santa Claus. It's easier to tell your kids lies and let them figure things out on their own. That's fine for parents, if that's the way they want to raise their kids. They shouldn't be surprised when their fourteen-year-old won't listen to them or talk to them, but they can raise them that way if they want. The problem with drugs is that it's one of the government's fairy tales. Those aren't lies designed to protect the innocent; they are lies told for power and profit."

Cal leaned forward to snag the pipe from the coffee table once more. "Drugs have always been a part of society," he said, inspecting the bowl for white or green.

He leaned forward again to get the baggie he had brought to the table. Sprinkling white powder over burnt shades of black, he watched a little mountain form. Satisfied, he sealed the baggie and tossed it to the table to slide across the surface. The next long careful hits he took were pretty much just cocaine. After two of them, he held the pipe out to its owner.

It looked like her eyes were going to go round for a moment, then Sarah shrugged and took the pipe and lighter.

This time he had put a pin in his thought, and Cal was able to continue where he had left off as an almost overwhelming numbness came over him.

"The war on drugs in the United States is really just a thinly veiled war on the proletariat." He smiled at her confused look. "The working class."

He went on while she smoked. "Rather than legal access and public education, this country chose a dangerous black market, disinformation and propaganda. It's no coincidence that prisons became privatized in the same movement that criminalized and demonized drugs. Other countries have chosen legal access and public education, and their people thrive and breathe in ways Americans seldom realize they are never getting a chance to. Most of us associate paranoia with recreational drug use, without realizing that it's not the drug responsible for the fear."

Sarah's eyes had gone glassy long ago, but she continued to gaze at him politely. Cal was used to hanging out with people that were way too excited about their own ideas to listen to his; it was nice to watch her wait for him to bring the train home, or send it toppling from the rails.

"When I realized drugs were not what my parents or teachers told me," Cal continued, delighting in not having to rush his words, "I started doing research. I kept running across a phrase, 'of choice'. I realized that everyone's body chemistry was different, and I decided to find my own drug of choice. Tyler wouldn't help me, so by the end of high school I knew where to get everything. I only like beer or pot once in a while, I knew that right away. I tried acid and mushrooms, and had a vision where a giant mushroom told me that we could be friends but we would never be lovers."

She was still paying attention, bless her heart. Cal knew it was entirely possible that she had left the train several stations ago, but she seemed to be on board.

Cal smiled, his thoughts on yesterday. "The rest of my vision was me playing in the snow. I thought it was funny, because I hate temperatures below sixty-five. When I went to school the next day, a buddy asked if I had ever tried coke. I said no, but I wanted to. We went out to his car and did a couple of bumps, and something clicked inside of me. This was what my unique body chemistry had been searching for. This was my white mistress. This was my 'of choice'."

"Forever?" Sarah asked.

"What do you mean?"

She smiled sweetly, put her hand disarmingly on his leg. "I mean, do you see yourself dealing blow when you're fifty?"

"Oh no," Cal waved his numb hand dismissively. "That would make me a bad drug dealer, or at least financially irresponsible. I save most of what I earn, half legitimately and the other half not so much. If I'm not retired in five years, it will be because people stopped liking cocaine."

Sarah eyed the one doorway that had been closed the whole time they had both been awake.

"Is that your legit income?" she asked timidly.

Cal laughed. "Have you been snooping?"

Frowning guiltily, Sarah gave the glass coffee table a long visual examination. "I looked around a little before you got up."

He was still smiling when she glanced his way again.

"They're so beautiful, Cal!" she gushed. "Do you make them?"

He nodded. "I buy the pieces and assemble them according to the directions. You'd be surprised how much people will pay for a lamp. Of course, mine fetch an even higher price since it's not actually lamps that put most of the numbers in the books. You can have one if you like. Most of the finished ones in there have been paid for at least once by now."

"Really?" Sarah's eyes were round despite her chemical cocktail. "Can I pick now?"

He rose from the couch, and she followed suit. When she stood, she reached for the shirt she had been wearing. Cal grasped her hand, shook his head, and led her naked into his craft room.

CHAPTER 13

When William was a man, music was something he heard from time to time. It was generally a pleasant background noise, a mix of alien sounds coming from strange instruments that often blended together in a rather pleasant manner. In those days, music was played by people live, and what singing he had heard was devotional. He had gone to church to hear the hymns, wondering at how his heart delighted in the music while his mind boggled at the Latin.

Music had changed, little by little, then seemingly all at once. William dealt with his immortality with varying degrees of success, and the sounds that assaulted his ears when everyone suddenly owned a radio were among his most difficult trials. He felt like an old man in a young man's body when he watched dancing devolve to drunken groping and music spiral into self-absorbed whining about the horrible tragedy of a self-absorbed person in or after a relationship.

Time and again, he would turn on the radio only to flip it off again. He tried, he really did, especially when he recognized that music was becoming such a big part of the culture he was supposed to belong to. Artist after artist lost his interest thirty seconds into the song, and the rest of their work failed the same chance. William was getting desperate, in his own quiet way, hoping against hope to find someone making sounds that stirred his soul.

He had quite nearly given up his fruitless search when William heard his first Rolling Stones song. Flipping on the radio one day, hoping, he had heard "Time Is On My Side".

Quite all of the sudden, William had had a favorite song and then a favorite band. He had chosen well, if indeed he had done the choosing, and was rewarded with a slew of great albums over the decades. He didn't turn the radio on much, but when he did it was to listen to Mick Jagger and Keith Richards weave their sonic magick.

Vanessa had told him to think about what he had had for breakfast, or about the last demon he had killed, or run a song over and over in his head. She'd said that was the best way to keep the Council from reading his thoughts.

A song seemed a good idea. He had thought first of "Sympathy For the Devil", then dismissed it immediately. That made him think of the small beautiful woman who had transformed his king and friend from frowning fighter to smiling lover before his eyes. Paul was the very thing he was trying not to think of. So he thought instead of the first recorded song that had climbed into his heart, set the needle of his mental record player in those old worn grooves, and thought of the last place he wanted to be right now.

Standing on clouds, eyeing the drab endless beauty, William tried to let his heavy heart be lifted by the Heavenly view. The voice in his head sang his musical mantra over and over, and he could only hope the words would turn out to be true for him. And for Paul.

'Time...is on my side,' said Mick Jagger in his mind.

"Walker William to see the Walker Council," he said to the blonde angel with the pretty eyes.

'Time...is on my side,' sang Mick.

"Follow the light please, sir," she smiled.

William turned to trail the orb that appeared at eye level. Before he could take a step, the receptionist politely cleared her throat behind him.

"Excuse me," she said quietly, "Walker William?"

He turned back to her. "Yes?"

"Is it true that you knew the Walker King?" she asked quietly.

William's dark eyes glanced meaningfully at the light over his shoulder. He turned up the volume on The Rolling Stones.

"I knew Walker Paul," he nodded.

She leaned forward across her desk, spoke even more quietly. "Is it true that he is coming back to break the Council and free us all?"

'TIME...IS ON MY SIDE,' William thought loudly.

Touching her hand on the desk, he said, "I don't know."

With his eyes, he tried to say, 'I hope so'.

She seemed to see it, or hear it. She smiled and squeezed his hand lightly. "Thank you."

Following the light to the doorway that winked out of existence at it's luminous touch, William hesitated before going in.

"Thank you," he said to the floating orb.

It glowed brighter, and then the Walker heard a distinctly feminine voice in his head.

'All hail the Walker King,' the voice sang along with the melody in his head.

Then it disappeared.

His thoughts were a happy whirlwind that was a hard thing to put in a box. He did it finally, nailing the box shut and setting the record player on the box in his mind.

Stepping through the doorway, he heard angels arguing in tense but hushed voices. The disagreement stopped as his second harness boot hit the clouded floor soundlessly, and an uncomfortable silence filled the room.

The Rolling Stones filled his head.

"I am here to report, as commanded." William nodded to the assemblage. None of them looked any happier for his being here than William felt.

"As requested." One angel spoke, one of the more historically vocal ones.

"Of course, Angel Stephan," William bent at the waist. "I apologize. I went below to request an audience with the Dragon Queen, as requested."

He straightened, waited. He listened to Mick's soulful croon.

"And?" As expected, the angel with the icy eyes and the icier voice spoke next.

William bowed a little once more, trying to imitate the regal air of an Eastern friend.

"I was met by a black dragon almost at once, Angel Listene," William replied, pronouncing the name carefully without losing track of the tune. He let the angel react to his respectful address before he went on. Listene sat up straighter and moved forward in his seat. He didn't smile, but he didn't look like he had just eaten a lemon either. Encouraged, William continued.

"I stated my name and my intentions, requesting an audience with the queen. The dragon tried to flame me."

"Did you tell the dragon you were the Leader of the Walkers?" Listene's voice was still cold, but slightly less so.

William nodded. "I did, sir."

"Did you fight back?" Stephan asked the next question.

"No sir," William responded. "I aborted the mission."

"You are authorized to fight back next time," Listene said. Stephan nodded his agreement.

"Give fair warning," Stephan said.

William had to let the song play in his head for a good thirty seconds before he gave himself permission to speak.

"With all due respect, to all of you," William eyed them each in turn, "I am not sure I can defeat a dragon, especially if I must give it fair warning."

"Is there a particular Walker whose life you would be willing to risk in aiding you?" Stephan leaned forward in his seat too.

Listene nodded. "Someone who has been particularly recalcitrant perhaps? A good way to establish your leadership role is to make an example of someone who doesn't obey."

William bit his tongue, so as not to make enemies.

"I will try again," he said at last.

He breathed, he listened to the song in his head, and he collected his thoughts as best he could without thinking them. When he trusted himself to speak again, the old Walker looked back and forth between the two speakers.

"May I make a request?" he asked.

Neither of them spoke, nor did any of the others.

"I am handling more demons than ever," William said. "Many Walkers are, after two telling wars. We can only train so many new Walkers, and it would seem that the type of people the keys are choosing are…different."

"What do you mean?" Stephan's eyes narrowed critically.

"You may want to review the records of the way Walker Chase handled his last demon," he suggested. "Two other new Walkers have demonstrated similar attitudes and abilities, and their training requires unique attention."

"What is your request?" Listene's voice was ice once more.

William tried to bow again, as imperceptibly as possible.

"I would like an upgrade that allows me access to the spaces Walker Paul used to learn and train." William spoke quickly, going back to the song in his head as a wordless murmur swept through the council.

The two speakers looked at each other, and Stephan shrugged.

"The platinum key is gone," Listene said plaintively. "Walker Paul's Agent is imprisoned in Hell because his key disappeared, surely. Did you not issue Guide Kris a key that is attached to yours?"

Stephan leaned forward in his seat again.

"Does Guide Kris still have a platinum key?" he asked.

"Of course not," William answered quickly, thinking of nothing but the Rolling Stones.

Stephan peered at him while the band played on.

William wondered if the song flooded the angel's head as well.

"You are authorized to request an upgrade from the Dragon Queen when you meet with her," Listene seemed pleased to make the pronouncement, and even more pleased when Stephan nodded his assent. "Do not forget our message."

CHAPTER 14

Naked and afraid, the man moved his bare feet absently to keep them from burning on the hot rock underfoot. He stood out in the open, watching distant flames and dancing shadows warily. His mind whirled with questions as his blue eyes searched the darkness.

"Paul!" The voice was a whisper and a shout. The voice and the name it spoke peeled back layers of confusion in his mind.

"Paul!" Again came the whisper, quiet but fierce.

He followed the sound, trusting, until small hands with slender fingers reached from the shadows to take his hand.

She pulled him into the shadows, then into her embrace.

"Ximena." There was a twinge of doubt as he said the name, but she nodded.

"Good," she said. "What else do you remember?"

He looked at her, his brow furrowed in concentration or confusion. Either way, his mind was awash in forgetfulness.

"I love you," he said simply.

Ximena held him tighter, hiding her disappointment by burying her head in his chest.

"Awww," she murmured. "I love you too."

After a sweet but too short moment, she pulled away and looked up at him.

"I found a place we can go," she said. "Jessica can't hear us there, and the demons have not discovered it."

Paul's eyes went round, begging explanation.

Ximena brushed his unasked questions aside with a smile. She held his hand for a moment, squeezing gently. Scanning the burnt terrain, she moved quickly to the next pocket of darkness, then motioned him to follow.

He darted after her, unhesitating, then watched her nude form sprint over open rock once more.

They traveled that way for some time, covering miles of scorched tunnel and sticking to the shadows. From time to time they exchanged a smile, or touched hands for a sweet forever moment. Mostly they ran, in quiet bursts, their voices silent and their breathing measured.

At last they came to a piling of rocks, giant stones that were stacked haphazardly against the tall rock wall. Ximena took one last look around, then clambered up one tall boulder after another. Paul followed, placing his hands and feet carefully and falling behind. Pulling himself to a small hard plateau, he looked up for a path to follow.

His eyes narrowed. She was gone.

Paul moved from one end of the rock surface to the other, watching. Ximena's head appeared between two boulders, smiling. She motioned him to follow.

Over one boulder and around another, Paul at last glimpsed a dark wide crack in the wall. Ximena slipped through it, turning sideways to disappear into the darkness. Pivoting and ducking a little at the same time, Paul squeezed through the opening behind her.

"Help me with this." Her voice came to him in the inky blackness, and Paul tried to follow the sound. Hands in front of him, he groped blindly until his foot struck a small rock. Stumbling, he lurched forward and struck his knee on a boulder.

Strong slender fingers grasped his arm, steadied him. Her voice found his ears again in the darkness.

"You can't see?" Ximena kept the disappointment from her voice. It showed on her face, but her face was just another layer of inky black to his eyes.

"No," he replied. "It's dark."

Her hand traced along his arm to lightly clasp his wrist. Gently guiding him, she placed his hand on the boulder he had whacked in his groping stumble.

"Can you lift this?" Ximena's voice was less than hopeful.

Paul moved to put both hands on the huge rock. He looked up at her, still unable to make her out in the darkness. She saw the incredulous look on his face and knew his answer before it came.

"No." Paul shook his head. "It's way too heavy. Why could I lift that?"

"Help me block the entrance with it."

For the next several minutes they moved stone, until what little light he had been able to see was blocked by their labor. When she was satisfied, she took his hand and led him to sit on a friendly outcropping of stone.

"Do you remember who you are?" she asked.

"Paul." He said the name doubtfully.

"Paul what?" she pressed.

He shook his head in the dark, despite the stone underfoot.

"Do you remember me? My other name?" She touched his arm.

Paul shook his head again, and frustration twisted his visage.

Leaning forward, she kissed him lightly on the lips. Pulling away, she watched his tongue lick his lips and his eyes widen at the taste.

"Brenna?" He said it like a question, but with confidence.

She smiled a smile he couldn't see. As she watched, he slapped his naked hand against the rock ledge they sat upon.

"Stone," he chuckled. "My name is Paul Stone."

"Good," she nodded for her own sake. "Do you remember what you became? Do you remember the accident?"

He stood up suddenly. "I was a Walker. You were..."

Paul trailed off, felt his way to sit by her side again.

Ximena braced herself, reading his face in the darkness.

"You were my world." His words were a sad whisper.

In the same moment that she realized he wasn't about to level who she was at her like it was automatically a horrific thing, Paul spoke again.

"I betrayed you," he said, his voice breaking. "I'm so sorry."

Tears in her eyes, she put her arms around him.

"I'm sorry too, sweetie," she crooned. "We have to save all that for later. Do you remember when we died together? Do you remember fighting the Dragon Queen?"

Paul squinted in the darkness, searching within. Sitting up straighter, he snapped his fingers.

"Jessica!" he said, brightening at the recollection only to darken at the memory. Then he shook his head.

"It wasn't just her," he said quietly. "My soul was falling. My time was counting down."

"Did your key choose another?" she asked.

"No," he answered. "I made another Walker, but his key was gold. Then Lilia killed him. His name was Mason."

The first was not a name she particularly wanted to hear, particularly from his lips. The second name seemed to crush him in its own way when he spoke it. She let him linger in his hurt while she dwelt in her own. It was only a few moments before he spoke again.

"This has happened before, hasn't it?" Paul asked.

Ximena nodded, then remembered that only she could see in this place.

"Yes," she said quietly. "You remember now?"

"I remember we talked." He squeezed her hand. "I remember you strangling me, and that I didn't fight back."

She put both her hands in his. "Do you remember why?"

Ximena let him think as long as she felt she could afford to.

"Your soul is falling," she said.

Paul said nothing. Ximena watched him try to predict her next thought, heard him sigh as he drew a blank.

"I think your key is still with you, I think it's what brought us here." Ximena paused, searched his face. "I think it's just hibernating, waiting dormant until your soul begins to rise again."

"And dying speeds my soul along." At last, Paul was remembering everything.

He stood, resolute. "I'm ready."

"Here's the thing." Ximena smiled at his commitment. "My soul is… well, it's different. A soul must be on the move, or risk becoming lost. Yet my soul and my counterpart's soul cannot dip and peak like others. Our madness would destroy the worlds, and our eventual migration would mean a Godless Universe. You might say our souls are bracketed, always on the move but never rising or falling beyond a certain point. Right now, my soul is falling again. I must be on the rise to truly speed your progress."

She watched his face, watched him try to put the pieces together, then try not to. Paul struggled in the silent darkness for several long seconds before he sat next to her again.

"How low are you going to go?" he asked.

The fall was upon him. Although he was physically the same man that he was before, the light in his blue eyes and the smile that lit his youthful features when she knew him then were gone. His shoulders hung dejectedly, his thoughts seemed slower. Paul seemed to be bearing up under it, but the thought of sending her into the same misery deliberately had him balking on every level.

"The lowest I can go is higher than any human," she consoled him. "I live in bliss, always, whether I am on the rise or the fall is upon me. Don't worry about me."

He shook his head, confused. "Are you an angel, then? I remember the Bible says so. Is that true? Are you not a devil at all, but the most glorious of angels?"

Ximena smiled in the darkness. "Every culture has its own view of who I am and what my purpose is. Some even paint me as the Creator, and my counterpart as the adversary. Usually I am considered evil. Necessary, but evil. And of course male."

She made a face that he couldn't see while she watched his.

"Most of the complaints my counterpart and I receive are of a similar nature," she continued. "We don't do the work for anyone, no matter what the stories say."

"I met your counterpart," Paul said quietly.

"I know," she answered, squeezing his hand in the dark. "And what did Love look like to you?"

He gave her a strange look, one he didn't think she could see, but Paul did not respond.

After a few sweet but short minutes together, Ximena leaned over and kissed his cheek lightly.

"It's time," she murmured.

Paul sighed heavily and stood up straight.

"After," Ximena said, "come find me. Bring me back here, remind me who I was and who I am."

"Then kill you again?"

"This is the way it has to be, my love." Ximena embraced him one last time, their naked skin pressing together along the full length of their bodies.

Turning in his arms, Ximena put his forearms across her throat.

"I might fight back," she warned him. "Be decisive, I'm stronger than I look."

Paul's forearm cut off her air, and she wheezed.

He loosened his grip for a moment, and Ximena dropped her hands to her sides and pressed bodily back into him. She felt his tears falling on her bare back.

"Do it," she said.

She was lifted from the rock floor then, her weight hanging from her neck as she gasped instinctively for air.

And then her world went black.

CHAPTER 15

William had fashioned his living room with a deliberate eye for human comfort. The wide flatscreen television, the plush sofas, the wall hangings and throw rugs and end tables were all subjugated to the same purpose. It was supposed to look like a human lived here, ate here, slept here. It was not supposed to look like it all happened on the sofa.

Both Chase and Daemon seemed content to live most of their lives on his comfortable couch. They talked loudly, watched television even more loudly, and they only seemed to be motivated to move when the move was to go get more vodka. The last trip they had made, the armful of bottles they purchased was accompanied by a deck of cards. The Walker was teaching the demon to play poker.

The last few days were taking their toll on William. He didn't need sleep, not really, although he usually made it part of his daily routine like any human. In mind and body, he was always sharp and fresh; over centuries, he had become accustomed to that. Yet somehow his spirit was renewed when his body slumbered, and he missed it when he missed it.

"Chase," he said, watching them together on the sofa.

Daemon and the new Walker went on laughing and talking and playing cards on the open cushion between them.

William cleared his throat, spoke once more.

"Chase," he said again, more loudly. He tried to keep the irritation from his voice.

They both turned.

"Hey William," Chase said brightly. "What's up?"

"We need to talk," He beckoned the new Walker to the dining room.

"Daemon too, right?" Chase did not seem willing to move until his question was answered.

William crossed his arms, began to shake his head.

"He's my Guide, isn't he?" Chase asked.

"Fine." William drifted to the dining room and chose a seat. When they were both settled in seats of their own, the old Walker glanced at each of them in turn. He frowned at Chase.

"How did you know what to do with that demon?" he asked.

Chase shrugged. "It seemed like the thing to do."

That was not explanation enough for the old Walker. "How did you know what to do?" he asked again.

The new Walker shrugged once more.

"I've seen strange things my whole life," he reminded the old Walker. "I read books, I talk to Daemon, I listen to my angels."

"Do you mean your demons?" William corrected him.

"It's easy to look up to angels," Chase mused, "just as it feels natural to look down on devils. Seeing the best in one and the worst in the other is almost automatic for those of us stuck between them, but that's really just perspective. If an angel comes at me with judgement, their outer form does not raise their character to some lofty status. If a devil opens their arms to me in acceptance, do their horns and tail truly dictate that I should automatically dislike them?"

"Roche is going to love this one."

They all turned to the voice.

Kris stood in the doorway, his arms crossed to hide his hands in the sleeves of his robe.

William thought that name sounded familiar for some reason, but as the thought formed in his head another took its place.

'Can we talk?' the Guide's voice came in his mind.

The old Walker nodded, unsure how to respond. He felt that old familiar wrenching feeling inside of him, and the next thing he knew he was standing on solid cloud.

William smiled. "Good thinking."

Chase materialized beside him, then Daemon.

Crossing his arms in his sleeves, Kris frowned at Chase.

"How did you get in here?" he demanded.

The new Walker was turning in a slow circle, tracing the luminous walls and ceiling with his sleepy eyes.

"Is this Heaven?" Chase turned to Daemon.

While the demon shook his head, Kris answered.

"This is Walker Paul's personal space," he said. "How did you get in here?"

The new Walker motioned absently at empty space.

"You left the door open behind you."

William watched the Guide's brow furrow. Kris turned to him, but the old Walker could only frown and shrug.

"What do you mean?" Kris asked.

Chase pointed. "See the doorway?"

Rather than watch the Guide, William eyed the place Chase was indicating. Focusing his eyes and his intention, he saw a shimmer in the space. It was faint, like a trick of the light or gas fumes rising through the air.

"It's fading now," Chase said, as William watched it evaporate.

When the shimmering had ceased altogether, Kris pivoted. As his eyes fell on Chase again, the questions began to pour out.

"How did you see that?" he asked. "How did you even know to look for it? How did you follow us?"

"There are doorways everywhere," Chase replied. "I've seen them my whole life, but I've never been able to walk through them. Now I can."

The new Walker held up his gold key.

"This makes me a doorway," he said. "When I walk between worlds, or when William does, we do not open doors between those worlds. Walkers are the doorway, able to move through layers of reality without leaving a trace. It's not the same for others; when a natural or supernatural being walks between worlds, they must create a doorway. When they have walked through it, they must either close it behind them or at least realize that they are leaving a doorway between dimensions open."

The Guide looked like he was deep in thought. William watched him while his own mind whirled with wondering.

"How do you close these doorways?" Kris asked at last.

Chase smiled, his clear watery blue eyes crinkling at the corners. "The same way you open them."

Kris nodded. "With intent."

"You can wave your hands or chant or do a little dance if it makes you feel better," Chase shrugged.

"Is it possible that those doorways are causing the problems that the angels are attributing to Walker activity?"

William tried to nod and shake his head at the same time. As a result, he ended up standing there still and silent while the new Walker schooled them both.

"Not all of them," he answered. "Walkers have been playing their part as well. Not all demons need to be dealt with violently, and even the ones that do have lights associated with them. Those lights need to be sent home when their demons are. The spaces between levels of reality are either cluttered with them or nearly absent of them, and they are either collapsing in on the emptiness or bursting with the overfill."

The Guide's gray eyes found William's, and the old Walker nodded his agreement.

"Where did you learn all this?" Kris asked, turning his attention once again to Chase.

"I go to class, I read the books, I talk to Daemon," Chase answered simply. His watery eyes found the floor.

"And I see," he added quietly.

"What do you mean?" Kris asked. "What do you see?"

His gaze chased a drifting cloud for a moment, and the new Walker kicked at it absently with one foot.

"I see…things," Chase spoke quietly. "I always have. Demons, angels, doorways, geometric patterns around and between people, hints of the future and what I should do or shouldn't do, you know…things."

William gave the Guide a solemn nod.

"He handled demons like I've never seen," he said. "Angels too."

Chase cocked his head to the side and squinted his blue eyes a little, regarding the Guide as if he were sizing him up. Kris waited, returning his stare while standing with balled fists on his robed hips. William noticed that Daemon was watching the exchange with as much interest and possibly as much confusion as William himself. The demon still tended to fade into the background when not being addressed or included, like attached demons faded from view when their host was happy.

The new Walker nodded, making up his mind about something.

"You said they were like rats in the walls," Chase said. "It's not a bad analogy, so far as I can tell. Do you know what would happen if there were suddenly no rats on Earth? Cities would have a problem with garbage pileup almost immediately, and flies would outnumber the oxygen molecules in the air. Rats are part of the cleanup crew, and without them the planet would suffer immensely."

"In much the same way," he went on, "demons and lights are not just in the walls, they are part of the function of these barriers. They insulate realms from each other, and they are meant to feed off the falling thoughts from the realm above and the rising thoughts from the realm below. They rise and fall like any other soul, finding new purpose in each new world while they carry the wisdom of the thoughts they have consumed. Like rats that eat the dead things or ants that aerate the earth, at this stage of consciousness reality needs demons and angels just to continue being reality."

"You learned all this in class?" Kris ventured skeptically.

Daemon wagged his head from side to side, watching Chase like he should respond though the demon knew he wouldn't. At last the demon sighed and answered for him.

"God speaks to him," he said.

"Really?" Kris asked. He didn't say it like an impressed bystander listening to a pro explain technique; the word came out sounding much like a parent responding to a six-year-old claiming they could fly. There was no hint of belief to it.

Chase shrugged and went back to examining the liquid light floor with his light sky eyes.

"God speaks to everyone," he said plaintively. "Not everyone listens."

"Did God tell you to drink a gallon of vodka every day?" Kris demanded. "Did God tell you how to cheat people out of money?"

The new Walker's eyes glazed at the Guide and then to the clouds underfoot again. He shrugged once more.

"God told me that the Walker King is not gone," he murmured.

Glancing all about him, looking for ears or doorways, the Guide narrowed his eyes at Chase. He opened his mouth to speak, but the new Walker cut him off.

"No one is listening," Chase assured him. "I knew you came here for privacy, and I closed all open or partially open doorways."

"I brought William here to talk," the Guide said icily.

Just in case Chase didn't get the point, he added, "to him."

Chase got the point. His hand fell on Daemon's shoulder, and they faded from view.

William fought the urge to smile as the Guide shook his head and gazed at nothing.

"There's more to that one than meets the eye, friend," the old Walker said, giving in to the smile.

The Guide laughed, a cold bark that reminded William of the king he had lost. Shaking his head, Kris arced an eyebrow at him.

"Maybe so," he responded. "I still don't trust him."

William chuckled quietly. "Paul once told me that if you met God you would find some flaw in his character."

"I have," Kris frowned. "I did."

Before William could express curiosity, the Guide spoke again.

"I went to Hell and tried to see Jessica," he said.

William's smile fell. "Me too."

"A dragon tried to fry me," Kris added.

William nodded. "Me too. I told the Council."

"What did they say?" the Guide asked.

"Try harder."

The Guide's eyes went round. "Seriously?"

William shrugged. "The good news is that they can't see everything, or even as much as I thought they could. They don't know that you still have a platinum key, or that we can get in here."

"Good," Kris responded. "We may have an ally, although I'm not sure yet how he can help."

The old Walker gazed curiously at the Guide, wondering who he might have trusted. He asked, "Who?"

Flushing a shade, the Guide shrugged. "My dad's demon."

CHAPTER 16

Cal stood and stretched, naked, letting the blanket fall completely onto Sarah. She sat cross-legged on the couch, her arm where Cal had just lain between her legs. Where her thighs came together, the blanket piled to hide all but the shape of her lap. From the waist up she lounged in nude comfort, leaning against the soft leather.

"Now I really do have to go," he said, looking down at her. Smoking weed and coke, having sex on the couch and on the bed and in the shower, watching television and talking had all added up to a well wasted day. Maybe it had been two days, even three. It didn't matter. What did matter was the collection of texts that had gathered on his gold iPhone.

Sarah blinked, her eyes going wide.

"Do you want me to come with you?" she asked.

"Nah." Cal waved his hand. "I'll probably be a couple hours, people are waiting on me. You can hang out here and make yourself comfortable."

Laying back, she sprawled her nude body across the soft yielding leather. The blanket slid slowly off her lap to puddle on the carpet. Sarah stretched, putting her hands behind her head and arching her back to display her scant height fully on the horizontal cushioning. Cal watched her belly flatten as her ribs stood out and her toes pointed straight. She shifted slightly back and forth, rubbing her smooth skin on the soft leather and giving him another glimpse of every part of her that he had tasted earlier.

She was still laying there, relaxed and nude and smiling, when Cal came back into the room dressed in his work uniform. Black shoes and slacks under a dark light buttoned shirt. The gold cross at his neck dangled in the air when he leaned forward to kiss her, and she caught her fingers up in the chain.

"This has always confused me," she giggled, inspecting the tall symbol. "Why do you wear a big gold cross?"

Cal grinned, reaching behind his neck to remove it.

"It's my insurance policy," he explained.

"Do you think everyone who wears a cross gets into Heaven, and everyone else goes to Hell?" she frowned prettily. "I don't think it works that way, sweetie."

Taking it from her with gentle hands, he pinched the top half of the cross with his left thumb and forefinger while pinching the bottom half with his right. Chuckling the whole time, he turned one hand slightly and pulled it away from the other. The top half of the cross came away from the bottom half, trailing a slender piece of metal that ended in a miniature spoon. The spoon had a little mound of white powder on it.

Cal snorted the little bump and grinned at her again.

"It's not for when I die," he grinned. "It's in case I run out of cocaine."

He reassembled the novelty and hung it around his neck once more.

"I'll be back," Cal said.

Walking a complete circle around his car in the parking lot, Cal only slowed a little as he passed the bullet hole.

It was less visible than it might have been if it were a little higher, but still more visible than he would've liked. He drove with an eye out for cops or people too upright for their own good for a couple blocks, then pulled into the first service station between his apartment and Raul's house. A quick trip inside, a quick cash purchase, and he slapped the bumper sticker over the bullet hole on the way out. With the pink mermaid-shaped lettering, he just looked like another Santa Cruz resident too stupid or too proud to put their bumper sticker on their bumpers. It was not his ideal image, but it was better than running coke in a bullet-riddled car.

He tried not to think about whether it was worse that he had spent all that time banging Sarah or that it had not seemed nearly as enticing as killing her. He tried not to think about how he had felt standing over Mikie's dead body. He tried not to think about how he might get that feeling back without murdering any friends or customers. He tried not to think of these things so hard that he thought of nothing else as he drove across town.

Parking on the street, striding up the walk and knocking on the door were all automatic actions performed in the swirling violent whirlwind that were his thoughts. Cal opened the door after Raul's muffled voice came through it and stepped into the familiar living space. The colorful cartoon images on the television caught his eye, a demonic-looking young girl cowled in purple and black playing delightedly with a pink pegasus doll.

Cal turned from the television to find Raul beaming at him.

"Whussup killer?" Raul stood and briskly crossed the room. He knelt below the giant screen, where a funny-looking little green dude was transforming instantly from elephant to ostrich to funny-looking little green dude once more.

"How's it going, Raul." Cal's gaze drifted to meet his lively glazed dark eyes. "Can I get an ounce?"

The safe was already open, and the dealer grabbed baggies while Cal dug in his pocket and counted cash.

Raul hefted the baggies, down on one knee, watching Cal count. When he reached the end and set the money on the coffee table, Cal noticed there was no gun adorning its surface. There was a mound of cocaine, but no gun. He could have sworn it was there a minute ago.

"Keep it coming, Holmes," Raul said, slow and low. "Protection ain't free."

Narrowing his tan eyes with suspicion, Cal kept his gaze locked on Raul's while he reached into his pocket again. Once he felt the soft click of the blade locking into place, Cal felt drunk with confident anticipation.

"Hey Raul," he said quietly, "Have you ever heard of the gun versus knife rule?"

At the sound of the word "gun", Raul brandished the pistol he'd hidden behind his crouch. Pivoting and standing at the same time, the swing of his arm met the swing of Cal's arm. Blood flowed, the pistol bounced harmlessly off the flat television screen, and the blade buried itself in Raul's low wide shoulder. Cal swung his weight hard, watched a wide red smile open at the base of Raul's throat. A splash of blood erupted from the wound, and the dealer's eyes went wide as his hands went to his throat to staunch the flow.

Cal reversed the blade and slashed downward, opening another gash across his chest. His eyes caught a glimpse of the white mountain on the coffee table turning pink down one side as it was doused in blood. Then he watched Raul reaching toward him, both bloodied hands questing blindly over the table between them to grab at him.

Slashing upward, Cal felt one arm catch on the blade, then the other. He ducked and stabbed stabbed stabbed, watching red slits appear in Raul's white tank top in rapid succession. Blood covered his arm and the knife and the coffee table, and Raul was painted in flowing shades of red.

Stepping back, Cal watched Raul fall to his knees. His hands dropped to the coffee table, one of them landing in the tainted pile of cocaine and raising a momentary cloud. His round eyes looked up at Cal, unseeing, as his body trembled.

"They say that a knife is almost always better than a gun at less than twenty feet," Cal said coolly, his light eyes locked on the glazing dark eyes of his victim. "I'm not sure it's always the case, but it certainly proved true here. Lucky for me."

Raul's dark eyes rolled back in his head, and he fell to the floor.

Watching the body, more for pleasure than out of caution, Cal emptied the safe and picked up the dropped bags and money. He moved swiftly and quietly, closing the door behind him when he left.

CHAPTER 17

William steeled himself, closed his eyes and let his thoughts fall. Burnt smokiness climbed inside his nostrils, and he opened his eyes to survey the hellish terrain. His armor was whole, the chains and buckles silent as he stood there staring into the smoke and thinking of his sword. There were no forms taking shape in the mist, no leathery flapping of wings or armored footfalls.

There was a voice, however, a lone distant voice that sang a bawdy drinking song with a haunting siren's sound. William moved toward the singing, prepared for a trap but still unarmed. As he came closer, the words came clear, and William stood and listened for a moment before proceeding.

> Well the dragons all breathed fire
> And the demons they all burned
> When each demon disappeared
> Five smaller would return
>
> In Hell's darkest hour
> We all began to pray
> Our fallen queen and the Walker King
> Would rise and save the day

Smiling, William stepped forward. He let his feet fall heavy on the burnt rock, to alert the singer of his approach. The voice paused, then went on as he continued to move forward. It seemed too lovely to belong in this place.

> We burned, we fought, we bled
> We all fell one by one
> We raised our prayers to bend God's ear
> The words burned in the sun

He saw her at the same time that she saw him, and William stopped walking in the instant she stopped singing. She was long of limb, lithe and slim under her flowing cape. Black and silken, the wide material was attached at her neck and her wrists with leather cuffs and collar. Straight black thick hair cascaded from the side of her head not shaved clean to puddle in her lap. Her hands clutched the pile of hair loosely, bringing her cape to cover her in folds from neck to knees.

Sitting on a scorched rock, the devil watched his approach with slitted eyes that danced with fire. Her small horns sat atop her head, close together and barely poking out through her thick silky jet mane. A ring of fire burned around her, a perfect circle of flame somehow guttering in the already burnt terrain. Her tail stretched out from under her cape, longer than her legs with a sharp barb at the end. It was the only part of her that moved while William watched, drifting over her bare calves and feet lazily.

William smiled and inclined his head in a friendly gesture.

"Please, by all means," he said. "Go on."

Her speaking voice was as beautiful and measured as her singing voice, finding his ears over the fire.

"We haven't the time, or the drink," she replied.

"So what happens now?" William's sword was in his grasp in his mind.

She lifted one arm slowly, the cape trailing her movement to make it appear as though she was spreading a black wing.

"Step into my ring of fire, Walker." She smiled, and he saw that her canines were unusually long. "I will make all your worries go away."

One long lithe leg appeared as the cape fell away, smooth crimson skin stretched bare over taut muscles. The whole right side of her body was naked, the left swathed in cape. Her tail began to wind its way around the length of her exposed leg, the barb snaking its way between her slim thighs as she opened them slightly.

The old Walker felt a flush begin to heat his face as his eyes moved away to begin tracing the ring of fire.

"I would have audience with the Dragon Queen," he said.

"Oh?" The devil lifted herself from the stone upthrust to stand before it. "And what words would you have for her?"

William returned his eyes to her cloaked form.

"I am William, leader of the Walkers," he said.

She smiled, showing her long biting teeth.

"I am aware of who you are, as is the queen."

William smiled entreatingly. "It is customary for the Queen of Hell to meet with the leader of the Walkers as well as the Walker Council from time to time."

A silent wave of laughter shook her shoulders, the gossamer cape rippling down the length of her body to where it puddled on the burnt rock. Her eyes narrowed and her hands moved almost imperceptibly under the fabric.

William took a step back, instinctively, and she smiled.

"Relax, Walker," she cooed, putting a long brown twisted length of something in her mouth and lighting it by touching a finger to it. A dark brown tendril of smoke drifted from the tip, to join in the thick cloud that issued forth from her lips. The acrid brimstone background stench was overlaid with the sudden smell of pencil lead rolled in roofing tar and set alight.

Rather than crinkle his nose, or ask her to stand downwind, William simply stopped breathing. Every breath he had taken since becoming a Walker had been a superfluous gesture, a breath drawn for pleasure or out of habit. Walking through the smoky casinos in Reno, he had shut off the habitual motion so often the shutting off had become habit. The occasional deep breath was all he needed to give his thoughts voice.

One side of her cape was parted where her arm bent to hold her smoke. William deliberately held her gaze, not glancing at the small round exposed breast or the smooth crimson skin along her slim torso.

"Is it customary for the Queen of Hell to stuff the dungeons with demons, or burn them alive for heat and light?" The beautiful devil took a long drag from the smoking stalk.

The Walker's eyes widened. "The Dragon Queen is…"

"No! You mustn't!" The fire in her slitted eyes danced as the devil's eyes darted left to right, looking for anyone that wasn't there. "She cannot hear me inside my ring of fire, but she can hear you out there. Step closer, Walker William, or behave as though I am rebuffing or seducing you."

"What are your orders?" he asked, dark eyes on bright flame.

She smiled and puffed away languidly. "To rebuff you or seduce you, find out what you know about the fallen queen."

"And then?" he arched an eyebrow.

Blowing out smoke, she shrugged. "Then I am to kill you."

The ring of fire was suddenly less inviting than before.

William considered his choice of words before taking a breath.

"What might the council or I offer the Dragon Queen to show our good will?" he asked.

She laughed again, more relaxed this time. Reaching her free hand behind her, the devil pulled the long flowing cascade of her silken hair over her shoulder. It trailed nearly to her knees, blending into another shifting shade of black over her robe. When she moved the smoking twist to her other hand, she was covered neck to toe with flowing darkness.

William relaxed his rigid stance and gaze, grateful.

"The queen wants nothing but revenge," the devil responded. "She would see you all burn before she would treat with you. The Dragon Queen cannot forge Walker tools as her mother could, nor does she have her complex ancient mind for strategy. All she knows is bondage and hate, and all realms of Hell are now her dungeon. Whether she is its most fearful guard or its most dangerous prisoner is both indiscernible and irrelevant. The inevitable outcome is the same."

William frowned, seeing that the fire burning in the devil's eyes was one of suffering, of longing, of hopelessness.

"What is that?" he asked quietly.

"First the demons all burn. Then the devils all burn. Then the dragons all burn. Then there is nothing left to burn but the Dragon Queen." The devil took one last long pull from the substance or mix of substances and tossed the rest into the ring of fire. She blew out a long thick stream of smoke.

"Get out of Hell, Walker," she said. "Do not make me carry out my orders."

"I must meet with the Dragon Queen," William frowned.

"I am the first line of defense between you," she replied, casting her arms wide so that her hair and the cape filled the air around her with flowing shades of silken black for a breathtaking forever moment. She changed in a heartbeat, transforming into a thirty-foot long black dragon. Her hair disappeared, but the cape didn't. It flowed down the length of her back, a decorative scrap of material clinging still to the shackles around her slim serpentine neck and wrists. When she flexed her wings, the cape was all but obscured by the wondrous black glittering dusting of scales that covered her wide wingspan.

The same sad intelligence gazed at him from behind her slitted reptilian eyes.

"I am not the last line of defense, nor the most formidable," she said, her voice bigger and fuller but much the same. "If you get through me, you will kill me or she will for failing. But worry not about my lost soul, for yours will be adrift soon after. If you kill me."

"I don't want to kill you," William answered honestly. "I want to help you overthrow the—"

A burst of flame cut him off, although the dragon gave him plenty of time to dodge it. William moved swiftly in a wide arc around the circle of fire, a few feet ahead of the stream of flame, until she stopped trailing him and paused to inhale.

"You must not speak of such things," she hissed.

Flapping her wings three times, the scaled lengths of them cracking loudly each time, the dragon rose into the air and extinguished the ring of fire at the same time. She landed bodily outside the scorched circle, rearing back on her haunches and glaring down at him.

"Dragons are loyal above all else," she proclaimed loudly to him and anyone else that might be listening. "I stand behind my queen in all things until the end of my life or the end of time."

She shot forth another burst of flame, with no warning this time. Rather than manifest a weapon, William ran. Pumping his legs furiously, he did his best to be nothing but a dwindling blur to his opponent's eyes. The flapping of wings began far too quickly, far too close behind him. The sound drew nearer as he ran, only to be joined by identical sounds coming swiftly from his left and right.

William skidded to a stop.

"Well, hell," he cursed.

Three gigantic black dragons descended from the acrid smoke, three rivers of flame joining to burn a hole where he had stood.

CHAPTER 18

Vanessa glided about the room, collecting empty candy bar wrappers and chip bags and vodka bottles. There was a faint touch of a smile at the corners of her mouth as she watched Chase and Daemon playing cards and talking excitedly. William stood quiet and calm behind them, neither willing them to see him nor willing them not to. He collected his thoughts while he breathed in the smells of home. He wondered if there was a word that described an intense fear of dragons, then realized any being in their right mind would be afflicted.

He sighed, shaking off the feeling.

Vanessa was standing between the sofa and the television, her arms loaded with container castoffs, peering at him with such concerned consternation that she looked downright distressed. The Guide crossed the room to stand before him, her arms bent to encircle the trash. Her eyes were round and luminous, her youthful forehead lined in a single shallow questioning crease.

"Did you go to Hell?" she asked quietly.

William nodded.

"Were you attacked?" Vanessa clutched the mess tighter to her robed body.

"Yes," he answered. "By three dragons."

"Did you fight them?"

The old Walker shook his head. "I ran."

"Good." Vanessa glided away from him, looking back over her shoulder to see if he would follow.

He did, trailing her as far as the dining nook and pulling out a chair.

"The council will not see it that way," he grimaced.

Her back was to him as she separated trash from recyclables and deposited each piece in its proper container.

"Have you seen Kris lately?" William asked as she drifted close.

Vanessa shook her head, moving even closer to encircle her arms about his waist. Her head leaned into William's chest, and he stroked her hair while breathing her in. The old Walker closed his eyes and let himself be happy in the moment.

"I am worried about you," Vanessa murmured quietly.

He pulled her closer, so she wouldn't see his frown. When he spoke, he did so slowly, measuring his words so they would show the emotion he wanted rather than the feelings he had.

"I know I am not your whole world, Vanessa," he said. "You have new abilities and old curiosities that you might explore rather than wait to see if this old brain can wrap itself around this new world or if my sword is long enough to reach anything important."

She moved away, not enough to release her embrace but enough to look up at him. Vanessa's eyes were round and curious and a little hurt as she peered carefully at him.

"I am your Guide," she reminded him. "I continue to exist in this form for the sole purpose of assisting you in your duties as a Walker. By definition, you are my world."

William nodded. "Not your whole world, though. I am your job, but I do not have to be your…I do not have to be anything more than that. If you do not wish it."

Now she did release him from her embrace, stepping back to regard him with open curiosity. He pretended his heart didn't fall as she did, as best he could.

Vanessa was frowning, crossing her arms in front of her. It was so hard to read her, so little of the depth of her being showed on her smooth young face. She began to speak, stopped, then began again. Her voice was as calm and as measured as his had been.

"Are you not comfortable with the direction our relationship has taken?" she asked plaintively.

William shook his head. "I do not want to risk you being uncomfortable with it due to the nature of our working relationship. I do not want you to feel—"

"Hey guys." Chase stepped around the corner, startling them both. Vanessa moved even further away, and the old Walker felt his heart sink lower. The smell of vodka filled the room.

"Am I interrupting something?" Chase's watery blue eyes went from one of them to the other, hesitating only a moment before going on. "I've got another demon calling, but there's another right after it that feels strange to me. I was wondering if you could come with."

The new Walker looked at each of them once more, smiling at Vanessa.

"If you have time," he added.

William felt a shame come over him, a dark cloud of a thousand voices weaved together to point out his failing. To be himself, William had to follow certain rules. For one, he never struck too soon or too late or without conviction. For another, he never disrespected humans or judged them for their demons. But most importantly, he never took a new Walker's training lightly.

Yet here he was, indulging his feelings like a teenager adrift in a sea of hormones, while this mysterious new Walker impetrated him for a little guidance. Rather than apologize, William flayed his fallen heart and questioned Chase.

"Two demons in one night?" William asked. "It's a little early for that."

This was the moment where he would ordinarily exchange looks or words with his Guide, pained by her beauty but attentive to the task at hand. Instead he kept his eyes locked on Chase's, wishing he had kept his mouth shut like he usually did when he felt something.

The new Walker shook his head, the corners of his mouth creasing in a deep frown.

"William," he said, "I have been answering countdowns every three or four hours since you took me on that first hunt. They seem to be coming even more quickly, as time goes on. That's another thing I wanted to ask you about. Do Walkers not get days off? Or a day? Or a night?"

"Your first hunt was with Walker Paul and I," William corrected him, allowing himself a smile at the memory. "You wouldn't take the sword, and Paul got impatient and killed your demon so we could get back to training."

The rest of the new Walker's words sank in.

"Chase, how many demons have you…" William trailed off, realizing all of his customary words didn't fit.

"Transitioned." Chase smiled, solving the problem. "I call it transitioning. I hope that's okay…?"

William nodded. "It's perfect."

Chase shrugged. "I lost count around twenty."

In life, William had always been chosen to train men, and he had shouldered the responsibility with utter seriousness in every instance. As a Walker, he had taken that seriousness to a whole new level as the sacred symbol glowed on his key time and again. It wasn't until he had met the Walker King, then scores of other Walkers, that he had realized how many more Walkers he turned than any other demon hunter. When Paul had told him, a certain pride had blossomed within William. Even among the exceptional, he was exceptional.

Now he looked at this young Walker, whom he had judged so harshly. William felt another layer of darkness descend upon him. He wished he could tell the enigmatic supernatural how he was feeling, how he wanted to learn from the new Walker so much that he felt inept trying to teach him. At this point he did glance at Vanessa, who stood still with her arms crossed before her to remind him just what he created when he spoke his feelings.

"That's too much activity for any Walker," William said, his words more gruff than he had intended. "I will speak to the council about it. Let me have your key for the night, get some rest. I must meet with them tomorrow. I will straighten this out."

Chase's eyes went round, coming alive. "No, no, that's okay. I'll keep at it. Would you accompany me next time?"

"Yes," William nodded. "When is it?"

The new Walker didn't consult the new ancient timepiece, or pause to think about it. "Seventeen minutes."

"I'll be right back," William said.

He hesitated, churning his thoughts and second-guesses.

"Chase," William spoke, resolved.

The new Walker raised his eyebrows attentively. "Yeah?"

"I am going to draw a symbol in the air," he said. "Normally I just visualize it, which will also work for you, but I am going to draw it to show you."

"You mean the symbol you use to access that cloud world?" Chase asked. His hand moved in the air, a slim line in pretty indigo trailing his pointing finger. The symbol William had been about to show him hung in space before the old Walker.

William nodded. "That's the one. Did Kris show it to you?"

"No," Chase replied. "It appears in the air whenever either of you go there. Except yours is a little different."

The new Walker's hand moved again, and as one symbol faded another formed to hang in the air. It was a small collection of mostly straight lines, a simple drawing of a longsword cleaving an arrow in two down the middle.

Chase pointed. "What is that?"

William felt a flush creep up the back of his neck. "My sigil."

Chase smiled. "Nice tag. Want to see mine?"

The old Walker smiled back, nodded.

It was even more simple, and elegant. With a few deft strokes of his hand, Chase painted a doorway within a doorway within a doorway. He looked at William, hopeful.

"I'm still working on it," Chase spoke his voice of doubt.

"It's perfect," William said once more, wishing for better words.

"Would you open a doorway to that place, please?" William asked him.

"Of course." Chase began to draw, though William suspected his ability to visualize rivaled that of the old Walker. He turned to speak a few words to Vanessa, or invite her along, but the Guide had disappeared.

William spoke as he walked through the sudden opening that appeared. "You do not always employ…the spirits when you form a doorway?"

The pause was not so much to pass through as it was about replacing his vernacular with the new Walker's. Chase seemed to notice, passing into the high place with a smile. He drew the same symbol reversed, noting William watching, and tagged it as doorway and momentary paint faded to nothing.

"That is more for them than me," Chase replied. "My key opened those portals, but the spirits helped hold them open. You don't need help, though, just ask the key to open the appropriate doorways or imagine them opening. It gets easy pretty quickly."

"Will you show me?" William asked.

Chase nodded. "In about…"

He trailed off, narrowing his eyes as some thought or realization was slowly striking him. Opening his hand, he raised it to peer at the gold watch face that appeared open in it. Still staring at it, he finished.

"…seventeen minutes." His eyes found William's.

William shrugged. "There is no time here, nor in the next place we are going. You can rest here or there when you wish."

Chase looked around, eyeing the small distant structure.

"It's empty," William replied. "There are bunks in there, but it smells like beer. There are more comfortable quarters in the next place."

"This is where you trained for the War of the Demon Horde, isn't it?" Chase queried him. "Is the next place we're going where the Walker King stretched a moment into eternity to learn the secrets of the universe?"

William realized Chase had spent more time reading about him than interacting with him, and let another wave of shame wash over him.

"Don't believe everything you read," he advised the new Walker, "especially in the book you were provided."

"It's not just the books," Chase responded. "All the Guides and new Walkers talk about it, in class and in the hallways between classes. You're a hero, Walker William, a legend in your own immortal lifetime. The obvious inaccuracies in the books just lend more to your mystique. And Paul's."

The new Walker sighed for some reason. "Especially Paul's."

"Is he still alive?" William pressed him suddenly. "Can you see where the Walker King is? Or his soul?"

Chase shook his head, sad. "I would have told you if I could."

They were both quiet, forever not ticking by.

Chase spoke at last. "Did you really kill a dragon?"

William smiled, despite himself. "I got lucky, once. Walker Paul was the real dragon slayer."

CHAPTER 19

Kris sat in the hard straight-backed wooden chair, reading an awkwardly bound hand-written tome. The couch was right behind him, and there were easier books to read, but comfort had long since stopped being a concern for the Guide. Besides, he wasn't about to be the fool looking for his key under the street lamp just because the light was better there. Paul had discovered enough in these pages to get them all into this mess; perhaps Kris could find what he needed to get them out of it here.

He had drifted ghost-like through every mile of scorched rock or packed dirt or woven cloud that waited between the seemingly endless layers of reality. Most were bare and barren, not a soul or soul-sucker from the beginning of tunnel to the end. As he got lower, demons were everywhere, but the angels either hovered out of view like him or weren't there at all. Kris saw no sign of Paul, or Ximena. He kept his eyes out for anyone doing the same thing he was, or looking in on him, making sure to close every doorway he opened or found standing open.

Marking his place with his flask, the Guide leaned back and rubbed his eyes. There was no point checking the time; it was the same as when he had arrived here hours ago. He considered moving to the nearby sofa, dismissed the thought and spread the tome open again on the table before him. Untwisting the silver cap from the flask, he gulped at the endless liquid as his eyes searched the page. Finding his place, Kris put a finger on the spot and set the drink aside.

He heard a sound, then smelled vodka.

"Hey Kris." Chase's voice sounded behind him.

The Guide turned in his uncomfortable chair, chambering some of his growing frustration to fire it at the new Walker. His eyes fell on William standing with Chase before he could speak, and Kris put the thought away.

"Chase," he nodded, politely enough. "How goes it, William?"

William returned his nod. "Harder and harder. You?"

"Much the same," the Guide chuckled darkly. "I have searched and searched, but..."

He trailed off, glancing at Chase.

William frowned, too lost in his own thoughts to notice.

"I went to Hell again," the old Walker said. "The good news is that the queen does not seem to be popular, even among her own kind. The bad news is that the least loyal dragon guarding the perimeter still tried to flame me. I could sure use some ideas here."

Kris shrugged. "I was about to try again myself. I thought I might just try to outrun the sentry."

Shaking his head, William replied. "I tried. There were two more dragons coming at me before I knew it, and probably more waiting beyond. I can't get within ten miles of the tunnels, much less the throne room."

"What about a series of doors?" Chase asked.

They both turned slowly, pivoting to regard the new Walker with annoyance and curiosity, respectively.

"What do you mean?" William asked.

"Well," Chase responded, "I assume you are transporting yourselves as close to the throne room as your key and the queen's magick will let you? Then proceeding on foot?"

William nodded immediately, and Chase watched the Guide carefully until he followed suit.

"It's not her magick," William pointed out. "It's her mother's. As is your key and mine."

Chase nodded, in acknowledgment or dismissal or both. "Your keys can make a doorway appear, from anywhere you can see to anywhere else you can see. You can use those doorways to get past the dragons, walking through them whenever one attacks you so you don't lose ground and have to reappear at the beginning."

Kris watched William start to nod right along with Chase almost immediately, and as soon as the new Walker finished his sentence the old one agreed.

"Good idea," he said. "Will you two help me?"

"I don't know," Kris interjected doubtfully. "What if it doesn't work?"

"Then we're right back where we started," William said. "Again."

"I'll help you," Chase volunteered.

"I don't know," the Guide repeated.

"The council is going to make me start taking Walkers with me to engage the sentinel dragons," William said. "The only way we stand any chance is if I bring an army, and even then Walkers will surely die. Our numbers have already dwindled recently, too much for me to put more of us at risk. I have to do this, even if the most important Walker's life must be put on the line."

Kris let his confusion show on his face. He had never seen the old Walker display arrogance in any form.

"Not me," William smiled. "Chase."

The Guide shrugged. "Okay. Let's go to Hell."

Chase gestured, and a doorway opened before them. The thin metal wall of the shed was an ordinary backdrop to the swirling otherworldly lights that framed the portal and the dark burnt terrain that awaited them on the other side.

Kris gestured. "Walkers first."

He watched William walk through, followed after Chase had passed. On the other side, he smelled sulfur and brimstone and dread. The new Walker was already motioning at the doorway, closing it behind them.

The three supernaturals faced the direction they all knew they needed to go, and Kris saw another doorway appear about thirty feet away. It was shrouded in smoke, blurred a little around the edges, but it was visible. Another doorway appeared, right in front of them, and Chase stepped through.

Suddenly he was standing thirty feet away, waving at them and smiling through the haze.

"Come on," William said, moving through the portal.

Kris sighed and floated along behind, then toward the next scintillating rectangle of light full of soot and smoke. Chase had just finished closing one door and was moving toward another when he paused.

"What's that sound?" he asked, curious.

"Dragon's wings," William responded. "Keep moving."

The sound was closer when Kris stepped from the next doorway. A chill ran up his spine, and he even saw William glance nervously in the direction of the noise. Only Chase seemed unperturbed, opening another set of passageways immediately after closing the last.

Rocketing from the sky, a huge black dragon angled its jaws to rend one of them and its front talons to slash the other two, readying its rear legs to flay them into a supernatural puddle of remains.

Instead, its face struck the rock, its claws slashed at nothing, and its huge body landed in an ungainly heap.

Thirty feet away, Kris could swear he felt the ground shake. He watched Chase move through a doorway, urgent to follow. Risking a glance back while William trailed Chase, the Guide saw the dragon lifting itself from the sunken landing zone. It pivoted its head, cranked open its jaws, and spewed fire.

Sixty feet from the dragon, the Guide sighed and faced forward. Chase was moving more quickly now, and Kris suspected it might be due to the fact that the sound of flapping wings filled the air once more. Another glance back confirmed that the sounds were not coming from behind them. The first dragon was still on the ground, slithering towards them swiftly. It looked like a giant lizard with wings and fangs and intelligent slitted eyes of fire, moving in a twisting four-legged crawl that left deep marks in the stone and brought it quickly within flame distance.

Kris felt his robe yanked rather violently forward, and he was dragged bodily through two successive doorways. William had ahold of him, one hand at his waist and the other at his shoulder. Before Kris could be annoyed at being manhandled, or appropriately amazed at the Walker's incredible strength, dragon fire burst through the doorway they had just come through.

William waved his hand, the doorway collapsed, and the dragon and its fire were a safe distance away again. Chase had already moved along, and was a stone's throw away and opening another set of doors. The presence of an actual dragon seemed to have sparked some fear or urgency in the new Walker, and he was moving with a speed that was beyond human. The Guide reached out mentally to link with Chase as he stepped through the fresh egress, felt himself pulled once more through doorways effortlessly.

"Keep moving," Kris said, appearing beside the Walker. "Go forward a few doorways and leave them open, then come back through one or two and wait there."

He did not have to wait long for William to catch up. As soon as the Walker appeared, Kris began to speak.

"Close that door," he pointed behind them, as William did just that. "Keep moving, but don't close any more doorways. When you catch up with Chase, wait there with him until I come through. Then get us all out of there, as far as possible. Chase will have a series of doorways set up for us to go through."

William moved forward and then disappeared. Kris saw him reappear through the haze, press ahead and vanish again.

Kris thought of praying while he watched the slithering monster pull itself over scorched rock toward him. He knew he was in Hell, and that God probably wouldn't listen to his request if it knew what was in his heart. Watching the woman he loved burn his best friends to a crisp had done nothing to fortify the faith he had never had. What good is a big ball of white light when everyone you loved is gone?

Considering where he was, he might be wiser to send his prayers downward. Once again, that assumed the existence of something he had watched evaporate before his eyes. Even if she still lived, the devil was surely busy. Kris had to rely on his own wits and timing to pull this off. So he watched, clasping his hands together in the sleeves of his robe to stop them from trembling, as the dragon moved toward him. Its whole body twitched and shifted with its gait, only its eyes remaining fixed in place as it rapidly approached. Narrowed to hateful reptilian slits, the dragon's burning crimson eyes were locked on the Guide's wide gray stare.

He knew he couldn't move until the fire started; the dragon would see. Kris held his ground, watching the monster pause to set itself and then rear back. It was so close, and he was so goddamned scared, the Guide uttered a helpless little one-word prayer despite himself.

"Please," he murmured, the sound lost in the whoosh of flames.

The Guide moved, one doorway then another. As soon as he came through, his robe was seized once again by strong Walker hands and he was dragged through two more ingresses. As soon as they were through, he pointed.

"Close that door!" he said.

A touch of flame came through, to sputter out inches from the Guide's face as the opening collapsed. Shrill and piercing, a scream split the air sixty feet behind them. Just as he had hoped, one dragon had descended on the waiting Walkers just as the other had shot flame through the doorway.

"What the hell was that?" William demanded while the sound of flapping wings filled the air once more. He still had ahold of the Guide's robe, and pulled him along as the other Walker made doorways. William waved his hand as they came through each one, collapsing it behind them.

"The one coming at us now is another dragon," Kris explained, allowing the old Walker to yank him through portals with a speed he couldn't hope to match. "I set those two against each other. Do you hear them fighting?"

"I know the nature of dragons," William replied coolly as they traversed rapidly through Chase's idea. "I am aware that it is a point of pride for a dragon to fight to the death any being who causes them injury, even if that injury is incidental or accidental or both."

The old Walker threw a stern glance over his shoulder as they crossed a stretch of burnt rock.

"You put Chase at risk," he scolded the Guide. "We mustn't—"

For some time, the sounds of flapping wings overhead and the fading sounds of battle had been the only evidence of dragons nearby. The flapping overhead had been a dragon watching, timing their appearances and disappearances from above and calculating when and where they might show up next. The beast was watching Chase, and timed its descent to intercept the new Walker's progress. That timing was a touch slow; and as Chase's foot retreated through a doorway, the dragon struck the old Walker with its right foreleg and the Guide with its hard narrow scaled chest.

One moment Kris was being dragged along most willingly and scolded by his only remaining friend; the next he was flying through the air with the shock of pain coursing through his entire body. He thought of the last time he had felt pain, the last time he had flown through the air to land dying on hard pavement. His thoughts raced as his body floated, and he wondered if it had all been in his mind, one last dimethyltryptamine dump from his pineal gland before moving on to the afterlife or nothing. He had time to wish it were so, that his mind had made up demons and angels and even God, and that his friends were still alive and human.

Then he hit the ground, hard, rolling to land in a pained tangled heap of robe and limbs awkwardly arranged. Kris heard the sounds of steel on scales nearby, but he couldn't see anything and his whole body ached. He wrestled with the folds of his robe halfheartedly for a moment, but every movement hurt and only seemed to confine him further. Kris relaxed with a piteous moan, letting the hammer of pain that pounded nails into his skull drive him into the awaiting embrace of unconsciousness.

Something grabbed at his robe, sliding him effortlessly over several feet of hard uneven rock. Kris let his body bump and flail while his mind tried to come back to life, wondering if the dragon was done with William already.

Strong hands flipped him over, the cowl was unraveled from his face, and Kris stared into Chase's watery blue eyes. Without a word, the new Walker tossed the Guide over his shoulder like a sack of potatoes and moved to the nearest door.

"William," the Guide gasped, as the Walker's every step shot pain through his body. "We have to help William. Where is your weapon?"

By the time Chase answered, they had already moved through several portals.

"He told me to keep moving if he was attacked," Chase said, transporting them deeper into Hell thirty feet at a time. "He told me to leave the doorways open behind us so he could follow if he got away. He gave me a scroll to deliver if he didn't."

"He won't try to get away," Kris cried out, from his pain or William's.

"He'll fight the dragon to the death, and any more that come, just to give you a chance to survive. We have to go back. We have to help him."

Kris tried to struggle, to roll off the Walker's shoulder and stand on his own two feet. Most of his struggle was against his own pain, and what little fight he had beyond that was no match for Chase's supernatural hold on him.

"I don't know how to fight," Chase said. "I'm not that kind of Walker."

Kris bounced along helplessly. "Give me your weapon then."

"I don't have one," he replied. "I'm not that kind of Walker."

CHAPTER 20

Jessica watched the crystal ball, her eyes narrowed to angry reptilian slits. She could barely see anything in the dark orb, as it served as dark window to the dark scene. They were just sitting there, swathed in darkness and talking to each other. It didn't help to see them if she couldn't hear them, and what little she could see told her nothing about where they were or what they were doing.

Still she watched, letting her anger build as they sat close to each other and talked, growling low in her throat as they kissed and held each other, feeling the anger layered over with curiosity and a little inexplicable fear as Ximena stepped willingly into a choke hold and then sagged lifeless in Paul's arms. Paul held her body close in a pathetic macabre embrace until it disappeared, then he began moving rocks from one place to another.

"What are they doing?" she growled, letting her gaze shift from the dark scene to the crone holding it in her hands. There was no reply, no shrug or shake of the head. The old crone's eyes held hers, unblinking and unanswering, until Jessica spoke once more.

"I must go there," she said, thinking of how she might imprison or destroy them once and for all.

"Walking between worlds is harder than ever now, even for Walkers," the crone croaked, speaking slow and low. "Only a platinum key or special dispensation from the Council of Walkers can reach a place like that now."

A low steady sound turned both their heads slightly, Matt chuckling humorlessly as he listened in.

Matt's cheeks were sunken and hollow, his skin reddened in an unhealthy flush, his dark hair matted to his forehead with sweat that had long since stopped pouring. A little fat, a lot of muscle, and far too much water weight had melted from the skin and bones he had become. His dark laughter was interrupted by a coughing fit that set his shoulders to shaking and caused his arms to twitch convulsively as he tried to raise his hands to cover his mouth.

When the coughing fit ended, he glanced up to make sure the queen still had her eyes on him.

"You should have told the council as soon as you saw them," Matt said, his voice a hoarse whisper. "They would have worked with you to imprison or destroy them. If you tell them about Paul and Ximena now, they will go there themselves and enlist their aid in destroying you."

Matt's gaze fell to the floor as he began laughing again.

Jessica didn't dare strike him, as much as she might want to. The most casual backhand from the smallest dragon could end the life of the most formidable human. She was not the smallest dragon, Matt was hardly formidable, and her backhands were seldom casual. The dragon queen had no desire to see what he might become when Matt breathed his last breath, although it appeared she would find out soon enough.

The great stone door opened, and a black dragon entered in his devil guise. Unarmed and unarmored, his lean muscled frame was covered only by a leather kilt that hung low on his hips.

"My queen," the devil intoned solemnly, dropping to one knee before her. The leather kilt rode up his thighs with the kneel, giving her a clear view of his huge flaccid crimson piece that dangled nearly to the floor.

"Rise," Jessica hissed hastily. She had gone right from a world of guys afraid to ask her out to a world where sexual invitations were thrown about like confetti. Jessica suspected that it would be as difficult to adjust to one as it had been the other.

The devil stood, giving her a salacious wink.

"My queen," he said again, as though he were being respectful, "there are two Walkers approaching. They seem to have devised a clever strategy that prevents us from attacking them. They are nearing the tunnels."

Jessica turned from the devil, her reptilian head pivoting to the crone. "Show me."

Holding the crystal ball out at arm's length, the crone narrowed her dark slitted eyes.

"They are not together," she croaked. "Here is one."

The clear stone orb lit up with a scene, a Walker in motorcycle gear with a longsword positioned defensively before him. A huge black dragon advanced on him, darting forward with teeth or claws at the ready over and over. Each swipe of talons was met by the sharp blade, every thrust of its head resulted in a long gash on its face or a painfully skewered eyeball. She watched for five seconds, as a score of such bloody exchanges played out in a series of rapid blurs. Then a swinging set of talons caught the Walker full across his ribcage, and he went flying in a satisfying burst of blood and flesh and leather. The dragon was upon him immediately, covering him in a mountain of heavy dragon flesh while all four legs writhed under itself to flay the Walker into a puddle of unidentifiable flesh.

"Show me the other one," Jessica said, pleased.

The orb went dark, the crone hesitated.

"He is moving very quickly." Her old throat crackled and popped as she sounded out the words. "It is difficult to catch a glimpse of…ah, there we are."

Lighting up, the crystal showed the queen an open empty expanse of Hell. While she watched, a luminous play of multi-colored lights appeared in the shape of a door frame. A blurred figure in black flashed out of it, opened another doorway before him, and dashed through it. Both tall rectangles stood open behind the figure, the only evidence that the black blur had not been a trick of the light or her eyes.

"Call together all the dragons," Jessica hissed at the reporting devil. "Tell them to set every rock and stone and speck of dust on fire in a three mile perimeter around the tunnel entrances. Let's see if the Walker can walk through fire."

"Yes, my queen." The devil began to kneel again.

"Go!" she roared at him.

The devil hastened to the exit to the soundtrack of Matt's dark foreboding laughter.

"Wait," she hissed when the devil's hand fell on the door handle. "If the old one dies, he dies. Let the other through. And send someone to fetch me a message stone."

"My queen?" The devil's brow furrowed under his spiked forehead. He hesitated, his hand on the door handle as he waited for her to change her mind once more. The queen nodded at last, and he sighed and pulled open the stone slab.

Jessica's head whipped around as the crone made for the open door.

"Show her to me," she hissed.

The crone made her way to the queen's side, holding the crystal ball out as it was lit within by dancing fire.

Ximena was running, skirting the patches of flame under her naked feet. It looked like she had been running awhile; a sheen of sweat covered every inch of her nude body, her hair was a wet helmet clinging to her head and neck and back. The muscles in her thighs and calves were taut and bulging, flexing in rapid succession to drive her rapidly toward or away from something. This scene had sound, unlike the cave; Jessica listened.

The devil threw a quick glance back over her shoulder just as the pursuing demons came into Jessica's view. They loped behind her, eight or nine of them clustered together in a tight hunting pack, howling and screaming, growling and slavering. Between seven and nine feet tall, each fanged taloned monstrosity was two to three times the mass of their prey. It was chilling to watch them close the gap, even from afar, even when it was just what she wanted to see.

A man launched himself from the shadows as Ximena ran past him, tossing her a sword and beheading the leading demon with a powerful backhand arc swing of the other sword he brandished.

Jessica gasped, her eyes skimming the room before returning to the scene. All she had seen was that he was dressed all in black leather, that he had long hair and a beard, and that he had appeared with two swords. Her mind had gone immediately to the dragon's boogeyman, the antagonist in every royal dragon's fairy tale bedtime stories, the fear that kept young dragons close to their mother's unnurturing breast, the Stone Walker.

Now she watched with adult dragon eyes, saw that the leather was cobbled together armor that demons had stolen from devils and that this ordinary bearded man had taken from those demons. She saw that the swords that he carried were long curved devil swords, not a long straight bastard and broadsword. She noted that both Paul and Ximena wielded the swords with two hands, the heavy blades taking their toll on their human strength as they swung them again and again at ordinary human speeds. She considered the possibility that her reign as queen would be eternally punctuated by tuning in to the only show she felt like watching while it continually showed the repeated bloody demise of the fiends that murdered her mother.

The wide tall stone door opened again, and another devil approached the throne. This one was wearing pants, at least, and bowed rather than kneeling. Holding out two taloned hands, palms up together to present the small round stone to her, he never took his eyes off the blue-green orb and its errant pathways of red and white and gray.

"Larimar," the devil said. "Perhaps the best stone for communicating with angels and—"

"How does it work?" Jessica hissed, cutting him off.

He glanced at the queen, then the crone.

Heaving a creaky sigh, she stepped forward and waved her hand over it. One of the white pathways became an open fissure, and white light emitted from the opening.

"Speak your piece," the crone croaked.

"I have a message for the Walker Council," Jessica hissed at the stone. "Let it stand as warning and law, from this day forth. Any angel or human or Walker, Guide or Watcher that sets foot in Hell will be committing an act of war in doing so. They will be tortured, imprisoned, executed, or all three. No more Walker keys or weapons will be spelled, and the next key I make will open a doorway to Heaven if these trespasses persist. Every dragon in Hell will ascend to burn every angel, light, cloud and sky to nothing. We will burn God if he dares oppose us. But make no mistake, Walker Council. You will burn first, and any fool Walker that comes to your aid will burn right along with you."

"Leave Hell to me," Jessica continued. "Keep your prying eyes and your meddling hands out of my realm, or accept responsibility for the fire that will burn every layer of reality until this corner of the Universe is but a great burning ball of flame that none will remember and none would dare approach for eons."

The stone went dark once more, perhaps even darker for the message it held.

CHAPTER 21

William felt the dragon's front paw catch him in the ribs, felt the air and the blood and a few cherished pounds of flesh go flying from his wound as his body flew through space. The healing twisted his face into a contorted mask of pain as he hit the ground and rolled, his longsword clutched along his torso and between his bent knees. When he stopped rolling, he was face down with the sword between his body and the hard rock and a thousand pounds of black dragon on his back.

The air whooshed out of him again as the dragon settled the rest of its weight on him, and William felt the bones in his crushed body crack and mend with painful regularity as the beast shifted its weight back and forth. If he could breathe, he would surely have cried out; but he couldn't, so he didn't.

Waiting for a shift, feeling his left arm morph agonizingly from puddle of gore to left arm, William got the hand flat on the ground and the elbow pointed upward just in time for five sword-like talons to slice his forearm into five quivering pieces. The arm reformed, only to be crushed flat from elbow to palm under the dragon's shifting weight.

The bones of his skull cracked loudly in his own ears, and William felt his eyeballs rolling back in his head as they tried to bulge from their sockets. His right arm was free, and whole, and angled in preparation for the Walker to attempt his first ever two-thousand pound one-armed pushup. He gathered every last bit of life and strength and heaved upward with all his might.

Suddenly he was on top of the dragon, facing the wrong way and holding his longsword. Then the momentum of the roll turned the beast sideways, and William slid smoothly off its scaled belly to regain his footing at last. Pivoting, he swung his longsword with all his returning might, watching bits of blood-soaked leather fly at his sudden movement. The blade bit before his eyes saw where it had landed, burying itself longways along the dragon's jaw several inches deep in its throat.

The beast coughed, then gagged, then spit hot purple blood in his face. William tried to yank the blade free, planting his boot on the dragon's chest and pulling with both hands and all his might. Blood spewed from the wound and from the monster's open screaming mouth, drenching them both. Ten sharp talons raked at the Walker's torso, and his blood flew in every direction to mingle with the dragon's as it flowed.

Just as William feared that he may be cut in two at the waist, the blade came free. He stumbled backwards on shaky uncertain legs as the dragon took flight, great scaled wings beating a hot downdraft that blew his hair back flat where it wasn't already caked with gore. The beast drew in a deep breath as the gaping wound in its neck healed, opening its damaged jaw to belch flames at the old Walker.

Backing up a step with his right leg, William drew back the string on the bow that his left hand now clutched. In the time it took for the dragon to complete its in-breath, the old Walker had shot three sharp wide hunting tips into the beast's exposed chest where all the books said its heart should be.

The dragon screamed, but still shot flame at him, and the old Walker barely got out of its path on wobbly legs. He backed up slowly, loosing arrows with the calm regularity of a ticking clock. Most of them burned up in the fire, but two stuck in the hollowed scaled skin under its left eye. He rolled as the beast dove, somersaulting under its flame to stand swiftly and shoot a half dozen more arrows at its back. The dragon dove again, and William's whirring battle-ax chopped off its nose and then its left foreleg halfway between elbow and wrist. Blood flowed once more, but not enough and not for long, and William backed away shooting arrows as the beast took in another lungful of breath.

Full strength and full speed, William disappeared the bow and ran a dizzying circle round the dragon. As it breathed fire in a blazing perimeter, William leapt on its back and hacked twice at its neck with the axe, right at the base of its skull. After the two wet thunks, the dragon's head canted unnaturally sideways and purple blood gushed from the cleaved flesh like a fountain, and William raised the stained gleaming blade for a third blow. The old Walker lost his footing as the dragon launched itself into the sky, flapping its wings mightily and moving its head in a bloody serpentine dance out of reach of sword or axe.

William stumbled, the axe tearing through one wing as he fell against the other. The next downward flap found him clinging to an axe wedged through a wide gash in the dragon's wing. Dangling in space, clutching the weapon's handle, William was tossed against one scaled wing and then the other. The wind was knocked from him, and a few teeth, but he held on and gritted the ones that remained against the pain of regeneration.

They were falling, and fast, and William didn't realize it until the dragon pivoted in flight to smash him against the ground. His axe became his sword with a thought, and William felt the handle puncture his sternum as the blade was buried to the hilt in the dragon weight crushing him to paste.

Rising from the imprint of their landing, the dragon stumbled a few steps and fell on the sword still sticking from its back. The hilt and handle disappeared under its weight, driving the entire sword deep into the wound. It tried to scream, but wheezed instead, and blood trickled between its rows of teeth to stain the rock where its head lay still. The dragon lay on its back, taloned legs splayed.

Painfully regaining the hundred pounds or so that had been squeezed from his body like a tube of toothpaste under a truck tire, William watched the mountain of still dragon with one eye while casting about for his sword with the other. The mound of scaled flesh quivered, twenty-something arrows trembled where they stuck out of its body, and the old Walker still couldn't find his sword. He could feel it, nearby, but he couldn't see it.

The dragon stirred, struggling to its feet only to roll sideways to lay on its stomach. William watched its legs tremble, its head loll to the side, and a small river of purple blood drain from its jaws. The blood puddled to form a pool on the hard burnt rock, and finally William saw it.

His sword rose from the dragon's back, hilt first, pushed out the same path it had taken into the beast's broad torso by flesh replacing itself. William watched the full length of the handle rise up, then the cross-guard followed by a foot of blade. He rushed forward, his feet skipping over the tail to land lightly between its leathered wings.

Using both hands, the old Walker pulled the sword free as fast and hard as he could. The blade cleared the dragon's scales in a shower of blood that dwindled to a few floating droplets as the blade went straight over his head. It began to fly, and William lifted off with it all of eighteen inches. Then the dragon's jaws clamped down about his bare bloody torso, and William felt teeth pushing ribs aside and puncturing a lung and blending his guts. The air whooshed out of him painfully.

Turning the sword, William changed it to a dagger as he buried it in the monster's eye, then back into a sword as he held it there. He used the dragon's squeezing jaws as leverage for his upper body, fully aware that the lack of feeling in his legs might be because they were no longer there. With the long handle clenched in both hands, William rocked back and forth, violently stirring the beast's brains.

The feeling was starting to come back in his legs, although sharp rows of teeth still held him firmly. It pained him to keep working the pommel of the longsword, but the drunken sideways crawl the dragon was doing and the loosening jaws were encouraging signs. When he finally fell free, the old Walker abandoned the idea of landing on his feet in favor of protecting his back. The long arc of the battle-ax split the empty air as he spun while the dragon staggered awkwardly away a few more steps, oblivious.

William dragged himself wearily but quickly to his new feet, feeling more shredded leather falling away as he rose. Looking down, he saw that his nearly naked body was covered in red and purple gore as thoroughly as the length of his sword. He watched the dragon turn, nearly every black scale painted red or purple despite being as whole as William.

It reared back, to fly at him or over him or douse him in flames, then paused on its rear haunches. The dragon cocked its head to the side, listening.

William heard it too. Dragon's wings.

He looked at the distant shimmering doorway wistfully. Even if he could reach it, and maybe the next one, they would catch up. There was no top speed for a dragon in flight; the further they flew the faster, if they wished it. The old Walker knew enough about dragons to save the others, at least from these two. As the sound of flapping wings drew closer, he realistically considered the possibility that he did not know enough to save himself, and thought of closing the doorway.

He shook his head, refusing to allow simple things like overwhelming odds and irrefutable evidence cause him to lose hope.

The dragon nodded, perhaps balancing the same scale in its mind. Still it watched him, aware that a split second glance over its shoulder was all the Walker needed to claim its head and even the odds. It watched him warily, waiting for backup and giving William time to reimagine his armor and remember his dagger. He even had time to remember refusing a second sword against Paul's advice, and kick himself for it. The old Walker had made up his mind to rush the first dragon as soon as the second emerged from the wall of smoke, when the creature did just that.

William froze, watching the dragon descend. It had two things that he could see over the first dragon's shoulder, both of which he knew the beast couldn't see without turning its head. So he waited, valiantly trying not to smile at Vanessa as she rode out the landing. The Guide clung to the dragon's black cape with both hands, her youthful brow furrowed in concentration, then leapt from her back as her feet hit rock.

Landing beside the first dragon, the second monster turned her head as if in greeting. When the first turned, the second belched fire in its face. For a hopeful forever moment, William watched the flame envelope the monster's entire head. Then it rolled away screaming, and launched itself into the air with its skull still trailing fire. The caped dragon pursued it, and for once William was glad to hear the sounds of two sets of wings.

He approached Vanessa with long strides.

"Thank you," he said, pausing before her.

Vanessa held up one hand, her brow still furrowing as she stared into the clouds.

"I've only barely got her," she whispered.

The old Walker's eyes went wide as he realized what she was doing.

"Let her go," he advised her. "Now that they have engaged, they will fight to the death. She has a better chance of surviving if she has her own wits about her."

The Guide relaxed, her eyes coming into focus as they came to rest on William.

"Thank you," he said again. "And I'm sorry. I can tell you how to shoot an arrow straight, or swing a sword in a way that maximizes your leverage, but every time I try to talk to you about how I feel I say something stupid or wrong or the opposite of what I mean. I'm sorry, Vanessa. I wish that I—"

"William." She cut him off. "You have to help her."

He frowned, and was about to point out that he couldn't fly, when two tons of dragon flesh hit the ground and set it to trembling. They rolled back and forth on the cracked rock, scratching and biting at each other with such speed and regularity that the ground under them was stained purple with their bleeding healing wounds. William watched for an opening, dashing forward in a way that gave his uncertain ally a clear view of his approach. As he feared, she batted him aside with a powerful swing of her head and shot flame after him.

William stepped to Vanessa's side, brushing off his leathers. His eyes went from the fray to the Guide and back again.

"She doesn't seem to want help," he pointed out.

Vanessa nodded, watching the bloody contest with him.

"You must strike as soon as one bests the other," she said, her eyes still forward. "You must kill the survivor and then remove one of its wings. You must move with haste, before the body disappears."

Frowning, William opened his mouth to speak.

Vanessa cut him off again.

"Now," she said urgently.

One dragon had the other by the throat, long rows of teeth rending scaled flesh as it bit deeper and began dragging the other bodily by the wound. With a series of well-placed slashes, the biting monster turned two feet of the other's serpentine neck into liquid dragon. One body dropped to the ground, headless, and the other rolled to rest beside it with a score of bleeding wounds.

William was on its back before it could rise or heal, his harness boot tangling in the cape and giving him pause.

The monster's head moved just enough for her to open her eye and look at him.

"I die this day," she hissed. "Make it count. Do it, Walker!"

Her wounds were surely healing, and still he hesitated.

"What is your name?" he asked, tears in his eyes.

"Turelia," she breathed.

William aimed his axe, shed a quiet tear, then cut off her head and one twitching wing.

CHAPTER 22

Kris trounced along on Chase's shoulder, counting the dull aching places on his body that became lances of pain with every step the new Walker took.

"I see tunnel entrances ahead," Chase said.

"Get in one," the Guide gasped, "then set me down."

The scant blurring light became a still near-darkness. Chase lowered him gently to hard rock, and a dozen lances of fire cooled to a dozen dull aches. Kris tried to rise, only to fall again as he put his left leg under him.

"I think my leg is broken," Kris moaned.

Chase's eyes darted behind them at the long series of doorways, then into the darkness of the tunnel.

"What should we do?" he asked.

"We need to wait for William," the Guide snapped.

"Do you still want to go back?"

"No," Kris replied. "Even if I could walk, it would be suicide."

"Do you have your flask?" Chase was swathed in darkness, and it was difficult to make out his expression.

"Of course." The Guide always had his flask.

"Drink from it," Chase said.

Kris opened his mouth to hotly retort, not fond of taking orders. Then he reconsidered, held his tongue and unscrewed the cap. A little numbness might go a long way right now. He drank deeply, imbibing more liquid than the container looked like it could possibly hold before recapping it and wiping his mouth on his sleeve.

"Hey!" the Guide said, standing easily. "I'm healed!"

The magick liquid seemed to have brightened the Guide's vision as well. He could make out Chase's slight smile as the new Walker gazed warily down the long tunnel.

There was a long slim blade in his hand, glinting in what little light the steel could find.

"You have a sword," Kris said accusingly.

"Of course I have a sword. I am a Walker." Chase's smile widened a little as he replied, but he kept his eyes on the downward path.

"But you said—" the Guide began.

"Hush!" Chase hissed, peering into the darkness. "Don't you hear that?"

Kris cocked his head, listened to silence.

"I don't hear anything," he whispered.

"Something's coming," Chase spoke in hushed tones as well. "Fast."

Chase whirled suddenly, looking behind them at the doorway within doorway within doorway view. Then he moved, grabbing the Guide's robe and pulling him aside. Kris bounced off the hard stone wall, nearly losing his footing, as a smoking black blur shot through the doorway. A second figure trailed the first, also swathed in black and moving in the first's wake with the swift ease of a shadow. Slowing as they came through the portal, the two blurs became two figures standing a dozen paces down the path, obscured head to toe in smoking black shadow. One of the shadows unraveled, and William's face came into view. With a few swift movements, he cast aside what looked like a stiff smoking blanket.

"Hey guys," William smiled. "Thanks for waiting."

The series of doorways collapsed behind them with a wave of Chase's hand as Vanessa shrugged off the second shadow.

"Vanessa!" Kris was happy to see the Guide. "What are you doing here?"

"Saving my ass," William smiled, glancing at her. "Again."

"All in a day's work," Vanessa quipped, dusting her hands against each other and returning the Walker's smile. William frowned as she looked away.

"What are those?" Kris pointed to the smoldering shadows.

"Dragon wings," William answered, his frown deepening. "Or more accurately, one dragon wing cut into two pieces."

Vanessa nodded. "The sentinel dragons were ordered to let you through, but to kill William. One noble dragon gave her life and her wing that we might get through."

The Guide whirled on Chase, fuming.

"We should have gone back!" Kris cried.

"Hush!" William put his hand on the Guide's shoulder. He looked up and down the dark passageway. "They know Chase and I are here, and likely Vanessa, but they don't seem to know you are with us."

"Probably because I carried him most of the way," Chase muttered. Kris felt his anger rise, but pushing against the hand on his shoulder was as fruitless as pushing against a brick wall. He clearly made out the new Walker's smirk while William nodded his agreement casually.

"Probably," the old Walker said. He turned his attention to Kris, still grasping his shoulder. "Are you alright?"

Vanessa stepped toward him. "Did you drink from your canteen?"

Kris sighed, deflated. "Yeah. You know about that?"

"Of course," she answered innocently. "Did you not go to class?"

The Guide shrugged as Chase smirked once more.

"I never really had time to finish," he admitted.

"Hush!" William said again, annoying Kris a bit. "We need to go."

The old Walker moved slowly away from them, forcing them to follow or lose sight of him in the darkness.

"Hey," Chase whispered as they traversed the inky black, "this thing has a flashlight, doesn't it?"

There was a rustle and a click, and the tunnel was suddenly aglow in yellow light. Kris smiled when he saw William glaring at Chase.

"Turn it off!" he hissed.

They were swathed in darkness once more, made darker for the sudden light bath. The group stood still for a moment while their supernatural eyes adjusted. William's voice found their ears while they waited.

"Chase, walk beside me when the tunnel is wide enough," he said. "We want anyone looking to see two Walkers approaching side by side. Hold yourself as tall and wide as possible as you walk so Kris can—"

William's eyes adjusted as he spoke, and he saw the burden Chase carried.

"What is that?" the old Walker demanded.

"It's the dragon wing pieces you discarded," Kris said. He had seen it in the momentary illumination of the flashlight. He shot Chase a disdainful look, pretty sure the Walker could see it.

"I thought we should make armor of it," Chase whispered. "Rather than waste it. I can leave it behind if you want."

William sighed. "No, keep it. Give it to Kris to carry. Kris, stay behind us and kind of crouch down as you walk. Be as small as you can."

CHAPTER 23

Matt sat hunkered by the queen's throne, withered and tired and longing for death. His body had lasted longer than it should have, but he could feel it finally giving out. First he had lost the strength to stand, then the strength to hold himself upright, then the strength to speak. The chains had been removed the last time he had tried to rise and failed miserably. Some friendly devil had propped him against the queen's wide seat, and he leaned against it waiting for the life to leave him at last.

He thought of the fading memories of the life he had lived, of his sister and his friends and his lovers. He thought of them as he would the story of another's life, the biography of some ordinary person before they became extraordinary. That's all life was, an unnoteworthy prequel to what he was about to transform into. Matt welcomed death like the caterpillar welcomed its chrysalis, and longed to burst forth a devil as it would a butterfly.

Already images flashed through his mind, memories of the devil he had been and would soon become again. His frail gaunt body felt like it was dying and coming alive all at the same time. Matt looked forward to the future memories that awaited, finding Ximena and Paul and helping his best buddy find a nice girl that wouldn't fry his friends.

If his eyes hadn't been on the entrance to the queen's chambers, it might have been too much for him to turn his head when all the commotion started. Since Matt was already looking that way, he saw it all play out from the beginning. First a rectangle of light appeared, dancing colors in the shape of a door. Then William stepped through the doorway, followed by the Walker he had been training when Matt met him. He had a funny name that Matt couldn't remember, run or catch or something that seemed more a verb than a name. Matt watched the new Walker, wondering why he stood at an odd angle before the portal and very close to the other Walker.

Another figure came out behind them, William's Guide. She too stood as though her uncomfortable stance was deliberate, close to William's other side. Matt couldn't see the rectangle of shifting light behind them at all for his position and theirs. He suspected it was nearly the same for the queen. Their hands were all empty, save the one Chase held a scroll in.

"Walkers," Jessica's long sinewy body unwound from the wide throne, and she moved closer to the visitors than they had expected. They backed toward the portal, crowding even closer together. The queen laughed humorlessly.

"Don't be afraid, Walkers," she said. "If I wanted you dead, you would be."

Matt remembered the orders he had heard her give. He wanted to remind her that she had wanted at least one of them dead, but he couldn't raise his hand or his voice. He breathed his difficult and shallow breaths and listened.

"I have a message for your masters," the queen said. Moving toward them, she held the small stone out to William.

"I have no master," William scoffed, taking the stone. "I will take this to the Walker Council. Chase, give her their message."

Jessica batted the scroll from his proffering reach, scorching it in the air.

"You have a whole team of masters," she hissed.

Matt saw the world begin to go dark, just as another rectangle of shimmering light opened in front of him. Kris stepped out of it quietly, swathed in his robes, and moved toward him. Many of the devils lining the walls in silence could see the intruder, but none spoke or moved. Jessica's back was to the Guide as he came close. Her words continued as he wound one of Matt's arms around his neck and lifted his emaciated frame easily.

"No," Matt croaked weakly. "Home…"

"That's right, buddy," Kris whispered. "We're taking you home."

The dragon queen turned at the sound, her eyes narrowing as they fell on Kris.

They went through the doorway, then another. The next one took them to someone's ordinary living room, where Kris set him gently on a couch and stepped back. The Guide produced a small silver flask and uncapped it, holding it up to Matt's parched lips. It was empty. It was just as well; he was having enough trouble gulping down his painful final breaths.

"It won't work, he's not a Guide." A female voice, soft and sad. Vanessa. The sounds of the room were fading, and Matt's eyes didn't want to stay open. He fought to see, fought to breathe, fought to wave his hands and scream at them to take him back to Hell. His queen needed him, his realm needed him, he had been so close…

"Get him some water." William, finally getting used to being in charge. Matt had enjoyed training with the old Walker, had looked forward to fighting by his side in the war to come.

"Here. Drink." The new Walker knelt beside Matt as his vision closed in on him. His hands were kind and gentle, lifting Matt's head to help him with the glass of water that he touched to his lips. *Chase*, he remembered now. *Not run, not catch. Chase.*

The glass felt cool on his lips, the water trickled down his chin and windpipe. Matt coughed, choked, then began convulsing. Kris was at his side, both hands on his friend as Matt stared at him with unseeing eyes. It took a forever moment for Matt to realize he had stopped breathing, another for him to realize that he was looking down on his best friend and his own body from a frightening vantage point.

His soul railed against it, silently screaming as two lifetime's memories slipped from him like stones dropped into the sea. Then a portal opened, one that even Chase couldn't see, a shimmering doorway of light that beckoned soundlessly. The last of his memories were burned away in the light, and voices joined the light in inviting laughter.

Looking down, the hovering soul saw a collection of strangers huddled around a horrific corpse. The body looked drained of all life, and the soul thought for a moment that it must have experienced great pain before passing.

More laughter came from the portal, the light burned away the thought as gently as it had burned away his memories, and the soul forgot all about the strangers and the body. It moved toward the opening, uncertainly at first, then more confident as loving warmth embraced it. The soul passed through the doorway and into the light.

Silent and unseen, the doorway closed.

CHAPTER 24

Cal drove back across town, staring straight ahead at stoplights with his hands at ten and two like there was no blood on his face or his hands or his clothes. He listened to Jack Russell singing about a city with a psychopathy while his mind raced and his heart danced. He had never particularly liked or disliked Raul, but no interaction they had shared had ever made him feel this alive. He wished he could rewind the scene and live it again over and over.

Cutting him up like that, feeling the blood splash and watching the light go from his lively eyes, had been much different than pulling a trigger a few times. Cal had felt connected to this kill, and the moments he had shared with the dying man had been intimate and special.

One part of him went over the details of the event, trying to count the wounds and measure the blood. Another part planned the last twenty-four hours of this life, the first twenty-four hours of the next. Thinking about it, Cal realized he would miss his car the most, and that he would be glad to have long hours to say goodbye. No part of him thought of how things might have gone differently, or wished he had not taken the lives he had. Cal's whole being was happily divided between driving and cultivating the dark tangle of weeds that had invaded his inner garden.

He might not have noticed the dark unmarked car if it hadn't been positioned so haphazardly in an illegal space. Cops and delivery guys seemed to have no thought for anything but their jobs and no consideration for anyone but themselves, in Cal's experience of keeping an eye out for both.

A quick sideways glance at his front door as he drove by set his heart to pounding. Two suits stood shoulder to shoulder with their backs to him. The door was open, and he assumed Sarah was standing in the frame talking to them. His quick glance and the way they stood made it impossible to be sure.

He drove further up the street, turning around when he was out of view. Cruising slowly, Cal watched for a parking spot that would show him a decent view and afford them little. There is was, behind a sport utility vehicle with twin bicycles on top of it. Cal's Acura eased in behind the tall truck, close to its bumper. He killed the already nearly silent engine, watching out the sliver of windshield that was not dominated by the other vehicle.

They talked for so long that Cal considered doing a bump, but he didn't want to push his luck. When they turned around and trudged back to the haphazardly parked sedan, they weren't looking around suspiciously or anything. Cal sunk as far into the comfortable driver's seat as he could, but it was hardly necessary. They got in their car with what felt like agonizing slowness to Cal, which probably felt like normal speed to them, and drove away.

Waiting for what felt like several minutes, Cal pulled away from the curb thirty seconds later and parked in his spot. Sarah was still standing near the door when he burst through it, her face pale and drawn. She held a calling card in one hand, with some detective's name and number on it. She looked at his clothes and face, handed it to him.

"The police want you to call them," she said flatly.

Cal took the card from her, holding her gaze with his own. He crumpled it and let it fall to the floor between them, his eyes still locked on hers. Sarah's hand remained extended as if she continued to proffer the card to him, and it began to tremble. She still stared at him, and he at her.

"Cal," she whispered. "Did you kill Mikie?"

He didn't answer, just kept looking at her.

"Was Mikie the one that robbed you?" she asked.

Cal smirked, still holding the eye contact.

"Him and his asshole druggie friend," she said. It wasn't a question this time. Her hand dropped to her side, but she did not drop her eyes. Sarah continued looking at him, with curiosity or fear or both. Cal considered throttling the little pixie, but decided to wait out her response to the situation instead.

"His name was Mitch, if it matters," she said.

Cal smirked again, shrugged. It didn't.

She lifted her hand again, slowly, to point at the blood on his clothes. He noticed it was no longer shaking.

"Who was that?" she asked, her voice as steady as her hand. "A customer?"

Cal shook his head.

"Your dealer?"

He shrugged once more, nodded.

"Did he try to rob you too?" Sarah sounded out the question slowly.

Cal nodded, just as slowly.

Sarah had not taken her eyes off his the whole exchange. They stayed on his as she asked one last question.

"Are you alright?" she asked.

Cal nodded, and smiled, and she was in his arms.

"I was worried about you," she said, burying her face in his bloody chest.

"No worries," he said, squeezing her to him and looking over her shoulder at no one with an incredulous look on his face.

The look fell as he held her at arm's length.

"And no time," he said.

He let go her shoulders and her eyes, fully expecting her to make for the front door as he made for the bedroom. Instead she followed and asked, "What can I do?"

Cal slid open the mirrored closet door, grabbed a rolling suitcase. Sarah came up beside him as he opened it on the bed.

"Sweetie, let me do that," she said. "You need to get cleaned up."

Cal looked down at his clothes, remembering. His hands went to his own face tenderly, like a thirteen-year-old checking on his first mustache. The blood was still there. Moving through the door, unbuttoning his stained silk shirt, Cal called back over his shoulder at her.

"Lots of socks and boxers," he said. "And the Alberto's."

"What?" He could hear her from the bathroom. "Socks and boxers and what?"

"Alberto's!" he hollered. "Black slacks, hanging up."

"Got 'em!" her voice responded as he turned on the shower.

Stepping out of his trousers and boxers and socks, he stepped into the tub. After five minutes of scrubbing and collecting toiletries in his arms, Cal returned to the bedroom dripping and dumped the items on the bed beside the suitcase. He was surprised to find Sarah still there, still packing.

"Lose the slacks and dress shirts," he said, "except these." Cal chose one pair of slacks and two neatly folded shirts and set them aside.

"There are jeans and tee shirts in my dresser," he told her. "Grab a few of those. And a couple wife beaters."

He went back to the bathroom to grab towels to dry himself and his product. There were jeans and tee shirts in the open luggage when he returned, and he grabbed some and dressed hastily. Cal sat on the bed to put on nondescript sneakers, tucking the gold cross under his shirt. Standing beside her, Cal looked down at her and smiled.

Moving away from Sarah, still smiling, he found his way to the bathroom once more. Cal bent to pick up his slacks where he had shed them, removing the folded knife from one pocket. He ran it under warm water, watching the blood swirl down the drain. Clicking it open, Cal rubbed his finger and thumb along the sides of the blade to break loose any stubborn spots. He dried it calmly on the hand towel, then returned to the bedroom.

Sarah was arranging the suitcase like a puzzle. She watched her own busy hands as he came up behind her, the knife clutched tight in his left hand. Cal put his arm around her shoulder, then her throat. Sarah stood up straighter, then leaned back into him provocatively.

Cal kissed her cheek.

"I'd like to show you a part of my apartment that I have never shown anyone," he chuckled, releasing her and stepping away from her. He moved to the wall and plunged the blade into it, a dozen times in quick succession. Sheetrock and paint chips clouded the air and littered the floor, turning Cal's arms white to his elbows. He set the knife aside, ripped a wider opening in the wall by pulling away the corners of the jagged hole, and began removing zippered plastic gallon bags full of twenty dollar bills.

"Dust these off and put them in there too," he said, tossing one bag after another to the bed. Each bag landed on the comforter with a puff of white cloud.

There were only a few small stashes of cocaine and cash in the apartment, and he looked at each familiar room one last time as Cal filled the rest of the suitcase.

"Grab anything you want, if you can carry it," he told Sarah, looking around the living room in silent reminisce. Without hesitation she went to the spare room to return a minute later bearing a lamp aloft in each hand. Cal was already outside, glancing up and down the street.

Sarah closed the door behind her.

"Are you going to lock it?" she asked.

"Don't worry about it," Cal replied. He moved towards his car, opening the doors with the remote. Cal tossed the suitcase in the trunk, shut it and nestled in the familiar driver's seat a few moments later. A quick reflexive reach under the seat confirmed that guns and coke and cash were still there. Clearing Raul's safe had not been as intimate or enlivening as stabbing him to death, but as a practical matter it had made sense.

"Where are we going?" Sarah asked after they had wound their way nearly to the summit.

"I'm taking you home," he responded.

"Where are you going?"

"After that?" Cal shrugged. "Canada."

"You don't…you don't want me to come with you?" Sarah's voice sounded sad and hopeful at the same time.

He hung in the right lane, passing the cars in the left lane that slowed on the corners like they had never driven Seventeen before.

"Sarah," he spoke patiently. "This isn't a vacation. I need to get out of the country. It could get dangerous."

Sarah nodded, looking at him like he was some hero vigilante who couldn't stand the thought of putting her in harm's way.

"Let's go to Mason's," she suggested.

He moved into the left lane for half a minute, passing a couple of cars that knew their place. Cal glanced at her as he got over again to pass someone slowing on a curve on a road characterized by curves.

"Did you get ahold of him?" he asked.

"No." Sarah shook her head. "I have a bad feeling about him still. I think something happened. I think he's…gone."

"Like dead?" Cal asked. "What makes you say that? You don't think that I…?"

"No," she repeated. "It just feels like he's gone."

Cal pressed a button on the dash. "Call Mason."

Over the speakers, it rang and rang.

CHAPTER 25

William waited until he was called in once more. Although the Walker Council was on the other side of the door, he did not trust them in this realm at all. He blasted the Rolling Stones full volume in his head, hoping against all hope that time was indeed on his side. He couldn't trust any of the thoughts that whirled under the tune.

He couldn't think of Kris over his friend's body, unreachable for his grief. He couldn't think of Vanessa comforting the Guide, or deciding with Chase that the two of them should listen to the stone and relay the message to William. He couldn't think of what they had told him, or why the angels were deliberating so long over such a brief and decisive proclamation.

So he waited, not thinking of any of these things as he tapped his harness boot soundlessly on the liquid light floor in time with the song. It seemed like an eternity, and not the kind he had imagined when thinking of an eternity in Heaven.

At last the door disappeared, and a voice called his name from beyond. William returned to the room, forcing hopefulness into his heart and the Rolling Stones through his mind.

"Walker William," an angel said as he took his place before them. "Did you listen to the message you brought us?"

"Angel Colin," William responded in the same tone of voice, thoughtlessly grateful for Chase and Vanessa's wisdom under the sound of his favorite song. "I did not."

The old bald white guy seemed pleasantly surprised to be addressed by name. He straightened in his seat and leaned forward as if to press on.

"Walker William," Listene spoke coldly, cutting him off. "We have an assignment for you. You are to deliver a message to the Queen of Hell, our response to her communication and her wanton destruction of the scroll. Should you encounter any resistance to your attempt to deliver this message, you and your party are authorized to engage. You are forbidden from using the cowardly method of approach that you employed last time, or from taking any Walkers but those we assign to accompany you."

William knew the list before the angel began to tick off names. "Walker

Samuel, Walker Lara, Walker Batu, Walker Tristan, and Walker Mikeo will go with you."

"And if we do not make it?" William ventured.

Listene smirked. "You are all on your way up, many of you will become angels. We will find replacements."

Stephan cleared his throat and glared daggers at the other angel. "Now that the queen has opened a line of communication, what reason do you have to think that your visit will not be well received?"

William shrugged, forcing the song through his mind, wishing he had picked a different tune.

"Why are you sending six of us?" he asked.

Stephan smiled. "It is the traditional number when sending an envoy to Hell. Have no worries, Walker."

William bowed his head rather than make eye contact.

"I had hoped to ask a favor of the council." William ventured.

Stephan raised an eyebrow. "Ask, then."

"Guide Kris rescued a man from Hell," he began.

"We are aware," Stephan stated flatly. "What of him?"

"He was the Guide's friend," William said. "I was hoping it may not be too late to save him."

There was a rustle of robes from every angel, a few words muttered that the Walker had not expected to hear in Heaven. Listene spoke first in clear, cold, concise tones.

"Are you suggesting a resurrection?" he demanded.

Stephan waved his hand to dismiss both Listene and the Walker with one gesture. His lively luminous brown eyes looked down on William as he spoke down to him.

"Matt Blanco was a fiction," Stephan said with condescending slowness. "For hundreds of years he lived in that body, with the retired Queen of Hell using her little remaining power to reprogram his mind and identity every few years. The soul that inhabited the body you knew as Matt was a soul in chains. Death set it free, and it has begun a new life."

Now William did make eye contact.

"How do you know that?" he asked.

"Don't you know?" Andre spoke, ignoring the glares of everyone in the room long enough to finish his thought. "Stephan is the Master Weaver of the Loom of Light. We are all but threads to be woven in or out of the Tapestry of Life to him."

Stephan sighed. "If that were so, do you truly think you would still sit on this council?"

The old angel glared at the new one long enough to ensure his ongoing silence, then turned his attention back to William. "Your request is impossible. I advise you to dispose of the body somewhere remote and inaccessible to humans."

Listene cut in again. "Is there anything else?"

William clenched his jaw and shook his head.

"Very well, Walker William," Stephan sighed. He held out one hand. "Here is the message stone. You are dismissed."

Clutching the stone, he closed his eyes in Heaven and opened them in his kitchen. William had hoped to find himself alone, to have opportunity to sit and stew in the cook room by himself before sharing with the group. Hiding his displeasure at finding the space already occupied, William pulled out a chair and sat with a Guide to his left and right.

"How did it go?" Vanessa asked.

William glanced meaningfully around the room, aware that any fly on the wall could be an angel.

"Fine," he answered, shaking his head.

"Did you ask about Matt?" Kris ventured hopefully.

"I did." William looked at his own helpless hands on the table in front of him. "I'm sorry."

The old Walker wanted to pound his fists on the table until only a pile of splinters remained, to cry out in anguish in hopes that it might flee his heart. Instead he breathed in deep, still staring down at his hands.

He raised his voice. "Chase. Daemon. Could you come in here please?"

"They're not here," Vanessa said quietly. "Chase said to tell you that he couldn't wait any longer."

"Goddammit," William swore. "Everyone is running out of time."

Even as he spoke, Kris stood and turned. He waved one hand in the air in a precise pattern that lit up in faint blue-white light momentarily, and when he was done a doorway opened. It was framed in that same crackling electrical blue-white light, and it opened into luminous clouds. The Guide gestured silently, and they all went through.

Kris closed the portal behind them, then asked, "So what actually happened?"

"They gave me this." William held up the stone, small and beautiful and terrifying. "They told me to deliver it and a few select Walkers to the Dragon Queen."

"What does it say?" Kris peered at the stone.

William shrugged. "I don't know."

Kris glanced at Vanessa. "Can you activate it?"

She shook her head. "Chase can."

The old Walker smiled. "I'm going to find Chase and help him clear his schedule. Would you two please go find Batu, Lara, Samuel, Tristan and Mikeo? Bring them here and wait for us."

While the Guides nodded, William closed his eyes and thought of the new Walker.

"William!" Chase's voice came to his ears the moment they reappeared. "Watch out!"

The warning came too late. The old Walker opened his eyes just as a powerful force struck him bodily. He careened off a wall and right back into the violent charge of his attacker. It was a demon, full size and full strength and full of hate. William saw the taloned hands reaching for him, the teeth that chomped hungrily at empty air.

William let himself sigh as he pushed aside the monster's grasping hands and caught it with an elbow to its jaw. A demon he could handle. Another carefully placed blow and the demon crumpled to the floor at the old Walker's feet. Stepping around it, William surveyed the scene.

They were in someone else's kitchen, one of the spacious modern granite and stainless steel showcases that characterized the common McMansion. There were enough ovens and counters and burners for a line cook and chef to work together in preparing meals for dozens of people, or for one weary career-laden parent to heat food prepared by someone else to feed a busy family. The recycling bin was filled with cans and boxes that told that truth, the dishes piled in and around the stainless sinks to hint that dinner had been long since served. The broken dishes and food stains on the floor looked more like deliberate violence than accidental spill, and the two pairs of figures huddled in opposite corners suggested the same.

A couple cringed near the tall stainless refrigerator, her shielded from the room by his embrace. The man looked over his shoulder in abject terror, watching whatever part of what was happening in his kitchen that he could see. A quick glance his way told William all he needed to know, that they were unhurt and unable to see him or the demon or the other pair of cowering figures in the opposite corner of the space.

William moved towards Chase and Daemon, manifesting his walking stick and whacking the demon on the head with it once more as it began to rise. The monster dropped to the floor again, still for another stretch of heartbeats.

"Are you okay?" William came up next to the new Walker and his unlikely Guide. They both nodded, mute, unable to take their eyes off the prone monster. Chase held his sword, a long slim straight modern blade that he could clutch easily in one hand. William was glad to see that the new Walker had armor and gloves on, but was not so pleased to see that the leather jacket was shiny and sticky with blood. Daemon looked both strange and completely natural in his Guide's robe somehow, more comfortable in it than the new Walker looked with a sword in his hand.

The demon rose from the floor, grasping at the granite countertop for support. Its long talons made a glass with a couple of ounces of clear bubbly liquid in it dance across the surface to go crashing to the floor. Across the room the couple cried out together, her with a surprised shriek and him with a hoarse shout.

"Please stop!" the man pleaded, clutching the woman to him. Another glass crashed to the floor, and he started. "Please! I won't hit her any more! I won't hit anyone ever again!"

William imagined a doorway to a cold killing field, watched it appear in what would look like the entry to the living room to the cowering couple. He nodded Chase and Daemon towards it, then caught the demon in his arms as it came at him once more. William let the momentum of the monster's charge propel them both towards and through the portal, and he closed the door behind them as they rolled in cold unpacked snow. The monster bit and clawed at him, but William kept his arms up so every blow fell on leather. Feeling the claws scratch at his arms, the old Walker timed a half-dozen short jabs between the clockwork assault. He watched the monster's head rock back with each crack on the jaw, and he let the demon roll on top of him as he calculated the next blow.

With the weight of the world behind him, the old Walker pulled his elbow as far back as it would go and connected a powerful left cross to its battered jaw. The force of the blow sent the monster flying, trailing powdered snow and flailing limbs across twenty feet of still mountain air. It landed with a quiet clouded burst of white and lay still, half buried in cold powder.

William was up and at Chase's side before the monster hit the snow. He felt his own fierce frown.

"Are you okay?" he asked the new Walker once more.

Chase nodded, trying to muster a smile.

"Did it hurt you?" William's frown still tugged at his lips.

"Yeah, he got me pretty good." Chase forced a chuckle, touching his face tenderly in remembrance. "I'm sorry, William. I really fucked up back there. I scared the hell out of those poor people. He was about to hit her, and I saw the demon right away. He saw me too, and came at me. I separated him from his host, but he batted me around their kitchen like a pinball for a minute there."

Chase was talking fast, obviously unsettled by the experience. He looked down at the sword in his hand like he was ashamed at the awkwardness with which he held it.

William shook his head, watching the demon.

"I failed here, not you," he said, meeting the new Walker's eyes. "You were bound to encounter a violent demon, and I should have prepared you for it. I have so much to learn from you, I forgot that I am the teacher here."

William approached the demon as it stirred, lifting its face from the snow. He pointed with his walking stick as he spoke, moving a slow circle around the prostrate monster.

"Striking a demon here, here, or here will usually render it unconscious for a spell," he said. "Most folks don't go out when you just knock them on the head like they do on television, and demons are no different. Hit them hard enough in the right place and they will, though. Go ahead. Try it."

Chase seemed hesitant to either approach the demon or relinquish the blade. He watched cautiously as the monster got up on one elbow, then the other.

"You need not fear demons," William went on. "Keep your hands up to cover your face if it comes at you. You are a Walker. You are power personified. You can move as quickly as you can think. You heal rapidly from any wound. You are a Walker. Strike, Walker!"

In a flash, the new Walker stood over the demon. It was driven face first into the snow by his blow, and its eyes closed in unconsciousness as they were buried in powder.

"Good," William said, waving his longsword. "Now the sword. Place the tip in front of you, high and to the left, slash downward and to the right, then mirror the move quickly the other way. Repeating that rapidly will make you difficult to approach."

The new Walker's sword flashed, over and over, quicker and surer.

CHAPTER 26

"I think it's time to call in the big guns," Kris sighed.

Vanessa looked questioning, either at the expression or who he might be referring to.

"Have you met Roche?"

She shook her head. "I do not believe so."

"He's a devil," he said.

Vanessa shrugged. "Okay."

"Do you want to come with me?" he asked.

She answered with a nod, and he opened a doorway that they might both walk through. Vanessa glanced through the portal at the scene beyond.

"That doesn't look like Hell," she mused.

"It's not," Kris nodded, indicating that she might go first. "It's San Francisco."

Stepping through the doorway behind her, Kris stood on the street beside her a moment later. He waved his hand, collapsing the portal.

Kris looked up at the wall above the covered windows, frowning at the four craters in the concrete overhead. He wondered what the cardboard taped up over the glass was hiding as he rapped on the door's steel frame with his dead knuckles. The door was thrown open immediately, and Kris backed up a step at the sudden movement. His retreating foot landed on the edge of the curb, and he canted backward enough for his adrenaline to start pumping.

Recovering his balance, the Guide looked up and down the empty street in somber melancholy before he turned.

"Roche," he sighed, relieved to see the familiar face even if it was drawn and strained.

"You!" Vanessa gasped, retreating onto the paved road.

"Vanessa," the devil sighed. "You remember me."

Kris watched her shrink away further from the devil, backing slowly into the street even more. He looked questions at Roche, who did nothing but shrug. The Guide moved to her side, took Vanessa's hand tenderly. He had never seen her anything but composed and graceful, and her wide eyes stared past him while her hand trembled in his.

"That's Roche," he said, leading her back to the sidewalk. "He's a friend."

She let him coax her to the door and through it.

"He's no friend of mine," she whispered fiercely as they passed him. "He murdered William's Watcher."

The lock clicked into place behind them. Roche turned, planting his meaty fists on his hips.

"Very few people would call sending a dead woman to Heaven murder," the devil mused, frowning. "One person in particular would say I was not the one to blame for the Watcher's death."

Vanessa faced him fearlessly now, her eyes narrowed and her voice strained with emotion.

"If the sun failed to rise tomorrow, William would feel that he must be to blame," she retorted hotly. "An overdeveloped sense of responsibility is his only shortcoming, but it doesn't make the evil of others actually his fault."

"Very well," the devil shrugged, nonplussed. "I will take responsibility for your Watcher's passing. In doing so, I must take responsibility for preventing your Watcher from betraying you along with many others during the War of the Demon Horde. I must take responsibility for your continued existence as a Guide, and William's continued existence as a Walker. I must take responsibility for taking ownership of this place before the Stone Walker's father's father's father's father had even heard of Ellis Island. I must take responsibility for the fact that we might just have a slim sliver of a chance of saving the world if we don't spend much longer trying to figure out who the best and worst of the good guys are here."

Vanessa was still glaring at Roche when her voice came in the Guide's head.

'Do you trust him?' Vanessa asked Kris silently.

He tried to put as much certainty in his shrug as possible. Vanessa's frown only deepened, so Kris sighed and nodded.

"Very well," she said, still eyeballing Roche cautiously. "Will you help us? Will you help us fight the Dragon Queen?"

"Absolutely not," the devil stated loudly. "That would be in direct violation of Walker Council law. I must tell you what I told Jessica when she came to me. Absolutely not."

As he spoke his vehement refusal, the big devil moved across the gutted and burnt remains of his business. When he finished speaking he opened the door that led to his office and rec room. Roche motioned them inside.

Kris stood on the blackened floor, wondering whether or not he should ask the question he was pretty sure he knew the answer to already.

"Who did this, Roche?" he said finally.

The devil let his smile fall for a moment.

"Jessica," he growled. "Obviously."

"Why?" Kris asked, incredulous.

"She's a teenager," Roche replied flatly. "I may have lived for longer than you can conceive, I may have unraveled the impenetrable mysteries of the Universe, but even I cannot tell you why teenagers act as they do."

The devil beckoned once more, insistent.

Kris moved past him. "She's almost five hundred years old."

Roche harrumphed. "A five hundred year old dragon. A teenager."

The moment Vanessa was in the room, Roche slammed the door behind them loudly. He advanced on Kris, one meaty fist balled up to strike the other repeatedly with a resounding smack.

"You killed Matthew," Roche growled.

"I tried to rescue him," Kris frowned, backing away.

Then he stopped, planting his feet.

"What, Roche?" Kris spread his hands. "Are you going to kill me? Beat me up? Somehow make me feel worse than I already do?"

Roche stopped as well, tears welling up in his black eyes as his hands dropped to his sides.

"You have no idea…" he said. Kris had never heard his voice sound so quiet, so gentle, or so sad. It made him want to cry as well, although he apparently had no idea why.

"I loved Matt," Kris moaned. "I risked everything to save him."

The devil nodded sadly. "I know, Guide."

Roche straightened suddenly. "So what's the plan?"

"I thought you weren't going to help us," Vanessa frowned.

"That was just out there, where anyone who knows how to listen can hear," Roche said, waving his hands dismissively.

"You lie far too easily," Vanessa noted, crossing her arms.

Roche let his eyes flash fire at her. "And you speak your thoughts far too freely."

"The plan," Kris broke in, "is to get the five Walkers that the council has set to be executed in a safe place, then gather an army to take them out."

"Take who out? The Walker Council?" The devil guffawed. "Have you ever killed an angel?"

"Have you?" Vanessa asked.

Kris moved deliberately between them.

"We don't have to kill them," the Guide said, "We just need to remove them from power."

Again, the devil indulged himself in a hearty peal of laughter.

"With a ragtag team of Walkers and two Guides who can touch things?" The devil's words were hard to make out in the torrent of mirth. "Oooh, scary."

Kris gritted his teeth. "Do you have a better plan?"

"Actually, I do." The devil folded his arms across his barrel chest and waited for him to ask.

"What, Roche?" Kris threw up his hands, exasperated. "What's the plan?"

Rather than answer, Roche moved across the plush carpet to open the door set next to the jukebox.

"In here," he said, motioning them forward.

Kris moved, but Vanessa's hand on his shoulder stopped him.

"Why?" she asked plaintively.

"It's my war room," the devil growled. "There is a table and chairs, so we can sit and plan. There's also a delicious bottle of aged scotch just waiting to lubricate the wheels of my old brain."

"Get your bottle and your chair," she retorted. "We will wait here."

Kris chuckled uneasily. "It's a pretty big chair. I'm sure everything is okay, Vanessa."

She turned to him, her youthful countenance a cloud of concern. Before she could speak an angel stepped into the room, then another.

"Please." One of the angels spoke in a sonorous voice, his friendly brown eyes dancing with light. "Join us."

The Guide thought of his key. He grabbed Vanessa's hand and thought them fiercely away from here, to William's, to Paul's space, anywhere but here…

Standing there, hands clasped, the Guides both frowned with internal effort.

"Guide Kris, Guide Vanessa, your keys are being blocked, as I am sure you have discovered." The angel's voice seemed friendly enough, and he smiled warmly at them. The doorframe behind him was filled with at least a half dozen more dour faces under halos. They peered out at them, not one of them smiling.

"I am Stephan," the smiling one said. "Won't you join us?"

CHAPTER 27

William circled Chase while the new Walker circled the demon, trying not to beam with pride. Daemon stood on a snowy plateau, watching it all and visibly trying not to shiver too violently. Chase's face was still painted in his own dried blood, but otherwise he looked as unharmed as he had managed to remain. The demon, on the other hand, was bleeding purple blood from a half dozen deep gashes. One of its horns had been sheared clean off during axe training, along with a slab of flesh and bone. The demon's brain pulsed in time with its adrenalized heartbeat, pumping steams of blood down the side of its face. A steady flow of steam was coaxed from the opening by the chill mountain air.

Still it came at him, diving at the new Walker's knees under the defensive swing of his sword. Chase leapt nimbly, kicking the demon as he rose out of its reaching talons. His harness boot jingled as it contacted the demon's jaw, hard, and the monster spun twice before striking the ground.

Chase landed neatly beside William, elbowed him playfully. "See that? Right in the jaw."

The new Walker beamed as he watched his foe lie still in the snow. William nodded, glad to let his pride show.

"Hey Chase," he said, as the demon began to stir. "Do you really believe that every issue has a favorable aspect to it? A good side, if you will?"

The new Walker smiled, then leapt into the air once more.

William watched him rise through the chill, higher than before, until he lost him in the sun. Chase landed heavily beside the demon as it struggled to its feet, driving it into the cold snow again with a violent whack of his walking stick. Another flying leap and he was by William's side, grinning.

"Sure," Chase said. "Don't you?"

William smiled, shrugged his broad shoulders.

"Do you not believe in God, William?" Chase watched his adversary, who lay unmoving with a fresh dent in its skull. A happy smile still played about his lips.

"Of course I do," William answered quickly.

"Just how big of an asshole do you think God is?"

William thought of all the things he had seen, all the people he had lost, all of the times his heart had been broken. He thought of how nice it was to feel himself growing close to Chase, and how only he had prevented it happening sooner.

The old Walker smiled. "Pretty big, I guess. When you put it that way."

"I disagree," Chase said. "I think this is the perfect framework for each part of God to work toward knowing itself completely. Our issues test our mettle, but there is no evil at the core of the darkest issue. Most of the things that trouble people exist in others' lives without causing any problems at all. When an individual treats a stepping stone as a stumbling block, it is not because the stone's evil caused them to. It's just a stone."

Still smiling, William asked. "Would you have had sex with that woman if I wasn't there?"

"The hooker whose name was not Angela?" Chase grinned. "Oh yeah. Why do you think I want some time off?"

William nodded. "I will see to it."

Chase held the battle-ax in his hand suddenly.

"We should wrap this up," the new Walker said, ticking gold glinting in his free hand. "It's almost time."

Peering at the glint of gold, William's smile fell.

"Your first Walker?" he said. "Already?"

It rose to its feet while they stared at the watch face together, both of their faces confused. Snow drifted from the demon's body as it dashed towards the Walkers, battered and bent but not broken. Chase rolled his eyes at William, already accustomed to his new speed and strength and weapon. If William had been an ordinary man, and taken that moment to blink, he would have never noticed Chase leaving his side.

William was an old Walker, though, and he did not blink. Instead he watched Chase glide over the snow, his axe going back over his shoulders in a wide two-handed swing. The demon was raising one hand as he neared, and it was removed from its wrist cleanly just before its head was removed from its shoulders. As the three dead grisly slabs of flesh struck the snow, Chase stood once again by William's side. The axe was gone, and he held up the countdown for both of them to see.

"We should get going," Chase said uncertainly. "Daemon is getting cold."

William glanced at the demon, watching them and shivering.

"Follow its pull like you do when you are hunting a demon," William advised him. "I will follow."

"I am," Chase said. "I mean, I did. I tried, but nothing happened."

The new Walker closed his eyes, but remained rooted in the same snowy spot. When he opened them, he looked at William in frustrated confusion.

Their next thought was a shared one, and both of them turned their heads slowly together to regard the one being on the mountaintop that was not a Walker.

Daemon stood there, shivering and watching them. His eyes went from Chase to William, and he stamped his feet in the snow as he hugged himself against the cold.

"What?" he asked, frowning.

Chase began to walk toward him, and Daemon backed up a step. William fell in behind the new Walker.

"Uh, you guys?" the demon retreated further. "What's going on?"

"How do I do it?" Chase glanced at William.

Coming up beside him, the old Walker matched his stride. "I usually stab them in the heart and give them the key at the same time."

When the dagger appeared in Chase's hand, Daemon's eyes went round and he waved his taloned hands before him.

"Oh, no," he whimpered. "What are you doing?"

Still ignoring him, the supernatural duo advanced.

"I don't know if it will work with him," William said, shaking his head. "You have to cut off a demon's head to kill it."

They were close enough now for Daemon to hear. He fell to his knees.

CHAPTER 28

The cruise control was set at exactly sixty-five, and that's how fast Cal's Acura moved towards the city. Sarah was puffing on her little nose burner, smoking the remaining drugs from the baggie. Cal had cracked her window three times already to keep the cab from filling with smoke; he had considered cracking her head against the dash twice as many times, eliminating the nuisance at its source.

She had cultivated an image of him that Cal had grown attached to. He was reluctant to spatter her blood about the car, and even more reluctant to shatter the illusion with it. It was far more appealing to see himself through her eyes, as some righteous vigilante escorting her home before going on the run. The further they drove along 280 the more her story seemed likely to become true. In her eyes, Cal was the victim here. He was not what he felt like inside, a cold-blooded killer delighting in his own psychopathy. He was brave, maybe even a hero.

Cal glanced at her, wondering how far she had taken it in her mind. Did she think he was sparing her a life on the run for her sake, for some festering love he felt? Or maybe that he had loved her at first sight, had been tortured by seeing her with Mason, and was similarly tormented by the thought of leaving her behind. He wondered if using that illusion might help him out in some way.

Nah, better to keep things at a healthy distance now that the sex was over. He pressed a button on the steering wheel, keeping his eyes on the road and his mind off the drugs and guns under his seat.

"Call Tyler," he said, enunciating clearly.

The sound of his brother's phone being alerted of Cal's intentions filled the car, playing over the speakers. Then his breathy strained voice replaced the ringing.

"Hey brother," Tyler squeaked.

"Hey brother," Cal smiled. "I'm with Sarah."

"You are?" Tyler thought for a moment. "Hey Sarah."

"Hi Tyler, how's it going?" Sarah's voice was sweet, but her momentary glance at him was a touch suspicious. Cal didn't care; he had learned his lesson many speakerphone calls ago. Before Tyler could answer, or Cal could smirk, Sarah spoke again. "Have you talked to Mason?"

Cal heard his brother sigh through the speakers. When his voice followed, it was even more strained and high-pitched than usual. Sarah awaited his answer, breathless.

"No," he said. "I assumed he was with you."

"I haven't seen him since the show," Sarah said.

"Neither have I," Tyler responded.

They were both quiet for a moment, and Cal didn't like any of the directions he saw their exchange going.

"Tyler," he said tersely.

"Yeah, brother?"

"We're headed to Mason's again to see if he's there." Cal hesitated, glanced at Sarah. "I'm going to drop Sarah off there. Then I need to disappear."

There was a lengthy silence. Then Tyler's voice came, sounding as sad as Cal had ever heard it.

"For how long?" he asked.

Cal frowned. "For good, brother."

The next silence lasted so long that Cal checked the counting digital display to make sure they were still connected.

"Cal." Tyler's voice came at last. "Did you kill Mikie?"

In his mind Cal pounded the dash, first with his fist and then with Sarah's head. Mentally he screamed, allowing all of the anguish to pour from his body as he coaxed the blood to pour from Sarah's. In his mind, he raged madly until the car flipped or rolled or flew off a cliff.

In reality, Cal gripped the steering wheel and frowned. The world could think him a monster, Cal might even think himself a monster; but not his brother. His mind spun on.

"Can you come pick me up at Mason's?" Sarah broke in. "I can explain what happened, Tyler. It's not Cal's fault."

"Yeah, Jason's here," Tyler said. "We can come get you."

"Actually," Cal said, coming back to himself, "you guys should go to Santa Cruz first. I left the front door to my apartment unlocked. You can have whatever you want."

"We can put it in storage for you," Tyler suggested.

"I won't be coming back," Cal reminded him gently.

"I'll meet you at Mason's," Tyler said.

Although his brother couldn't see it, Cal shook his head.

"No," he said. "I'll only be there for a minute. I am already putting Sarah at risk, and I can't stand the thought of keeping her at risk any longer than necessary. I can't put you at risk too."

Cal checked peripherally to make sure Sarah was consuming the bullshit he was feeding her. She was.

"I love you, brother," Cal said sincerely.

"I love you too, Cal."

He pushed the button to hang up the phone.

Sarah was watching him with that hero worship in her eyes again. He didn't need to turn to see it; Cal could feel it. He needed to do something about that, something other than pistol-whipping her and tossing her onto the rushing asphalt like his imagination kept suggesting.

"I could come with you," she murmured quietly.

Smiling inwardly, Chase called upon his inner asshole.

"You would be a liability," he said, watching the road.

Sarah frowned. "What makes you say that?"

"You're used to guys that follow you around waiting to do your bidding," he shrugged. "I'm not that guy."

"Mason didn't do my bidding," she objected.

Cal nodded. "And look how upset you got, and how you reacted."

"Mikie didn't do my bidding," she said hotly.

"And that's why you cut him off, right?" Cal watched the road. "I can't afford to deal with the drama that comes with you. I know the fairy tale, and how it's always most romantic for most ladies if the guy dies saving them or defending their honor or dealing with some other situation that he wouldn't have had to deal with if it weren't for her."

Sarah was watching the road as well. Her mouth was frowning ever so slightly, but otherwise she showed no emotion.

"That's not what I want," she said quietly.

"Do you want to stop singing?" he demanded. "YouTube is international, you know. Every time you open your mouth in public it would put me at risk."

"I don't want that," she said, more quietly.

"What do you want?" he persisted. "What long-term scenario do you see playing out where you and I are together and we both get everything we want?"

They rode in silence for a while.

"I know what you're doing," she said at last.

Cal didn't answer, just stared at the road.

"You're trying to push me away," she said. "For my safety."

This girl could psychoanalyze Hitler and still be convinced there was a saint in there somewhere, Cal mused to himself.

He drove, not speaking or looking her way, letting her project whatever she wanted onto his blank screen.

The only way to keep from pulling over and stabbing or shooting or bludgeoning her was to imagine that he was, and that's what Cal did while he watched the miles go by. Or maybe strangle her, watching her eyes bulge and feeling her go limp in his grip. That way there wouldn't be any blood, or bullet holes; and he could just open the passenger door and push her corpse out into the weeds.

He remembered Tyler, and that Sarah was his ticket to keeping his brother's image of him intact. As soon as he thought of it, his brain went to work on the problem: how could he make it look like an accident, or like she had turned on him? It seemed unlikely, but unlikely was not the same as impossible. Surely his clever coke-fueled brain could think of something.

They moved along the freeway, him devising ways to get away with murder while she painted a picture on his deliberately blank canvas of a fairy tale that couldn't come true.

CHAPTER 29

William was pretty sure they were purposefully making him wait. He was not a hang out kind of guy, having made a happy habit of keeping his hands and mind occupied learning and building. Waiting on the Walker Council had William feeling nervous for the first time in a century of learning. He had chosen another song to blast over his thoughts before he had come, a different Rolling Stones tune of course. William had thought the choice to be random until he was given time in a Heavenly waiting room to consider that there is no randomness where a choice is made. The consideration was done at length, under the blasting sounds of "Gimme Shelter", and led him to consider the title of the album the track had been released on with grim irony.

If this was what an eternity in Heaven felt like, the other option might just hold more appeal. William shuddered, thinking of devils and dragons and the Rolling Stones.

"Walker William." He leapt to his feet at the sound of his name, and the liquid light seat he had taken disappeared into the clouds it had sprung from. He walked resolute through the sudden open doorway. As soon as he stopped walking, stood and faced the council, he began to speak.

"Gentleman of the Walker Council," he said. "I fear that Guide Kris and Guide Vanessa have been captured or killed. I sent them to gather the Walkers you had requested me to take to Hell with me, and I cannot locate the Guides or the Walkers."

William noticed that Stephan would not meet his gaze. Listene did, however, staring him down while he spoke.

It was Listene who responded when he paused.

"William," he said coldly, "Guide Kris and Guide Vanessa have been captured. They are in our custody."

The urgent song screeched to a halt in his mind. William felt his key come alive in his hand, first taking shape and then tugging itself from his grasp. He tried to activate it, to cling to it, to go home or to Hell or to a peaceful icy mountaintop in Montana.

It was wrenched from his hand, uncurling his fingers against their will to float through time and space towards Stephan. William sensed that the magickal device was just as perturbed by the separation as he was, and just as helpless to prevent it. Three hundred years ago he would have scoffed at the thought that an inanimate object could have feelings; today he would just as surely scoff at the suggestion that this particular item didn't.

Stephan reached out his hand, as if expecting the old pocket watch to leap into it. Instead it swirled through the air like a feather caught in an errant wind. The glinting device moved left, then right, then floated above the angel's head to hang suspended out of reach.

A transparent box formed around the key, fine light woven into what looked like a glass cage or plexiglass display case. Within its confines, the gold disc raced back and forth the few inches it could. The box itself descended slowly to Stephan's waiting grasp.

"William," Stephan said, dropping the Walker title as Listene had, "you are charged with serious crimes against this council, and you have been scheduled for rehumanization."

"Isn't that up to my key?" William objected. He knew how to read it, and how much time he had left. William might be old, but he was anticipating ancient status long before handing over his key and weapon. He let his thoughts blast as loud as the Rolling Stones in his mind, churning with fury and frustration set to boil to rage. The gold watch pressed at the transparent wall closest to him, straining at its constraints as liquid light manacles appeared to similarly constrain the man. That's what he was, too; William realized it as he pulled with ordinary human strength: just a man at the mercy of a group of supernaturals. He sagged against the weight at his wrists, defeated.

"The Walkers must learn to obey the Walker Council," Listene said. His voice actually sounded happy for once, even a touch giddy. "They will not learn under the command of a miscreant such as yourself. The keys must learn to obey us as well. We consider ourselves better equipped to choose when Walkers are made, and what kind of candidates to put in place, than devices that were forged by dragons in Hell."

William glared at him. "What if the keys do not agree?"

Stephan tapped the transparent container soundlessly. "We will deal with the keys that will not cooperate, and the Walkers who will not cooperate, in whatever ways we see fit."

"We suggested that you make examples of some of your less…team-oriented Walkers for a reason," Listene beamed. "The strategy is well-known for causing naysayers to fall in line."

"All Walkers are independent thinkers," William scoffed.

"Not any longer," Stephan said sternly, and just a little sadly.

William gazed longingly at his key.

"It's not just an object, you know," he said quietly. "I suspect that none of them are. There is a consciousness in that key that easily engulfs the scope of my own, or any of yours. I don't pretend to understand it, and I have never spoken aloud of it until now, but I have puzzled over it and paid close attention to it for centuries. The only thing I can say for sure is that it is not evil."

"We will take your opinion under advisement," Listene said dismissively. "We will of course weigh its value against yours, and that of your reputation."

Stephan cleared his throat, then spoke.

"Before you are sentenced," he said soberly, "the council would offer you a chance to redeem yourself."

William raised an eyebrow, curious but hardly hopeful.

"You want to make a deal?" he asked, disbelieving.

"In a manner of speaking," Stephan shrugged.

"And I would keep my position?" William was nearly laughing.

"Of course not," Stephan replied gently. "We will choose a new leader. You would return to the life of a Walker, although you will not make any new Walkers or interact with any existing ones."

"Upon penalty of death," Listene said, grinning broadly.

Stephan turned his head slowly, his hands still holding the invisible box and its contents. For a long cold moment he glared at Listene, until the other angel frowned and look away.

"I get it," William said, too engrossed in his own predicament to be amused by their infantile dynamic. "What do you want of me?"

Stephan turned his gaze on him full force, imposing his will on William as best he could. William let Mick Jagger plead his case at full volume, hoping he might somehow still have some secret worth guarding.

"The Walkers that were to make up your envoy to the lower realms are nowhere to be found," Stephan said. "We know you have them stowed away somewhere. Turn them over to us and you can go back to your old life."

"With Vanessa?" William asked. "And Kris?"

Listene mumbled something that sounded dark and foreboding, but William's human ears couldn't make it out.

"They await trials of their own," Stephan responded. "We will consider the possibility of returning one or both to assist you in your duties should you all cooperate completely."

"Gimme Shelter" blasted so loud that William wondered if he could damage his inner ear. He fought a smile, tapping his harness boot in time to the music.

"I have no idea where they are," he said, his own voice lost in the sacred soup of sound.

William saw his key pressing insistently against its container, and he redoubled his efforts at straining against the feathery chains. He wondered if it had heard what he had said, if the simple metal object knew that his feelings ran deeper than his words could express.

Stephan waved his hand, and two tall statuesque angels entered the room. They looked nearly identical to each other, and the rippling muscles under their light robes made the lightning swords they carried seem unnecessary.

"Place him in a containment cell," Stephan instructed them.

William was tired from holding up the weight of the liquid light manacles; he had no chance against either of the giant light sources holding them each in their free hands. They were nearly to the luminous door frame when Stephan called out after them.

"Where are the keys that Walker Paul collected?" Stephan asked. "Where are the keys you collected? How many Walkers did you make during your time as leader?"

William spread his hands as much as the manacles and the angels would allow. He listened intently to Keith's rolling guitar.

"I have no keys," he responded, trying not to smile. "I assumed you had taken them to be re-issued. I have made no Walkers since becoming Leader of the Walkers."

It was actually all true enough, what he had said. It was the churning undercurrent of thoughts that he was drowning out.

Stephan gestured again, and the tall angels led him gently enough out the doorway. William followed them up a long lighted hallway made of clouds, glancing up as they began to speak to each other as though he wasn't there. They towered over him by a head, and even as humans would have outweighed him by at least fifty pounds. When he threw the wings and the swords on the scale, it tipped precariously in his mind.

"Another prisoner," one angel said, glancing at the other. His voice was a low rolling thunder, beautiful and musical and like to coax tears from William's old eyes.

"We must follow orders," the other responded.

His voice was as beautiful and as musical as the first's, and William's heart was lifted by the sound despite his circumstances.

"What were those orders?" the first spoke again, smiling a beautiful perfect smile as he turned his head once more.

They locked eyes over his head, moving slowly down the hallway, and the one to William's right began to grin as well.

"Place him in a containment cell," the angel responded, in a voice similar to Stephan's but comically whiny at the same time.

"Which containment cell?" The angel to William's left nudged his shoulder playfully, as if attempting to include him in the banter. William nearly collapsed under the weight of the blow, reeling breathless against the other angel.

"Careful!" the angel to his right said, catching William gently in the curve of his elbow. His hard muscles felt like marble against William's yielding flesh, and his winced.

"Don't hurt him," the angel said, putting his heavy arm around William's shoulders. William struggled to keep pace under the crushing weight.

"Here we are," the thunderous one said, and William felt the burden eased at last.

They had entered a room, and William saw a gigantic version of the transparent box his key was captured in at the same time as he saw the two Guides contained within it.

"This looks like a containment cell to me," thunder boomed, followed by laughter.

William looked from Kris to Vanessa, then at each of the angels in turn, as they pushed him towards his friends.

"Thank you," he said, as they retreated unresponsive from the room.

Vanessa's arms were around him, and William held her to him as fiercely as he could with his diminished strength. He breathed her in, fighting tears of gratitude or joy or hopelessness.

Stepping back, he welcomed the other Guide's brief embrace as well. William saw the frown creasing Kris' face.

If he made it out of this mess, William knew what he would learn next. He had so many questions, and no silent method of asking them. Instead he leaned on the one crutch he had, blasting music loudly over his whirlwind thoughts.

"Relax," Vanessa said soothingly. "We have privacy. Nothing gets in or out of this space."

William sighed and let his thoughts come back to him.

"You got to them before the council," William said, clapping Kris on the back. "Why so grim?"

The Guide looked at him, confused. "What do you mean? We got to who?"

"Paul's generals," William responded. "The Walker Council cannot locate them."

Kris shook his head. "We never got to them. We went to get help first."

"From who?" Now William was confused.

Kris sighed. "From Roche."

There was that name again, ringing some old bell in his memory. "Who?"

"The Original Walker Demon," Kris shrugged.

"The devil that murdered Sylvia," Vanessa added.

Kris glanced at her, then hung his head. "He was working with the Walker Council. He led us right to them. He betrayed us."

CHAPTER 30

"We could have used the Guides, devil."

The low voice roused him from his reverie.

Roche slumped in one of the nine silver or gold or platinum thrones in the room, watching coins glint in the light from the luminous manacled angel against the wall. He turned his attention to the source of the voice, a short stoic Walker that stood patiently rather than claim a throne. His face looked like it had been carved from rock with a broad and sharp chisel. Wiry dark hair sprouted from his head to brush his shoulders, and even in an overcoat he looked lean. His face wore no hint of an expression, as if it were truly hewn from stone.

"It was them or you, Walker Tristan," Roche grumbled. "If I had been planning a party, I would surely have chosen them over you."

"But we are planning war," a strident feminine voice broke in. "The devil chose wisely."

Roche turned his attention to the beautiful young woman, remembering that she was neither young nor human. Lara's dangerous allure was no illusion; even in an army of Walkers she was among the fastest and fiercest.

Mikeo sat in a silver throne in silence, his posture suggesting that he actually perched on a simple cushion. Roche had watched his eyes go from Walker to Walker and devil to angel with alert attentiveness a dozen times in the last hour. The devil had yet to hear his voice.

"Five Walkers and one devil against an army of angels." Walker Samuel's slow drawl pointed out the obvious to everyone in the room, not without a tone of humor. "That sounds more like suicide than war."

Batu's sword appeared in his hand, a long curved weapon that seemed extra sharp somehow. He beat it three times against his breastplate loudly, his long hair and beard shaking with his intense movements.

"Five of the most formidable Walkers that ever lived, you mean," Batu said fiercely, "and the Original Walker Demon."

"Very well," Samuel drawled. "It sounds like slow suicide."

"Let me gather an army of Walkers," Batu insisted, disappearing his sword to implore them in turn with piercing green eyes.

Roche and his counterpart both shook their heads, her laughing musically while he frowned.

"As soon as anyone leaves this place we show up on their radar," Roche pointed out. "We wouldn't have time to gather enough Walkers for a fútbol team, much less an army."

Samuel's cowboy hat tilted as he cocked his head to the side. "You mean soccer?"

Roche was glad to see nearly every immortal eye in the room train itself on the lone American with proper disdain.

"Is she clear of the darkness?" Batu asked Roche, indicating the imprisoned angel with a wave of his hand.

"Release me and find out," the angel sing-songed, her voice a threatening haunting lullaby.

The devil shook his head sadly.

"It looks like we're the army," he grimaced.

CHAPTER 31

When they saw the first demons coming up behind them, they began to run. He looked at her in confused anguish, his only memory that he had something of vital importance to remember. She had only just found him, they had only just begun walking, when the trio of monsters appeared. He knew that he knew her, that he could trust her, and that was why he had followed her. She was beautiful and familiar and was not threatening him with either of the heavy curved swords she held.

"Do you remember?" she had asked. Hope had lit her dark lovely eyes, and that alone had made him want to answer in the affirmative. He couldn't, though, not honestly; so he hadn't.

"Remember what?" he had responded. His heart fell when her face did, but only because she was so breathtaking.

"Let's go," she had said, visibly trying to hide her evident despair.

And then they had started walking. He had barely had time to be aware of his own naked and unarmed state, or curious about the strange crimson leather that the beautiful woman wore, when the demons gave chase. The sight of the three horned behemoths jarred something else in his memory, as did the weight of the sword that she tossed him. Between hurried steps and ragged breaths he cried out to her.

"Brenna?" he called, uncertainty in his voice.

She may have been a head shorter than him, and female, but she was a good stride ahead of him. He got the feeling that his top speed was somehow her holding back. She threw a smile at him over her shoulder as she ran, and a flashbulb burst in his brain.

"Ximena!" he cried.

She glanced over her shoulder at him to treat him to another precious smile when three more demons stepped from the shadows to block their path. Ximena ran bodily into one, bouncing off his muscled abdomen like she had struck a wall. Somehow Paul caught her in one arm and swung the sword with the other, his own speed startling him. The added momentum of catching her made slicing through the monster's thick neck easier than he had expected; he couldn't possibly be that strong.

There was no time to think as they each tried to dispatch a demon before three more were upon them. Ximena seemed faster and stronger than she should be, and maybe he was too; but the demons they faced were nine to ten feet tall and armed with ten slashing talons each. When their sword-like claws were not sweeping at tender flesh and a thin demon skin dress, their massive heads were dipping to chomp at them with huge slavering maws dripping with saliva and teeth.

They didn't stand a chance, he knew it before he felt long biting teeth sink into his shoulder. The pain brought with it a stab of memory, and he gasped his own name as his blood drenched his naked back and belly.

"Paul!" he cried. "Paul Stone!"

Ximena's eyes went round, and she tried to meet his gaze while a monster seized each of her arms.

A third monster stepped between them, blocking his blue eyes from home. Paul struggled against the arm about his torso and the teeth in his shoulder.

"Walker Paul Stone!" he cried out. "Ximena! I remember!"

He couldn't see her, or know if they had torn her apart. Paul moved despite the pain, eyeing his sword on the charred rock where it had fallen. He willed it to come to him, to fly into his hand or into his foe's throat. Then he heard the demon that stood between he and whatever was left of his love speak in a guttural grunt, and he knew she yet lived.

"Hold her," the demon grunted. He doffed the leather vest he had been wearing and went to work unlacing his leather pants.

Paul lurched forward, leaving half of his shoulder and several cups of blood in the demon's jaws. He felt the arms that held him turn to talons as he escaped the embrace, flaying his naked torso until bare ribs showed. The sword on the ground shifted, then lay still, as Paul advanced on the demon's wide back empty-handed.

His raging charge was halted from behind, as the demon that had held him caught Paul up once more. He thrashed about in the demon's arms, splattering blood about the other's back. He turned, a look of annoyance on his twisted hateful visage, and took his clumsy hands from his lacings. They were proving hard to untie, with gigantic taloned hands clearly meant more for the task he had turned to.

The demon described a wide arc before him with those talons.

Paul's face and neck and chest were sliced open in five wide gashes, any one of which would have proved fatal. His remaining blood painted the demon that was holding him in a wide swath across his torso, and a small cut was dripping purple blood from his arm. He cast aside the lifeless body and stepped forward to push the other demon aggressively, then step back and point at the blood welling on his muscled forearm.

Neither of them noticed that the body disappeared before it could hit the ground, or that another shadow rose in the valley of shadows as it did.

Swathed all in black leather, the shadow took shape and stepped forward. A low modern cowboy hat was tilted low over his eyes, but they gleamed from the darkness with blue electricity. One black glove held an old sharp bastard sword, the other clutched a gleaming platinum broadsword, and his voice sounded out as confidently as his boots falling on the burnt stone.

"Let her go," he called out, stepping closer.

Ten hate-filled eyes turned his way, swirling black on scarlet on rage. One hissed at him, another growled, but they didn't release their hold on her.

"I won't ask twice," he growled, planting his boots.

Three of the monsters moved to advance on him while the remaining two held her. Ximena struggled against them almost absently, watching Paul erupt instead.

He moved as though time stood still, whirling and leaping and slashing a beautiful fatal dance among the demons.

Ximena's wide eyes barely tracked his movements as he blurred towards her, five gigantic horned heads striking the burnt ground at once as he gathered her in his arms. A wide puddle of purple blood formed behind them, bubbling and smoking and filling the air with an awful stench. They clung to each other, heedless of the grisly scene or the bloody smell that surrounded them. His swords had disappeared before the heads had hit the charred rock underfoot; and she felt his gloves disappear as he held her, that he might feel her flesh.

"You're bleeding," he said, stepping back to inspect her arm. Blood flowed from a gash on her elbow, red and dripping but not spurting or flowing.

"That?" Ximena shook her head, taking his hands. "That's just a scratch."

She smiled when she said it, and he smiled too. Then she turned and let him see the five long gashes down her back. Her bare legs were clothed in her own blood, and fat drops of it joined one narrow stream to form a puddle at her feet.

"It's those I'm worried about," she said, her back still to him. When she pivoted towards him again, her knees wobbled and her eyes rolled back in her head.

Paul rushed forward, catching her and clutching her to him once more. He pressed cold metal into her hand insistently.

"Ximena," he cried. "Take it. Take the key."

She lolled in his arms. Tears stained his cheeks.

"Brenna," he whispered. "I need you to take the key."

She coughed, her knees straightened, and Ximena's beautiful dark eyes came into focus on his. She reached out slender fingers, feebly, until they closed about the gold pocket watch in Paul's hand. The disc glowed, then melted into her hand, and she collapsed once more into his embrace. Paul lifted her easily, cradling her gently in his arms and tilting her head to rest on his shoulder. He carried her over burnt rock as easily as a mother might carry a newborn, and as tenderly. He had walked for nearly a mile before she lifted her head from his shoulder and smiled at him.

"You made me a Walker," she giggled into his neck, wrapping her arms about his shoulders and squeezing.

Paul shrugged, feeling her lively weight shift with the motion. She kissed his cheek over and over while he answered, and a wide smile broke out across his face.

"I sure did," he grinned. "No more fucking dying, for either of us. Got it?"

His face grew dark as he cursed, then brightened again as he kissed her back.

"Got it," she answered solemnly.

"I love you so much," he said, as both of their tears salted their kisses.

She giggled and clutched him tighter. "I love you so much."

Ximena drew back, still smiling. "Where are we going, love?"

Paul halted his smooth hurried pace, felt her precious weight shift once more in his arms.

"I was taking you to the cave we have been spending time in," he explained. "You said Jessica can't hear us there. I was going to leave you there while the key turned you into a Walker. It typically takes about three days."

"I'm not typical, sweetie." Ximena kissed his cheek and smiled. "You can set me down if you want."

He held her weight for a sweet forever moment, and she pressed herself close to him.

Paul set her down, held out dusters in each hand.

"Brown or black?" he asked.

Ximena crinkled her nose and chose, whirling the supple black leather round her shoulders. She accepted the hat and boots next, putting them on with a mirthful solemnity. Paul watched, smiling, watched as she closed her eyes and transformed the armor before his watchful gaze.

The hat was gone, everything else changed. The boots were still boots, but the heels were a couple of inches higher and the snug leather now reached beyond her knees. The overcoat had gone from a loose flowing cloud of leather for her to float around in to a form-fitting dress that covered her arms to her elbows but left most of her lean muscled thighs exposed. Paul stared at her shamelessly while she moved before him, making minor adjustments that further perfected her perfection.

She smiled at his attention. "Do I get a weapon?"

Paul nodded. "Actually, you get two. New policy."

Soon she was holding a longsword in one hand and a short sword in the other. She clutched them easily before her, black leather gloves curling around the handles and covering the better part of her slim forearms.

"Ah, the strength of a Walker," she murmured, waving the heavy metal before her like they were hollow plastic toys.

"Is it enough?" he asked.

"It's not what I'm used to, but it will do," she shrugged. "For now."

Paul frowned, nodding. "Are you coming with me?"

Her swords disappeared, and she was in his arms.

"Come find me," she breathed. And then she was gone.

For the first time in lifetimes, Paul breathed in air that was not swirling with smoke and reeking of soot. He hadn't bothered to close his eyes before the shift, and he saw the devil before being seen.

Roche sat alone at the end of the long table, his bulk tilted sullenly in the giant chair. An empty glass sat next to an empty bottle, which was next to another bottle half full of aged scotch. The devil stared at the empty bottle, dejected.

Paul cleared his throat politely.

"It's not too late in the game to have a drink, is it?" he asked, watching the devil straighten in his chair. Roche launched himself from his throne, crossing the room in the blink of an eye. He caught Paul up in a bear hug that lifted him from the floor and squeezed the air from his lungs. Roche seemed perfectly aware that the embrace would have been pained torture for anyone else, and laughed loudly in the Walker's ear for some time before setting him down.

When his boots finally found the floor again, they stepped along the table to the waiting bottle.

Paul didn't pour it in a glass or ask permission, taking the liberty of upending the bottle for a long drink. Roche watched him, grinning unabashedly and still chuckling. He stepped toward the Walker as he drank, and stood by his side as he finally lowered the glass container.

"Roche," he said, handing him the bottle. "I believe you have something that belongs to my beloved."

The devil nodded, gulping at the drink.

"The Walker Council has collectively gone mad with power," Roche said. "They had to put Marcus in charge of the Loom of Light, but they imprisoned his Guide and Watcher to maintain control of the device as best they could."

Paul was just looking at him, waiting. Roche misread the look.

"Sorry," the devil said, passing the bottle back. "The Loom of Light is—"

"I know what the Loom of Light is, Roche." Paul cut in quietly.

"Oh. Okay. Good." The devil nodded. "The council made Marcus—"

"They made Marcus freeze time in Hell, giving you an opportunity to take Ximena's stone while Jessica took the opportunity to burn us," Paul cut in once more, smiling. "I know."

"How do you…" Roche beamed suddenly. "You can see."

The devil held out a necklace, a simple chain with a simple agate oval dangling from its length. As soon as Paul took it, a gleaming platinum key took its place.

"What?" Paul frowned playfully at the devil's sheepish pose. "Do you not wish to be my Agent?"

Roche bellowed with laughter. "Is that allowed?"

Paul shrugged. "You'll never guess who I made into a Walker."

The key disappeared into the devil's meaty paw.

"Ximena has returned, then," Roche mused. He appeared to be considering whether or not he was pleased by the news.

Paul nodded, obviously delighted.

"She has," he said. "I need to bring this to her."

"Of course," Roche nodded. "But first…"

The Stone Walker gauged the amount of liquid still in the bottle, tipped it; looked at it again, then tipped it once more. He handed it to Roche as he objected.

"Oh no, not that," the devil protested, taking the bottle and draining it nonetheless. "I want to show you my trophy room."

Paul laid his hand on the devil's shoulder, and they were there.

The devil whirled on him.

"How the hell did you get in here?" His eyes swirled with crimson fire as he confronted the Walker, heedless of the semi-circle of similarly formidable Walkers around them.

"I had to find Ehcor," Paul said with a smile. He turned the smile on each of the Walkers, and even the angel, before turning it back to the devil. Each Walker lit up in their own way when they made eye contact. Tristan somehow seemed taller and harder, his face still expressionless while his eyes danced unblinking laughter. Mikeo grinned broadly, Batu dipped forward in a fierce and regal bow, and Lara stood to happy attention. Samuel tipped his hat at Paul, winking and smiling. Even the angel smiled, and seemed to glow a bit brighter.

Roche was still pretty pissed off.

"Is that where my gold went?" he demanded. "Did you steal from me, Walker?"

Paul shrugged again, still smiling. "I had a war to fund. If it helps, I knew that you had taken Matt's key. I thought of it as more of a rental fee that you didn't know I was charging for a valuable device that you thought I didn't know you had taken. From the right perspective, neither of us really ever stole anything from the other. Don't you think?"

The devil finally matched his smile.

"No need to ask who you've been spending time with," he chuckled.

Pivoting in place, Paul made eye contact with each of his generals once more, addressing them with a sober smile.

"Walker William, Guide Vanessa and Guide Kris are being held by the Walker Council, but they yet live," he said. He saw them sigh with collective relief. "I intend to rescue them if I can. I have only dealt with one angel, and it was clear that I was no match for her. No one gets judged for sitting this one out."

They all laughed at him, except Tristan. It did look like maybe he was considering it. Ehcor's sweet song came to him over the laughter.

"Not all angels are as powerful as I am," she sang. "Stab them through the heart as you would sever a devil's head."

The generals looked from the angel to the devil, as one. He nodded his agreement, as did Paul.

"My king," Batu bowed once more. "I understand that I may be rehumanized for revealing this, but I have stayed in touch with key members of my family for many generations. If you have the ability to make them into Walkers, they could probably get ahold of a MiG-29, or at least a MiG-21."

Roche looked like he was about to go off on another tirade. Paul spoke before he could.

"We don't have time to make an army of Walkers, and we cannot risk our decimated ranks," he responded.

"And no one is flying a jet into Heaven," Roche added.

Paul nodded his agreement. "We are not the only wave of attack, my friends. When our reinforcements arrive, I am told there will be at least one dragon among them. Do not risk yourselves any more than you must. Our primary objective is locating and freeing Walker William and the Guides. There is no need for all-out war unless she declares it."

"She?" Samuel drawled. "You mean The Devil?"

Paul nodded, smiling at the cowboy. "Yes, I mean Ximena."

A platinum disc appeared in his hand, more to show them his train of thought than to check the time. Paul was one with the key, tuned in to it to his very soul. There was no need for him to ever look at it again, if he didn't want to.

"See that, Walker?" Roche growled, eyeing the device.

Paul smiled. "It appears to be broken, do you think?"

They all gathered around, watching the countdown clicking one moment forward and then one back over and over again. The disc changed to a book in his hand, bound in leather and uniquely characterized by a digital display set in the cover. A series of nines appeared across the display. The last number became an eight, then a nine, an eight, and then a nine again.

"The Walker Eternal," the angel's enchanting voice found all of their ears. "At least one of you seems to stand a chance."

CHAPTER 32

"My queen." The crone's voice crackled, snapping Jessica from her dark reverie. She had dismissed the creepy old seer when she reported that she could not find any of the things she was looking for in her magick orb. She brought her head around slowly to consider her, resolved that if it wasn't good news the bitch was getting fried.

"What is it?" she hissed.

Her milky eyes peered from under the dark cowl, and her raspy voice issued forth from it.

"I found it."

Jessica stood straight on all four of her scaled legs, towering over the slight figure. She did not need to ask what she was talking about.

"Show me," she said, lowering herself slowly and snaking her head toward the crone's crystal orb.

She recognized the room immediately, as well as its two occupants. Jessica watched Paul and Roche standing near the devil's table, swilling whiskey and swapping words she couldn't hear. She knew better than to ask the ancient battered being to turn up the volume; she was lucky to have the view into the devil's space.

Jessica saw the devil offer Paul the item she had been searching for since coming into power.

"Roche, you goddamned sonofabitch," the queen hissed. "I'm going to kill you."

"No." A new voice issued from the shadowed depths of the cowl. "You're not."

The crystal ball fell to the floor, crashing into a million pieces.

The heavy cloak drifted to the floor, three sudden reactions coming all at once.

"Ximena!" Jessica hissed the name, rearing back to strike.

A flash of crimson light crossed the room in time with the sound of a sword clearing a scabbard, and Charine was pressing a sharp curved blade against Jessica's throat.

Laurentis exploded in place, sending devils flying in every direction and seriously damaging the wall behind him as he became a huge black dragon. His giant black head slithered to within a foot of Jessica's, watching her with anticipation and a complete lack of fear as a cloud of dust drifted to the floor.

"Shall I dispatch her, my queen?" Charine asked, grinning at Ximena and showing long sharp biting teeth.

Ximena shook her head, turning in place to look at every devil that would meet her eyes.

"I am the cause of this situation," she said calmly. "If you need someone to die for it, it should be me."

A tall, lean devil stepped forward. He was dressed in dark flowing robes, and steepled his hands before him.

"My queen," he said, "the rules clearly state-"

"To Hell with the rules," Ximena snapped. "They are the other cause of this situation."

The devil's eyes went wide, but he did not protest.

"What is your name?" she asked him.

He shifted uncomfortably, eyeing the devils about him. "I am Taltono, High Priest of the Seventh Realm. I serve the people. My master is the High Priest of the Nine Realms."

"How do you serve the people?" she asked.

"I guide them, I advise them. I preach The Word."

"Whose word?" Ximena's eyes remained dark, but flashed with anger. "Mine? God's? Yours?"

"Your word, my queen," Taltono replied. "The Queen Lilia Version, to be sure, but times have changed. Certainly you will agree?"

"Don't tell me what I will think, about anything," Ximena crossed her arms across her breasts. "Are you compensated for your service?"

The priest's hands went quickly from a humble prayer position to being clasped behind his back. Apparently he was hoping she hadn't noticed the collection of rings on his fingers, glinting with precious metals and gemstones.

"A pittance, my queen," he replied dismissively. "Barely enough to live among my constituency."

"Is your constituency made up of those you claim to serve?" She pressed him. The devil looked around once more and made as if to bring his bejeweled hands into view. He stopped mid-motion, kept them clasped behind him.

"Of course not," he scoffed. "Only dragons can vote."

"I do not claim to serve," he added, disgust still dripping from his words. "I *serve*."

"For a paycheck," she clarified. "Do you not know my books? Was Book Two, Chapter Nine, Verse Three removed?"

"Of course not," he bowed regally. Taltono looked as though he very badly wished to place his hands in a somber prayer position before him, but once again he resisted the urge. He began to recite memorized words to her in hallowed tones:

> "Each soul hath a value that can be brought to market
> Each market hath a place for thou that wouldst toil;
> Caring for thine family is caring for thine self
> Care for thine realm by mining the soul or the soil"

He bowed his head, quite pleased with himself.

"Are you serious?" Ximena was now glaring at him. "Who the Hell wrote that drivel? Who the Hell added 'thees and thous' and removed the actual message?"

Taltono frowned. "I was not on that board. I am told that the original verse was quite lengthy, and didn't even rhyme."

"My queen," the devil holding the sword to Jessica's neck ventured politely. "I would love to hear the original."

She shifted slightly as Ximena met her eyes and smiled.

"Charine, yes?" Ximena asked.

The devil nodded, starstruck.

It was all those little things that added up to make the next moment altogether different than if Paul had appeared a few seconds earlier or a few seconds later.

Her sharp curved blade hovered over Jessica's throat instead of pressing a threat into it, and Charine's attention was almost entirely on this legendary figure. When the Walker winked suddenly into existence, what little attention she had to spare went to assessing his presence and identity. She saw the hat, the duster, the blue eyes of the Stone Walker, and then the simple necklace he had in his hand. Charine was so overwhelmed by the moment that she didn't notice the way the dragon's eyes widened at the sight of the gemstone, nor did she react quickly enough to stop her sudden movement.

Jessica's reptilian head flashed forward and chomped down, consuming the necklace and Paul's left hand in one sudden shocking bite. Laurentis and Charine both moved, but Ximena held up a staying hand.

She glanced at Paul. "You okay, sweetie?"

The Walker held up his new left hand. "Not a scratch."

Jessica looked back and forth between them, incredulous. Then her slitted eyes went round, and she gave a surprised little dragon cough. She blinked twice, then her eyes rolled back in her head in time with it hitting the floor. Her wings fluttered, then began to grow, until they touched the walls on both sides of the room. They flapped, listlessly, driving a dozen devils to the floor under their descending weight. Then they burst into flames, and all Hell broke loose.

Devils were screaming and running, and several of them were on fire. Some were caught under the burning wings; they were screaming as well, but the sound was lost under the blanket of flames and the crackling of fire. The unconscious dragon began to twitch convulsively, then tremble, then thrash about blindly in place.

Laurentis took his tall devil form, crowding close with Ximena, Charine and Paul. The four of them watched while devils made for the door or disappeared under a thrashing flaming wing or a pile of the boulders that began to fall from above. Two of the walls were on fire, and the flames had climbed them both to begin licking the stone ceiling high above them. Chandeliers fell one after another, each hundreds of pounds of wax and metal, as the cables that held them burned in the dragon-fire. For nearly a minute the room was a pandemonium of shoving and screaming and burning and running, while four figures stood together in the still eye of the storm.

After a minute the only devils in the room were the ones whose toasting dead flesh filled their nostrils and the three standing with Paul. And the dragon queen. They watched her eyes go wide once more, unseeing and pure black, as her burnt wings began to grow back. The left one sprouted, twenty feet of bloodied bone, so fast that it struck the far wall and set the room to rumbling once more. More rocks fell, and Laurentis took dragon form again to stretch his wing protectively over the other three. Paul watched a stone the size of a small automobile bounce harmlessly off the shelter, and tipped his hat in thanks.

Before it could finish forming, the bloodied length of bones burst into flames. Jessica began thrashing about as the second wing took shape. The way she was positioned, the dragon was propelled toward one of the burning walls. She struck it where the rising stone met the ceiling, bouncing from wall to ceiling to the floor again. Her right foreleg was on fire, and began to grow grotesquely as it burned. Soon it was the size of her body, then it engulfed her body in size while engulfing it in flames as it filled the room. Stones fell to strike her repeatedly about the head and wings and giant arm, but the size of her flaming appendages kept her from moving about enough to damage the room more than she already had. The cushions on the throne had long since caught alight, and the flames had climbed one dragon's form to dance along its carved teeth as though it were breathing fire.

Jessica had become a writhing mass of grotesquely misshapen dragon flesh that smoked and bubbled and burned before their eyes. Charine, Laurentis and Paul all divided their attention between watching the dragon twitch and watching Ximena for a call to action. Ximena stood calm amongst them, watching the dragon burn with her full attention. They all wondered what she was waiting for; if she noticed that all of the walls were on fire now, or that the exit itself was awash in flame. And then it happened.

The dragon's eyes opened once more, and this time they could see Jessica in them. The could see pain as well, and a tormented confusion. She coughed another little dragon cough, and the gemstone leapt from her mouth to skitter across the floor. There was no chain, no setting, no hand with it; it was simply stone, lying there still in a small puddle of dragon bile.

Almost immediately, Jessica's body began to resume its natural shape. Her wings morphed into a reasonable size, looking like proper dragon wings instead of sheets of flame. The monstrosity that her foreleg had become shrunk back to its normal shape, and she was able to roll back and forth to put out the fire. In the space of a long calm breath, she extinguished the flames on her body and in the space she occupied. Jessica faced them, as still as Ximena, her eyes on the gemstone between them.

Ximena glanced at each of her companions in turn.

"Please do not kill her unless it is absolutely necessary," she sighed. She stepped forward and knelt to retrieve the gemstone. The moment she took her eyes from the dragon's, Jessica struck once more. She swiped and bit at her at the same time, and Ximena was lifted bodily from the stone floor. She flew several feet, the arm that had been reaching for the gemstone bitten off at the elbow and spurting blood as she spun through the smoky air. In the same moment that she struck the burning floor and rolled, Laurentis opened his gigantic maw and took the smaller dragon's head in his mouth. The motions of Ximena hitting the floor, rolling and standing up whole were almost soundless. The dragon's action was punctuated by a loud and distinct cracking sound, the noise that issues forth when a dragon's black spine is severed in one bite.

Laurentis chomped again, another foot of Jessica's long neck disappearing between his jaws with another loud crack. The dragon continued delivering one fatal blow after another, slicing and swallowing Jessica bit by bit as her scaled limbs twitched with her death throes. He was nearly to her shoulders when Ximena stepped from the flames and began walking towards him. Her hair was on fire, as was her leather outfit in many places, but she walked calmly forward despite the intense pain she must have been enduring.

As soon as he saw her, the black dragon dropped the remains of the red one. He rose up on his hind legs, bending his neck so his head would not strike the high ceiling. Stretching out his wings, Laurentis wrapped them about Ximena with the gentle care of a mother swaddling her newborn, as Paul and Charine watched Jessica's headless torso spurt purple fountains of blood.

Laurentis straightened his wings, and Ximena stepped forth whole. She watched Jessica's body, sadly, as it began to fade from existence. Then she glanced up at Laurentis, who was picking at his sharp teeth with a long talon and looking rather pleased with himself.

"I would say that was absolutely necessary," Paul ventured, looking from Ximena to Laurentis to Charine. Ximena frowned, and Charine nodded; the dragon continued picking his teeth.

"Please burn everything that is not us or already on fire," Ximena addressed the dragon. In a few moments the exit was lost behind a sheet of flame, the carpets and tapestries were all on fire, and the throne was nothing but a melting burning misshapen inferno. Jessica's gory remains were gone, burnt or faded or both. All that was left of the throne room was flames and falling rock.

Ximena bent to retrieve her gemstone once more, and this time no one moved to stop her. As she picked it up, it melted into her hand, and the entire room began to tremble. Ximena stood, her eyes closed, and breathed deeply in and out. The others watched as the walls of flames that surrounded her breathed with her, as more broken rock tumbled from the walls and ceilings to strike the flaming floor. They watched her skin flush as two tiny sharp pointed horns sprouted from her head and a short barbed prehensile tail ripped a hole in the back of her leather dress. Then she opened her eyes, and they swirled with scarlet and black and promise and hope and eternity.

Charine dropped to her knees, and Laurentis grinned and stopped picking his teeth. Paul watched her transform, watched her new eyes meet his. His eyes were wide, his face expressionless. Ximena cocked her head to the side, uncertain.

Paul stepped forward, his gaze still on hers.

"I see now," he murmured, breathless. "I see everything in you." Tears shone in both of their eyes, and they fell into each other's arms. A ripple of light or energy danced through the choked air, and the four of them were out in the open on some Hellish plain as they broke the embrace.

"Gather the dragons and the devils," Ximena said. "Release the prisoners in the dungeons who reside there for acting against the laws or powers of the dragon regime rather than acting against a fellow citizen. While violent crimes are clearly a result of societal pressure, we must deal with those who have taken to violence on a case-by-case basis when we have time and resources to do so. Remove the jailors from their posts and replace them with those that you release, as you see fit. Give them the resources to make the remaining prisoners comfortable and safe. The punishment for violence shall not be caged violence, or neglect, or rape, any longer. The punishments for going one's own way without doing harm to another shall cease. The punishment for imposing one's will on another, for taxing any individual's spirit or paycheck, will rain down on those who might rise to tell others what to do or how to live or when they might speak and what they might say. From this day forward Hell shall live without masters, and I will remain to see that it does."

CHAPTER 33

Chase blinked at his new surroundings, checking to make sure Daemon and his angels were with him. He saw the new sheets on the mussed bed, the old blue and white guitar next to a new black one, the speakers and amplifiers and coiled cords and the ashtrays on every surface. He settled himself on the dingy little sofa at the foot of the bed. Chase didn't have to peek into the two darkened doorways to make sure no one was in the tiny kitchen or the cramped bathroom.

He was early, and he hoped to have the precious few minutes remaining on the countdown to sit and relax. Since he had become a Walker, his life had been nonstop. Chase thought of it all as one long day, since he hadn't slept, but he knew the sun had risen and set at least once or twice as the endless day flew by. As far as he knew, it could easily have been more like a dozen.

Daemon was quiet, as usual, moving around the studio in slow measured steps. He had watched the other Guides touching things and people, and had taken to practicing picking up small items as part of his routine of fading into the background. Now that he was a Walker he had no problem touching things, yet for some reason he was still indulging in the affectation. He put everything back where it had been, and spent a lot of time going back to the older guitar, but he was doing no harm.

The new Walker ignored him politely, as he did the three swirling flashes of light whirlpooling through the air. He stared at the blank television screen and let his eyes delight in the complete lack of action or adventure. He didn't notice Daemon kneeling next to the old guitar, touching the strings and crying softly.

After a few blessed minutes of silence for Chase and quiet tortured grief for Daemon, voices sounded on the other side of the door and a key slid into the deadbolt. Chase sighed, raising his consciousness beyond human perception and his body from the dingy sofa. The deadbolt rotated, the doorknob followed, and the door swung into the apartment. Two humans entered, strangers to Chase, a pretty young couple from the looks of them. They were talking, but Chase wasn't listening. He was paying attention to the lumbering demon with one beefy taloned hand on the young man's shoulder. He had other demons; but they cowered on the other shoulder, as far from the oversized monster as possible.

"Cal," the girl said, her pretty green eyes going wide as she addressed him, "you should take Mason's car."

The man looked around the apartment distastefully.

"Why?" he asked her.

His demon was whispering in his ear, and its hateful mantra seemed to have hooked his attention more than the girl. Chase stepped back a step at the words it chose.

"Kill her," it whispered, in the tones of someone professing their love, or speaking of them. "Hit her, strangle her, break her bones and make her bleed. Remember the glory of watching life slip away in your hands, the pleasure, the intimacy, the power…kill her…kill her!"

Chase saw that he was fiddling with a knife clipped in his front pocket, but otherwise the young man showed no outward signs of being a killer. He looked like a cokehead, if Chase saw anything, but not a killer.

"They won't be looking for Mason's car," the girl shrugged. "And I don't think he's coming back."

"What if he does?" the man asked.

She shrugged once more. "I'll tell him to wait a few days and then report it stolen."

To her, it likely looked as though he was considering her suggestion; to Chase, it looked like he was listening intently to his demon. The new Walker tuned out the grisly description of what the monster thought the man should do to the young woman. Averting his gaze along with his attention, he saw the demon's face.

"Daemon!" Chase stepped around the people and to his side. "Are you alright?"

Daemon nodded, wiping away the tears that continued to spill from his eyes. Then he nodded again, indicating the couple.

"They were Mason's friends," he said quietly, sadly. "She's right. He's not coming back. He's gone, and it's my fault."

Chase closed his eyes, letting his vision wander to a place he had never looked.

"Mason was your Walker," he said.

"Mason made me," Daemon responded, wringing his clawed hands. "Then I got angry with him, and led him to his death."

"Daemon," Chase said gently. "Mason didn't make you, any more than parents make a child. He was no more deliberate in your creation than a mother is in the act of gestation. His thoughts and actions may have set the stage for your creation, but your soul is your own. Besides, you didn't lead him to his death; the angels did that by manipulating the Loom of Light."

Daemon looked at him, hope and uncertainty and tears in his eyes.

Then a strange thing happened, and his attention snapped back to the task at hand.

The couple was talking, exchanging words that he was tuning out as he focused on Daemon. One of the man's smaller demons stirred on his shoulder, stood and walked right up to the man's ear. It addressed him calmly, ignoring the two simultaneous conversations and the huge demon's grisly suggestions.

"Hey Cal," the demon said, casually gripping the man's ear with one tiny hand, "it's about time for a line, don't you think?"

While Chase was pondering the possibility that the way to keep demons small is to give in to every temptation, the large demon reached out to seize the smaller one. Squeezing it in his powerful clawed grasp, the large demon ate the little one in three bloody bites. The demon grew even larger, taking up his Hellish rant once more after swallowing the last bite. Blood dripped down his chin, and the veins in his temples began to throb visibly.

"Kill her!" the demon shouted. "Hit her! Cut her! Shoot her! Kill her!"

A loop of leather fell neatly about its sinewed neck, and the demon broke off to whirl on Chase. It grabbed the staff stretched between them and pulled fiercely. Chase shifted slightly, but kept his balance and his place. His new strength was a part of him now; and no demon could compete with that, no matter how unnaturally overgrown the monster may be.

"Do you know what I am, demon?" Chase asked the struggling monster. It growled and hissed and swiped razor talons at him, but otherwise it didn't reply. The new Walker waited for it to blink, and when it did he moved. As the monster's eyelids came together, he changed the snaring staff to sharp sword and cleaved the connection between the demon and the man. As its eyelids came apart again, the loop of leather held him once more.

The demon's eyes went wide, realizing what had happened in the blink of an eye. It wailed, then turned to lunge at its host just as it had tried to lunge at Chase. The new Walker had no trouble holding it in place, and it pivoted in the tight snare to glare at its captor.

"Do you know what I am?" Chase repeated. He held the taming tool in one hand and the severed end of the connecting cord in the other.

The demon swiped and spit at him, its intensity and strength ebbing visibly. Its feet slid on the worn carpet, losing purchase over and over as it strained feebly against the leather snare about its neck.

"Walker!" it hissed, giving Chase his answer. The spirits began to move in deliberate patterns, framing space in three places to support the Walker's way. Chase shook his head, however, and waved them off. Turning to Daemon, he plunged the connecting cord into his sinewed chest. Daemon stepped back, surprised, but the demon came to life with renewed strength. It strained at its tether with mounting intensity.

"The Walker Council has influenced the Loom of Light directly in one way or another many times in recent history," Chase said. He was holding the demon with both hands now, but he was addressing Daemon. One demon continued to struggle with its physical captivity while the other battled his own emotional confinement.

"Walker Paul was not a scheduled transformation," Chase went on, ignoring one struggle to give his full attention to the other. "Mason was not slated to ever be touched by the world of Walkers in any way. He was certainly not ever meant to find out about Walkers. Walkers operate in secrecy. The world knows about Guides and Watchers, Vampires and Reapers and Zombies and nearly everything else out there, even if most people don't understand their functions like they would like to think they do. But Walkers do not exist, as far as the world is concerned, and the council has gone to great lengths to keep it that way. Some who have stumbled upon knowledge of the Walker have become Walkers themselves. The others have all died."

Chase sighed as the demon suddenly became as dejected as its new host.

"Mason was a good person," Daemon murmured sadly, "but he was on the way down. It's still all my fault. I told him too much, I took him to Hell."

"You were manipulated by the Council," Chase corrected him gently. "Mason was affected by the accident in a way that needed to be controlled. People and events other than you played a part. If you hadn't played the part that you did, someone else would have. Mason was doomed from the moment his car struck Paul."

Daemon was wringing his hands once more, lost in thought. The demon watched him, breathing heavy and frowning fiercely but no longer struggling at the tether. They spoke at the same time, almost the same words.

"I should have never been made," Daemon whispered.

"You should have never been born," the demon hissed.

They looked at one another, each surprised in his own way. Chase shook his head, interjecting.

"Would you take Mason's time with Sarah from him?" Chase demanded of both of them. "Would you take the moments that he spent expressing his soul at last with that very instrument?"

He pointed at the blue and white guitar with one hand, barely holding the staff with the other. The demon was rooted in place by its new attachment and the exchange.

"What about the way he felt about you?" Chase pressed him. "He cared about you like a friend, like a father. He loved you. Would you erase that? Would he want you to?"

Both demons considered the words and each other in stillness. Chase frowned and prepared to do the thing he hated most.

"Daemon," he said carefully. "The Walker Council filled your mind with their thoughts several times in an attempt to kill Mason. You had no control when you told Mason what you did about the world of Walkers, or when you took him to Hell."

Daemon frowned. "That's not true."

Chase turned so his Walker might see him while the demon could not, and threw Daemon a cheesy wink.

"Yes it is," Chase countered. "Think back, remember and vividly imagine those moments in which your mind was not your own. The Walker Council manipulated you. The Walker Council controlled you. The Walker Council murdered your best friend. The Walker Council destroyed Mason's soul."

Daemon caught his drift right away, and was carefully creating a mental scene of merciless angels tearing a helpless human soul to shreds or something of the sort. The connecting cord between him and the demon pulsed with energy, anger and hate and bile pumping into the monster. It growled, shaking its head violently, and started to scream.

"The Walker Council!" it screeched. "The Walker Council must die! The Walker Council! The Walker Council must die!"

Chase waved his hand, and a doorway appeared right where the entrance to the kitchen had just been. Light poured through the opening, clouds billowed beyond it, and Chase changed the snaring staff to a shining straight sword. He pointed the blade at the doorway as the demon continued its rant.

"The Walker Council is in there," Chase said. "Go get 'em, big guy."

In a flash, the demon was through the doorway. Chase cut the cord behind it, collapsing the portal with another wave of his hand.

Daemon crossed his arms across his chest.

"And the truth?" he asked.

Chase smiled. "The truth is a bit more complex than the fuel I needed to properly fire up that demon."

There had been human activity amongst the supernatural scene, and Chase had paid little attention after separating the demon from its host. He had been peripherally aware of the guy doing a line, of her lighting a joint, and of him going out the front door and coming back in minutes later. There was no hint of danger about their interactions, no need for the Walker to pay but the most scant attention. He had felt a silly connection to the girl, for conspiring unknowingly to send a cloud of pot smoke into Heaven, for a moment. Then he realized they probably had the best of everything up there, and dismissed the errant thought.

Now he checked on them, tuning in to their conversation as they sat close on the loveseat.

"I'm sorry, Sarah," Cal said, shaking his head.

He leaned forward and signed a piece of paper that he had brought in from his car and laid on the wooden coffee table. After signing it, he handed it to her.

"This is the title to my car," he said. "It's only a year old, and just has the one bullet hole. You can give it to Mason if he comes back, if you want, but I don't think you should. Keep it, cash it in, trade it in, do whatever you want with it. I'm sorry I…I'm sorry for getting you caught up in all of this."

"I can't, Cal," she said, taking the slip of paper. She looked it over, making sure everything was in order. "Are you sure?"

Cal nodded and stood up, avoiding her embrace as she rose beside him. He moved to the front door.

Although still reluctant, he let her wind her arms around his waist as his hand fell on the doorknob.

"Sarah," he said, squeezing her shoulders lightly with one arm. "I have to get going."

He tilted his face to brush lips against her forehead, but Sarah raised herself on tiptoes to press her lips against his instead. He opened the door and let his arm drop from her shoulders, moved his mouth from hers.

"Goodbye, Sarah," Cal said. He shut the door behind him.

"Goodbye, Cal," she whispered at the door. She moved to sit on the sofa, fishing around in the ashtray for a smokeable.

Chase turned to Daemon, satisfied.

"Your thoughts were your own, I know," he smiled, "but you were still manipulated by the council. They would have found a way to kill Mason no matter what, but one council member objected strongly to the method they were entertaining. He stepped down and volunteered to take Mason's soul to the next world with him in order to save it. Mason's body went with you to Hell, but his soul was already on its way to a better place."

Daemon's eyes filled with tears once more, fresh happy tears.

"Truth?" he asked, as though a demon couldn't tell.

"Truth," Chase said resolutely.

He waved his hand, and the luminous doorway appeared again. Chase motioned him through, glancing back over his shoulder at the young lady on the loveseat as he followed.

Sarah picked up her phone, swiped and tapped and tapped some more. She held it to her ear.

"Robert? Rob?" She blinked, and her eyes went wide. "Hey. How's your hand?"

CHAPTER 34

Ximena stood before a crowd of devils and dragons, still swathed in a Walker's black leather. Charine and Paul stood nearby with Laurentis, each of them gazing at her with a different brand of adoration. They waited for Ximena to speak, as did the endless sea of Hell's denizens.

"I am Ximena," she said at last, needlessly. Although she hardly raised her voice, no one strained to hear her words. The crowd was more than a crowd; it was a carpet of devils squeezed together to form an unbroken sea of crimson in every direction as far as the eye could see. Not all of them could see her, but they all heard.

"I was once Queen of Hell, and as queen I lived by a clear definition of what that meant. My methods evolved over time, but the definition of what a queen was never did." Ximena smiled at the gathering. "Does anyone remember the rules by which I lived, the only edict I ever pronounced that was not up for debate?"

A small percentage of the vast assemblage began to speak, all at once in all different cadences. Ximena smiled at the roar of garbled unintelligibility while Paul strained to listen to one distinct voice or one complete sentence. He made out a word here or there, or a string of them, but the meaning and the message was lost on him. She saw his confused look, and that most everyone gathered around shared the look. Nonetheless, a cheer broke out as the voices died down; and Ximena waited for silence to descend once more before continuing.

"That's right," she smiled, then repeated the edict:

"The queen will only serve, but never rule.
The queen will only give, but never take.
The queen will tax only her resources, never another's.
The queen will contest only those that would politick, police or teach under any other ethic.
The queen will allow the community to evolve unmolested."

Charine mouthed the words with her, smiling like Paul had never seen.

Her eyes were round in awe, and glistened with tears.

As the queen fell silent, voices erupted from the crowd once more. They began as uncertain grumblings and soon grew to clear shouted complaints.

"I am a teacher. Did I just lose my job?"

"I am a jailor. I already lost my job!"

"Where am I supposed to get my demons?"

A tall devil stepped from the crowd. Laurentis sniffed at his approach, a sign to him or to the others that he knew what he was. His scaled skin was dark, leathery and weathered. His eyes glittered black with slices of scarlet. Most of his lean frame was swathed in the blackest of robes, which swished at his feet and dared any mote of dust to attach itself to it; none did. A wide sash cut across his abdomen, somehow darker than the blackground of the robe. Twin horns jutted from his forehead, thick and long and curved all the way round to point wickedly forward. A black crystal glittered between the base of the horns, a dark third eye hanging from thin platinum chains.

Ximena watched him approach, crossed her gloved arms.

At ten paces, he stopped and bowed.

"Ximena," he crooned. "Welcome back."

"Staurale," she said, her voice slightly less beautiful as it dropped to low cautious tones. "Speak your piece."

"Much has changed since you renounced our realm and abandoned its people," the dragon said. "I have come to rule second only to the dragon queen. I am reluctant to give up my post or my income for some old-fashioned ideal. I suspect that many of the dragons that hold important positions in the government feel the same. Hell is no longer enthralled with your words or subject to your law. You left."

Her eyes were sad, but Ximena's voice was beautiful and strong once again. "Those that remember the old way, those that loved someone who remembered the old way, have you passed on your passion and your fervor to your young? Do you speak of yesterday's yesterday, and how we will never survive to see tomorrow if we do not revive its principles? Or has your passion been incinerated in this eternal fire, in this burning of beauty to light the world for a day? You trade in demons until the demons run out; then you feed on each other while the dragons feed on you; then only dragons remain, left to consume one another in a burnt and broken paradise. If you see the folly of the dragon's way, even if you are a dragon, I ask two things of you today. Please be still."

The crowd was stirred by her speech more than once, and not every stir was gentle. Devils shouted or booed, and more than one shoving match broke out. At her final simple request, nearly every sound ceased immediately; those that didn't were gone soon after, and one could hear a tail swish.

"First," Ximena smiled entreatingly, "I would beg your forgiveness. I left you for my own selfish reasons, in a state of what looked like eternal abundance. Dragons were kind protectors when I left, and their collective contribution to society greater than my own. I had no inkling of how things would change in my absence. I would earn your forgiveness by never leaving again after this day, if you would have me."

It couldn't have been all of the voices cheering, but it certainly seemed like it. Paul felt his ribcage tremble with the sound, and he smiled and shook his head in wonder.

"Please," Ximena said once more, "be still."

And they were, shouts fading to murmurs fading to a sea of whispers that became stillness.

"Second," she continued, "I would ask that you remember a world with me in it; a world where a day's toil bought a month of living; where teachers were people who had learned by succeeding at life and had the resources and sense of purpose to help others build theirs; when politicians kept their jobs by listening to the people, and lost them the moment they took anything from anyone. Remember those days, or speak with someone who does, for me. Ask yourself if you are ready to work for gold and gems instead of copper or demon labor or demon flesh. Ask yourself how long this can go on before the flesh on the fork is your own. And then join me when I return, and give me the opportunity to keep my promise to never abandon this realm again."

Staurale had been deflating visibly under her words and the black dragon's baleful stare. As she finished, he straightened.

"You are leaving again?" he asked. "Already?"

"The Walker's way has been misinformed. It has been the cause of the constant stream of demons into Hell, as well as the recent flood," Ximena frowned. "I must go above to face the Walker Council and see them change their way or step down."

Laurentis brought himself up to his full towering height. His thunderous voice did not reach every ear as hers did, but it reached enough.

"Those that do not need to forgive the queen for seeking something for herself after giving us so much," he boomed, his giant wings trembling, "those that do not need to take time to ponder her words, and those who would follow me should I ask, come with us to Heaven. Fight by our sides to remind Heaven that Hell is a part of its function, and that our freedom is not subject to their rule or anyone's. Rise up, and raise your arms!"

The clamor that followed was deafening, and the army that began to form was immense. Devils came together before Ximena in loose orderly ranks, standing at attention in lines that began to stretch into forever in three directions. Somewhere in the commotion, Staurale had slipped away. Many followed his example, drifting away from the scene to consider their positions or rally their forces. Ximena gave Laurentis a slow smile of gratitude as she let the sound settle, then turned her attention to the troops.

A strained voice reached her, followed by the slow rumble of tens of thousands of footfalls.

"My queen!" a demon called out, pushing his way through the crowd. He was thin and wiry, his face a pale red sheen of sweat. His clothes were rags, old and unwashed, and drenched through in perspiration. It looked like he had been running for a while.

"My queen," he repeated, panting between words. "The demons have heard you. If what you say is true, if you would free us and help us find the way to ourselves, we would fight this war with you as well."

The rumbling became a horde of demons that appeared at the edges of their vision to swell their numbers beyond counting. Smiling at the queen's smile, the demon spoke again.

"The dragon city is piled high with more demons," he said. "Many are huge and fierce, as the Stone Walker can surely attest to. If you free them, they will certainly fight for you as well."

Ximena sighed. "Those demons are not just the product of the Walker Council's slave trade with the dragon queen; they are the products of war. We need to separate the demons that have been consumed from those that have consumed them, and give them all the same opportunity at life and purpose as the rest of us. We cannot press entwined spirits into military service."

"My queen," the demon frowned. "You speak as though demons have souls. Is that true?"

Laurentis glanced at the queen, and she nodded.

"The queen left us with one last message all those years ago," his voice boomed out. "We are none of us beings with souls; we are all of us together one soul. Remember that in all that you do!"

CHAPTER 35

The hallways of luminous cloud all looked the same to Chase. He followed the swirling spirits and his inner vision until they led him to a wide and open space. He saw William and Vanessa before they saw him, and Kris in a far corner of the cage with his back turned. Chase beamed as the old Walker finally glanced his way, then looked behind him to make sure everyone was with him.

Daemon had entered quietly, his eyes wide with wonder. He made his way to the transparent wall and pressed his palms against it. The spirits were already in the room and swirling about the cage looking for an opening. The other two were missing, and Chase held up one finger to assure William he would be right back before rushing back up the glowing hallway. There they were, talking and touching a wall.

"It gives way if you ask it to," the demon was saying, as his hand disappeared to the wrist in the lighted fog.

The man chuckled. "Ask it, eh?"

He pressed against what appeared to be flowing solidity.

"Will it," the demon urged him. "See it so."

"Simon, Duncan," Chase called to them. "I told you to be quiet and not to touch anything."

They dropped their hands to their sides.

"It's really not the time to be debating whether or not the walls are alive," Chase pressed. "They are, by the way. Everything is."

"Sorry," Duncan said, and the demon echoed the sentiment.

"Come on," Chase said, "we have a rescue to pull off."

"No," a voice boomed behind him, "you don't."

Chase sighed, and turned to face the speaker.

"Angel Stephan," he said, eyeballing the spectre. "I thought you would be taller. And not so fat."

The angel's triumphant smile fell to a terse frown, which deepened when one of the guardian angels flanking him sniggered to himself. The other guard held Daemon, his giant hand nearly engulfing the demon's entire upper arm. He glanced over at the laugh, smiling but maintaining his stoic silence. Two other angels were there, and Chase saw fit to let them know a little about how much he knew.

"Andre," he said, throwing caution to the wind, "the worthless piece of shit turncoat. And Listene. You look exactly the way the books describe you."

Chase spit into the clouds at their feet. "Disgusting."

"Hold him," Listene hissed. The second guard stepped toward Chase, his sword sheathed and his grasp reluctant. He nudged Chase playfully, apologetically, barely gripping his arm.

"Do not be frightened," Stephan said soothingly to Duncan and Simon. "We do not intend to hurt you. Who are you, and what is your business here?"

Chase spoke to the angel's wide back. "I brought them to—"

"Shut up!" Stephan whirled on him. Chase felt the guard's grip go even more lax on his arm, and he remembered that he still had his weapon. And his training.

"Shut up!" Stephan screamed once more, advancing on him until their noses nearly touched. "No more words from you!"

Chase blinked three times, then shrugged, but didn't speak. Stephan stood there, nose to nose with him and trembling with anger. At last he glanced up at the guardian angel holding the new Walker and backed up a step.

"No more words from that one," he hissed at the guard.

The guard glared down at Chase dutifully while Stephan watched, only to elbow him playfully once more as the angel turned.

"Now," Stephan said, "where were we?"

He studied the wary visitors, then pointed at the demon.

"You," the angel said, "state your name and business."

The demon drew himself up proudly, his vest parting to show his scarred torso. Raising his remaining hand to his forehead in a mock salute, he grinned. "I am called Simon. I am the human Doug Reed's demon."

Simon hesitated a moment, then added, "Retired."

Stephan ground his teeth. "What is your business *here?*"

"Oh!" The demon brightened. "I am here to testify."

Duncan nodded. "As am I."

Stephan looked daggers at both of them in turn, and the human mistook his look.

"Sorry," he said. "My name is Duncan."

"And what are you here to testify to?" Stephan asked.

They both shrugged and looked to Chase. The angel was loath to turn to him, the new Walker could tell as he did.

"Chase." Stephan pronounced the name like he didn't want to get any on him. "What are they here to testify to?"

"Well, primarily," the new Walker gulped, "they are here to testify as to the upright moral character of one Walker Paul, the Stone Walker."

"The Stone Walker is dead," Andre said behind him.

He sounded frightened.

Chase smiled. He didn't bother turning.

"Don't be so sure," he said. Chase was glad he hadn't moved his attention from Stephan; the angel dimmed visibly at his words.

"Duncan was seriously traumatized by his wife's passing," Chase said quietly. "Walker Paul found him on the street, wasting away, and he helped him. Simon was spared by Walker Paul so that he could go on to undo the damage he had done. They are here to testify, as the rules dictate. One victim from any realm and one human from the middle? Isn't that right?"

"Where did you learn that?" Listene asked coldly. He turned his icy attention to Stephan. "What kind of Walker is this?"

Stephan waved his hand, frowning. "You said they are primarily here to testify on Walker Paul's behalf. What else are they here to attest to?"

Chase gulped once more. "They are here to testify against the Walker Council, to prove certain members unfit for duty."

Listene moved more quickly than Chase would have expected. The angel stepped toward the guard holding Daemon, pulling his long sword of light from its sheath in one fluid motion. He advanced on the pair, swinging the blade blindly before him. Duncan and Simon got tangled up in trying to escape, and he was upon them before anyone could act. They both held arms up defensively, crouching in the clouds. Duncan lost a hand and then a head, and Simon rolled away with a gash on his already severed stump.

Stephan seemed to be waiting, giving him a chance to finish the demon. Listene was heaving with the effort of so much movement and the weight of the giant sword, and he glanced back as if hoping someone might be coming forward to restrain him. No one was, so he moved down the hallway.

The demon reached into its vest pocket, digging around for something as the angel dragged himself and the heavy sword forward. He grinned then, and held up a platinum key; then Simon disappeared.

"Enough," Stephan sighed. "Retrieve your sword."

Stepping forward, the guardian angel left Daemon standing alone right next to Andre. The angel that barely held Chase was on his other side, not watching him at all, and Andre realized that nothing stood between them in the same instant that the new Walker did.

Andre tried to move, his eyes going round, but he bounced off Daemon instead.

Wrenching free of the guard's half-hearted grasp, Chase appeared his sword and grinned wickedly as the blade flashed. He could have sworn the angel holding him cracked a smile when he broke free, but he was too preoccupied with his own precise movements to be sure.

Chase flashed forward and plunged the blade deep into Andre's heart. When he was close enough, he grasped the angel's shoulder and pulled him further along the blade, speaking as the angel gasped in pain.

"Now the Walker Council is only eight in number," he said as the gasp became an explosion of fireworks and Andre died at last.

CHAPTER 36

Cal watched the speedometer closely, cursing Mason's piece of shit car for the umpteenth time over the last few hours. There was no cruise control or power windows, and the air conditioner only blew hot air. He hadn't noticed the missing cruise control until he had gotten on 101. Cal had almost turned back for his Acura, but had thought better of it. When he got to San Jose he had switched on the air, and ended up wishing he had gone back.

Now he was on I-5, already seeing signs for Los Angeles and going a fairly steady seventy-five miles an hour. The Malibu was among the slowest cars on the road, save when he had to change lanes to go around someone driving a bigger piece of shit than he was. Cal tapped out a line onto a CD case on the passenger's seat, driving with his knee along the long straight freeway while he snorted the line.

He knew he couldn't sync his phone up to the stereo, so Cal had grabbed the one CD that was in his car. He must have listened to Psycho City three or four times all the way through by now; and as it started over with a violent and threatening message, he pushed a button. The radio came on, some cowboy singing about girls or trucks or beer in a nasally tone that made him punch the search button before he found out. The next wave of sound that flooded the car was a happy upbeat tune that he sang along to, moving his shoulders subtly.

"El mismo sol," he crooned, in time but off-key. He didn't know all of the words; but he knew some, and it was good practice.

Cal listened to a few more tunes, singing along where he could. He watched for cops, but not in a worried or hopeful way. The Cal he had been just a few hours ago might have consciously or unconsciously done something to attract attention, so he might use one of the guns under his seat one more time before crossing the border. Now he felt like his old cautious self once more, and found himself wondering what had gotten into him. He had gone overnight from lovable old Cal to a psychopath who virtually salivated at the thought of hurting people.

He turned off the radio, counseled himself aloud in the ensuing silence. "It's just post-traumatic stress or shock," he said. "We all have it, in varying degrees, and we all deal with it in our own ways."

Cal sighed his relief at the label, even if it didn't fit.

"You got rolled, dude," he said to himself. "Twice. You were violated, victimized, you were robbed. You were in a state of shock when you killed Mikie and…"

Sarah had told him the name, but flipping through the filing cabinets in his brain wasn't producing any results.

"…and that other guy," he frowned. "You were still in shock when she told you his name, which is probably why you don't remember it. New experiences and knowledge were rolling off your consciousness like water off a duck, even when you killed Raul. When that crazy voice in your head kept telling you to hurt Sarah, it must have snapped you out of it. You're okay now. Hell, you're not even enjoying the cocaine."

CHAPTER 37

The enraged demon snapped, spit and charged its way through Heaven. It leapt from one cloud to another, sometimes sprinting on two feet and sometimes dropping to all fours to gallop through the mist like a mad animal. Every once in a while it would stop and stand in place, shaking clenched fists at the sky and screaming.

"The Walker Council!" he roared. "The Walker Council must die!" Anyone who heard it felt hot prickles down their spine, and promptly moved on to things more angelic.

At last a doorway opened, tall and grand and wide enough to admit an ordered army. They poured through the portal, hundreds of demons and devils and dragons armed to the teeth and collectively crying out for battle. The demon watched, still for a moment, as did a few haloed bystanders. Then the beast began to bay and beat its chest, and the bystanders sprouted beautiful white feathered wings and wisely flew away.

"The Walker Council!" he bellowed at the stream of crimson flesh still flowing steadily through the luminous doorway. "The Walker Council must die!"

"Hey you!" A comely devil with a spear and a leather armor dress that hugged her every curve called out to him. "You're with us!"

He began to lope toward her, then slowed his approach as the devil standing beside her became a towering black dragon. The comely devil climbed the dragon's massive foreleg, clambered over his shoulder and settled on his back. She motioned for him to follow.

The demon hesitated. "The Walker Council must die."

One gigantic eye peered at him, and the dragon's rows of teeth were revealed in a terrifying smile.

"Indeed," Laurentis boomed. "The Walker Council must die." The dragon's tremulous tones caused his ribs to tremble, and the demon launched itself to the dragon's scaled back. As soon as he was settled, they were in flight.

Heaven was not to be surprised. Already a league of angels were battling their way to the portal, flashing swords of light spraying hot purple blood all over the pretty white clouds. Paul stood near Ximena and watched, glad to see as many starburst explosions as he did splashes of blood. Most of the dragons had flown off to set the realm afire, but one held its ground near the doorway. It bit and slashed at the winged warriors, flaming them to nothing every time it got hold of one.

Paul took her hand. "I need to go. I have to find Kris."

She nodded. "I'll come with. I need Chase."

"Chase?" Paul frowned his confusion. "The new Walker?"

Ximena smiled. "In the stories, they will call him The Next Walker. I need to convince him to teach and lead and work to free the forgotten."

"Okay." Still confused, Paul nodded nonetheless. "What about the doorway?"

"Would you close it please?" Ximena watched the lone dragon fend off a small army by itself, watched the army continue to swell its ranks as reinforcements arrived.

"The last thing we need in Hell are a bunch of angels." she mused. "That would ruin even the best neighborhoods."

The portal collapsed, and they shifted together. Paul hadn't realized how loud the sounds of the battle had been until he stood in clouded silence.

"We must be close," he said, squeezing her hand. Even his voice was muffled, absorbed by the cumulus walls of the vacant lighted hallway. He moved forward, but after only a few steps a voice called out behind them.

"Paul! Walker King!" Sharp and strained, the voice was followed by another.

"Walker Paul!" This voice was lower. "We ran out of beer!"

By the time he had turned around they were upon him, Yarson giving Paul a crushing bear hug while Rikar shuffled his feet excitedly in place and waited his turn. They both seemed to realize who his companion was at the same time, and their knees dropped into the clouds as their heads bowed together.

"Queen Ximena," Yarson rumbled.

"Oh, bright and shining one," Rikar breathed. "You are returned."

"Rise, devils," she smiled, touching each of their shoulders before she did. "Time is of the essence, as always. We are looking for the imprisoned Walkers and Guides."

"So are we," Yarson grumbled. He held up a platinum key and echoed Paul's sentiment. "We must be close."

Paul smiled. "Let's go."

They weren't moving for long when they heard muffled shouts and the sounds of melee. Paul blurred ahead, then stood at the doorway laughing and gazing into the lighted open space. The others came up behind him.

The cage was transparent, but they could hardly see the prisoners through the thick streaks of bright blue blood that painted its walls. Most of the room was taken up by the huge black dragon, who was making a game of chasing council members into the arms of the enraged demon or the lithe devil that seemed to wait at every turn. Charine was caught up in the game, and poked at angels with her spear without piercing any hearts. Plenty of the blood on the cage and on their tunics had been drawn by her carefully placed jabs, but most of it had been sprayed haphazardly about by the demon's uninhibited rampage. All of the angels were bleeding, and two lay motionless in the drifting mist that was the floor. The blood glowed fluorescent blue wherever it puddled or streaked in thick dripping swaths.

Stephan was in a clouded corner, wielding a long blade of light warily whenever devil or demon came close. His white robe was stained in blue all down his left arm, and blood dripped from his empty fingers. He paled visibly when he saw Ximena appear beside Paul in the doorway, then launched himself at the rampaging demon with renewed vigor. Laurentis brought his tail around to catch Stephan along his ribcage and send him sailing into a nearby wall. The substance did not give at all, and the angel struck the wall hard and then the floor even harder. The dragon belched a stream of flame in his direction as Stephan fumbled about trying to rise, and the angel backed into a far corner once more.

Paul could hear the devils whispering as they came up the hallway behind them.

"She touched me!" Rikar said amidst a mad quiet giggle fit.

"Yeah." Yarson spoke lower, slower. "Me too."

Ximena called out to the dragon, her voice not without mirth.

"Laurentis," she sang, "I would set the prisoners free."

The dragon whipped his head about, smoke puffing from his nostrils. He frowned, but only a little, then craned his neck to see the clear encasement under him. William, Vanessa and Kris were crowded together in the middle of the space looking up at him. Laurentis changed, and stood on the transparent surface still watching the captives. He strode to the edge of the cage and stepped casually off the side, his knees bending like springs as he struck the ground. Expressionless, he took three more steps and found his place behind Ximena.

"My queen," he murmured.

She looked at the prison, at the bodies on the floor; she shook her head sadly.

"This will not do," Ximena pronounced.

By the time she finished the sentence, a fluid wave had washed over the entire space. The transparent cage was clean and clear, all traces of blood erased. Kris, William and Vanessa were free, and they rushed forward to embrace Ximena and Paul. Looking over his best friend's shoulder as he squeezed Kris tight to him, Paul saw eight unhappy but whole angels crowding the space within the transparent walls. He clapped Kris on the back, released him.

"I missed you," Paul said. He held the Guide's steady gray eyes to show he meant it.

"Me too," Kris nodded, his eyes going to Ximena. He smiled tentatively, then let the corners of his mouth fall into a frown as she shook her head. He knew what that meant, but he still had to ask.

"Jessica?" he ventured quietly, looking from one to the other once more.

Ximena shook her head again. "I'm sorry, Kris."

He sighed, in relief or in grief; Paul couldn't tell. The Guide stepped toward Ximena and gathered her up in his arms.

Paul grinned at William. "I missed you too."

William smiled and extended his hand. Brushing it aside, Paul embraced the old Walker for the appropriate three seconds. He stepped back, smiling.

"Sorry for the mess I left you," Paul said.

"No worries, boss," William quipped, waving his hand. "I think I've got everything pretty well handled."

Paul touched his hat, watching the old Walker curiously.

"William," he smiled, "did you just crack a joke?"

Vanessa drifted up to William and wrapped her arms about his waist. She smiled at Paul.

"Hello, Walker King," she said. "William is getting in touch with his sense of humor."

"And my feelings," William said, pulling her close.

Paul smiled, his eyes going to Ximena as they filled with tears.

"I see eight council members," Paul blinked, waved a hand at the prisoners. "Where is the ninth?"

Ximena turned and strode through the impenetrable wall like it wasn't there. Hands on her hips, she glared at Stephan. On the other side, they couldn't hear the questions she asked or the answers he gave. They did see him heft his long light sword as she turned her back, and they all rushed forward at various speeds. Pressed against the glassy wall, Paul and Laurentis sighed in relief as the others reached their view.

Without even turning, Ximena caught the long blade in her hand. She held it easily while Stephan wrenched and tugged uselessly at the other end. Then she did turn, and smiled just enough to show the angel her fangs and the twin infernos that were her eyes. Stephan let go the sword, falling back into the clustered bureaucrats. They watched him react to whatever she said, going pale and backing further into the other angels fearfully.

Stepping through the wall as if it did not exist for her at all, Ximena joined them on the other side once more.

"Walker Angel Andal stepped down," she frowned, met Paul's eyes. "Andre replaced him."

"Andre?" Paul was frowning too. "So where is Andre?"

Now she smiled a little. "Walker Chase killed him."

"Oh." His frown softened. "I like him better already."

Ximena nodded, still smiling and casually holding the sword the angel had attacked her with by the blade. She held it out, the hilt pointed in Charine's direction.

"Charine," Ximena said, watching the pretty devil light up at the sound of her name coming through those lips. "Would you help Laurentis keep an eye on the prisoners?"

Charine looked at the sword, at Ximena, then at the tall devil. Laurentis nodded when her eyes found him, and he even smiled just a little tiny bit.

"I cannot wield an angel's sword, my queen," she breathed. "I am a devil."

Ximena smiled. "You are a beautiful and bright being. You are not angel or devil or human; these are but outfits you wear along the way. Take the sword. Should anyone ask why you wield it, tell them you are my angel."

The spear she had brought with her was forgotten as it fell harmlessly to the clouded floor. Charine stepped forward and grasped the hilt of the proffered weapon, taking it gently from Ximena's hand. She hefted the blade, slashing at empty air to feel the sword's scant weight and perfect balance.

"I am Ximena's angel," she murmured, testing out the phrase as she tested out the blade. Charine let the sword hover still in the air as she looked between them again.

"I hardly think Laurentis needs my help with much of anything," she said, glancing at the sullen captives.

"He doesn't need your help," Ximena said quietly. "He desires your company."

"He does?" Charine's eyes went round at the thought, and she turned them on the dragon. "You do?"

"I do." Laurentis nodded, then met her eyes and smiled. "Your beauty shines with your bright rise, you fight and speak and walk with breathtaking conviction. I would keep your company so long as you desire mine."

She looked at the sword, then the dragon, then the queen.

Ximena was gone.

CHAPTER 38

Chase paced the misty floor, stopping every now and then to press his palms or pound his fists against a transparent wall. Daemon watched him, silent, his arms crossed over his chest. The other two captives sat calm together in a corner, talking quietly and laughing occasionally in the same hushed tones. Their placid state seemed to be feeding his restlessness. He stopped pacing to stand before them.

"Is it just age?" he asked, smiling at his own impatience. "How old are you? How many years did it take before you made peace with the way things are no matter how they might go?"

The woman smiled. "We are older than your history would believe. And no, it is not just age. David did not find his peace until we became angels."

The other matched her smile. "Lillian found her peace long ago, and she has been a touchstone for reality for both Marcus and me for some time. Without her, we would have both surely gone mad before he began to see or I sprouted wings."

"Marcus can see?" Chase asked, hopeful. "Can you?"

David shrugged. "I can now, but not like you or Marcus."

"What do you mean?" the new Walker pressed.

"I see the past," David explained. "My vision goes very far back, and I can see things that happened long ago as if they are playing out right now. Sometimes I get glimpses into the present, but they are not so clear. You are like Marcus, in that you can see anything happening anywhere so long as it is recent or current. You get glimpses of possible futures, but they are again only glimpses. You must be on constant alert, as must Marcus, to ensure that the best path is chosen."

Chase nodded. He glanced at Lillian.

"What about you?" he asked. "What do you see?"

Lillian's shrug was peaceful. Her smile was ecstatic. Her words were a quiet calm mystery.

"I see nothing," she smiled. "I see everything."

David's voice boomed out in laughter at Chase's befuddled frown. He clapped the Walker on the back with a surprisingly strong hand. Still chuckling, he tried to demystify her response.

"She sees the future," David explained. "Her glimpses are of whatever lies beyond the future."

Chase felt his frown deepen. "What could lie beyond the future but more future? Does that mean the future is fixed?"

Lillian shook her head. "What lies beyond the future is the past, Next Walker. The future is only fixed if the past is fixed as well."

The look on Chase's face caused David to burst out laughing once more. His mouth was uninhibited, his whole being went into every loud guffaw, and Chase found himself smiling despite himself.

"At last," David grinned, "someone who understands why my peace was so long in coming."

Chase began pacing again.

"The Watcher, the Walker and the Guide template was designed around you," he mused. "Imagine if we could all see so well."

David glanced at Lillian, and she nodded in solemnity.

"So what now?" Chase asked. "What does a man of action do when he cannot act?"

"He waits," Lillian smiled. "He waits for what he cannot see while he dwells in the thing we can all see if we look for it."

"Hope?" he asked.

She shrugged.

"Ah, yes." Chase smiled. "Love."

"And what am I waiting for?" he asked. "What is it that I cannot see?"

She held up one finger, her single word a trigger for another round of David's explosive laughter.

"Wait," Lillian said.

Chase put his hands impatiently on his hips. "Do we have time for you to explain how I might dwell in love while waiting for whatever it is I can't see coming?"

David grinned, and looked as though he may lose himself in another fit of mirth. Lillian shook her head, and her finger went from pointing straight up in the air to pointing over his shoulder.

The shimmering walls stopped shimmering as he turned, and Chase smiled at the eternal couple. He strode forward, speaking as he did.

"Walker Paul," he said. "We met before, I don't know-"

"Walker Chase," Paul cut him off. "The Next Walker. Do you know my companion?"

Chase felt the Stone Walker's crushing grip pumping his hand as his eyes went to the breathtaking devil.

He bowed his head. "You prefer Ximena, I hear?"

Her smile was even more breathtaking, her handshake a gentle firm grasp that set his whole body to tingling.

"I would hope that you of all people would not take this the wrong way," Chase ventured, giddy at the contact, "but I have always been a big fan."

Ximena turned a deeper shade of crimson. "You flatter me, Next Walker. Do you not realize that it is I who am an admirer of your work?"

Chase watched Paul go to the others; he had met Daemon, and the demon was introducing him to Lillian and David. Ximena gave them all a little wave over his shoulder, and Chase realized that everyone knew the devil in some way. While they exchanged pleasantries, Ximena spoke to him.

"Chase," the devil smiled. "I would ask the world of you."

He gulped, and answered honestly. "I would give it if I could."

"You can," she nodded. "You can teach Walkers to deal with demons and lights. You can teach Watchers and Walkers and Guides to see in their own ways, and to work together to make each team's vision complete."

Chase laughed a little uneasily. "The only things I can teach is how to drink and how to gamble. I'm afraid I would fail if I were to try anything beyond that limited wheelhouse."

He glanced at Paul. "And Walkers already know how to drink."

"You will not fail," Ximena responded. "Not if you try. I am certain of it. Will you do that, Chase? For the Walker's way? For the world? For me? Will you try to teach the Walkers?"

Chase bowed his head once more.

"Of course," he breathed. "I will try."

"Walker Chase!" Paul called out to him.

Chase turned to Paul, ready to correct him. The angels had taken his weapon and his key, and his spelled armor had transformed to regular old biker gear as his strength had ebbed.

In one hand, Paul held out a gold pocket watch; in the other was a sword. Chase grinned and dashed forward to seize the items and reclaim his identity. A wave of power washed over him, his leather growing firmer and getting lighter all at once.

Chase watched Paul dole out keys and weapons and armor to the angels, then glance Daemon's way.

"Do you fancy yourself a Walker, demon?" Paul said kindly, with a sly smile.

"Chase made me," Daemon said quickly. "With William's help. His key told him to. Please do not punish him. If you would pronounce judgement on that clear violation, punish me."

Paul shrugged. "I made Ximena a Walker. I just made two angels into Walkers. Would you question my judgement?"

Daemon shook his head and looked to Chase.

"Relax," Chase said. "He's just messing with you, like a person. Like a Walker."

"Did you have to kill him?" Paul asked Chase, curious.

Chase shook his head. "He was already dead. He had already begun to work on touching things, but once he learned to engage his Walker's will and strength he didn't have any problems."

Paul clapped Daemon on the back. "You are in good hands with the Next Walker. Glad to have you onboard. Any questions?"

"Will I have a Guide?" he asked, enlivened by the feel of the immortal hand on his shoulder.

Paul nodded. "You will. His name is Simon. You will find that the two of you have a lot in common."

Turning to Chase, Paul said, "Your Guide will be my former Guide, my best friend Kris. He will help you and William forge the new way of the Walker, along with Vanessa."

Chase frowned. "What about you?"

Matching his frown, Paul glanced at Ximena.

"If I am welcome," he said slowly, "I will be spending the rest of my life in Hell."

CHAPTER 39

For a little while, their biggest problem was keeping the mad demon occupied. It slavered and snarled and lunged repeatedly at the transparent walls, only to bounce off and charge at another angry angle. Charine stood near Laurentis; her swordless hand nearly touched his, but not quite. Each time the demon screamed its hateful mantra, they shared a little smile.

Charine began to speak a few times, but held her nervous forked tongue. She could not put the stories from her mind, or set aside her companion's legendary status for long enough to think of some triviality they might swap words about. Every time he smiled at the demon's cry, Charine's heart skipped a beat as she smiled back. Then he spoke at last, still watching the monster pound against the soundless invisibility, and she was glad for her hesitation.

"What they say about dragons seems to be true," he said, glancing at her and then away again. "At least it was in my case."

Charine waited for clarification, sharing another smile with him as the demon raked long talons across the cage. They say a lot of things about dragons.

"The Walker Council!" he screamed. "The Walker Council must die!"

Laurentis nodded, in agreement with the demon or with some inner resolution.

"I went mad with my own power," he said, "and nearly brought about my own demise because of it. Fortunately my power was greater than my madness, and I survived to seek a solution to unraveling the death urge within me."

The dragon fell silent, and watched the demon rage.

Charine watched the demon as well, but only to be polite. Her attention was on his words and presence as much as it could be while her gaze was averted. The stories told of his fierce and fearsome presence on any battlefield, but any conflict that he may have waged within was a story left untold. With both her celestial father and her loving mother here in Heaven with her, Charine prayed to both of them that he would go on.

"I began to integrate all the parts of myself into one whole," he said at last. She breathed out, suddenly realizing she had been holding her breath for some time.

"I sat in silence with myself," he said. "Mortals call it meditation, and I suppose that's the tool I used. I certainly didn't invent any technique; it's more like I found an existing thought sequence that had lain dormant within me. Once I activated it, my desires and my thoughts changed."

Now he looked at her, and it was almost too much. Charine had seen younger devils look away from her for some time now, or grow uncomfortable holding her eye. Even some of the older devils had begun to do it in the last few hundred years, and nearly all of them after the Stone Walker had so neatly jumped her soul upward. She had chalked it up to her rising state until her integration instructor had told her to expect it one day, long after that day had passed. Under his steady gaze, after that long glimpse of eternity that was looking in his eyes, Charine began to understand what those young souls must have felt. She was trembling, but she wasn't; and instead of looking away she stepped toward him and clasped his hand.

He poured into her, and she into him, and they gazed into each other's eyes while that calm rushing current flowed between them.

"Then I began to see you," he said quietly. "At first I just thought I was imagining some breathtaking young beauty, or remembering some devil I had caught a glimpse of. I watched your life like it was a human television show behind my eyes, watched you train and learn and love and lose; I watched you grow more beautiful over the centuries, and watched you turn every loss into a victory somehow."

Charine wanted to ask the dragon to pinch her, or bite her ever-so-gently; she was sure she was dreaming. The dragon was telling her her own story in reverse, except that she had known the star of her internal visions was real. How many times had she considered telling her integration teacher of the visions, knowing she never would? Even if some breathing technique or visualization sequence would banish the sights from her mind, guaranteed, she would never use it. Laurentis had been a part of her her whole long life.

Still lost in his eyes, Charine's heart devoured his words.

"I saw you begin to learn integration," he smiled, squeezing her calloused hand tenderly. "I wondered if you saw me behind your eyes as well."

Charine nodded, not trusting her voice.

"I began to see visions of a future where we were together," he continued, and she nodded once more. "I feared that I was going mad once more, living so much in this elaborate inner reality. Then I saw you, in the flesh. You were walking with the Watcher turncoat, telling him about the importance of loyalty."

Charine frowned. "I tried every subtle and not-so-subtle method of propelling that one down the right path. To no avail."

"I wanted to destroy him then, burn him to nothing and hold you at last in my arms," Laurentis hissed.

She sighed. "I wish you had."

"I got my chance with him," he said, smiling. "Now I would have my chance with you."

Laurentis knelt on the clouded floor, holding her gaze as he lowered his body. Without reaching into a pocket, he presented her a ring carved from midnight on his upturned palm.

"Would you be my lady, Charine?" he asked, forever gleaming in his eyes. "Would you let me cover your fingers in jewels and fill your life with love?"

If the lighted sword hadn't disappeared when she willed it, she would have tossed the damned thing into the clouds. It did, however, to her pleasant surprise; and Charine clutched the hand he proffered with both of her own.

"I'm not a dragon," she protested, cupping his hand but not taking the ring. "I know what that is; I cannot wear it."

"The only rules that apply to us are the rules we decide to apply to us," he said, placing his other hand gently over hers. "The rules of Heaven burn in dragon fire as we speak, and the rules of Hell will follow suit tomorrow. Tell me you have not seen glimpses of our future."

Charine nodded, tears streaming down her face.

"Impossible visions," she said, "of an impossible future."

"Tell me," he said, taking her left hand in his. He splayed her fingers with the feather trailing touch of his own.

"I saw us," she began, then sniffled, "I see us all of the time, living in the dragon city together. I see us with…with a family. I see me as a human, still living in Hell with you, then as an angel. I see so many lifetimes of love ahead of us. Impossible lifetimes."

While she spoke, he slipped the ring on her finger. It was as if the current that had been flowing between them multiplied in amperage or voltage or both, and Charine dropped to her knees to embrace him there on the misty floor.

"You there!" A voice called out. "You're not supposed to be in here!"

Two tall angels stood in the doorway, watching them embrace. They were both on their feet in a flash, but they stood their ground rather than act. Holding her hand, Laurentis glanced over his shoulder and smiled.

The enraged demon saw the angels at the same time as they saw him;

and as their eyes moved to view the cage's current captives, it beat its taloned fists against its broad chest and howled at the clouded ceiling.

"The Walker Council!" he bellowed. "The Walker Council must die!" Then he went to all fours and galloped toward them, thick strings of saliva dripping into the clouds every time his arms came down on them.

As the demon blazed past them, the angels shrank back through the doorway. Charine felt his arms around her once more, and she sank into his tender embrace and rested her head on his hard wide chest. She marveled at his gentle touch as he disengaged and turned.

Suddenly a huge black dragon was standing between her and the open doorway, and just as suddenly the doorway was bathed in flame. Charine heard screaming from the hallway, and edged around him to see. At last the dragon's breath ran out, and she could see the doorway once more. It was framed in flames; and as she watched, a burning angel burst through the door. His sword was a forgotten accessory, dangling from his huge limp hand as the flames engulfed him to rise crackling over his burning halo. A few strides into the room he tripped and fell to the floor, then lay there unmoving under a sheet of flames.

Laurentis heaved in another powerful breath, and Charine nudged his giant tail with her elbow.

"Let some of them through, would you?" She appeared the light sword again and waved it at the doorway. "You don't get to have all the fun."

As of in answer, a statuesque winged warrior dashed into the room. He looked at the dragon, then backed away as a fresh stream of flame cut off his exit and flooded the hallway. More screams rose above the crackling sound of burning clouds and angels, and the guardian angel turned to find a pretty little devil grinning and beckoning to him. He barely had time to wonder where she had gotten an angel's sword, or the dragon bone ring on her finger, before she was upon him. She slashed and stabbed and whirled a lethal dance before him.

Her sword glanced off his twice, giving off a quiet but impressive explosion of light each time. The other blurred movements had opened his white tunic in half a dozen places, and the neat wet slices were outlined in blue. The angel looked down, incredulous, as the network of gashes began to mend. Backing up, he bumped into the dragon's tail. Reflex or instinct twitched the huge serpentine muscles, and the angel was tossed stumbling toward her again.

This time her first motion brushed aside his sword, bursting a blinding fireworks display in his eyes. The angel didn't see the next moves to her fluid lethal dance, but he felt them. His throat was opened, and a gush of blue blood poured over his broad chest as the light blade was plunged into his heart. The angel exploded in a brilliant burst of light, and Charine turned to the dragon.

"Let two through next time," she complained, rubbing his rear haunches affectionately. "I can handle it."

She saw him watching out of the corner of one slitted reptilian eye as she danced with the next two angels. He filled the hallway with a wall of flames almost absently, his eye tracking them across the clouded floor. Both of the angels were bleeding, and tiring, while Charine danced a painful figure eight around them. She felt like they were naked and alone, the clouds and the fire and the angels all just a backdrop to the smooth rhythmic movement that she danced just for him. Burying the sword in one heart, then another, she winked at him as one burst of light turned to two.

The stream of fire ceased suddenly. Charine could see pretty far up the hallway, and it was all flame. She turned to Laurentis just as he turned into a devil, and saw Ximena between the dragon and the doorway. She had gathered even more companions.

Ximena kindly took a moment to introduce them all to Charine: first was the Guide's Guide, then the Next Walker; and then the First Watcher and the First Guide. Walker William and Guide Vanessa had the same humble demeanor she had read about, and it made her think of them both by name rather than laden them with a stack of prophetic titles in her bookish brain.

Ximena stepped to the glassy cage. As the walls shimmered one last time, she spoke to the cowering angels.

"Your political offices are all burned," she told them, "as are your homes. The lights you have enslaved are set free, and the army you paid to die for you is doing just that. I am left with a choice. Do I turn you over to the hands of those whose lives you have subjugated and whose sons you have forced into military servitude under threat of poverty? Or do I evaporate your filthy souls?"

"You do not rule in Heaven," Stephan said. He looked to his companions for support, but the other seven angels were content to huddle together and study the luminous clouds underfoot.

"You are exiled from this realm," Stephan said, his voice growing stronger. "God will not stand for this."

Ximena laughed. "What do you think I was made for?"

Charine moved as Ximena spoke, as did Laurentis. They each stood between the devil and the angel, out of the line of sight but angled for interception. No one was going to rush at her with a sword while they stood watch.

"I was separated from God by God's will and design," Ximena said. "I was not sent to the lower realms as punishment but to serve. We both saw the potential for creativity in the Great Separation, yet we also saw the dangers of subjugation. I went to Hell to ensure that the theme of life there would be finding one's purpose and fulfilling it. My theory was that souls dedicated to their own highest calling would naturally help others on their way to finding their own, and that fair trade and a robust economy would grow naturally from the seeds of principle."

Ximena glanced at Charine, briefly. She wondered if the devil had seen the love in her eyes.

"My theory was sound," Ximena said as her gaze found Stephan once more. "Hell was a vibrant utopia for so long that I committed the greatest of all sins: I became bored. I wanted something else, and so I left. The souls rising from Hell under my watch were self-sufficient innovators, free thinkers who had never known any other way to think. I came to Earth expecting to see a realm greater than the one I had left, a realm that combined the purpose of every soul with a hundred methods of shining light on that purpose. Instead I discovered a world enslaved by such deviously subtle methods that many of the slaves called themselves free, a world where those taking the coin call themselves servants while those giving it can only dream of such wealth as their masters hoard."

Ximena turned a slow circle, mist drifting at her dainty feet. She frowned.

"It's a bit stuffy in here," she mused, then waved her slender fingers absently. In an instant, the clouded walls around them dissipated and they stood out in the open in Heaven. Ordinarily that might be nice, and Charine had had glimpses of this place in her visions that had made her look forward to feeling glowing clouds underfoot while the very light of God shone on her face. Today Heaven did not look anything like she had imagined or foreseen.

Everything was on fire; well, almost everything. Turning in place, Charine could see flames in every direction. From close up to far as she could see, clouded structures burned and the air was choked with smoke. If she had closed her eyes and tossed a rock, it would have either landed in a fire on in a frenzied melee. Devils and demons were locked in combat with lights and angels, some fighting on burning clouds while others battled in the air. Charine had never seen so many devils aloft, and was not surprised to see that many of them faltered in their flight. Devils hate flying.

Except dragons, of course. Charine followed his gaze as Laurentis watched a red and a blue dragon working together to eviscerate any light or angel that got close enough. One dragon would seize an angel, chomping down on its head or clamping taloned claws down on the angel's shoulders; then the other dragon would disembowel the warrior from the belly up or just begin eating at the feet or groin. When enough damage was finally done to the angel's heart, there would be an explosion of light and they would both belch fire merrily; then they would switch, and the one who got to kill last would reach out fangs or claws to snag another victim. Both dragons were soaked in blue blood.

Laurentis watched the scene with an obvious mix of pleasure and envy for a little while, and Charine watched him as he did. They were both smiling.

Bursts of light filled the sky, swords or spears piercing angel hearts to put on a pretty lethal fireworks display. Blood was everywhere, blue and purple staining clouds and blades and clothes and drenching the fires to fill the air with a thick acrid stench. Horned heads dropped disembodied from the sky or rolled around on sticky clouds or found their way into the fire to burn along with everything else. Glorious battle scenes raged all around them, and Charine fought the same itch that she watched Laurentis resist.

"Let all the souls of Heaven hear me," Ximena said, and they did. Not everyone stopped fighting, but a few did.

"I am known by many names," she said, "but most here once knew me as God's counterpart."

"We call you The Other," Listene hissed behind her.

Ximena nodded at him, as if in thanks for the helpful information. Listene frowned and crumpled in disappointment.

"Of course," she smiled. "God is The One and I am The Other. How perfect is that?"

She glanced Charine's way again, and she nodded dumbly. Charine's nod was not so much in agreement as it was an affirmation of her starstruck state. Ximena could have asked her if she thought all angels should be transformed into doughnuts and would have likely gotten the same response.

"God and I both set out to guide the Earth plane to its own highest evolution," Ximena said to everyone. "We tried the direct approach for some time, and many an ugly tussle ensued. Then we withdrew from the middle, each of us vowing to no longer interfere in the lives of mortals. I set out to rule by serving, to help every last soul find their purpose and the means to pursue it. God was more pained by the damage of our efforts than I was, and withdrew even beyond Heaven's politics. God sought to rule by serving in a different way, by filling Heaven and all its denizens with light everlasting."

Ximena sighed. "God expected the highest angels to embody the highest ideals, as the light would shine on them the brightest. Yet as those souls fell they sought to use their greater power to take the light of those below them. Rather than pass on the love and light and hope that is God, these angels have hoarded it for themselves; and rather than honor what little everyone else had left, they taxed the last of the hope from your hearts and locked your creativity inside your servitude. Then these souls fell to Earth, where they learned to speak for God or for the people in soothing tones while taking what they wanted."

Some battles still raged on, but more and more died down as she spoke quiet words that everyone could hear. The sky was darker than ever with smoke, and the occasional starburst of light from a dying angel did little to light up the clouds. Many unarmed lights and angels had appeared while she addressed the realm, and soon a ring of them came together around her. As far as Charine's eyes could see in every direction, the huge halo of light formed by the gathering angels was the only bright light that remained in Heaven. Even the dragon fire was burning low, guttering out and smoldering with low constant irregular crackling sounds.

"Many of you feel that you do not belong here," Ximena said, "and you are right. The angels in power have taken the lights from their proper places and turned their labor into currency for themselves and their slaves. You have taken from these lights as your masters have taken from you, as the dragons in Hell have dealt in demons. You soothe your own conscience by telling yourselves that they have no souls. But do me a favor and consider this possibility: what if we are all one soul learning to know its many parts through separation? What if nothing we see or touch is without soul? How then should we act? How can we then see one part of ourselves caged by another part of ourselves and rest easy in our own confinement?"

Almost all of the fighting had stopped, and the ring of hovering angels about her had grown considerably. Ximena glanced at Charine once more, and she suddenly realized where the queen wished she could be. Her heart swelled all the more as Ximena spoke again.

CHAPTER 40

Chase had honestly never expected to see Heaven firsthand; he certainly hadn't anticipated that it might be on fire when he did. Busting in and trying to free the others had started out as a grand adventure only to end in epic failure. It had shown him nothing more of Heaven than some hallways with walls made of clouds and a cage that he couldn't even actually see.

Since being sprung from captivity, he had taken in as many sights and sounds as he could while taking as few lives as possible. Not many attackers had approached the clouded dais on which they all stood, and Laurentis or Walker Paul dealt with any threat with startling haste. The occasional silent explosion of light nearby signaled that an enemy had come too close, although it was difficult to tell which lightening attacker caused each burst. Chase wouldn't have even known what was causing the light show if he hadn't noticed each of them vacate their attentive posts for a hundredth of a second, using all his Walker tools of attention.

Every time one of the council members made as if to move, Chase would step forward menacingly and wave his sword at him. It was usually Stephan, and Chase delighted in it every time the angel fell back at the threat. He had found a way to help Ximena and still listen to her words. If Heaven felt the way he did about her speech, there was bound to be some cheering or commotion at some point, and Chase figured Stephan was just waiting for a chance to slip away.

The new Walker smiled grimly at the angel, waving the sword and letting him know that Chase was hoping he would move. He mouthed a series of increasingly vile insults at the angel, each silent sentence beginning clearly with the words "Try it, you…" and ending in a string of profanity that degraded the angel in every way he could think of. He didn't realize that Ximena had turned his way or said his name until she said it once more.

"Chase," she said, smiling. The new Walker snapped to attention.

"Would you help me show these lights their way home?"

Chase gulped, imagining a sky full of lighted doorways.

"I'm sorry," he said. "It's too much."

A hand fell on his shoulder, and Chase turned.

"Walker souls have been rising to Heaven for a very long time now," Paul said quietly, his hand still on his shoulder. "Not all of them came straight here after their lifetime as demon hunters, but many did. They know now how they failed, because of you. Feel them all around you, feel their wills galvanizing as one with yours. Feel my will behind you, Next Walker. Do what must be done."

Electricity crackled in his limbs, and Chase saw a thousand pieces come together within him at once. He held his arm out, up and out to the sky, and his key began to glow like a little pocket-sized sun. Portals began to appear, round and square and rectangular frames with glowing worlds beckoning from beyond. There was no need for prompting, as one light after another disappeared through this doorway or that simply because home lie beyond and they knew it.

"The worlds between worlds are calling to you," Ximena said. "Heed their call, enjoy the abundance that awaits you there. Let every light in Heaven hear my voice and know that you are free, that your purpose calls you. Step from your posts, cast aside your chains, and find your way home."

The sky was full of them, thousands turning to hundreds of thousands of lights streaking across the sky at every given moment. Chase felt his upturned face aglow with the bright illumination of millions of lights finding their way home. Some stopped near the cloud they stood on, taking brief humanoid form to give the Walker Council the last bitter piece of their minds; but most of those who stopped spoke words of forgiveness and understanding to the angels, or thanked Ximena. Some even thanked Chase, and soon his heart glowed brighter than his skyward visage. Most of the streaking lights cometed across the sky to plummet full speed through their chosen exit, however, and Chase watched them like it was pieces of his own heart going home.

When he had become a Walker not so long ago, Chase had felt so enlivened and awakened that his every cell seemed to tingle with the power; now his whole body seemed to vibrate as he harnessed the will of countless Walkers. He was a happy open conduit, the hollow bone through which their power flowed. His mind was a thousand minds, each holding open a set of doorways and watching every light that slipped through. Somewhere in the vast network of thoughts that he had to choose from, it occurred to him that all of the Walkers should see this.

As he thought of it, it was so. Walkers from around the globe suddenly appeared all around him, standing on clouds that were not only no longer burning but beginning to glow again. The smoke in the sky was clearing, and bright light was spearing through the remaining smog in a handful of spots. Their eyes to the sky, the Walkers bolstered his will and confidence even more; and the Next Walker felt free to throw a glance at Ximena.

He was glad he did.

A light had stopped to talk to her. As Chase let part of his dynamically layered attention focus on them, he heard the light's concern as it was voiced.

"I feel a world calling to me," he said, wringing his hands and throwing a wistful glance at the portal in question. "I don't want to go through it without my counterpart. I lost her long ago, but I have always hoped to find her again. I know I belong in another world; but even more deeply, I know I belong with her."

Chase saw her glance at Paul and smile.

"I think I understand," Ximena said. "Do you see those lights hovering near doorways, uncertain? They are waiting for their counterparts as well."

He hadn't noticed before, but Chase saw them now. Hundreds of lights stood still in the sky, close to one portal or another while not blocking its flowing ingress. The light glanced up at them and then back at Ximena.

She pointed again.

"See the demons gathered in the clouds below?" she asked.

Once again, Chase followed the light's eyes. He frowned as the angel nodded. The demons that had stopped fighting had gathered under the collection of hovering doorways. As one, they gazed wistfully at one portal or another.

"I see them," the light said. "She is not among them."

"What if she was?" Ximena asked plaintively. "What if one of them was your counterpart, and you were trapped in Hell or killed in battle or unable to resist the call of home? What if all those demons below are like your love, waiting for the one being that cares for them to find them and take them to the next world?"

The light was looking down at them, fear battling concern to dominate his features. Every one of them had fangs and talons; many had swords or spears that still dripped with luminous blue blood. He gulped.

"I should help them, then?" The light asked the question like he hoped it would be brushed aside.

"No one can tell you what you should do," she said. "That is what your heart is for."

He nodded. "Very well. My mind fears that they will attack me, but my heart longs to go to them."

Ximena placed her hand on his shoulder, and he brightened visibly.

"If they attack you, I will come to your aid," she assured him, with the confidence of a parent dismissing the monster in the closet. "I will gather your bright soul up in my arms and take you to your love and then home myself."

The last of his apprehension melted away, and the light stepped from her side to drift to the clouds below. Chase kept his eyes to the sky, and soon he saw the light float upward past them again. He had a demon in his arms, and he carried it to the doorway that one of the monster's long talons pointed insistently toward. When they got close the demon leapt from his arms to disappear through the portal, and the light descended once more to aid another.

After three or four similar trips, the lights that hovered overhead began to drop from the sky to the demons below. One after another, angels descended to lift them up and take them home. The clouds began to glow brighter than ever, and the light was shining like Chase had never seen. Nearly every fire had sputtered to nothing, and the smoke had cleared or dissipated or burned up in the light. The fighting had not just ceased; angels and devils gathered with demons and lights and Walkers on clouded islands, talking quietly together and tending to the wounded. Bloodied weapons had been cast aside absently or shamefully, and unlikely groups came together under the light to shake hands and talk and embrace.

Chase felt his many minds rejoicing as one at the scene. He held the doorway open still, but most of the lights and demons that wanted to go had gone. He glanced at the remaining council members for the first time in what seemed like ages. They looked deflated, defeated and not likely to move under the watchful gaze of the Stone Walker and the black dragon.

CHAPTER 41

Paul watched the Walker Council with one eye and Ximena with the other. He was resolved not to let any of the angels or any of her words escape him. As the doorways began to collapse in on themselves and disappear, as the last of the lights disappeared through them, angels began to fill the sky. Ximena spoke, and they all heard.

"Your currency became the lives of others after I left," she said sadly. "These angels had opportunity to correct a tragedy borne of ignorance. Instead they capitalized on it, enslaving the innocent and subjugating the entire realm. They dealt in souls, right out in the open, with those they called evil or enemy. Yet the evil was their own, and their actions made it clear that the only enemy was them. They gave power to those that would wield it as directed, and took it from those that would show you the truth."

Ximena sighed. "From the bitter light's perspective, it would seem that only the guilty remain in Heaven. Nearly all of you benefited from their toil, although you were surely too caught up in your own endless toiling to notice. What might I do to make an impression that might last long enough to undo lifetimes of conditioning? Shall I reverse the power structure to see how well the public servant can actually serve? With the work of a thousand souls on their shoulders, how many would delight in watching their former masters crumple under the weight? Shall I imprison them with no comforts, under the threat of daily violence and rape? Shall I press them into war without proper education or training, to do evil in my name and carry those scars for life while trying to raise a family broken and broke?"

Ximena pointed at Stephan. "Shall I treat them as they have treated you?"

It was a good thing so many lights had gone home. The luminescence of Heaven was bright like Paul had never seen before. Rather than blind him or warm him, the excess of light seemed to soak through his leather and skin to sink into his very bones. The lights that remained cheered Ximena's harsh sentence, but they were few and far between. Much of the glow came from the angels that had gathered, and they shifted uneasily at the thought of punishment for privilege. As the brightness in the sky reached incredible intensity, the glow gathered at one place to burst forth from the clouds. The voice that came with it was a familiar stranger to him, and its words seemed to sound in his mind as clearly as they rang in his ears.

"Ximena," the voice said, not unkindly. "Your compassion wears thin."

Her brow furrowed, then she grinned up at the sky.

"So it does," Ximena said, with a shrug.

"Somehow your creativity and generosity never find their way into the stories," the voice mused, still with kindness. "It's always fire and punishment, damnation and deception. Why is that, my dear counterpart?"

Ximena laughed easily and shrugged once more.

"Serve your realm as you will," she said, "as I will serve mine."

If a cloud could sigh, this one did. Its voice was full of love as it spoke again, but there was a hint of sadness.

"Why must we always seem to be at odds?" it asked. "You light your realm with your love just as I do mine."

"Actively," she responded, waving a hand at the gathered souls. "I do not force anyone down any path, but I do not stand by as others try to take up that task either. I help souls find their own purpose, their own meaning. I give them the tools to propel them towards that meaning. I watch these souls grow and change, evolving into something altogether different through their journey. What do you do? Watch? Wait?"

"My dear Ximena," the voice said, with nothing but sincerity and gentle kindness texturing the words, "I have seen what you are doing, and I am as pleased with it as I could be. But I am not just watching, nor am I simply waiting. The spark that you long to see in everyone's life is not easily woven into the fabric of the soul. Each purpose must be crafted to perfectly suit the individual, and to do the appropriate amount of reminding. Too much, and such frustration ensues that nothing gets done; too little, and such laziness ensues that nothing gets done. More and more souls come here from other realms every day, curious about this process playing out in our lonely little corner of the universe. That process is of no one's interest more than mine, or yours, for that process is the one you insisted we begin."

Ximena's whole face was lit up with the glow, her dark horns absorbing the light like happy antenna.

"You craft each soul's purpose?" she asked, her voice full of wonder. "When I see that light in their eyes, is that because you put it there? When I see a soul evolve, is it because of you?"

"Evolution is not there because of me," God responded simply. "Evolution is me. When you see that light in their eyes, you are looking at me."

"Look behind us," the voice suggested gently. "Rather than always looking ahead at how far we have to go, look back at how far we have come. Violence did not abhor you so much not so long ago; and causing the bumbling apes that souls used to be to do anything creative was simply too much to ask. Now we are both watching less violence happen in all the realms, save the occasional war. Individuals are treating each other with kindness more than ever, despite the mounting pressures of society that concern you. The oversoul is evolving, formed by your frustration at that which you see as being wrong combined with my certain hope that everything will be all right. It does of course require time in which to do so."

When Ximena glanced at the council members this time, her eyes were lit with love rather than anger.

"If only I could say I have not committed sins as great as your own," she smiled.

"These angels have lived a great long time in these bodies, with these memories," the voice considered lovingly. "As they fell they made new rules, and the only rising soul saw fit to rise above the entire situation recently. I would think that they would be the lowest of angels if they were to pass now, or falling humans. Perhaps they will find themselves in your realm, with no memory of this long life and no explanation for your treatment of them."

Stephan's eyes widened as the voice spoke, but the other angels all frowned in confused consternation. Their faces froze that way for a moment, then disappeared in eight bursts of light. Paul shielded his face against the fireworks.

"Walker King," the voice intoned. Paul straightened, tilted his hat.

"I would pass that title to one more worthy," Paul said. "Walker William serves the Walker's way as a king should. I used my power to find what I wanted, for me. I have found her. Now my only desire is to remain by her side. The only reason I would use my power now is to fulfill that desire, and that is not very kingly of me."

"You have learned much in a very brief time."

"It didn't seem so brief," Paul grumbled happily. "And I would say that I have much to learn, at the risk of quoting the Walker that I would nominate as king."

They were all there, Paul had noticed them appear during the mass exodus of lights. The Walkers started to cheer his words; first a handful, then all of them. He glanced at William, a grin stretching his lighted face. The old Walker was shaking his head and clearly fighting a smile.

"I would serve the Walker world in any way that it needs serving," William called out, "except that."

The clamor died down as quickly as it had begun.

William's eyes found the sky. "Is there any way that Walker Paul might remain king and counsel us?"

"There are some souls that never fall or rise beyond certain boundaries," the voice responded. "For the sake of all of life we never pass into new bodies or lose our memories. I would extend this honor to three souls on this day, given that each of you agree to the conditions I set forth."

The voice paused, and the light swelled.

"Walker Paul," it said, and he stepped towards it involuntarily. "Your soul shall rise and fall alongside Ximena's as you wish. You shall reside solely in Hell. Should you attempt to rise above the highest level of Hell, you shall pass into the next life and lose all memory of this one. Do you accept?"

Paul turned to Ximena. "Do you want me with you?"

She nodded once. "Always."

"Forever?" he smiled.

Ximena mirrored his smile. "Always and forever."

He raised his eyes to the sky once more.

"I am happy to accept the terms," he responded. "But how am I to deal with demons or turn Walkers from Hell?"

"You won't," the voice responded with kindness. "You will act as liaison and advisor to any Walker that would come to you. You will work with Ximena and Walker William to help the Next Walker educate your army of immortals. Your key will no longer count down to demons, and you will turn over all of the keys you have gathered to Walker William except one."

Paul cocked an eyebrow. With each pronouncement he felt a shift within him, and he watched inner doorways of possibility slam shut as he was ushered down the hallway of his destiny. The last shift was a buoyant weight lifted from his heart, dozens of starfire spots of consciousness drifting away in a bittersweet goodbye after lifetimes in his care. He saw William stir and close his eyes for a moment, and Paul knew the burden would lift the old Walker just as it had lifted him.

Paul held his gloved palm out, and the gold disc glinted in the great bright light. His platinum key was a part of him, he saw that now more clearly than ever; its destiny spoke in his ear as if it were his own, and perhaps it was. He no longer needed to look at it because he somehow always looked through it now; yet he knew he would spend long happy hours peering at it in wonderment nonetheless. The golden object in his hand was different, a friendly alien consciousness that spoke someone else's internal dialect. He looked at it as he held it up.

"So who is this for?" he asked the shining cloud.

"Charine," the voice said. The devil looked up, startled.

"Me?" she asked.

"You have done much to master yourself and your life," the light said to her. "Should you pass, this realm may lose you altogether. Would you join my desire to your own, and remain in this life as Walker forevermore?"

Looking closely, Paul thought he could see the comely devil's tail trembling slightly at the tip. Her eyes were no longer on the sky as she spoke, but on Laurentis.

"In what realm would I reside?" she asked.

"You may go where you wish," the voice responded.

"What if I wish to raise a family?" she asked. Charine hesitated, her eyes still on Laurentis. "With a dragon?"

"Of course," the cloud glowed brightly. "Did you not know that when a devil becomes a Walker she is able to mate with a dragon? Isn't that right, Ximena? I'm sure that's written down somewhere that is very, very sacred."

"Of course," Ximena giggled. "I remember."

Charine looked up at the sky at last.

"What do I have to give up?" she asked. "What are my conditions of eternity?"

"Don't leave us," the voice answered simply. "This world needs you."

Tears streamed down her face as Charine moved to embrace the dragon. He bent, wrapping her in his long arms and holding her close to him. Paul smiled and turned to William.

The old Walker frowned and shook his head sternly.

"Walker Chase," the voice said. The new Walker started, glanced around him.

"Um," he said, "yeah?"

"You are standing there imagining that every soul here wishes it were next, that Heaven will be filled with disappointment when I make my final pronouncement. You imagine that anyone would do anything for forever." The voice fell silent while Chase stared up at the sky in wonderment. Paul couldn't tell if it was Chase's smile or God lighting his face. His smile broadened as the voice spoke again.

"Isn't that right?" it asked.

"Of course," Chase breathed. "There is so much, especially to this life. Forever is only barely enough time for it all."

"Not all souls feel that way, Next Walker. There is a weariness that takes hold that can only be shed by moving on and letting go. Most souls look forward to that as much as they do every other part of their journey, even if they do not remember it until they dwell in it. You see life a different way than most, and I would have you see it forevermore."

"Okay," Chase nodded. "Conditions accepted. Are there any?"

CHAPTER 42

Chase was the first one through the huge portal he created, and stood back to watch the ranks stream through it behind him. He had hardly needed the key to open the passage; or perhaps the key had hardly needed him. Regardless, the single doorway was easy to hold open no matter its size and traffic; the act that would have been an impossible dream to him a week ago was reduced now to an afterthought in his quicksilver eternal mind. Demons and devils and Walkers flowed into Hell, as did a few dragons. All of them looked changed by what they had seen. Chase certainly was.

Among the last through the portal were the ones who most needed to see what awaited them. As the weary wounded warriors lined up in bedraggled rows, they faced a fresh army of demons and dragons set to advance on them. There were a few devils swelling their ranks, but it was the other fearsome figures that Chase felt his eyes returning to over and over. Even the small dragons were terrifying, and the larger ones just looked like ridiculously overgrown killing machines. Most of the demons were huge as well, though not ancient dragon size. Chase figured the large leading ground troops averaged about twelve to fourteen feet tall and surely tipped whatever scale you could get them onto at over a thousand pounds. They were muscle-bound monsters in leather, and many had somehow gotten their hands on weapons that matched their size. Swords as tall as people and shields as big as cars dotted the crowd.

Chase could not have been more relieved when William and Daemon came through, followed by Laurentis and Charine. By the time Paul and Ximena materialized together, the black dragon was already in the air. He floated high above the open space between the two armies, drifting with the occasional flap of his powerful wings. Charine sat astride his back, perched as though she had been riding a dragon for centuries.

There were still devils returning, and Chase held the passage open for them while he moved closer to Ximena and Paul. The Stone Walker nodded to William.

"They are already gathered," Paul said, pointing. "Would you see to it that your army vacates this realm or handles themselves with utmost caution if they must stay?"

William shook his head. "No one is leaving, and no one is holding back. You stand behind the rightful queen of this realm, and we stand behind you. I will go to my people, and there I will await your orders."

It looked to Chase like maybe William's hand was trembling a little, but the old Walker turned and strode away before he could be sure. Chase wondered if he might have survived more dragon encounters than anyone alive, and if the Walker health plan covered post traumatic stress disorder. His wonderings scattered when Ximena spoke.

"We are weary," she said, both to her army and the opposition. "We have battled angels this day, and those battles have taken their toll. Yet we did not simply fight; we won. We did not simply battle; we triumphed. We did not just bring our enemies to their knees, we brought justice to their realm and freedom to their people. We did not just see the power of the righteous cause; we heard the very voice of God cheer our efforts."

Chase smiled. It sounded so pretty, the way she told it. The doorway was no longer vomiting devils, so he closed it so he might pay closer attention to her colorful interpretation. The devils behind her cheered, and the ones crammed in between gigantic monsters across the way began to exchange nervous glances. Her words seemed to have little effect on the dragons or the demons, except to incite them. A few dragons belched flame at the sky, and some demons began to howl wordlessly, but they were drowned out by the thunderous cacophony of happy cries.

"Those that would reconsider their allegiance," Ximena continued, "may do so at any time. Retreat to safety or take up arms against those you wish you did not stand beside. Those that would stay true to the cause of slavery, or whose imagination cannot see a world without subjugation, will all die this day. The Next Walker will help all of the demons that want to find their way home when this is all over. Those demons that have grown by consuming others will be separated from those they have consumed through a peaceful process if they lay down their arms. Otherwise be warned: you will surely die twice. The first death will likely be quick, as the tireless Walker army tears easily through your ranks. The second death will come at the hands of those separated from you by the first, and will surely be long and painful."

Ximena turned her back on the opposition, although they still heard her words. She spoke as if she addressed only her army, but the power of her message touched them all.

"We are strong in numbers," she said, "yet numbers are the very least of our strengths. We have the oldest and greatest dragons on our side. Nothing in the Universe is more powerful than a self-actualized dragon, and they all stand behind us. They are few because most dragons are self-serving and eventually self-destructive. Their ranks are swelled with this type of dragon, too full of their own hubris to realize that they came here to die this day. The few dragons that are with us consider all life in all realms to be as precious and sacred as their own. It is clear that they have more dragons, just as it is clear that we have more dragon power."

A cheer arose as she pointed to the sky. Laurentis made for a fine example, a beautiful gigantic weapon of mass destruction drifting peacefully overhead.

"Is there a devil here who does not know of the mighty Laurentis?" Ximena called out over the clamor. "Has ever a war been fought in this realm where he did not fight on the side of justice? Has Laurentis ever been a part of a losing army? Now the great dragon has found his love, a warrior who fights with as much conviction and ferocity as he does. If those two had their way, they would send us all home and vanquish our enemies themselves."

There was a ripple of laughter amongst the cheering, then the cheering grew louder as Laurentis filled the sky with fire.

Ximena's voice went louder, riding the rolling din like a surfer riding a wave. Rather than cutting through the clamor, her words were the clear lyrics to a song whose sole instrumentation was thousands of raised voices and the endless off-beat clanking of armor, and rose over it.

"Walkers do not gather unless the cause is clearly righteous," she said, "and even then, Walkers seldom interfere in the lives of any realm. Yet here they stand, every Walker that lives, prepared to fight by our side. Alone they could take Hell today; they could best this army we face with little or no loss of life, as I am sure many of these great warriors are itching to do."

The Walkers had been standing by, stoic and calm. A few smiles broke out among them as she spoke, and by the time she finished praising them they were cheering too.

"If we were left alone this day," she cried over the thunderous sound, "with no dragons and no Walkers, we old devils would surely triumph. Those of you who remember a world of personal responsibility, those of you born too late to know it but whose hearts long for it, those of you who would live in a realm lit by love rather than the burning corpses of your brothers and sisters, I know you. Our hearts are the same, and if there were only two of us I would fight by your side for your freedom and mine to the very end. Yet there are not just two of us, there are many of us, and we know what our enemy has never learned. We know how to reach into the very depths of ourselves for the sake of something higher, something greater than us. We know that their darkness will evaporate in the light that we bring. We know that the fires that burn today are not burning the lands or its peoples; the fires that burn today burn those that have done the daily burning. We devils could tear apart this army if left here alone with them."

Ximena was shouting now, and grinning, as the stone beneath them trembled with the sounds of agreement.

"Yet we are not alone, are we?" she cried. Somehow the deafening roar grew louder. "We have the Walkers, we have the greatest of the dragons, we have the Stone Walker and even God on our side."

When she said "God", Ximena threw her arms apart in a wide embrace that seemed to encompass the entire realm. The sky was lit by a beautiful brilliant glow, and rays of bright white light speared through the smoke to touch the scorched rock at their feet. Everywhere it reached the ground, a little plant or patch of grass sprouted.

By the time she turned around, there were very few devils standing on the other side of the field. Not all of the dragons were gone, but enough had slunk away to make a noticeable difference. The gargantuan demons all stood their ground, save one. It had rushed forward as she spoke, impatient for the fray. Barely shifting in flight, Laurentis had adjusted his attitude slightly to swoop in with a fountain of flame.

The demon burned in a fiery flash, to be replaced by a half dozen regular-sized monsters. As if to illustrate Ximena's earlier point, five of them converged on one in a whirlwind of blood and flesh.

As they tore the monster apart, Laurentis circled round to turn the gory assemblage to ashes. The remaining opposition watched them burn but stood their ground. Those that were going to leave had left. As the smoke cleared, a giant blue dragon came forward.

"You left us," he rumbled, his voice deep and tremulous. It didn't have the magical effect that hers had, to find its way to every ear and burrow into every mind. It was loud and clear nonetheless, and even from across the wide open space Chase felt his bones jangle with the sound. He glanced at Ximena, saw her frowning.

"You left us," the dragon said again, "and we did what we had to do to survive without you. While you were gone we have worked hard to make a workable society. We did not have your magick or some stamp of approval from Heaven to feed us and clothe us, and the rules you left were so simple. Times change, and those of us that have changed with them would be fools to give up our vast holdings for some pretty principle. Our system may have flaws, but it is ours. We are mighty, and we aim to keep it."

While the dragon spoke, Chase noticed Ximena lean in to say something to Paul. He listened in without thinking, his curiosity heightening his hearing instinctively.

"Many devils left," she whispered, "and even some dragons. We might just stand a chance."

Paul's look was a perfect out-picturing of what Chase felt when he heard the words. His eyes went round, and he frowned.

"Are you serious?" Paul whispered back. "But you said…"

She poked him, mirroring his frown.

"I can't really say I think we're all about to be fried by dragons," she hissed.

Paul looked around then, and it was the same moment that the dragon's voice died down. Another deep rumble began, and Chase realized it was the army beginning to clear the gap. The crack of thousands of dragons' wings flapping filled the air, and Chase felt himself shudder even as Paul's eyes fell on him. He gave the Walker King a wink and a nod, then pointed to the sky. First it was just smoke and dragons, and Charine firing arrows at the five winged forms converging on Laurentis and her. Then doorways began to open, and lights poured out of them like rivers.

Chase broadcasted his distress signal through the doorways, and his own immortal army spilled forth to engage the enemy dragons. They swirled around them, overwhelming the monsters in sheer numbers and disorienting them with the flashing fireworks display of their movement. As the Walker army flooded forward to meet the gargantuan demons first on the battlefield, streaming quicksilver spirits lit the sky above them with luminescence while tearing dragons to pieces and raining blood down on the battle below. The blood was blue and purple and plentiful, and covered the crimson skin of the devils as they came up behind the Walkers. Sheets of slick stickiness layered many of the devils before they even reached the fray.

Chase had watched Paul pause to kiss Ximena on the cheek before dashing off in a dizzying blur even Chase couldn't track. He imagined that the Stone Walker might have waited to see what was coming next if he had known what was coming next. Chase was pretty sure he would never forget the image, even if he indeed lived forever. Ximena threw back her head and cried out a name he had heard before, three times and louder with each repetition.

"Roche!" she cried. "Your exile is lifted! Roche! Your home needs you now! ROCHE!"

A huge devil appeared at the sound of the last name, as tall and wide as the demons being torn apart and tearing apart others on the battlefield. His horns were huge, long and curved and daunting. Massive canines showed when he smiled down at her, and the curved sword in his hand surely weighed as much as Chase did. Giant leathery wings unfurled behind him, and suddenly they were flapping and he was gone. Chase watched Ximena's hair pressed flat in the downdraft, then saw an explosion of light and blood in the sky some ways away. It was followed by another violent burst, then another. Then Chase turned, in time to see Ximena's own glorious transformation.

She burst forth from her own skin, and for a moment there was nothing but dark swirling smoke where she had stood. Watching the darkness, Chase felt his eyes go round as the towering cloak of wings and teeth and claws and burning red eyes rose above him.

In the next moment she was gone, and Chase was left watching a dark streak flash across the sky towards the nearest dragon. It was engulfed in her completely, and began to scream as it fell from the sky. Sets of gashes appeared all over the dragon's body as they dropped together, raining more blood on the battle below. The lights that had been attacking the dragon drifted away, or found another target; and somewhere between them being clear of it and the violent cloud hitting the ground, the beast burst into flames. The fire was hot and fast, and the cloak of fangs left nothing but ash to drift into the fighting.

Chase watched the Walkers and devils on the ground for a few minutes, wondering if maybe he should join the fight. He didn't want to close the doorways, or interrupt his distress call, since lights were still coming to their aid to tip the balance. While he watched more than one Walker went flying, cut in half by some monstrous demon with a monstrous sword. The devils were not faring nearly as well, dozens falling in a moment's raging stampede of hate and steel. They fought on as their brothers and sisters fell, bravely pushing forward and barely slowing the demons they met as they did.

This was the realm where the demons were at their strongest, and their peaking power showed in the way they fought. There were so many demons and so few Walkers by comparison; the devils were losing numbers at an alarming rate, and less lights dotted the sky with every passing minute.

Chase had to consider the possibility that the lights were not enough as he turned his eyes to the sky. The dragons were shredding and chomping and burning them with rapid-fire precision, and most of the blood raining down on the fighting below was blue now. A few dragons had broken free of the cloud of violence to zig-zag back and forth through the fray behind a sheet of flame. The sky was lit by the network of fire, and burning lights fell from the sky with the blood and ashes of their fallen comrades.

On the ground, every demon that was overcome by a mound of devils or a streaking flash of Walker steel spewed a fountain of purple blood to be replaced by four or five or six fresh demons. Some of them turned on each other, but most turned on the nearest Walker or devil. They couldn't wield the giant sword or heft the humongous shield the monster demons had carried, but nothing stopped them from choosing from the selection of devil arms that had collected at their feet. They were all covered in blood from angels and dragons above and the dying and dead all around them. From a distance it was hard for Chase to tell who was demon and who was devil, and the only Walkers he could pick out for sure were the ones in blood-drenched cowboy hats. Then he lifted his eyes to the sky once more, and an involuntary cry escaped his lips.

"No!" he screamed. "Laurentis! Walkers! DRAGONFIRE!"

He watched the three dragons that had broke apart from the overhead fray come together toward the battlefield from three angles. As they converged, they dipped low and breathed flame.

A wide sheet of blazing inferno spread out before them, with such searing heat and deafening sound that Chase was driven back a step from far away. The layers of burning roar and sharp crackling were not the only sound he could hear, however; tortured strained screams rose in the wake of the dragons' smooth destructive glide.

Chase was relieved to see a network of blurs streaking back and forth before the flame. The Walker army was not simply saving themselves; they were moving their allies to safety one or two at a time, throwing devils and demons over their shoulders and running them to a stretch of rock nearly a mile away. Thousands of Walkers made a handful of such trips as he watched, and Chase looked up just in time to see the trio of dragons meet their fate.

Ximena was streaking toward them from one angle, a long streaming cloak of darkness and fangs and talons set to meet them head-on. Roche was coming up behind them, a giant winged warrior with a sword that could likely take them all in one swing. It was Laurentis that reached them first; or rather, it was his flame. Charine stood upright on his broad shoulders, firing arrows through his flame as they approached. The shafts caught fire as they passed through the sheet of flame; and by the time the fire touched the first, all three of them had a half dozen flaming arrows stuck in their scaled hides. Then the fire washed over them like a wave, and they became three dark falling winged fireballs that struck the burning rock and exploded.

The fire continued to spread, and thick smoke filled the air along with the stench of burning blood. Chase had a moment of detached reflection as his mind tried to withdraw from the horrors that assaulted his senses, in which he was grateful that at least most of the bodies disappeared in death before they could burn. Then there was a click and a clack in his mind, audible only to him, as another realization struck him.

Both the devils and the lights that had fallen had surely risen by now. Devils would be appearing all over Hell, just as lights would be awakening in their own realms. Those that had not shifted direction or graduated to another reality would remember their life and the battle. Even the demons would be beginning new lives, but with their lights there to guide them.

As another set of dragons approached the fresh ground battle with a joined sheet of flame, Chase opened yet another series of doorways. He sent out a more complicated and, if possible, more urgent distress call. While he watched Ximena turn the team of winged flamethrowers into a harmless cloud of drifting ash, Chase watched the doorways with his other eye. He waited, holding his breath.

The lights came first, flooding the sky once again. There were more than before, and the dragons' numbers had diminished noticeably. They overwhelmed the flying monsters immediately, and the sky glowed with the brilliance of what looked like one gigantic busy light. Then devils and demons began to stream through the new doors, looking more interested in fighting by each other's side than in battling each other. They were fresh and clean and coming to fight with bows and arrows instead of swords and spears. As soon as the dragons got a handle on the lights by flaming and clawing and biting frantically until the big bright light became a series of small ones dotting the sky, a cloud of arrows filled the air. It was followed by another flaming volley, and then another. Once again the battle on the ground moved slowly as the battle in the sky rained fresh fire.

The dragons flew at the devils, directly into the endless rounds of flaming shafts. A few faltered in flight, and two fell, but the rest descended on the army with flame and fangs. As they did, a cloud of flaming arrows found them in flight from behind. Chase watched Walkers and devils and demons lining up in orderly ranks and loosing arrows across the field of fire.

Some dragons turned to face the army they had left behind, reversing their course to close the gap as it was filled once more with arrows. The rest landed amidst devils and demons Chase had called forth, writhing through the crowd to leave a trail of smashed and bloodied bodies in each dragon's deadly wake. Just a few hundred dragons devastated the countless numbers of devils and demons that had come forth in minutes, and they were rising into the sky to cross the field of fire and similarly devastate the other army. The first of the returning dragons were spewing fire as they approached, and the Walkers were once again blurring back and forth to carry others to safety. The last few dragons that lifted off doubled back to incinerate the few surviving archers and the ground they had stood on. There was nothing but fire as far as he could see in two directions, and it looked like yet another field was set to burn.

Then a fresh stream of lights poured from the portals in the sky, and the dragons were overwhelmed once more in the air. They fought viciously and valiantly, but they were less than before. Ximena and Roche and the few dragons fighting with them were making a bigger dent in their numbers than ever, as the math shifted in their favor. A fresh army of devils emerged before the lights could be extinguished, and the dragons began to fall from the sky like bleeding burning pincushions. Ground troops swarmed the monsters as they fell, dealing a swift and sure or slow and bloody demise.

It seemed like days of raining blood and dancing fire and choking smoke to Chase, watching the dragons fall until only a few remained. He felt exhausted and enlivened through it all, taxing the limits of his mind to continually flood fresh souls into Hell. He knew they came for their own gain, to leap their souls forward time and again; but he knew that it was a brave choice to make over and over, and that they made it for the realm as much as themselves. Chase reveled in the challenge, awash in the flow of love that was his own selfish service.

He was the Next Walker.

- THE END -

Epilogue San Francisco

Roche came up behind the young woman, placing her between him and the busy bar.

"Rachel!" he barked. The girl jumped, startled.

"Every time you mix a cocktail it's either heavy or light on the booze," he scolded her. "Good goddamned Hell, girl, what's wrong with you? If you're going to be inconsistent, at least be consistent about it!"

Customers were shouting drink orders over the busy bar, and she glanced between patron and boss a little helplessly. Through it all she kept moving, pouring drinks under Roche's watchful eye as he hollered. Rachel kept calm, pushing the drinks across the bar and taking cash from two different customers. Her dress was form-fitting, and showed off her long legs below and perky cleavage above. Her simple pretty face was framed by long dark hair cut all one length to touch her shoulders, and was momentarily clouded by a slight but attractive frown.

"Sorry, Mister Roche," she said, breezing past him twice. "I'll work on it."

Roche grumbled and harrumphed to her bare back and bulbous buttocks for a half a minute, frowning happily.

"See to it that you do!" he barked.

Rachel jumped once more, and he almost smiled.

Tromping his way upstairs, the devil paused mid-flight. He turned on the steps, looking down on the band and the packed dance floor. The band had really hit their groove in the last couple of months, and it had been nice to watch the members all show up for every show.

Jason beat the drums, smiling slightly as he laid down a rolling rhythm that you could set a clock to. Tyler's eyes were closed as his fingers danced over the four fat strings stretched tight across his fretboard. Rob mirrored Tyler's spot on the stage, playing his keyboards and backing up Sarah's vocals when it was called for. Sarah shared the front half of the new stage with their new lead guitar player, some skinny fellow with long stringy blond hair. Roche had pulled her aside when she found him, to ask if he was the next Mason.

"Oh no," she had said, shaking her head. "He's a dime-a-dozen guitar player, like most of them are. He's laid back, though, and he has a great ear. As arrogant as he may be, he's not half as bad as most dime-a-dozen guitarists. But no; he's no Mason."

She had told him the kid's name, but the devil hadn't bothered remembering it. He had enough names to remember, with the five pretty young ladies he had hired to wait tables and tend bar. Instead he just called the guy "Guitar Wizard" whenever he needed the kid's attention, and the kid answered no matter how much he made his gravelled voice drip with irony.

Roche listened to them rock the house, Sarah belting out the strained soulful strains of "This is War" by Thirty Seconds to Mars, as he watched his attractive staff work the floor. It looked almost as it had looked before, except there was no busy blonde dragon behind the bar. Roche sighed and shrugged, then pivoted on the step to ascend the remaining stairs.

There was already a tall glass of aged whiskey on the bar when he took a stool, and the devil drained it while his eyes adjusted enough to look at her.

"Ah, the perfect pour," he grinned, setting down the glass. "Ehcor, your drinks are always the best."

The angel smiled, the manacle at her ankle shifting as she moved in closer.

"I pour with love," she said sweetly, pouring him another round. He drank it down and thanked her with a grumbled sound that sounded like gratitude to him. Roche hefted his weight from the stool and moved to descend the stairs once more. As he reached the final step, he called out to the nearest waitress.

"Amanda!" he hollered, stabbing a meaty finger to her left and then to her right as she turned. "That table and that table are both covered in empty glasses!"

"Sorry, Mister Roche!" she cried. The curvy redhead moved to the nearest of the two tables, leaning over to clean the drinks and listen to the seated patrons order more. She glanced up nervously halfway through both tasks, afraid a fresh critical barrage might be headed her way.

Roche was already gone, shoving drunken dancers rudely aside as he made his way to the back room. He glanced wistfully at the island bar as he passed, certain he had seen a flash of blonde hair or perfectly painted fingernails scrubbing away at something. Looking closer, he saw Becky's dark hair and short unpainted nails moving as she poured drinks for a waitress. The band segued into Cheap Trick's "Surrender" the moment his hand fell on the doorknob, and the devil stood there listening through the first chorus. Smiling, Roche went through the door and closed it behind him.

"These books are a mess," Kris said happily, looking up from his interminable task. "You make money pretty well for someone who can't seem to count it."

Roche made another grumbling sound as he passed the Guide, then moved through the second door without breaking stride. He made sure Kris didn't catch him smiling.

Epilogue San Diego

Cal steeled himself, trying to look as relaxed as possible, and fell in behind a handful of hooting and hollering pedestrians. They followed the signs, he followed them, and his rolling suitcase followed him. He felt the shifting bulges under his loose clothes, tried not to pay them any mind. All too soon the familiar scene came into view, guards armed with automatic rifles standing along a set of tables. They watched the stream of white weekend warriors with little concern, letting most of them move into Mexico with nothing more than a nod.

As usual, they were looking through women's purses and men's knapsacks when they had them, and Cal was not surprised when one of the strapped police waved him over to the table. He hefted the case, confident in his repacking job. Cal had used the same secret compartment in the same suitcase to transfer most of his wealth over the border in the last few years, making a trip every quarter. He had dumped the guns and the coke, since neither would be hard to find in Mexico so long as he had cash. It would be ridiculously stupid for him to get busted at this point for bringing drugs and guns into Mexico.

The guard messed up his careful packing job like he had taken a class on it, but he didn't feel the money layered into the flat back. After a minute of ruining all the careful folds and rifling through all of his harmless toiletries, the guard pushed the case closer to Cal on the table. He made a motion, indicating that Cal should lift his shirt.

He did, lifting it nice and high and completely ignoring the uncomfortable bulges in his pants. Cal had his passport in his hand already, and he held it out while fervently hoping the man wouldn't take it.

The guard waved his hand and motioned for him to move on. Cal smiled, stuffed the bulging contents of the suitcase back into place, and did just that. He was almost to the one-way gate when a voice called out behind him.

"Señor!" It was a man's voice. He kept moving.

"Hey, mister!" The voice called out again. A hand fell on his shoulder, and Cal resisted the urge to run. He turned, his heart beating out of his chest.

"This yours?" The guard was holding up his gold chain cross, dangling it before him with the gold chain wound round his palm.

Cal gulped and nodded, feeling the blood slowly come back into his face. He set the rolling suitcase upright, took the chain and lifted it over his head. He patted the cross as it fell into place.

"Gracias," he smiled, grasping the handle and tilting the suitcase. He stepped through the revolving doors, and let the sights and sounds of Caminó de la Revolución wash over him.

EPILOGUE HEAVEN

Marcus smiled as he felt tender arms wrap around his shoulders. He was seated, his feet working the pedals while his blurred hands wove threads into and out of an endlessly flowing tapestry. He didn't have to glance at a clock or watch to know how much time had passed; the tapestry could tell him anything he wanted to know about any moment.

Turing his body on the simple stool, Marcus spun inside her embrace to smile up at her.

"You love me so good," he murmured into her robed breasts.

"And for so long," she whispered, tousling his hair. "The Loom of Life would have us here forever, together, if I am hearing it right. As would I."

Marcus squeezed her to him tighter. "And I as well, my perfect angel."

He stood, and their noses nearly touched as he did.

"I was afraid I would lose my link to the loom if I helped the council," he breathed, "but I was terrified at the thought of losing you."

Lillian kissed him, her lips pressing against his for a sweet forever moment. She smiled as she leaned away, just an inch from touching his lips with hers again.

"Your love is my strength," she smiled, "just as my love is your strength. You will never be without it, or me."

"Alright!" A booming voice cut through the pleasant stillness, followed by a rolling round of laughter. "Break it up, you two, or leave me alone to my work."

Marcus smiled, giving David a happy wave as he followed his angel through the door.

Epilogue Hell

Paul sat on the wrought iron swing next to Ximena, his arm around her shoulder. They looked out over an ocean of lava that stretched as far as the eye could see and lapped at the shore with the sounds of searing and scorching. Little puffs of smoke filled the starless night sky with drifting fog, and the light from the lava cast a beautiful eerie glow on the clouded shapes. It was breathtaking, and Paul traced a light's flight as it streaked across the sky to wherever it wanted to go.

He smiled, nudged her playfully.

"I guess we don't need windows after all," he said.

Ximena was more beautiful than ever, busy all day dispensing love to the realm and busy all night sharing a life and a home and a bed with him. She was glowing like working tirelessly was her natural state, and she thanked him every day for being here with her.

And every day, Paul smiled and responded that the only thing that he could have lost that would have felt like giving up something was her. It was true, too, and he couldn't have imagined a better end for himself than forever anywhere with her.

As it had turned out, Hell was not so bad after all.

Paul watched Ximena in her own beautiful reverie, turning slowly to him to acknowledge that he had spoken, surely abandoning some train of thought that would have carried food or supplies to thousands. He felt her attention gather up a little at a time in his direction until it was fully on him.

"I'm sorry, lover," she smiled. "What was that?"

Paul chuckled. "Nothing, sweetie. I'm sorry. Go back to your thinking."

He leaned over and kissed her cheek, to show he wasn't hurt. Ximena turned as he pulled away, her lips pressing softly into his. Then she leaned over and fetched the two tall crystal chalices on the metal table before them. Paul swirled the deep red liquid in the glass, stuck his nose in as far as he could and breathed in deep. He took a long slow drink.

"Mmm," he said. "You still haven't told me what this deliciously powerful drink is."

"Sure I have," she smiled, sipping at her glass. "We call it 'The Blood of our Enemies.'"

Paul frowned, as he had when he had heard the name before. Still, he took another drink; it was the only thing in centuries that had given him a decent buzz. He nudged her again.

"Really?" he asked. "What is it?"

Ximena sighed. "It's a grape-like plant that only grows here, and only if dragons plant it and care for it. Soon it will grow again, and I will show you the fruit and the process that turns it to a lighter, more mellow version of this. Then I will show you how to turn that to this. It keeps virtually forever, and I was lucky to find some still stashed in my old cellar."

"Hmm," he mused. "So it's like port?"

"The Blood of our Enemies is to port what a hydrogen bomb is to a firecracker, my love," she smiled sweetly.

They sat in silence, watching the lava glow and the smoke reflect the glow back to it. They held hands for a long while, one turning every now and again to kiss the other. After some time, Paul spoke again.

"Sweetie," he said, "do you know why God would want me to stay in Hell, or be so adamant about ending me if I left?"

Ximena sipped her drink, then set it aside. She took his hand in both of hers.

"There is a prophecy that says that The Walker Eternal will rise one day to challenge God," she said.

Paul felt his brow furrow. "Why would I do that?"

Ximena patted his hand. "I'm probably not the best person to ask that particular question to, do you think?"

The Stone Walker chuckled, replaced his frown with a smile and kissed her again.

"Paul," Ximena murmured quietly. "When you saw God, what did you see?"

He watched the thick swirl of deep red in his glass.

"It's a hard thing to put to words," Paul said. "An old wise man or big bright light would have been easier."

She waited, letting his thoughts whirl to clarity.

"It looked like a wiser, better version of me," he said at last. He shook his head. "Or the best parts of me staring back at me. Is that awful? Or arrogant?"

Ximena smiled. "It's beautiful."

She fetched her glass from the table, lifted it between them.

"To God," she breathed. "To you, to Hell, to us together forever."

"To us," Paul smiled, "together forever."

They both drank deeply. The glasses were never quite empty, apparently one of the fringe benefits of chilling with the devil herself. They drank and talked long into the starless night, cuddling closer with each passing hour and drinking the precious blood of our enemies.

Dear Reader,

You made it to the end! Hopefully everything turned out in a way you were at least okay with, all your questions were answered, and you feel as satisfied with reading 'The End' as I did writing it.

Actually, there's more to this story…but let's talk about the journey we just shared together first.

Everything I had been through seemed to come into play when it came to writing this trilogy. From trying to form a band back in the day, to learning about all the strange ways in which we humans choose to love, to all those books I tore through looking for the meaning of life…my own past gave me compassion for the diabolical as they schemed, and for the ignorant as they blundered. This story helped me reconcile everything that had come before writing it, in my own life. Sharing it with the world started me on a whole new journey, with the perfect partner by my side; but it took readers like you to make that road feel real underfoot.

Hearing from people who have enjoyed reading my books has showed me a whole new aspect of writing. Some folks are kind enough to leave reviews letting the whole world know what they thought, while others reach out to me and share how they have been affected firsthand. These books led to that initial feedback, and it meant even more to me that I had thought it might. It all came together inside me, along with my own need to create; the only thing to decide at that point was what to write next.

Almost every character from this series became a point of focus for me while writing these books. In order to understand each of them, I had to delve into their pasts more than I could really share in the pages previous. An idea for a set of nine more books came to me before I had even finished this one, where we get to see where the characters that clashed and came together here started from…but there was a small problem with following up this final book immediately with the first of those.

The last thing I wanted was to be stuck in a box of my own creation, unless it was a box I could live comfortably inside of. Before I could expand on this world, I had to create other worlds…in other genres…but that is all stuff you can find on my website. What you need to know now is that I have come full circle, and recently wrote the first book in that series I thought of while writing this trilogy.

If you have read these books in order, you have already gotten a couple invitations from me to join my newsletter. Hopefully, you've done that; if not, you can always jump over to JayNorry.com and make sure you start getting those updates. All my books are available at the website as well; and that's really the best place to get a feel for the widely narrow lane I write books in.

However…in light of what you have just finished reading…

What you might want to do is go to wherever you got this book, and look for that other book I've been telling you about. The best way to relate this story is from the beginning, through the eyes of the only soul who was there to see it all. '*The Demon Be Damned*' takes us back to that beginning, when the demons people were making first started to be a problem. Roche may have been created to help deal with this, but he must first decide whether he is here to save the worlds he can walk between or destroy them.

I hope you enjoyed the trilogy you just read, and that you pick up your copy of '*The Demon Be Damned*' so you can get started on it right away.

Thanks for reading!

All the best,
J.K. Norry

What did Roche do to get
himself exiled from Hell?

Why did Echor go mad?

And where the hell did that
fedora come from?

Learn more in this preview of

The Demon
Be Damned

PROLOGUE

The first thing he knew was everything.

He knew the form his consciousness had taken was the body of a devil, that he was capable of taking many forms, and that each was more powerful and destructive than the other in some way.

He knew the power guilt carried, and that the humans on Earth had only begun to toy with this great power. They were creating demons from that guilt, demons they couldn't see. Demons they couldn't resist.

Demons they couldn't stop.

In the first moment he was, he saw it all. The past stretched forever behind him, the future trailed off into eternity, and he saw every ecstatic and agonizing moment of it before he had taken his first breath.

He knew the one that created him was obligated to ignore him forever. In the same moment he had been made, he had been cast out. For the same reason he had been made, he had been cast out. In seeing it all, he saw there was no reason and no purpose to asking why. A million whys would be answered by a million silences, and he knew before he asked the silence would be too much to bear.

He knew his name was Roche, in that first moment.

In the next moment, he breathed in.

A darkness entered him along with the breath, invading every part of him. His ecstatic vision of a moment ago was gathered up in the darkness and swept away with his breath. Everything he had just known was gone, replaced by a bottomless emptiness within him. Now he saw where he was, in a place of light and clouds. Although he had been made here, he did not belong here. He knew it like he had known everything a breath ago, as a certainty that knew no doubt.

Then he saw her.

She was like him, but different in every way. Her soul was pure and clear and empty, and on the rise. Her mind was without thought, without reason and without doubt. Even her name was the same as his, while being exactly the opposite of his.

"Ehcor," he murmured.

She turned, and the light shone forth from her. Lifting a hand to cover his eyes, Roche felt his skin soak up the blinding luminescence. The pain was almost too much to bear, yet his skin seemed to hunger for the light. While the pain soaked in, the hunger rose up to greet it; and as he stared through splayed fingers he saw her clearly within the brilliance.

Twisted in hate, her face moved to form the first words he had ever heard spoken. The words were thrown at him violently.

"You!" she cried. "You don't belong here! You are cast out!"

Roche felt his own voice trying to burst forth. He listened to the whirling thoughts in his head that told him they were the same, that she was a part of him and he a part of her. While he hesitated, she acted.

Two bright hands of light burst forth from the cloud of light enrobing her. She extended them toward him, hands bent at the wrists to show him her palms. A ball of light erupted from between them, and shot toward him. Roche felt his eyes go wide as it hit him, felt his arm thrown back over his head, and felt his body go skittering helplessly across the soft clouded floor.

Somehow he slipped over the side, or through what they had both been standing on, and Roche felt himself falling. Lights and sounds passed him as he fell, but he could find no way to grasp anything. His body began to spin as it descended, and his eyes rolled back in his head as Roche felt his consciousness slipping away from him.

CHAPTER 1

Just because it wasn't home didn't mean he couldn't learn to live here. The only home he had ever known was in a mind that would never think of him again, and he had to live somewhere.

Roche surveyed the landscape, and smiled for the first time.

He had come awake on a low hilltop, with gradual slopes rolling in every direction away from him. The land was nothing more than dirt, but the soil was streaked in blacks and browns and golds in a way that made it seem alive. Off in the distance he could see where the rise began again. Gradual at first, the soil became rock and the rock became a wall. The wall stretched up and out of sight, as did the similar vertical face far behind him.

Surely it met to form a stone ceiling overhead, but Roche couldn't make out its features for all the light shining down on him. Warm and invigorating, the light kissed his skin and put another smile on his face. He let his eyes wander the horizon once more, and spied a dark spot where the ground became wall.

Roche left his vantage point behind, moving forward over the packed dirt. He thrilled at the feel of the wind on his face, his feet against the ground, and the sweet pungent scent that entered his nostrils with every breath. The only other place he remembered had been odorless, the air itself without texture. In this place he could nearly taste the dirt as he strode across it.

Had he not been so caught up in the experience of being alive, Roche surely would have noticed the forms gathering behind him. First two came together, matching his pace; then three more fell into step with them, and moved along with him towards the dark spot in the distant rock face. When the last two caught up, a lone voice called out from the group.

"Ho there," the voice said. "I think you may be lost."

Roche stopped, and turned.

He watched them as they continued to move toward him, spreading out to form a loose circle around him. They looked like he did, sort of; yet there was some distinct difference he couldn't put his finger on.

While he glanced from one to the other, without turning to see them all, Roche heard one speak behind him.

"He looks like an old devil," he said.

Roche whirled toward the new voice, only to hear another comment from one of the devils that was now behind him.

"Old and senile," he said.

This time when Roche turned the last one that had spoken continued talking. He had gotten a glimpse of each of them, of their metal coverings and their array of weapons. Most of them carried a curved sword, with a dagger sheathed and hanging from their belted waists. Two had spears, and one hefted a club with metal spikes sticking out from every angle around the rounded thick end.

The one with the club was still speaking.

"Who else would wander around naked and alone, this deep in Hell?" he asked no one in particular. "Only a new devil or an old one that has lost his mind."

One of the swordsmen nodded.

"Look at the size of him," he said. "And those horns. He must be ancient. He probably lost his mind a long time ago." Roche stood still, letting his eyes flit from one devil to the next as they passed the thread of comments. The next voice came from behind him, and he didn't turn to see who it was.

"He's got nothing," the devil said. "And maybe he hasn't lost his mind. Maybe he likes to battle bandits. We got nothing to gain by finding out."

The armor they wore was finely wrought, contoured to each of their bodies to give their muscled torsos room to flex and move. A single piece of steel bent over each devil's shoulder to cover their backs and chests by simply fitting it over their heads. From the waist down, they were covered in loin cloths that hung between their naked legs. Although they were a ragged band, with hair and beards that looked both unwashed and uncut, the armor lent a uniformity to the group.

That was not the difference between him and them that Roche couldn't figure out. He was bigger than all of them, but a couple were near his size; yet somehow he could feel they were all the same in some way, some way in which he was different.

One of the largest of them was directly facing Roche. He had been doing much of the talking, and he leaned to one side to speak once more.

"Someone is scared," he sneered.

He was looking past Roche when he said it, narrowing his eyes at the devil that had expressed his doubts. After speaking, he let his eyes find each of the others in turn.

Roche sensed movement behind him.

"I'm not scared," the one behind him responded.

The words were followed by an audible gulp, and hesitant footfalls.

Roche felt a different internal response to this movement. Everything inside of him seemed to stand still, while his senses all became immediately and almost painfully heightened. He turned, to see what approached from behind. The turn was not rapid, or panicked; yet he could see that he was moving much faster than the devil as he brought his sword up over his head and stepped forward once more. Roche had time to cock his head curiously to the side, and narrow his eyes, before the curved blade began its arc toward him.

With no hurry to his movements, Roche easily moved aside and grabbed the devil's sword arm by the wrist as it passed harmlessly through the spot he had just been standing. The motion was punctuated by a loud cracking sound, and the devil howled in extended slow motion as he dropped the weapon. It had hardly fallen when Roche let go the devil's wrist and grasped it by the hilt. He swung the blade three times before his opponent could react with anything but a look of shocked surprise.

The first swing was awkward testament to the fact that he had never held a sword or seen one in action. It glanced off the devil's breastplate, driving him further off balance but doing no real harm. Stepping back and swinging again, Roche felt as though the blade had become an extension of his arm. He cut the devil just below the shoulder, and the appendage with the crushed wrist fell cleanly to the packed dirt at his feet. Before blood could flow, Roche swung the blade once more.

Another arm hit the ground with a thump, and Roche drifted back as the dark syrupy spray began to fountain from the devil's stumps. Purple wetness covered the soil, coloring it as it sunk in. It began to puddle immediately, in several small pools. When the devil made to take a step, still howling, he slipped in his own blood and pitched backward.

His head struck rock, and the devil fell silent.

Roche glanced at the others. A few were staring wide-eyed, but the rest were clearly seeing a challenge where those few saw danger. Two of the larger devils rushed forward; one from behind, the other from his right.

Whatever had slowed the world down or sped him up was still with him, and Roche imagined and discarded three possible ways to respond before he chose one and acted. He stepped forward, letting them crash awkwardly into each other, spun to face them and brought their skulls together with a satisfying thunk. One went down, his eyes rolling back in his head; the other dropped to his knees and swung his spiked club at Roche's legs.

He let the blow land, curious what effect it would have. It nearly drove his legs out from under him, and the points of pain that dotted the larger concussive ache almost made him cry out. Roche held his ground, and pried the weapon from the devil's hand and then from his own leg. Bringing it down on it's owner's skull, Roche watched the light go out of the devil's eyes as his body dropped lifelessly the rest of the way to the ground. He had stepped back again, to let the body fall; and he had stepped right between two others when he did.

Two blades were coming at him, and each bit into his torso in the same moment. First he felt the pain, and a fury rising within him; then another shift washed over him, and the scene stood nearly still.

Roche felt a thirst deep inside, a pure killing steak that wanted to turn his body from what he was to what it was. Part of him wanted to let it loose, and watch the cloud of darkness rain stark destruction on the remaining devils. Another part of him feared that transformation, and wondered if he could even make it happen if he wanted to.

The time he spent warring internally over whether to resist the impulse or surrender to it felt like a brief eternity to him. For the others, it was a passing moment; they remained nearly still, moving in exaggerated slow motion while he contemplated the choices he didn't know he had. The fury rising in him passed in that eternal moment, and Roche calmly spun in place. What felt like a measured response to him looked like a whirlwind blur to them, and their weapons were yanked painfully from their taloned hands.

He spun again, and the swords let go the flesh they had bitten to fly in opposite directions and clatter harmlessly outside the broken circle. By the time he stopped twirling the wounds were healed. Roche pushed the two devils away with a casual explosiveness, surprising himself with how far they sailed away from him. He saw the first that had fallen rising again, and saw the arms he had chopped off growing back slowly.

Roche dropped the spiked club and grasped the hilt of the curved sword with both hands. Some instinct within him told him what to do, and the next devil was already rushing at him. Roche let him come, swinging the sword with all his might at his charging adversary. The blade cut past the charge, between the devil's defenses and through his neck. His body took one more step before it fell and began gushing thick purple blood.

A moment later the devil's head rolled to a stop at Roche's feet, eyes vacant and unseeing. While the other wounded regained their feet and their limbs, the headless one stayed down.

They all came at him at once, and Roche found himself wondering if he would die should one take his head from his shoulders. The thought was fleeting, and was left behind as he stepped gingerly around the converging attack. One head after another fell behind him. By the time he returned to the place he had begun the thought, seven crimson corpses dotted the field. An equal number of heads lay lifeless in the dirt, streaks of purple describing the paths they had taken away from their bodies.

Roche felt time begin to settle into its previous slow pace, just as he saw another devil approaching from the distance. At first he saw every feature of the figure as it neared; giant legs pumping as he ran, he seemed to be moving at the same rapid speed Roche was watching in. As his perception slowed, the devil became a dark red blur streaking across the landscape.

Distant and thunderous, a rumbling sound punctuated by regular cracks seemed to be coming near at the same pace as the racing devil. The noise grew louder as the blur came closer, and Roche expected it to cease when the devil halted a dozen paces short of him. Rather than stop, the rhythmic rumbling continued to increase in volume.

The devil didn't seem to hear it at first. He looked at the carnage surrounding Roche, glared hatefully at him, and howled his rage to the sky. The roar was deafening, and Roche could feel his chest trembling with it. While he was being attacked by the smaller devils, Roche had briefly wondered for the first time whether or not he could be killed. Now he stared at a devil nearly twice the size of any of his previous opponents, and considered the possibility that he was about to get a very final answer to his earlier internal question.

When the devil's roar fell silent, he noticed the approaching sound at last. His face went from a mask of rage to a confusing mix of surprise and terror, and he began to lift his eyes to the sky.

In a startling blink, Roche was no longer looking at a devil. A deep scarlet winged serpent stood where the devil had just been, in a trench created by its halted descent. The ground trembled beneath Roche, while dust and rock and liquid devil rose into the air only to fall all around him. He stared at the creature, wondering why time had sped up at such an inopportune moment. All he wanted to do was run his eyes over the scaled torso, to examine the reptilian visage, and take in the wonder of this horrific killing machine.

"You're a dragon," he breathed.

Roche didn't know how he knew the word, or how to register the flood of knowledge that accompanied the statement. He only knew the teeth and claws on the monster made the swords and spears the devils had carried look like so many playthings.

The dragon laughed, and Roche breathed out.

"I am a dragon," she said, inclining her scaled snout.

Her voice was melodious and flinted at the same time, almost musical. Roche let the surprise show on his face for a moment, and she misread his expression.

"You didn't know dragons can talk?" she said.

Roche shook his head.

"Actually, I did know that," he said. "Somehow. But I've never met a dragon before, and I didn't know a dragon's voice could sound so…"

She interjected, impatiently.

"Normal?" she said. "Intelligible? What?"

Roche shrugged.

"I guess…" he paused. "Beautiful."

A slight smile had settled on her lips while they talked, upturning the corners of her mouth. Roche had thought it was meant to be threatening, as it showed him a considerable number of teeth he couldn't see when she spoke. Now he watched the line take a downward turn, and realized how threatening a dragon's face could be. Her eyes narrowed to slits, and flashed with fire.

Then she laughed, the sound rolling over the field and echoing back to them from the distant walls and subterranean ceiling. Roche noticed a cruelty in it he hadn't heard when she spoke, a sinister note that made him wish time would get on with slowing down again.

When she returned her eyes to his, the slight smile was back.

"The queen would see you," she said.

Her voice had gone flat, as though she had deliberately tried to remove the musical tone. Now he could hear the cruelty in it. He shrugged his shoulders, to show her he didn't know what she meant.

"Who?" he said.

The dragon's body seemed to inflate, as she pulled in a deep labored breath. Roche remembered somehow that dragon fire was not to be trifled with, and had a good long moment to wonder if perhaps he was about to learn more details about that inner caution.

She sighed, and turned away.

"The queen of Hell," she said. "She wants to know where you came from, why you arrived here, and why you began your visit with a killing spree. After you talk, maybe she'll let me kill you."

Roche had begun to approach her, mistaking the way she had positioned her body as an invitation to climb on and ride her. At her last words he stopped, and stared.

Pulling back her wings, the dragon leapt into the air in time with the first powerful down-thrust. That newly familiar loud cracking sound accompanied the motion, as did another blast of dust and rock. Roche was pushed away by the explosive takeoff, and staggered backward a few steps while the thunderous sound filled the air again. He heard her call out to him, barely.

"Try to keep up!" she cried.

The carefree lilting tone was back in her voice, and she was already a dwindling dot overhead. Roche took a good long look at the crimson and purple puddle of goo in the trench she had just vacated. He wondered, while he stared, what sort of creature might command a monster like that.

Roche began running.

CHAPTER 2

The number of possibilities drifting by was a little dizzying. Minutes seemed to stretch to hours as they walked endless corridors carved through solid rock, each punctuated at irregular intervals by entrances to adjacent passageways. They turned one way and then another, seeming to double back directionally without ever revisiting the exact same stretch of tunnel. Some passages were dark and empty, and he followed her footsteps down them more by sound than sight; others were illuminated by torches or candles or mysterious light sources he couldn't see, crowded full of devils going from one unknown place to another.

At the entrance to the cave, she had waited for him in her intimidating reptilian form. She had behaved as though he took a great long time to arrive, but he could tell she had put forth real effort to stay ahead. Once he started running, Roche was able to feel time wanting to stretch until it seemed to stand still. He engaged the feeling, somehow, and was able to make the moments tick by nearly as slowly as he had while doing battle. Every time he had looked up, she was above and a bit ahead of him. She hadn't gotten out of sight until right at the end, and he heard her hit the ground harder than she might have wanted to if she didn't been rushing for effect.

As he had approached, she had transformed. One moment she was a monster, watching him over her shoulder as if he had kept her waiting for some time; the next she was a devil, with an outward form to match the voice he had heard earlier. Smaller than him nearly by half, her face was fierce and unlined. Scarlet and orange curls that looked more like dancing flames bounced with the slightest movement of her head, and her eyes seemed to contain actual fire.

Without a word, she had turned and slipped into the cavern. Since then she had walked quickly, keeping far enough ahead of him to make the only conversation possible between them brief echoed exchanges. Roche remained silent, and watched her lead him deeper into Hell. Whenever they approached a tunnel with anyone in it, she would call back to him not to talk to anyone. Then she would press on, silent but for her swift quiet footfalls.

Everything about her was alluring, an intricately layered attraction that was either completely natural or carefully constructed to appear as if it were. The way she walked, her entire body moving like a flickering candle's flame. How she tossed her flowing red hair over her shoulder, and flashed her fiery eyes at him. Her voice, melodic and lilting. Even her smile threatened to overwhelm his senses, and stir a deep hunger within him. She had become clothed when she transformed, in a flowing swath of fabric so dark it shifted from black to deep purple as she passed through lighted and unlighted sections of the endless passages. Hugging her at her breasts and hips, the dress covered the entire length of her legs and trailed behind her along the path.

Only her laughter pierced the illusion of her beauty. Roche heard it again when she saw some of the devils in the crowded areas stop and stare as they passed. Nearly all of them wore coverings of some type, from a simple loin cloth that left little to the imagination to layered robes that showed nothing but brief glimpses of crimson skin. The larger the devil, the more they seemed to wear. Roche was one of the few without clothing of some kind, and the only one of his size. He did his best to ignore the curious gazes, along with her cruel laughter.

He was convinced she was leading him down a deliberately circuitous path. Without intending to, Roche saw a map drawing itself behind his eyes. The tunnels went from a labyrinthine mystery to a familiar network as they walked. By the time she halted before a closed doorway, he was sure he could find his way back to any and all the places they had been. In trying to confuse him, the dragon turned lady had instead given him a clearer idea of how the passages were laid out.

Turning to him as he approached, she pointed to a spot in the worn rock floor and met his eyes. She had to look up to do so, and he got the feeling she didn't much care for raising her gaze to find his. At the same time, she kept herself from staring at his nakedness like the others had. For the first time Roche realized he was an imposing figure, even among the largest devils he had seen. Next to her, he was a small giant.

Knowing she could turn into a creature that dwarfed him in size in an instant, Roche took no pleasure in towering over her or witnessing her reaction to it. He tried to keep his expression respectful, and diminish the effect of him looking down at her.

"Wait here," she said, still pointing.

Roche glanced at the place she indicated. He nodded, and stepped sideways to be exactly where she was telling him to be. She glared at him a moment longer, then turned and pushed the door open. Disappearing into the space beyond, she closed it behind her to leave him standing naked and alone in the hallway.

Less than a minute passed before the door was pulled open once more. This time Roche was able to see into the room beyond. Spacious yet sparsely furnished, it was wide from wall to wall and spanned overhead in a tall smoothed rock ceiling. Bookshelves dominated most of the wall space; they stretched high beyond his reach and were loaded with volumes bound in everything from stone to steel, from cloth to clay. A few chairs were loosely arranged on the mostly open floor space, and a dark figure rose from one as he watched.

For a moment she was an amorphous fog in shades of black, flowing from the chair to begin drifting languidly toward him. The dark cloud coalesced into a simple but lovely figure, and he shook his head to clear it. Nothing remained of his original vision as she approached, and he took in her dark swirling eyes and black flowing hair as carefully as he took in her midnight robes. Nearly every inch of her was covered by the dancing fabric, which resembled shifting shadows more than any material he had ever seen. Only her hands and her head were clearly visible, and they were lovely in a way that made him think of danger like he never had before.

The dragon lady had slipped behind him, and he felt her hand on his shoulder before he sensed her movement. Suddenly she was pushing on him, trying to drive him to his knees. Roche let himself be surprised at her strength, and grateful for his own. Resisting still, he heard her whisper behind him.

"On your knees," she hissed. "Bow before the queen."

He couldn't take his eyes off the dark vision before him, but Roche continued to stand up straight. Apparently the dragon was stronger than he had thought, in this form; she continued to push harder, and his legs were beginning to tremble with the effort. Before he could step aside, or lash out at her, the approaching figure spoke.

"Lilia," she said. "Release him. That won't be necessary."

The sound of the dragon lady's voice had been pleasantly disorienting, the first time he had heard it. Just as he had nearly grown accustomed to one sound, Roche was spun in a whole new direction by another. The queen's voice was smooth and sublime, musical layers that carried her soft but sure words beyond his ears to shake the core of his being. One part of it was a sweet and caring young girl, another a kind old woman; altogether it was the most moving sound he had ever heard.

His knees would have buckled, had Lilia not stopped pressing on his shoulder in that moment. The dark figure came closer while he found his breath, and stopped a few steps inside the room.

"Won't you come in," she said. "We have much to discuss."

Denying her may not have been impossible, but it seemed such a ridiculous notion he saw no reason to try. Her presence drew him in with warm comfort, her voice beckoning him gently with every softly spoken word. Roche stepped forward, crossing the threshold into the stark space. A scent climbed into his nose as he entered the room; the smell of something that had been burnt, extinguished and burnt again.

It was not at all unpleasant to him.

Lilia was following, until she saw the dark form shake her head slightly. Her face twisted into a momentary mask of anger, only to relax into its placid beauty once more. Without a word, she turned and stepped into the hallway. Another look from the queen, and another paroxysm of fury crossed her face. Again, she relaxed visibly. She pulled the door shut behind her.

Suddenly alone in the room with her, Roche was even more conscious of the dark being studying him. She was so small, and yet it was hard for him to remind himself of that; the power that flowed from her was nearly palpable, pulling him in and pressing him back at the same time. For the first time he became keenly aware of his nakedness, and he shifted awkwardly under her gaze.

Turning, she flowed like a shadow into the room. He watched her, until she turned and gestured at the entire space with a slight subtle wave.

"Please sit down," she said, "if you wish."

Finally tearing his eyes from her, Roche tried to let his gaze drift about the room in a way that appeared natural and relaxed. He found the task nearly impossible, felt the irresistible urge to yank his attention from whatever it wandered to back to her.

"In all honesty," he said, "I really don't know what I should be doing. Surely there is some way to interact with you that shows great respect, and countless ways to behave that would imply my disrespect."

He was looking away, then back at her again, as he spoke. When he paused, his eyes found hers for a moment. She smiled.

"Of course," she said. "You are new, and I understand. Please, make yourself at ease. You have nothing to fear from me."

Turning, Roche glanced at the door that had been closed behind him. He felt Lilia's presence still on the other side, found himself wondering if she was listening somehow.

"Your dragon would disagree," he noted. "She is under the impression that if you don't like what I have to say, you will order her to kill me."

The dark lady's laugh did not resemble the dragon's at all. Like tinkling glass, it was full of humor and delight.

"My dragon?" she smiled. "You mean Lilia? She is not my dragon; she is my friend, my confidante. I would not have the relationship with the dragon community that I have were it not for her. Although she is a little standoffish at first, I'm sure you will warm up to each other."

Roche cast another glance over his shoulder, eyeing the door as if he was afraid the dragon would burst in flame first. The dark one laughed again, and drifted to the seat she had been occupying when he first saw her.

"You are like me, I think," she said. "Created on high, only to be cast out. There will be those that say you don't belong here, as they did when I first arrived. Do not let them trouble you. So long as I have a place in Hell, you will have one too."

Now his attention was drawn to her in a whole new way. Something about the way she laughed, the way she spoke, or the way she seemed to blur about the edges as he focused on her.

"The queen of Hell," he said, almost to himself. "You are like me. That means you have an opposite, another much like you that rules in Heaven. That would mean you are…"

Roche drifted off, and watched her raise her eyebrows in anticipation of what he might say next. When he didn't speak, she smiled and finished his thought.

"The dark one?" she said. "The devil?"

Shaking his head, Roche frowned at the thought.

"You are not like the one who made me," he said.

She smiled again.

"The one who made you also made me," she said. "As well as my counterpart. We were separated from that creative force out of necessity, a necessity that also demands we are given great power."

It was Roche's turn to laugh, and be frank.

"Great power?" he said. "I feel as though I know nothing, as though I could do anything if I could only figure out what to do and how to do it. I feel like a very small point in a very large reality, and I feel as though I am only getting smaller."

He looked down at himself.

"I know I appear to be old, and fearsome," he went on. "But only because I have seen others since coming into being. On the outside I seem to be a powerful devil, but within I feel as though all I am is stuffed into a tiny box I cannot open."

He heard his own voice become strained, exasperated.

"I don't even have any clothes," he blurted out.

With a wave of her hand, a change came over him. Roche felt as though giant arms were encircling him in an enormous embrace. The tension drained from his body, his racing thoughts were slowed until his mind was wondrously still, and another more tangible weight settled over him. His sense of delight at the calm within him made it seem only natural that a set of soft flowing robes appeared about his body. They were dark, edged in crimson and deep purple.

"You are not what you clothe yourself in."

Roche heard her within the comforting reality of her presence surrounding him. Her voice was in his mind, and more beautiful than ever. Much as the soft fabric of the robes tickled his skin, her words thrilled him within.

"These coverings are for those like us," she said. "Rulers of the dark realm, and those who reside here. Yet they cover only one form, the form others see when they look at us. Beneath that is the truth only some of us can see, the light that must be ignited to cast the darkness of our shadowy form. In that light you will always find yourself."

He shook his head, and the sublime presence drifted away from him.

"I remember that," Roche said. "But I cannot feel it like I remember feeling it. In that place I was whole, I saw and knew everything."

Suddenly he did need to sit down, and she sensed his need. Once more, she gestured her invitation. Roche settled across from her, and sighed. She looked so small, and so ordinary, sitting before him. He wondered how bright the light must be, to cast such a shadow.

"You will see that place again," she said. "But first you must fall, so you may rise. Things are sure to get worse, I am afraid. Yet then they will shift, and your inner vision will become clearer than ever. By the time you see the light again, you will understand it as only one who has dwelt in darkness can. In the meantime, I am happy to offer counsel and comfort."

Roche stirred in his seat, threw up his hands.

"I don't even know what my purpose is," he cried. "I don't how you might counsel me, or if I would be wise to heed your counsel."

She nodded, understanding.

"Lilia will show you the common areas," she said, "and the place that has been set aside for you. You may come to me as you wish, and make your way as you please. Despite my reputation, I am here to guide the path this reality cuts through existence in much the same way you are. There are not many like us, and I may need your counsel and comfort one day as well. The only beings that need fear me are the ones not comfortable facing reality as it is."

Meeting her gaze again, Roche lifted his eyebrows.

"You seem to have me at a disadvantage," he said. "You know much about me, and I know so little about you."

She smiled, and waved her hand in a gesture that seemed to take in the whole world.

"Then go," she said. "Learn, and live; and know you can ask me anything, when the time comes for us to speak again."

She paused, and he didn't realize he hadn't heard her utter his name until she said it.

"Roche," she said. "You are a special being, with a unique purpose; but only you can define and determine that purpose. Your urges and desires will find context in the world as you make your way in it, and the light within you is there to guide you."

He nodded, wishing he knew just what she meant. Before he stood, Roche let himself soak up the reality of her presence a moment longer.

"Thank you," he said. "I feel you are doing me a great kindness, and I may not be properly appreciating it; yet I do thank you for this meeting, and for your words. You have given me much to think about."

Rising, he found himself feeling awkward again as he looked down at her. She appeared completely at ease, even as she gained her own feet and drifted toward him.

"You know my name," he said. "But you referred to yourself as others do. Surely you have a name, that I may think of when I think of you?"

Her eyes deepened, the shifting shadows going completely black for a moment. For the first time her smile was less than kind, a twisted smirk that reminded him how dangerous she must be.

"I am indeed called many things," she said, "and many are the names I answer to. With you I would share the name of my choosing, the one that fits me best."

Roche nodded, waited.

"Ximena," she said. "When you think of me, you will be thinking of Ximena. And I do so hope you will find yourself thinking of me."

* * *

READ THE REST OF ROCHE'S STORY IN

THE DEMON BE DAMNED

www.ingramcontent.com/pod-product-compliance
Lightning Source LLC
Chambersburg PA
CBHW031225120726
47905CB00002B/474